THIS edition, issued in 1957, is for
members of The Companion Book
Club, 8 Long Acre, London,
W.C.99, from which address par-
ticulars of membership may be
obtained. The book is published
by arrangement with the original
publishers, Michael Joseph Ltd.

THE ANGEL IN THE CORNER

"A blessed companion is a book"—JERROLD

THE ANGEL
IN THE CORNER

*

MONICA DICKENS

THE COMPANION BOOK CLUB
LONDON

Made and printed in Great Britain
for The Companion Book Club (Odhams Press Ltd.)
by Odhams (Watford) Limited
Watford, Herts
S.1157.ZSA

To
PRUDENCE

I

IT WAS cold outside, and the winter afternoon was dropping darkly down to tea-time. In the nursery, the coal fire was a solid orange glow, capped with sticky black. Woollen underwear and towels were drying on the high brass fireguard, and the old nurse sat in the low chair, fumbling a darn with arthritic fingers.

Virginia was at the table, doing homework. When the flowered china clock on the mantelpiece struck the half hour, the nurse looked up and said a little crabbily, for she distrusted studying: "Time to put the books away, and set out the tea things."

Virginia looked over her shoulder at the darkness gathering outside the window, and slid quickly off her chair to draw the curtains. Once she had seen a face looking in, and although it was only her father, she had not forgotten the terror of seeing it there in the shadows beyond the glass, like the face of a drowned man, washed over by the sea.

"Tiny." She went to the chair of the bunchy old woman, who had nursed first her mother as a baby, and then herself. "Don't forget what I told you about not dying."

In the ugly, chilly house, half shut up to save expense, and restless with the noise of her mother's heels, always in a hurry to go out somewhere, and her father's petulant voice, the nursery was her refuge, and quiet, unchanging Tiny her best friend.

"I'll try, dear," Tiny said, in the same comfortable tone with which she added: "Get the cups and plates out."

As Virginia went to the chipped, oddly proportioned cupboard, which had held nursery china and toys for so long that it did not look ugly any more, the door from the hallway opened, and Virginia's mother came in quickly, as she always moved. She was a firm-bodied, brisk woman, with dark, darting eyes and a disgruntled mouth. She shut the door behind her, and leaning against it, moved her mouth into a grin, although her eyes, looking everywhere about the room, had no smile in them.

"Well, Tiny," she said, with an abrupt, strident laugh. "It's happened. Just as I told you it would. You didn't believe me, but you were wrong, you see, as usual."

Virginia stood still by the cupboard, with a pink patterned plate in her hand. The old woman by the fire raised her eyes, screwing up the reddened, crepey lids.

"He's left me." Again the unnatural laugh, mocking at emotion. "He's gone. Never coming back. Never coming back, don't you understand?" She raised her voice irritably, in an attempt to ruffle the nurse into some reaction.

"Mr Harold?"

"Who else? Mr Harold. My beloved husband. Your father, Jinny." She narrowed her eyes at the schoolgirl, who still had not moved.

"Miss Helen—please. Not like this." The nurse was shaking. She nodded towards Virginia. "Tell me about it later."

"Why not now?" Virginia's mother sat down at the table and lit a cigarette. "She has to know about it sooner or later. She's ten. I'm not going to hide things from her, or feed her with fairy stories that will make it easier for her and more difficult for me. Jinny!" She turned her sleek, black head sharply. "Don't stand there like a piece of furniture. Say something."

Virginia came forward with the plate in her hand. "Daddy's gone?"

"Yes, dear heart, and why should you care? He was never much use to you, and you can't pretend you haven't said you hated him."

"Hating," Virginia said, taking a breath, "is like a pain. But then, loving can be, too. You don't always know which is which."

"Oh, don't talk to me in clever riddles," her mother said. "It's that school. You've been doing too much homework." She got up and took the exercise books off the table, moving about restlessly, looking for something to use as an ash-tray.

She chose the fire. She came to stand sideways in front of it, leaning her hip on the fender, flicking ash at the coals.

"Thank God I've got my job," she said. "I shan't stay here. It's *his* house. He can have it if he wants it. I've always hated it. Damn mausoleum." She sometimes swore in front of Virginia when Tiny was there, because she knew that it shocked the nurse. "It was always much too big, anyway. We'll get a flat—Kensington, perhaps, or Bloomsbury, near the office. Much better for the two of us."

"Three," Virginia said quickly, but the nurse shook her head, as if she knew what was coming.

"Tiny will go to her sister," Virginia's mother said. "You know she's been wanting to go for years, haven't you, Tiny one? You and I, Jinny, will find ourselves a nice little flat, and be happy as two pigeons in a roost—probably happier than we've ever been. What do you say—on our own, eh?" She held out her hand to the child, but Virginia backed away. She held on to the edge of the table, fighting the pricking sobs in her throat. She would not cry until her mother had left the room.

After her mother's heels had gone tapping through the hall to keep a dinner engagement—"just as if it was an ordinary night!" the nurse exclaimed to herself—Virginia wept again in bed. The nurse came up, her humped shadow preceding her up the stairway wall. It was more familiar to Virginia to hear the nurse's creaking steps than her mother's swift feet. For as long as she could remember, it had been Tiny coming up at sleep time, Tiny with the stories and kisses, Tiny with the illicit chocolate, Tiny with the hot lemonade for coughs.

Tiny sat on the bed, breathing heavily after the climb, trying to thread a bent pin back into her sparse knot of hair. Her arms were so stiff and fat now, and her chest so sunk into her lap, that it was difficult for her to reach her head.

"Who will do your hair for you when I'm not there?" Virginia asked, with a child's quick recovery from voiceless sobs.

"Why, my sister, of course. She's younger than me, you know. She still has all her powers."

"Will she let me come and stay with you?"

"Will Hilda? Of course she will. You'll have to take the couch, though."

"I mean, will Mummy let me?" Virginia said gloomily. "I don't know what it will be like, living with her. Does she know how to look after children?"

"If she doesn't," the nurse said sadly, "it's time she found out." She put her hands on her knees and got up from the bed. She was not much taller standing up than she was sitting down. "You'll be all right, dearie," she said more briskly. "You'll see. Things will turn out." Wretched as she was at this sudden ending of an era, ending of her nursery days, ending of the only life she could remember, she was tough enough not to make it worse for the child by mourning with her. "And there's still the angel, don't forget." She nodded towards the corner of the room, where a street lamp threw a barred patch of light.

"Will he go with me?"

"I've told you often enough. He has to go with you, in every room, to watch out for the corners of life."

Virginia sighed. "I wish I knew what he looked like."

"Chances are you never will," the nurse said, going to the door, "because you believe he's there. It's only when you think you're alone, that he might show up, to prove you wrong. It would depend though. I don't know. Angels are funny people—if you'll pardon the liberty." She bobbed her head towards the corner of the room, where she had taught Virginia to believe that her angel stood to guard her.

2

"You're so terribly noisy, Jinny," Helen Martin complained. "Why are you always so noisy? You don't get it from me, but your father could shout loud enough in temper, in which, I feel constrained to say, he frequently was."

"Stop picking on the poor man." Virginia continued to bang the broom against the skirting-board as she swept. "It's done with. Let the past bury its dead, Helen." Now that she was grown up, she called her mother that. They treated each other as equals. On Virginia's side, that meant a certain indiscipline, a thinly-veiled disrespect, but a guarded friendship that had somehow evolved from the difficult years when they struggled as mother and child together.

On Helen's side, their equality was tainted with rivalry. At forty-eight, she thought she was better-looking than Virginia was at twenty. As an unattached woman, she considered herself still in the running for any men who came along, even if they were nearer her daughter's age than her own.

"Your father," Helen continued, leaning stiffly back on the sofa, closing her eyes tightly, and recrossing her legs, for she was "resting," which was more an active than a passive occupation, "your father, poor man, suffered from being the greatest egotist the world has ever known. What he really couldn't stand was the fact that I was more successful in my career than he was."

"Were you?" Virginia eyed her mother, thinking that if it were not for her legs, she was still a fairly well preserved woman. "We seemed to be quite well off in those days, and you didn't have the position on the magazine that you do now."

"Ah, yes—*in those days*," her mother said darkly, flexing her fingers, and then raising them in the air to make the motions of drawing on gloves. "But how is he doing now?

That's the question. He was the sort of man whom one always saw as doomed to failure."

Since she had become quite a person in the magazine world, and uplifted the souls of several thousand women every month with her limpid editorials on love, marriage, and what she called The Things That Count, Helen had taken to a certain artificial precision of speech. She always put in her whoms punctiliously, and could insert subjunctive clauses flowingly into her conversation, without pausing for breath.

"I'm going out," Virginia said abruptly. She flung the broom into the kitchen cupboard, and came back to her mother wearing a camel hair coat drawn tightly round her enviable waist. Helen opened her eyes and calculated how much smaller the waist was than her own. She shut her eyes again at the deduction, and asked, "Where are you going?"

"To work, of course. You know I have an evening class today." Virginia was studying journalism at a college on the other side of London. When asked whether she hoped one day to be a magazine editor like her mother, she was apt to reply that if she were, it would only be on the way up to something better.

Eager and confident, Virginia was full of a limitless ambition, which arose from her vitality and her youthful belief that the world was hers for the asking. She had experienced, by normal standards, an unhappy childhood, her parents divorced, her mother sending her away to an illiberal school and not knowing what to do with her in the holidays; but it had not quenched her enthusiasm for life.

She ran down the stairs outside the flat, and went eagerly out into the pungent London darkness. The flat was in a mews off a Bloomsbury street, converted from a garage, which had been converted from a stable. Some of the buildings were still garages. As Virginia walked over the cobbles to the arch of the mews, she greeted with a smile a man who was working on the engine of his car by the light of a street lamp and a torch. She did not know him, but

14

he looked troubled, as if he did not know as much about the engine as he should.

He smiled back. Virginia was tall, not willowy, but healthily supple, with a wide mouth and thick, dark hair plunging over her high forehead. She was feminine enough, and slight in her bones, and yet there was something rugged about her. Although she was only twenty, and had seen nothing of life, she looked as if some day, if she had to, she would be able to stand a lot of abuse.

The man saw some of these things dimly, resisted a desire to shine his torch directly on her, and said: "Hullo." He liked her vivid look. Even in the pale coat, she gave the impression of colour in the half-darkness. You could pass thirty girls in coats like that on the street, but only turn to look back at this one.

Virginia replied amiably, and stopped walking when the man asked if she lived in the mews. He told her that he had just come to live in a flat above the garage with a friend who was also a doctor, and they stood for a moment and eyed each other speculatively, before the man said: "Hm," which might mean anything, and Virginia said: "Oh, well," and walked on.

The man had looked about thirty-five. Refreshing after the coltish boys at the college. Life was full of the excitement of brief contacts. Always something new. Virginia walked down to Oxford Street to catch her bus. The tall houses, cramped yet dignified, like duchesses in an Ascot crowd, were dark and abandoned, for most of them were offices. Although it was early, there were few people about, and those who were in the street hurried along it to get out of the cold. At the corner of Oxford Street, the man selling newspapers wore a Russian cap with fur ear-pieces, given to him by an American soldier, but his coat was threadbare, and his mittens had more than finger-holes in them.

The light and bustle of the Tottenham Court Road were stimulating after the dark reaches of Bloomsbury. The people here were mostly out for the evening, not just hurrying home. Coloured men in dashing hats walked with white girls unhurriedly, as if they were parading, not going

15

anywhere in particular. Outside the cinema, a small crowd was marshalled into line, as meek and chilly as if they were waiting for bread. Virginia felt fleetingly sorry for them, reminded herself that they were not forced to go to the cinema, and ran across the road just in time to jump on her bus as it moved forward with the change of lights.

Virginia was taking the extra evening classes at the college because she wanted to complete the course as quickly as possible. She was almost certain that she could get on to the women's magazine of which her mother was the editor. Her mother did not know about this yet. When Virginia had started to study journalism, Helen had said: "Don't expect me to get you an easy job in the office. For your own good, and of what else must I think, you'll have to find work for yourself, the way I did. In any case, I don't approve of parents and children in the same organization."

Virginia had replied that she would not dream of asking her mother for any favours; but she did not add that the managing editor, who liked her better than he liked her mother, had half promised to find her an opening when she was ready.

The Earl's Court Road looked as uninviting as it has always done, and as it presumably always will, a depressing thoroughfare of fairly respectable poverty, down which the buses hurry, as if anxious to reach the more adventurous air of the river. The college was three terrace houses turned into one building, with the same peeling paint and smutted ledges as its neighbours.

In the basement where the evening classes were held, Virginia kept her coat on, for it was cold. She sat next to Mr Benberg, one of the older students, who wore a raincoat with the collar turned up. He had a long, grey face with weak eyes, and a recurring downward twitch to one side of his mouth, which interrupted any lifting of his expression and brought it back to bondage.

Mr Benberg worked during the day in an insurance office. He had no intention of trying to change it for a newspaper office, but he came down the Earl's Court Road each night in pursuit of a secret dream of being the greatest writer in the

16

world. He was not very good at the work. His efforts and failures to please Miss Thompson were tragic, although neither he nor she saw the tragedy.

Miss Thompson, with her acid jokes and her hair which looked like the dying foliage of an autumn plant, was talking tonight about newspaper make-up, and criticizing, as despairingly as any school-teacher, the homework of her grown-up class.

"It is quite clear," she said, coming round from behind the high desk, which was a mistake, since her figure was better above the waist than below it, "it is quite clear that none of you, at this moment, is ready to make up the front page of a national daily."

Her voice spelled sinus trouble. She finished her sentence with a high little hum at the back of her nose, and looked round for laughs. She got only one, from Bobby, a printer's apprentice who saw himself going all the way, like Lord Beaverbrook. He laughed at all Miss Thompson's jokes, to show that he was following the trend, but the others merely sighed and waited for Miss Thompson to stop wasting time and get on with the business before the pubs were shut, or the last train left.

For their homework, the class had been given a selection of photographs and columns of newsprint with the head-lines cut off, which they were to paste on to a large sheet of paper, as if making up the front page of a newspaper.

Mr Benberg did not change his expression when Miss Thompson, announcing that she would show the class a perfect example of how not to make up a newspaper, held up his page. Mr Benberg, who had been following the proceedings mildly, twitching his lip, and tapping his fingers to some rhythm in his head, continued to look mild while Miss Thompson tore the page to pieces, first figuratively and then actually, dropping the pieces into the wastepaper basket and dusting off her hands.

"Never mind." Virginia reached over and patted Mr Benberg's cold, dry hand. "I thought it was good."

He turned his gentle eyes on her. "I didn't. She was right, I dare say. It doesn't matter." They were talking softly, under

17

cover of Miss Thompson's droned dictation about type faces, which Virginia had already taken down, and Mr Benberg did not care to.

Mr Benberg leaned closer to Virginia and whispered more tensely, like a conspirator coming to the crux of a plot: "It's the words that count. Let someone else worry about how to print them. Words, words . . ." He tapped a pencil on his knee, making little pock-marks in the grey flannel. "Words . . . springing alive out of your head, like Athene from the head the Zeus. Words . . . so insignificant on their own, so powerful when fused together by the miracle of man's brain. Look here, Miss Martin, I tell you. There's nothing in the world as romantic as words." His weak eyes were glistening. He twisted the pencil round in his hands as if he were tightening a tourniquet.

"You really want to be a writer, don't you?" Virginia tried not to stare at the corner of his jumping mouth.

"Want to be? I am one. In the bureau drawer at home, I've the manuscripts of twelve novels—unpublished, of course—and I'm half-way through my thirteenth now. Oh——" he glanced round quickly at the scribbling class. "That's a secret. No one knows, except my dear wife, of course. I shouldn't have told you. I don't know why I did, but you're—well, anyway, I don't think you'll betray me."

"Of course not." Virginia was puzzled. "Why do you come here?"

"I'm looking for the clue. There must be something I've overlooked, or my books would be published. I thought I might find it here." Mr Benberg looked round anxiously, as if expecting to catch it lurking in a corner of the draughty basement.

At the college a few days later, jovial Mr Deems stopped Virginia in the corridor. "Greetings, my young friend, and congratulations," he said.

"Oh, good. Have I won the Christmas hamper?"

"Better yet. You have won, by your honest efforts, a two-weeks' stint on the staff of the *Northgate Gazette*. Not a job, you understand. Just a part of your training. They oblige us—for favours returned, of course—but they oblige. Lovely people. You start today."

"Now?"

"When else? You should be there now, my young friend." He looked at his watch, shook his fat wrist violently, glanced at it again, and scuttled away down the corridor like an egg with legs.

The lovely people lived two flights up above a bank on the corner of the High Street of Northgate, which is a western suburb of London. Its name is the only illogical thing about Northgate. In every other respect, it adheres logically to the standards set for it by the other outer suburbs which jostle each other in a rough circle round the metropolis, joined to its mother-life by the umbilical cords of the underground railway. Virginia had seen its like many times before, and yet today, as she walked from the station, it did not look familiar or dull. It looked like fresh and promising country, where anything might happen.

She was a reporter. She was The Press. Any moment now, something might happen, and she would be on the spot to get the story. Any one of these women, pushing their babies so arrogantly into the road under the very wheels of cars, might find herself knocked down, to reappear as a headline on the front page. "ACCIDENT ON PEDESTRIAN CROSSING. NORTHGATE WOMAN GRAVELY HURT. By Our Special Correspondent." Any one of these shops might yield a smash-and-grab raider, backing out of the door with pistol cocked, then running for his life, with Virginia after him. At any moment, a top window might fling up, and a woman's head look out with a wild cry of: "Fire!"

The citizens of Northgate went calmly about their dull Monday-morning business, unaware that an ace reporter walked in their midst, waiting for them to make news.

Virginia climbed the two flights up to the offices of the *Northgate Gazette*, undaunted by the narrowness of the wooden stairway and the smell from the lavatory half-way up. This was a place where work came first and appearances second.

19

At the top of the stairs, a door with a pane of glass, opaque with dirt as well as frosting, said: "Enquiries." Virginia stepped in. There was not far to step. Immediately in front of the door, a linoleum-covered counter ran from wall to wall, leaving a space only a few feet wide in which the enquirer could stand. You had to lean on the counter, or lean back against the wall. Virginia leaned on the counter. Opposite her, leaning on a table, was a fatigued girl with greasy hair and two cardigans thrown over her thin shoulders. On the wall at her side was a small switchboard, with a few wires lying on its edge, not plugged in anywhere.

She looked at Virginia without interest. Then she picked up a pencil and asked: "Small ad., dear?"

"Oh, no," Virginia said. "I've come to work here. I'm from the Latimer College."

"Oh, one of those." The girl looked resigned. "You can go inside, I suppose." She jerked her head towards the door at her back, from behind which came the sound of a stumbling typewriter. "Lift the flap."

Virginia looked at the counter. At one end, the solid front was cut away beneath a flap covered with the same mottled linoleum. At that moment the door to the back room opened, and a boorish young man in a muffler and heavy shoes clumped out, lifted the flap, ducked under, pushed past Virginia and went outside. The hole in the counter was apparently the only entrance to the offices of the *Northgate Gazette*. Bending her long back, Virginia went through it, hesitated at the farther door, glancing at the girl, then went through it and stood in the inner sanctum itself.

Rather, the outer sanctum, for within this room, boxed into a corner with plywood reaching three-quarters of the way to the ceiling, there was a dog-kennel of an office with a door bearing the word Editor, and some disrespectful newspaper cartoons tacked on to it. The flimsy walls of the kennel were decorated with pencilled telephone numbers and memoranda. Up at the top, in black, indelible letters, someone had written: "What a lousy life!"

There was one long, littered table in the room, which was thick with the stale air of cigarette smoke and windows closed to keep the winter at bay. At the far side of the table, a stringy man with a woebegone face typed inexpertly, screwing up his eyes against the cigarette which dangled from his lip. At one end, a round-faced boy in round spectacles corrected galley proofs with impatient flicks of his pencil.

Virginia stood awkwardly, wondering whether two weeks would be enough to make her feel at home in this ungenial room. Where would she sit? There was only one empty chair, which must belong to the young man with big feet. The soft wood of the table was scarred with names and pictures inked and carved into it. She would write her name there, and in years hence, people would come to see the place where her career had started.

The stringy man looked up from his typewriter. "How did she get in here?" he asked the boy.

"Under the flap," Virginia said. "I'm from the Latimer College. I'm to work here for two weeks."

"Oh," said the man, going back to his typing, "one of those."

"You'd better see the old man," the boy said, more kindly. He nodded at the door with the cartoons.

"What shall I—shall I just go in?" Virginia was accustomed to the office of *Lady Beautiful* where it would be unforgivable, if not impossible for any outsider to penetrate the phalanx of immaculate receptionists and secretaries, who guarded the elegant secrets of her mother's office.

"Sure," said the boy, in passable American. "Help yourself."

Virginia opened the kennel door, which was very light, and opened with disconcerting speed. Inside, at a desk which took up most of the space, was a middle-aged man, with deep indigestion lines running from his bony nose to his mouth, and a long, shining bald head, with a pair of black-rimmed spectacles slung up on it.

"I'm from the Latimer College." Virginia began her piece once more.

"Oh," said the editor, crossing something out, "one of those."

The lovely people did not seem glad to see her. Virginia wondered what could be the favours for which they so grudgingly obliged Mr Deems.

Then the editor looked up at her and smiled. It was a difficult smile, as if the muscles of his face rebelled against it, and Virginia was grateful that he had achieved it for her. Because he was a newspaper editor, and he was to be her employer for two weeks, and he had smiled encouragingly at her, she felt a rush of admiration for him, and pledged herself to please him.

"Well, I'm sorry, Alice," the editor said quite pleasantly. "There's nothing for you today. We go to press on Fridays, so things haven't begun to warm up round here yet."

Virginia felt blank with anticlimax. All she could think of to say was: "My name's not Alice. It's Virginia. Virginia Martin."

"No doubt it is," said the editor. "I call them all Alice. It saves remembering a new name each time. Come back tomorrow. You can make the Bovril, or something."

"But I——"

"I told you." He began to be less pleasant. "There's nothing for you today."

Virginia went into the other room. The feeble lock on the door did not close properly, and the voice from the kennel yelled: "Shut that flaming door!"

She looked at the clock, from which a wire was looped into the ceiling light along with another wire from a lamp, in a perilous arrangement of plugs and knotted cords. It was only eleven o'clock. The important day had fallen away to nothing before it even began.

The entrance to the offices of *Lady Beautiful* was designed to impress. Thick carpets, pale polished woodwork, a faint aura of perfume, and an assortment of glossy girls in sweaters combined to give the impression that life was in truth the easy and glamorous thing that the stories and articles in the magazine would have its readers believe. The reception-room was like the cover of *Lady Beautiful*, a lovely and shining thing designed to attract the eye and dispose the mind in favour of what lay beyond.

Virginia nodded to those of the girls she knew—they were always changing in the reception-room—and walked through the wide satiny door to what lay beyond. The carpeted corridor continued to breathe elegance and success, but Virginia knew that if she were to open any of the doors on either side, it would be like passing from a grand restaurant through the swing-door into the kitchen. As the doors opened and shut to the comings and goings of men and women, most of whom smiled at Virginia, she could see the desks and typewriters and filing-cabinets and drawing-boards, and ceiling-high piles of back issues of the magazine. She longed for the day when she would be behind one of those doors, sitting at one of those desks, using one of those constantly-ringing telephones.

It was not that Virginia had a consuming passion to work on a woman's magazine. She had set her sights on it because there was a chance for her in this place, and she might as well succeed here as anywhere else. Her lively ambition was catholic in its aims. If something other than journalism had come her way, she would have grasped it with the same eagerness. It did not matter where she succeeded in life, as long as she did succeed, and in her young arrogance, she knew that she would. She had luck. Things went well for her, just as Tiny had always said that they would; only Tiny had not called it luck. She had said it was the angel.

Her mother's secretary greeted her in the neat little office which guarded the door to what the staff called the throne room. Grace was a smooth, discreet girl, unobtrusive in her efficiency. Virginia wondered whether she ever let herself go at home, and said wild and foolish things and went without her girdle. When she saw her in the office, she was always correct, from her parting to her rubber heel-tips, never speaking a word out of place, unruffled by crisis or triumph, accepting with the same half-smile both Helen's splashes of twinkling *camaraderie* and irritable flings of temperament.

23

She picked up the telephone. "Virginia is here. May she come in, Mrs Martin?" she asked, in her voice which could not help being tactful, even when there was nothing to be tactful about. Virginia could hear her mother replying at voluble length.

"She says Yes." Grace replaced the receiver with a slight, well-bred smile.

The throne room was as large as the reception-room, and quite as exquisite. Armchairs and a sofa stood at tastefully planned angles on the carpet, as if it were a drawing-room. The curtains were off-white, tasselled with gold, and on the walls hung lavishly-framed reproductions of the classic paintings of beautiful women.

Helen's desk, a sarcophagus of carved and moulded walnut, stood in the exact centre of the carpet, with a padded swivel-chair, from which Helen could see and be seen by anyone anywhere in the room. She had picked up a telephone as soon as she finished talking to Grace, and Virginia wondered whether it was so that she could wave her daughter to a chair with the gesture of a gracious, but busy woman. There were two other women in the room, with notebooks on their knees. It was evidently a conference, which was what any conversation between more than two people was called.

"Do that, Robert darling," her mother said into the telephone. "A million thanks. I am in your debt for ever." She rang off, and swivelled round with a push of her thickset legs to where Virginia sat on the ledge above the radiator. "What can I do for you, dear heart," she said, slipping into the affectionate mother-and-daughter relationship, as if it were a *peignoir*. She could just as easily slip it off.

"I came to see if you would take me to lunch."

"Lunch? My dearest child, I'm much too busy. Marigold and Judy and I have barely broken the back of the knitting pages."

Judy, the elder of the two women, stood up, honest and square, and so unrelievedly plain that it was a miracle she had ever been taken on to *Lady Beautiful*. However, Virginia knew that she was more use there than a dozen

24

of the fetching girls whom her mother hailed as geniuses one week and fired the next.

"We can finish this afternoon," she said, wanting lunch herself. "There's plenty of time."

Helen frowned, as Judy and Marigold moved towards the door. She did not like her staff to leave the room until she dismissed them.

"Please come," Virginia said. "I've got something to tell you. I've got a job." She had not meant to say it here in front of the others, who would exclaim, and want to hear more; but, as often happened, she had blundered into telling something she had planned to recount in a quiet moment, over a corner table, with all her words for it prepared.

As she feared, the two women stopped on their way to the door. They knew and liked Virginia well enough to be interested in what she did. "A job!" Marigold said. "How exciting. What is it—on a paper?"

"Yes. Well, not exactly. At least, it's on a paper, but it's not a job really, just part of the college training."

"What a good idea," Marigold said, her clever face crinkled into an encouraging smile. "What's the paper?"

"Well," Virginia knew how the words were going to sound and be received in this pretentious room, "it's called the *Northgate Gazette*."

"The *Northgate Gazette*." Her mother cocked her head as if she had not heard aright, and sounded out the words as if they were a foreign language. "That sounds quite enchanting. Tell us more. Stand still, Jinny, and don't fidget about the room. Tell us about it. First, what is Northgate?" She put inverted commas round the name, as if it were a word Virginia had made up.

Virginia glanced at the others. "It's a suburb. One of the outer suburbs."

Seeing Helen's critically-raised eyebrows, Judy wanted to say something that would enable her indirectly to oppose Helen. "That's grand for you, Jinny," she said, clasping her notebook on her wide chest. "It will be a wonderful experience. You're reporting for them, is that it? What's their circulation? Some of these local papers have a huge readership."

"This isn't very big, I don't think," Virginia admitted, "judging from the size of the staff." She had to be honest with Judy, but when she saw the amused look on her mother's face she began to exaggerate stubbornly, until the *Northgate Gazette* began to look like a rival to the *Manchester Guardian*.

Helen was neither deceived nor impressed. "A job is a job, I suppose," she said. "It will keep you in nylons, at least. What are they paying you?"

"I told you, it's only part of the training. They don't pay anything."

"*I* see." Helen's patronizing lilt closed the subject. When they went out to lunch Helen did not ask any more about the *Northgate Gazette*, and Virginia did not want to talk about it.

Later that day, as Virginia turned into the archway at the entrance to the mews, a man turned into it from the opposite direction. He was wearing a black overcoat and a new black hat, which had not yet accommodated itself to his small head. It was the man she had met the other night, the doctor who had stopped working on his car to look at her.

"Hullo." His face had been set, as if he were thinking while he walked, but it dissolved into a smile when he saw her. "Going home?"

"Yes."

"So am I."

They could think of nothing more to say until they reached his doorway. He did not immediately take out his key, and she thought that he was trying to think of something to say to detain her.

"Do you have a job?" he asked. "I mean, are you on your way home from work?"

Virginia told him briefly about the college and the *Northgate Gazette*. He had tolerant brown eyes and a slightly crooked mouth, which tipped his whole face a little to one side when he smiled. She thought that he might be quite good-looking without the overbearing hat, which sat too low on his head, with the brim too straight, like the hat of a wooden figure from Noah's Ark.

"So you got your first job today," the doctor said. "Don't you think this calls for a celebration? Would you—no, darn it, there's Robert. I was going to ask you if you would come up and have a drink, but the chap I live with is working on a paper. We've only got one room, and he can't bear it if I ask people in."

"Come up to our flat then," Virginia said. Why not? Helen would not mind. She never minded seeing a personable man.

Panting a little to keep up the pace which was Virginia's normal rate of going upstairs, the man told her that his name was Felix Allen, and emboldened by talking to her swiftly-climbing back, he added breathlessly that he had hoped he would see her again after the other night.

When they went into the flat, and he took off his coat and hat and sat rather gracefully on the sofa in his well-fitting striped doctor's suit, she saw that he was indeed quite attractive in an unsensational way. His hair was educated by good barbering, and he looked very clean. His crooked smile gave his face a slightly whimsical air, which made the things he said seem more witty than they were.

Virginia guessed that he was neither whimsical nor witty, but really quite earnest. He had a quiet, deep voice, which must work wonders with his female patients. She imagined him sitting at bedsides and soothing neurotic women out of thinking that they were going to die, until their bulging eyes relaxed into dog-like devotion, and they murmured that they did not know where they would be without him.

Helen had not come home yet. The front door of the flat opened directly into the living-room, and when she entered in a flurry of furs, with a cross, tired face, she halted at the sight of Virginia and the nice-looking man and the cocktail glasses, and changed her expression swiftly to charmed surprise.

"This is a neighbour of ours," Virginia said. "Doctor Allen."

27

"A doctor. Well, well." Helen sounded as if that were the one kind of man she wanted to see. She let her gloved hand linger in his for a moment. "How strange that we haven't met before."

"I've only just come to live here," he said. "I met your daughter the other night. I beg your pardon. Have I made a mistake? Is it your daughter?" He favoured Helen with his quizzical smile, and leaned a little forward, as if to see better. "You look more like sisters."

Virginia wanted to run to a mirror to assure herself that this was not true. Was he being automatically suave, or did he really want to pay her mother a compliment? She bit at a nail. Damn Helen and the unaccountable way she had of making men say things like that.

Helen took off her hat, patted her smooth cap of hair, in which the grey streak was cunningly arranged to look as if she rather than nature intended it, and announced that she had had a desperate day and was exhausted.

Virginia went to pour her mother a drink, but Felix was there before her. They talked for a while. Helen did most of the talking, occasionally bringing Virginia into the conversation deliberately, as if she were the odd man out at the party.

She told Felix, as Virginia knew she would, that it was always fascinating to meet a doctor, because you felt that he knew so much about you. Virginia had heard her say this before to doctors, and had watched the variously baffled ways with which they dealt with it.

Felix did not attempt to deal with it. He sat looking quiet and friendly. Helen asked him what was his particular line, and when he said it was gynaecology, her eyes took on the glazed, Narcissus look with which women recognize an opportunity to talk about their insides.

Terrified that she was going to tell him about her fallopian tubes, Virginia got up and created a diversion with the cocktail shaker.

"I've had three," Felix said. "I think I need something to eat. How about letting me take you out to dinner?"

He was looking directly at Virginia, who was standing over

28

him with the shaker, but a cadence of chunky bracelets from the chair behind made her involuntarily look over her shoulder, and Felix took this as a reminder that his invitation should include Helen. Or had he meant to ask her anyway? Hearing Helen's feigned: "Oh, you don't want to take me," and his gallant assurance that he did, Virginia felt disgustedly young. She vowed that she would have nothing more to do with men in their middle thirties until Helen was old enough to have given up the struggle.

Felix, who appeared to be fairly sophisticated, took them to a club in Knightsbridge, where the only illumination was from candles on the tables and the intermittent flames of *crêpes suzettes*. There was a three-piece, dark-skinned orchestra and a handkerchief of dance floor. After the smoked salmon, Felix danced with Virginia. She was disappointed to find that she was a little too tall for him, and wished that she had not been so foolish as to change her working shoes for high heels before they came out. When he danced with Helen after the *tournedos rossini*, their heads were at the right levels. Helen talked excessively to him all through the dance, but he smiled, and did not seem to mind. Virginia finished her glass of wine, and then drank up her mother's, since the waiter did not come to pour her any more.

Tackling, with a forced smile, the difficult feat of trying to look as if you are having a good time when you are sitting alone, she watched Helen moving slowly in Felix's arms among the other couples, and tried to imagine what she was talking about with so many little flicks of her head and circular waves of the hand that lay on his pin-stripe shoulder. What did a mother talk about to a man who was really her daughter's friend? Was she talking like a mother, discussing Virginia fondly, and being a little maternal with Felix, so as to draw him into the family? Not a chance. Helen was having a good time. She looked like a woman dancing with a man, not like a mother dancing with her daughter's boy-friend.

Could Helen be her mother? She was so restless that it was impossible to imagine her ever being in such a bovine state as pregnancy. Virginia looked at her dispassionately, appraising the well-kept figure and the square face, whose ageing skin and captious lines were successfully disguised by candlelight under the careful make-up. Out of doors, in daylight, cosmetics could not do much more for Helen. It would not be very long before even kind lighting would be too cruel to mask the legacy of the discontented years.

Virginia tried to imagine how Felix felt. She remembered from childhood the odd feeling of being jammed up against the firmly-bouncing bosom of the dance mistress. Dancing with Helen would feel like that. Virginia imagined herself as Felix, and felt the supported, rubbery resilience pressed against her chest. But of course it would not feel revolting to him. It would feel pleasant. That was why men held you closely when they were dancing, so that even though they were comparative strangers, they could experience, with perfect propriety, a sensation normally reserved for intimates.

That was why Felix held Helen so close; closer, it seemed to Virginia, peering through the candle shadows, than he had held Helen's daughter when they danced. Or was Helen holding him? Virginia knew that ever since her father had walked out, her mother had been looking for a man, had found several temporary ones, and, at forty-eight, had not yet abandoned the search.

Back at the table, Felix talked with impartial politeness to Virginia and her mother. In the taxi going home, he sat on the little seat opposite them with his knees discreetly drawn away, and spent most of the journey with his head turned to the window, watching the streets.

They stood on the cobbles outside the entrance to the flat. The ping of the taxi meter and the small rattle of its engine sounded very loud in the deserted mews.

"I hope I'll see you again before too long," Felix said.

Virginia opened her mouth to answer, but Helen said quickly: "Of course. Please do feel free to come up to the flat whenever your industrious friend turns you out. Thank you so much for a very charming evening. It was extraordinarily kind of you. The club is delightful, and you were the best of hosts."

When her mother had finished being debonair, Virginia tried to express her thanks, but Helen had used up all the phrases.

"It's for me to thank you," Felix said. "You were good to come out with me. I don't know when I've enjoyed myself so much."

He lifted the unbecoming hat to the two of them standing in the doorway. Which one was he looking at—Virginia or Helen?

"A nice evening, didn't you think?" Helen said the next morning, when Virginia brought the tray to her bed.

"Yes, it was all right."

"A charming man, I thought, and clever too. Did you know he was on the staff at Westminster? They don't give those posts to just anybody, though one might be forgiven for thinking that they did, judging by the treatment one gets in some hospitals." She slit an envelope with her little brass paper-cutter. "Of course, he's much too old for you." She said it in a detached, superior way, as if it were indisputable.

Virginia put her hands in her coat pockets and stuck her head forward. "Maybe. But he's much too young for you," she said.

Helen looked up. The hair-net and lack of make-up gave her a peeled look. "But, dear heart," she said, refusing to take offence, "don't be absurd. As if I would dream . . . He's your boy-friend, I thought."

"He's no one's boy-friend," Virginia said abruptly, going to the door. "I'll probably never see him again."

The first person she saw in the mews was Felix, getting out his car. It was a new but sober car, prosperous enough for a successful young specialist, but not as dashing as it could have been if he was going to spend that much money.

It was a raw, grey morning. The cracks between the cobblestones were puttied with dirty ice, and in the sharp wind, Felix's face looked small and pinched under the mushroom of a hat. When he offered to drive Virginia to the station, she said that she wanted to walk. He stepped forward to persuade her, but she went quickly away from him, her heels ringing on the frosty cobbles. It was too cold to bother with a man just now, and her mother might look out of the window and see her getting into the car, and think that she was being sly.

3

As THE week drew to its close, things began to hum a little more busily at the *Northgate Gazette*, but Reggie Porter, the young boor with the big feet, who liked Virginia no better than she liked him, saw to it that she was not included in the hum. She spent most of her time, at his uncivil behest, running to and from the printers with pages of copy or galley proofs, and on press day, which she had thought would be the high-spot of the week, she spent all afternoon hurrying through the windy streets with pages of wet news-print. She wanted to ask many questions, but the other reporters were too busy to answer, and the editor was having his weekly press-day bout of indigestion, and seemed to have forgotten who she was and why she was there.

The printers were housed in a shabby wooden building in a yard off a side-street two blocks away. They had many other matters on hand besides the *Northgate Gazette*, and to reach Mr Couliss, who was her liaison there, Virginia had to step round and over piles of posters and pamphlets, and little mean-looking magazines devoted to such eclectic subjects as nudism and muscle culture.

Mr Couliss was short and full of spittle, in a greasy-backed waistcoat and gym shoes, and he grew quite racy with her as she came and went on press day. If she asked him a question about the printing of the paper, he would run his tongue over his lips and say: "You don't want to bother your head about things like that, a nice little dish like you."

Virginia, wishing to fall in with the way of things, had started off by being quite pert and chummy with him, but as the day advanced, and his jokes advanced with it to a grosser degree of innuendo, she wished that she had kept her distance from the start.

When Mr Couliss, frothing a little, informed her that she was a hot number, and that he was game for a bit of fun too, any time she liked to try him, she slammed back through the counter flap into the office, and told Reggie that she did not want to run any more errands to the printers.

"No doubt," he said, "you'd like to sit in the old man's office on your big, fat fanny and run the show. Old Couliss made a pass at you, I suppose." Reggie put his hands in his trouser pockets and stuck his stomach out, pursing his thick lips with a worldly air 'You women are all the same. Lead a man on as far as you dare, and then turn round and run screaming for help if he takes you up on it."

"As if I would," Virginia said disgustedly. "He's a horrible little man, and he's got a mind as foul as some of that trash he prints down there."

"By which I suppose you mean the *Gazette*?" Reggie rocked back on his heels and lowered his head at her like a bull.

"I didn't, but you can take it that way if you like."

"You may go home. You may leave," Reggie said grandly, his thick, throaty voice spoiling the high-toned effect for which he was trying. "Get out of here, and don't come back next week neither."

"On the contrary." The editor came out of his kennel with a bottle of tablets in his hand, looking for a glass of water. "I want Alice in early Monday. I've got a top job for you, girl. Interview with Doris Miller. She's opening in panto at the Empire. Not quite our district, but near enough for us to cover, and beat the *Courier* on their own ground. I've a good contact at the theatre, and I've got it lined up for you to go and see her. Exclusive. Thought I'd try you out."

"Now look here." Reggie blustered up to him like an unsubtle boxer coming out of the corner of a ring. "You can't do that. You can't go over our heads and send that girl out on a job like that. She don't know anything."

"We'll find out whether she does." The editor poured some souring milk into a cup, and swallowed two tablets, his face grey with the discomfort within.

Virginia sat in the dusty stalls of the theatre where Doris Miller was in the toils of a last-minute, scrappy dress

34

rehearsal. She felt neglected and anxious. She had been allowed into the theatre, although Mr Askey, the editor's contact, was not there, and no one could say where he had gone or when he would be back. She had been shown into a seat by an elderly man in a fisherman's sweater and dirty plimsolls, and told to sit still and keep quiet.

Virginia sat still and quiet for a long time in the fusty gloom of the dilapidated theatre. There was nothing else she could do. The time went by, and Mr Askey did not come, and she fretted about the interview and what the editor would say if she did not return with her story soon. He had given her this chance partly to annoy Reggie Porter, but partly, she believed, because he did think quite well of her, and wanted to see what she could do. She must do well, or she would let him down as well as herself. He was a cranky, disgruntled man, but she admired him, because he was an editor, and she liked him, because he had been nicer to her than he need have been.

On the stage, lit by all the harsher lights in the electrician's repertory, a dozen girls with goose-flesh on their thick thighs went dispiritedly through their paces, were shouted at to stop, and stood about dough-faced, rubbing their arms, until they were jerked into action again by the agitated voice of the producer.

At intervals, Miss Doris Miller came wearily on to the stage in different changes of costume. She was a sharp-featured henna-head, with the powder thick on the pouches under her eyes, an old-fashioned hour-glass figure, and legs that tapered like cones into wondrously slim ankles and tiny feet. Since she was the principal boy, her costumes consisted of various tunics and jerkins over the long, pyramidal stretch of black nylon tights. The tights were the most expensive part of her costume. If a stage-hand brushed past her with a piece of scenery, she would clap her hands to her thighs and shriek out: "Mind my tights, you clumsy sod!"

Each time the principal boy left the stage, Virginia wondered whether she could get up and go through the pass-door at the side of the stage, and beard her in her dressing-room for the promised interview. Each time, just when she had mustered enough nerve to do it, Doris Miller, who only had to change from the waist up, was back on the stage again in a new outfit, and Virginia had lost her chance. The little old man in the fisherman's jersey went in and out of the pass-door all the time, grumbling to himself. Virginia moved to the end of the row so that she could tackle him as he went by.

"What can I do?" Virginia appealed to him. "I must see Miss Miller. Does she know I'm here? The interview was all arranged. Do you think I could go backstage and find her?"

"You can't do that," the old man said. "Backstage is like a mad-house, and Miss Miller don't talk to anyone. My, what a temper! I wish you'd have seen her just now. Created bloody murder when she heard there was a chap from the *Courier* at the stage-door. And language! Had him thrown out, block and tackle."

"Oh, good." Virginia's spirits rose to the challenge. Although she could not understand why Doris Miller was so squeamish about the publicity she surely needed, the eviction of the *Courier* was a good chance for its rival, the *Gazette*. She must take the chance.

"Side by side!" squeaked the chorus, their thin voices failing away from the note as they kicked their way breathlessly off-stage, arms on each other's shoulders. Virginia waited until the producer was watching the Lancashire comedian in one of his Dame costumes, and slipped excitedly through the pass-door to the chaotic world backstage.

She found her way past ropes and pieces of scenery and gimcrack boats and coaches to a narrow stone passage-way, which led to a twisting flight of green stone stairs. Flattening herself against the wall as an avalanche of sturdy girls in feathers and cockatoo bustles clattered past her with darned woollen shawls over their shoulders, she climbed the stairs to an upper passage where the dressing-rooms were. She walked along the scarred and peeling doors, which appeared to be always kicked open, and looked at the half-obliterated numbers. There were no names on any of them.

A man came out of one of the rooms in a tail-coat with

36

frayed satin lapels, his dickey and clip-on white bow-tie stained with ochre grease-paint. When Virginia enquired for Doris Miller's room, he asked: "You her daughter?"

"I? No, of course not."

"Well, kid, I just thought. She's got a grown-up daughter, I know. Sings in cabaret up West. But I don't suppose she'd let her come down here. She doesn't like to be seen with her, they say. Made the girl take a different name, so no one would know she had a daughter that old." He lit a cigarette and leaned against the scribbled wall, holding the cigarette downwards into the palm of his nicotine-stained hand.

"What's she like?"

The man seemed friendly. His painted smile was wide, showing chipped, badly-spaced teeth.

"The daughter? Bit of all right, from her pictures."

"No. I mean Miss Miller."

"Her. Oh, kid, she's a sow. One of the original pigs. I've met some cows in my time, but never such a horse-faced goat as our Doris."

"I'm supposed to interview her," Virginia said, "for my newspaper. Which is her room?"

"You born yesterday?" The man shuffled his cracked patent-leather shoes in a tiny dance step, without moving his shoulders from the wall. "You've got a hope. You think she wants it splashed on the front page that she's come down to appearing in a tenth-rate show like this? She's only doing it because she's practically down and out. But she's keeping it dark. She's always thinking she's going to make a big come-back up West. You know what these old-timers are. She doesn't know she's finished. They never do. Anyway," he added casually, dropping his cigarette and turning his foot on it, "she's gone home."

"Oh, no!" Virginia was aghast. "I can't go back to the office and say I haven't seen her. This was a sort of trial for me. The first big job I've been sent on. I can't mess it up like this."

"I used to feel like that once," the man said. He looked at the end of his cigarette and gave a short laugh. "Thought I'd die of shame if I bungled a step. Now I dance like a

37

bull's foot most of the time, but I don't care as long as I can hang on to the job. Time was though, when I——"

Virginia cut him short. Nice as he was, and with a life, no doubt, seamed by tragic disillusionment, she had no time to get nostalgic with him. "Do something for me," she said. "Tell me where that woman lives, and I'll get her at home. I'll make her see me. I won't be beaten by her."

The man winked at her. "As it happens, I know," he said. "She'd have me shot for telling you, but if you won't let on and since I've a daughter myself—here, got a pencil? Ambassador Hotel, Lulgate Square. That's somewhere in Paddington, I think. Look, kid, she won't see you. She's a bitch on wheels. I'm telling you."

"What do you bet she won't? Get the *Northgate Gazette* on Saturday and see if I didn't get my story!"

Lulgate Square was across the Paddington railway tracks, between the Harrow Road and Edgware Road. The tall Edwardian houses, with stone steps rising over the basement entrance, had been built in the Square's palmier days, when servants toiled up and down the many stairs, and nursemaids walked prim children in the little railed garden between the houses. Now the paint and plaster had fallen in lumps and not been replaced, and the rows of bells and name-cards by the doorway of each house showed that they were no longer family homes.

The spear-tipped area railings still remained, but the little garden was fenced with wire, since the railings had long ago been taken away for scrap metal, and had not been renewed after the war. The wire gate was padlocked, but many children and dogs had climbed in over the sagging fence and reduced the grass to a dust-patch and the shrubbery to a few straggled bushes, dying slowly under the layers of soot and sulphur from the railway.

Two houses at one corner of the square had been shattered by a bomb, and had never been rebuilt. No one had thought it worth while to repair war damage which had only hastened the decay already begun long before the Germans made a target of Paddington Station. The bomb-site showed the foundations of old cellars, like bones exposed in an open grave. There were rusted tanks and cisterns in there, broken shoes, and saucepans and rags, and a blackened little bath lying on its side among the caked earth and weeds. On the high, blank wall of the house which stood next to this desolate plot, there showed quite clearly the marks of fire-places and the steeply zigzagging staircase.

The house from which the buildings had been torn away was the Ambassador Hotel. The name was painted on the fanlight above the door. There were five bells of different sizes, but none of the cards tacked beside them said Miller. After a while, Virginia rang the bell marked Caretaker. She heard a jangling far away in the house, and presently a woman in slippers and a flowered overall looked out of the basement door, and squinted up at Virginia on the steps.

"Doug's out," the woman said, "if it's him you want."

"I'm looking for Miss Miller. Miss Doris Miller. I thought she lived here."

"Are you from the furniture company?" the woman asked, drawing in her mouth. "You're not? Oh, well then, her bell's the third one up. The name's Porritt. That's her married name, you see."

Virginia thanked her, and the woman rubbed her hands and observed that it was cold enough to have a white Christmas yet, and went back into the basement.

As Virginia reached for the Porritt bell, the front door opened and a woman with a shopping-bag came out, leaving the door ajar so that Virginia could go inside. Here was a stroke of luck. She had been wondering how she could get in if Doris Miller felt too misanthropic to answer the bell. She calculated that the third bell up must indicate the first floor, climbed the stairs, and came to a halt on a small landing with two doors. The voices of a man and a woman could be heard behind one of them. Doris Miller was evidently at home in domestic bliss with Mr Porritt.

Virginia's knock was answered by Mr Porritt, in a colour-less cardigan and baggy tweed trousers. The room went back to the right at an angle, where the foot of a brass bed, hung with clothing, stuck out. Virginia could not see Miss Miller on the bed, but could hear her impatient voice: "Who is it, George? What do they want? I'm resting."

"What do you want? She's resting," George repeated obediently. He was a paunchy man, with a square head of grey hair and a resigned blue eye.

"I'm from the *Northgate Gazette*," Virginia said. "I was supposed to interview Miss Miller at the theatre, but I'm afraid I missed her there, so I thought, if she could spare me a few moments——"

"Go away," said the voice from the bed. "Get out of here. I'm not seeing anyone from the press."

"Go away," repeated George, softening the words. "She's not seeing anyone from the press."

"But Mr Askey promised. He arranged for me to see you." Virginia pitched her voice to reach round the corner of the room.

There was a grunt and a creaking of springs, and a foot could be seen kicking under the tumbled blankets at the foot of the bed. "Mr Askey can go to hell, and so can you." The voice was less distinct, as if it had gone to ground.

George did not like to repeat this. He smiled uncertainly, and Virginia smiled back, even more uncertainly.

"Has she gone?" The blankets heaved again, and the voice was clearer, as if Doris Miller had sat up in the bed.

"Please let me talk to you just for a moment." Virginia took a step forward into the room. She could not step farther without treading on Mr Porritt's stockinged feet. "I want to write something that will be good publicity for you. You can see it before it's printed, if you like."

"Get the hell out of here!" Miss Miller cried. "How dare you come here bothering me, making fun of me. Don't think I don't know your kind. The press. I've had some. All they want to do is tear your guts out."

"No, honestly, I——"

"Go away, or I'll call the police."

"Go away or we'll call the police," George said half-heartedly.

"Don't just stand there, George. Go and call them! No, wait a minute—what did she say the paper was? The *North-*

gate Gazette. Go downstairs and ring up the editor and tell him what I think of him for sending this woman here to meddle in my business. She's trying to make trouble for me, but I'll make worse trouble for her."

"You can't afford, you know," Virginia said, trying to keep calm, "not to work with the press. Every actress needs publicity."

"I'll get all the publicity I want my own way," Miss Miller retorted, "and that won't be from some twopenny-halfpenny scandal sheet in the back end of nowhere. George, get down to that telephone and lay it on hot. And you—get going, or I'll get up and kick you down the stairs myself."

"Get going," George said, looking at Virginia sadly, "or she'll kick you down the stairs."

Virginia backed on to the landing, and lowered her voice. "You won't really telephone the editor?"

"I'll have to," George said. "You heard what she said. Just got to get my shoes." Virginia went dejectedly down the stairs. In the hall, she saw the telephone hanging on the wall, with a box for money below it. She thought of cutting the wires, but what good would that do? She could not cut the wires of all the telephone boxes in Paddington.

When Virginia went into the reporters' room, Reggie was alone, looking very pleased with himself.

"In there." He poked his thick thumb towards the dog-kennel. "The old man's waiting to see you."

"A big help you turned out to be." The editor sat leaning back with his hands on the edge of the desk, his pill boxes and medicine bottles ranged before him like boy scouts. "I've had Doris Miller's husband on my tail, and the theatre too. It seems you were very rude and insulting. Quite a credit to the *Gazette*."

"But I wasn't! I swear it."

"You must have been, or she would have talked to you. You must have been damned rude for an actress to kick you out. I've never known one yet who didn't crave to see her name in print."

"You don't understand," Virginia said. "She thinks it's

a terrible come-down to have to do pantomime at the Hurleigh Empire. She's afraid that if we do a story on it, one of the dailies will pick it up and make fun of her. She thinks it will spoil her chances of a come-back. Poor old soul, you can't help feeling sorry for her, in a way."

"Better start feeling sorry for yourself," the editor said sourly. "And for me. You may not think the story was worth much. She's a has-been, I know, but she's the nearest approach to a star we ever get in this backwater. Of course we should write her up. You've made a mess of it, and made me look a fool, and more of a fool for giving you the chance. I tell you, if old man Deems wants to send any more of his half-wits round here, I'll tell him where he can put them. I've tried to make this rag into a decent newspaper, and I can't have the people who represent it going about insulting everybody right and left."

"You won't believe that I didn't, will you?"

He shook his head. "The subject is closed. I'm through with you."

"Can't I even stay till the end of the week?"

He rocked the front legs of his chair down to the floor. "How can I let you, you idiot, with that big oaf in there crowing his head off at me for taking the wrong chance on you? He thinks I only tried to help you because I—— Oh, well, skip it." He rubbed his head and muttered: "But when it comes to being called a dirty old man——"

"I'd better go then," Virginia said. She wondered whether he would manage his smile for her, but his face remained seamed with displeasure.

As she turned, he suddenly stood up, and stretched out his hand across the bottles and pill boxes. "Come and see me when you're editing the woman's page of the *Sunday Express*," he said, "if you ever remember we exist." He shook hands gravely, and Virginia went out.

As she shut the door, Reggie lunged forward, with a jeering remark ready in his mouth. Virginia pushed him out of the way and went down into the High Street, which had become so familiar in the last week, but was now already a part of her past.

When Virginia arrived home at the flat, she discovered that part of the turmoil inside her was a gnawing hunger. All the way home in the train she had brooded and fretted, and gone over and over all the small, distasteful scenes of the day which had led to her downfall. Emotion always stimulated her appetite. She felt ravenous. She went straight to the kitchen, found bread and butter and the end of a ham, and went into the living-room, chewing on the thick sandwich, thinking, with unfocused eyes.

She was startled to find Helen sitting at her little walnut escritoire, writing letters.

"Do I have to account to you for all my movements?" Helen said, when Virginia asked why she was there. "I am not a stenographer, chained to the office from nine to five. I might ask what you are doing here. I thought you were running around the suburbs being an ace reporter."

"I was." Virginia sat down, too dispirited to invent a story. "They threw me out."

"Dear heart, no!" Helen rose and swung round to sit with Virginia, all in one swift movement of whirling skirt and jingling jewellery. At first, while Virginia told her glumly what had happened, she was too sympathetic. Virginia did not want that. She did not want pity and soothing nonsense, as if she were a child weeping over a broken toy. She wanted fighting support, a rugged belief in her, which would help her own stamina, and push her ahead again.

"You're very sweet, Helen," she said, getting up and brushing crumbs off her skirt. "It's nice of you to be so concerned, when I know you thought the whole thing was ridiculous anyway. But you're making me feel worse. I feel awful." She went to the window, and looked down into the mews, where the first small flakes of snow were feathering the cobbles.

"I'm a failure." She said this hoping to be contradicted, but her mother, turning off her sympathy as swiftly as she had turned it on, said crisply: "All right then, so you're a failure. You've fallen down on this, but what are you wailing about? It isn't the end of your career, and if it were, there are plenty of other things in life besides newspapers."

"You don't understand," Virginia said, wondering how many girls were saying that to their mothers at this moment. "I know there are other things, but since I had decided on this particular one, I just had to be good at it. Look, it's snowing."

"I shall have to buy boots," Helen said absently. "Grey suede this year, I think. And I do understand, even if I am your mother. I know you've always thought that you could do anything you turned your hand to, and mostly you could. Rather sickeningly successful. I'll admit to you now, Jinny, though I held my peace at the time, that it used quite to embarrass me with the other mothers on Speech Day at the school, that in anything at which you'd happened to try, you came out top. Look how you won the tennis tournament, although you had taken up tennis long after most of the other girls. Well, he who exalteth himself shall be humbled, somebody said somewhere."

"Oh, Helen. *Christ* said it."

"I know, I know. Don't always talk to me as if I were a heathen, just because old Tiny pumped you full of sentimental twaddle when you were at an impressionable age. *My* God, I'm thankful to say, is not to be found in hymn singing and pretty pictures. My God is in the air around me, the streets, the sky, the open fields. I like to think that my religion is in the life I lead," she said simply, pleased with the phrase.

"That's the sort of facile thing everyone says who can't be bothered to go to church," Virginia said. "You didn't bother to bring me up to believe in religion, and now I haven't got any. I don't know anything about it, and I don't know where to start. I just know the things that Tiny told me, about angels, and Now I lay me down to sleep. They're childish, but at least she made me believe in them."

"There is no need to get bitter with me," Helen said, "just because you're disappointed with yourself today. You're not often disappointed, I must say, but you've found out now what it is to fail at something, and I have no doubt the experience will be a salutary lesson for you."

"Please don't preach at me," Virginia said. "I came home to get some help."

"No, you didn't, because you didn't think I would be here. You came to get a sandwich," Helen said triumphantly. She went back to her desk, lifted and shook her hand to run the bracelets up her arm, and began to write again.

"I'm going down to the college," Virginia said. "Don't wait supper for me. Or are you going out?"

"Yes, I'm going out," Helen said without looking round. "And don't ask me with whom, because I shan't tell you. I have a new boy-friend."

Could it be Felix? Oh, the rat. But presumably it could be. He might have decided that there were choicer pickings to be had from ripe fruit. The back of Helen's head, and the clipped nape of her neck looked very smug.

It was the last evening class of the course. Virginia did not have to attend it, and the Latimer College seemed trivial and useless now that she had been in and out of a newspaper job; but some mulish element in her dejection forced her to make the worst of a bad day.

Before the class was over, she was disconcerted to find that the heaviness on her chest was moving into her throat, up through her face, and trying to squeeze itself out of her eyes in tears. She stared at Miss Thompson, and Miss Thompson wavered and blurred. Virginia hardly ever cried. She had found that by straining her eyes wide open and thinking of something else, she could usually avoid it. It did not work now. A tear spilled out of her eye, and slid down her cheek. She turned her face quickly away from Mr Benberg, sought for a handkerchief, found none, and had to use the back of her hand.

After the class was over, the students said farewell to Miss Thompson and to each other, with the illusory regret of people who have been brought together by chance, and are not likely to see each other again. As Virginia walked despondently along the dark passage that led to the basement stairs, there was a touch on her sleeve. It was Mr Benberg, in a bright-blue belted overcoat, multi-coloured woollen gloves and a limp-brimmed hat, turned down all the way round.

"Forgive me," he said. "We've said good-bye, I know, and you're anxious to be away, but I had to say—well—you were crying in there."

"No. Yes, I was." She hoped that his kindly look would not make her cry again.

"What's wrong?" He matched his step to hers as they went down the long passage, which smelled of unwashed floor and wet raincoats.

"Everything. I did everything wrong today, and they threw me out of the newspaper office."

She thought that he would tell her that there were other fish in the sea, but he seemed to understand. "Going back to your mother?" he asked.

"No, she's out."

"People shouldn't be alone when they feel low. Don't go home. Come back with me, do please, and have something to eat, and meet my wife. I've told her so much about you."

"That's very kind of you, but I——" Virginia began. Then she changed her mind. Her own company was dreary at the moment. The company of Mr and Mrs Benberg was not likely to be stimulating, but perhaps it was better than being alone.

Mrs Benberg had a steak and kidney pudding waiting in its steaming cloth, and there was enough for Virginia, and still some left over for the small brown dog which lay on the ledge under the table.

"Disappointment doesn't take the edge off your appetite, I'm glad to see," Mrs Benberg observed, slicing treacle tart. She served it with flourishes and large gestures. She was a big woman, bigger both in height and breadth than her husband, and everything she did and said was expansive, and a little wild. Her hair was wild, like a frayed rope, and pins scattered out of it when she energetically nodded or shook her head. Her clothes were strange and disordered, as if she had put her hands into drawers with her eyes closed, and put on whatever came out in a dark room.

Mr Benberg was entirely and happily dependent on her. She undressed him like a baby, stirred his tea, and put salt and pepper on his plate for him. He was a quiet man, surrounded and washed over by his wife's vitality, like a stone in a torrent. He did not mind. He appeared content to be submerged beneath a personality that was livelier and noisier than his. Anxious at first about Virginia's visit, his lip twitched more than usual, but as the meal progressed, and Virginia's smile returned, the spasms came less frequently, and his mouth settled to rest.

In the little dining-room, stuffed full of furniture, books, old magazines and curly china ornaments, Mrs Benberg charged the air like a dynamo. Everything except Mr Benberg was abundant, like herself. The food was bounteous, overflowing the dishes and the plates on to which she piled it. Thick slices of bread tumbled off the board, and the crammed fruit dish spilled grapes and nuts on to the table-cloth. The monstrous, overgrown plants, which stood in every corner, were bursting out of their pots with the energy they drew from Mrs Benberg through the watering-can.

Virginia began to feel better before she was half-way through the rich steak and kidney pudding. Mr Benberg was so cordial, with his long, mild face and his nervous mouth. Mrs Benberg was so welcoming and enthusiastic, and so crazily affectionate, jumping up at unexpected moments to plant a smacking kiss upon Virginia, and tell her that she was a great girl. "Top hole, oh, absolutely the tops," she cried, loosely slangy. "If only Jim were here, eh, Father?"

Jim, in the uniform of an officer in the Merchant Navy, looked down at them cheerily from an embossed silver frame on the dresser. He looked nothing like his father. The exuberant blood of Mrs Benberg coursed in his veins. His cheeks were bursting with rude health, his eyes twinkled, and his hair sprang up from his head as if all the brilliantine in the world would never tame it. His mother kissed the picture wetly after she had shown it to Virginia, and then kissed Mr Benberg, to show that there was no favouritism.

47

"Feeling better, aren't you, love?" she said, watching Virginia grow more relaxed, watching, it almost seemed, with her bright, erratic eyes, the thoughts in Virginia's head clearing and sorting themselves out, and casting away the depression.

"You had a bad time today," Mrs Benberg said, pouring strong, dark tea from a fat teapot into outsize cups. "But it's nothing to fret over. A lovely young girl like you—why should you worry about such a potty concern? To the devil with them, I say. Who cares for the *Northgate Gazette*?" She waved the teapot over her head like a banner, sprinkling brown drops on her hair, and Mr Benberg called out thinly: "Hurry!"

"You're destined for higher things than that," Mrs Benberg said, dumping the teapot, and suddenly drawing her thick brows darkly down so that her eyes were glittering slits. "Don't argue with me. I'm prophetic. I see these things, don't I, Father? I see great things for you, love. Money, success, fame——"

"A tall, dark stranger?" Virginia laughed, realizing that she had not laughed all day.

"Ah," said Mrs Benberg, "that we don't know. Sex is the great mystery of life. Even the prophetic eye can't always fathom it out. However, drink up your tea, and let's have a look at the shape of the leaves."

"*I know where I'm going,*" she sang, in a rowdy, cracked voice, as she stared into Virginia's half-pint cup. "*And I know who's going with me*—— Not a thing. I must be off form tonight." She got up suddenly, scattering hairpins and paper napkins. "*I know who I love, but the dear knows who I'll marry.*" She sang gaily to herself as she swept out to the kitchen with a pile of toppling plates.

She continued to sing raucously in the kitchen, running gallons of scalding water into the sink, and making mountains of suds, while Virginia went with Mr Benberg to look at his manuscripts. The house was very small, but one of the ground-floor rooms had been dedicated for use as Mr Benberg's study. Mrs Benberg was just as earnest about his writing as he was, and equally convinced that he

48

would one day be acknowledged as the greatest writer in the world.

There was a fine desk in the study, an expensive typewriter, and a literary-looking chair with a leather seat and brass studs, which Mrs Benberg had given her husband on his last birthday. The rest of the space was taken up by a gigantic wardrobe, which housed camphor-laden clothes at the top, and the neat stacks of manuscripts in the bottom drawer.

"Here they are," Mr Benberg said, a slight croon coming into his voice, as he opened the drawer and reverently handled the thick piles of typescript, tied with pink tape from the insurance office.

He took one pile out, and cradled it, smiling. "All these words," he said. "All my nights and nights of words, taking meaning, taking shape, growing and flowering to fulfilment. Here it is." He held the manuscript a little away from him and beamed at it. "It does me good just to look at it."

"Have you really got twelve books in there?"

"I have. Twelve finished novels, which the world has never seen."

"Some day," Mrs Benberg appeared suddenly in the doorway, with a dish-towel round her waist and her arms covered in suds to the elbow, "some day the world will know and acclaim, and then you, Virginia, will be able to say: 'I knew him before you did. I saw his works in manuscript,' and people will shake you by the hand. Go on, read a little. Father won't mind."

Mr Benberg put the bundle of pages down on the desk, and Virginia sat down and began to read, while the Benbergs stood by, he clasping his hands and watching her closely, she wiping a plate round and round with a sodden cloth.

At first, Virginia's eye was caught by the beauty of the words in which Mr Benberg had framed his immortal thoughts. The phrases were lyrical, the choice of words romantic.

"But this is lovely!" she said, looking up at the end of the first page. "It's beautiful writing. Surely someone would want to publish this."

49

Mrs Benberg put her wet arm round her husband's waist, and they stood there, nodding and smiling and watching Virginia confidently. She had read several pages before she realized that she had no idea what the book was about. Thinking that she had been inattentive, she went back and read some of the paragraphs again, but they still conveyed nothing. She had read some half-dozen pages without grasping anything. There was nothing to grasp. The whole thing was meaningless. It was merely a florid collection of lyrical phrases and bell-like words, woven together lovingly, but with no thought for their meaning. There were no characters in the book, and no recognizable scene or incident. It was just, as Mr Benberg had said, words. Words carefully set down for the sheer joy of the individual sound of each one, but with no sense in the juxtaposition of one to the other. It was not difficult to understand why no one would publish Mr Benberg's books.

She looked up. "What did I tell you?" Mrs Benberg crowed. "Isn't it staggering?"

"Yes," Virginia said. "Yes, it certainly is. I—I am quite stunned." She was at a loss what to say, but this seemed to satisfy them. They were not asking for her opinion. They were merely expecting her to confirm theirs. Mr Benberg straightened the pages, retied the tape, and put the bundle tenderly back among its baffling fellows in the drawer.

They went into the sitting-room, and drank cherry brandy in tumblers before a blazing fire. Jim stood on the mantelpiece in a tortoiseshell frame, beaming on his parents. How happy they were! Mr Benberg with his kindliness, and the beloved illusion that brought him such joy night after night as he typed his beautiful nonsense, Mrs Benberg with her great moonstruck heart, and her magnificent zest for life.

Virginia was happy too, sitting there untroubled and warm, with the two of them so generously glad to have her. Strangely, although Mr Benberg was only an ineffectual dreamer, and Mrs Benberg seemed at times as mad as a hatter, they had managed to give her the help she had looked for in vain from her mother. Mrs Benberg's enthusiasm was catching. Her optimism restored Virginia's belief in herself, and enabled her to see the day's setback as a mere stumble on a staircase that she was bound to ascend.

Mrs Benberg raised her glass. The cherry brandy was touched with points of fire from the flames in the roaring grate. "A toast!" she cried. "To your health, Virginia, and jolly good luck to you!" She threw back her untidy head, tossed down the brandy, gasped in satisfaction, then settled back in her chair and suddenly picked up a length of orange wool from the table beside her and began to knit furiously.

"Things will go well with you, love," she said, her eyes swivelling to follow the points of the long, thick needles. "Things will come to you. I feel that. I'm prophetic, did I tell you? Father knows. I see more than I should sometimes, don't I, old friend?" She chuckled over her knitting, wagging her head.

"I've always felt that I might be lucky," Virginia said, leaning forward to stroke the harsh fur of the little brown dog, who lay with distended stomach on the hearthrug. It was almost on her lips to tell them what Tiny used to say about the guardian angel. Involuntarily, she glanced into the corner where a flourishing begonia tumbled its myriad little pink bells in a waterfall of blossom. She felt so safe in this room that it was possible to imagine that her angel stood there with calmly folded wings and a serene face, approving of her choice of friends.

Mrs Benberg flung down her knitting, and several stitches slid off the end of the fat needle. "Luck!" she said scornfully. "There is no such thing as luck. Luck is a reward, not a chance gift. It's only for those who fight for it. The people who say they're unlucky don't know that. They think they have been badly done by, when really they've done badly by themselves. But I tell you," she dropped her voice to a Biblical chant, "To him that hath shall be given. You know what that means, I suppose?" She leaned forward with her skirt straining over her spread knees, and stared at Virginia with glowing eyes.

"Yes, I think so. It always sounded unfair to me."

"Not unfair! Not, not! Why, it's the very plum-stone and essence of fairness. It doesn't mean that the rich people are going to get more money, and the poor are going to lose their pennies. Ridiculous notion. What it means is this. It means: to him that hath the courage to stand up to life shall be given chances, but to him that hath not the courage shall be taken away even those chances which he hath."

She got up and walked about the room, making the furniture tremble. She was excited by what she had said. She grunted to herself, and made jerky upward movements of her hands. Then she stopped in her tracks, the light went out of her face, and she grew calm. "Time to let the dog out, Father," she said mildly. "It's after ten."

Virginia said that she must go home, and Mr Benberg and the dog took her into the frosted garden and let her out of the little creaking gate. He stood by the gate and waved, and Mrs Benberg waved strenuously from the front door, and called gaily after Virginia until she was out of earshot.

Virginia rode home on a bus through streets that were at first unfamiliar to her. The Benbergs lived far out in the north-west of London, at the end of one of those long roads, once a coaching way out of the city, and now winding and narrowing and broadening past changing stretches of small factories, garages, houses, shops, school railings, and the long, dirty wall of a gasworks. The bus stopped and started, picked people up outside cinemas, let them down to hurry away round the corners of dark side-roads, and pursued its interminable course again unhurriedly, as if the driver were not anxious to get home to his wife.

As the bus moved in and out of the different boroughs, the street lighting changed. Here there were concrete poles, swan-necked and hideous, flooding the road with a shadowless blue light that turned the people on the pavements into ghosts, stark-faced, with dead lips. Then the bus passed into the shadows, as the fluorescent lights gave place to old-fashioned lamps, which cast pools of dim yellow light through the leafless plane trees, and left wide patches of darkness, where the few late walkers trod like poachers, mysterious, up to no good.

Then again the roadway was lit by globes of orange light, hanging in pairs like giant fruit along the middle of the road. Half asleep in her seat, Virginia grew alert to realize that she knew these lights, or some just like them. Memory opened, and she saw again the men on the high red trolleys, hanging up the lights, while she and Tiny, out shopping for vegetables, paused among the staring people on the pavement, and stared upwards with them.

She heard the disapproving things that the people were saying: "Hideous, that's what it is."

"Great overblown Belisha beacons, I call them. Why can't they leave things as they were?"

"That's the Council for you. Always something new. And who's to pay for it? That's what I'd like to know."

"Who always pays? Just wait and see if the rates don't go up!"

Virginia remembered that there was talk about the lights for quite a while, but presently the lights became part of the High Street, and after a time they were not new any more, but already old-fashioned compared to the glaring illuminations that other councils were erecting in other parts of London.

She looked out along the glowing edge of the pavement, and saw that it was not only the orange lights that were familiar, but the pavement itself. Here was the imposing double pillar-box, with an oval top, and one slot for Country and one for London and Abroad. Here was that same draper's shop, with the gilt lettering and the cards of hooks and eyes hanging on the door, unchanged amid a row of shops that had been modernized. Here was the post office, with the clock slipped a little to one side, so that twelve o'clock pointed to the magnetic north, and here was that very vegetable shop with the green awning, under which she had stood with Tiny and watched the men on the trolley putting up the lights.

This was the corner where the dogs lifted their legs against the bins of potatoes. This was her own corner, where you turned to plod up the hill for home.

She had never returned to the cold, unfriendly house since she and her mother had left it nine years ago. When she was still seeing her father, once during every school holiday, he did not live there. He had let the house, and Helen used frequently to regret that her disgust with the house had made her so hasty in relinquishing it, since she might now be getting the rent herself.

Virginia stood up and reached for the wire of the bell. When the bus stopped, she walked back to the corner, and then up the hill past the dark houses to the one with the shrubby garden which had once been her playground. It was very cold. She remembered that it had always been colder at the top of the hill than down in the busy High Street. The snow lay in a crust along the garden wall, and made two white skull-caps on the stone balls on either side of the gate.

She had no idea how she would get home. There might not be another bus, and taxis did not cruise at night in this part of London. She began to regret having jumped so hastily off the warm, lighted bus. She had seen the house now, and that was all there was to it. Standing by the gate, with her hand on its cold iron scrolls, she felt no emotion except the remembrance of how she had always been glad to go out of the house, and never very pleased to come back to it.

The house looked just the same; too big, too square, too unimaginative in its arrangement of windows and chimneys. She turned away and began to walk down the hill, slippery with freezing snow. As she reached the first corner by the house where the old lady with the cats had lived, a taxi climbed past her with its engine knocking, and stopped just beyond.

She turned, thinking that she might be able to ride back in it, and saw that it had stopped outside her old home. A man and a woman got out, she with a fur coat and a scarf over her head, the man lean and leggy, unfolding himself with difficulty from the taxi.

The woman hurried up the steps to the front door. The man paid the taxi, lifting the skirt of his overcoat, and squinting for change under the lamp light. As Virginia went forward to hail the driver, she saw that the man was her father.

54

4

"BUT I tell you, Helen, I saw him. Why won't you believe it?"

"The whole thing is too impossible. You must have been crazy trailing up there in all that snow and cold. No wonder you started imagining things."

"I didn't imagine anything. I saw him." Helen's refusal to believe that Virginia had seen her father made her wish that she had said nothing about it. For a time she had not meant to, but then she had rashly come out with it in the unsuitable setting of the fitting-room at Helen's dressmaker's, where Helen was buying her a new suit for Christmas.

While Virginia stood in her slip, waiting for the fitter, she had been overtaken by an impulsive mixture of tactlessness and honesty, and had told Helen suddenly: "I saw my father last night."

Helen argued, sitting upright on a brocade stool in the corner, her feet neatly crossed, and her slender rolled umbrella between her knees.

"He would never go back to that barrack of a house," she said. "When last I heard of him, several years ago, he was still living in that depressing flat by the river. A man on his own, why would he want to go and rattle about in a house that size? Absurd as he is, he was never absurd in that way. He was always practical, if nothing else. I could have killed him at times for being so practical, when what I wanted from him was a little imagination. Just a spark, that was all I asked, but it wasn't there in his soul. The man could not produce it. Not that he tried, I might add."

Virginia closed her ears. She was tired of her mother's post-mortems, from which, after all these years, Helen still derived a certain macabre pleasure.

To check her in mid-grievance, Virginia told the rest of

the story. "He isn't a man on his own. I haven't told you. There was a woman with him."

Helen frowned. "Don't be absurd. You're inventing. I never heard that he had married again."

"Why should you? You never took any interest in what he did. You've told me often enough you wanted to lose touch completely."

"Perhaps it wasn't his wife," Helen said, her displeased face brightening a little to the hope of scandal.

"I think it was. They looked married. They looked—well, you know how people look."

"Just because you saw them together doesn't prove—oh, here's Miss Rainier. Good afternoon, Miss Rainier. What a long time you've been."

Miss Rainier, whose father and brother had died in the Maquis, and who had been violated by three German soldiers in one night, came in humbly, her nose puffed from a cold, the worn tape-measure hanging round her neck like a chain of bondage. She took measurements swiftly and expertly, clucking at the admirable size of Virginia's waist, turning her with gentle hands, excusing herself, implying her apologies for the crude necessity of a customer having to be appraised by anyone as inferior as herself.

Helen fidgeted on the stool, telling Virginia to stand still, fussing at Miss Rainier and giving sharp little commands about the suit, manifesting her annoyance at what Virginia had told her.

When Miss Rainier had left, effacing herself with a duck of the head through the curtain, Helen asked the question that had been tormenting her all through the fitting. "Jinny —did you speak to him?"

"No, I didn't. I waited until he had gone through the gate before I grabbed the taxi. He didn't see me. Would you have minded if he had?"

"You know I would. You know we agreed you shouldn't see him again, and he agreed to it too. Not unwillingly, I am constrained to add. Don't give me that silly, quizzical look. It wasn't any hardship to you not to see him. I used to have to positively drive you there. Positively to drive you there," she said, amending the split infinitive.

"I was a child then." Virginia pulled her skirt over her head. "I was embarrassed by him."

"He would embarrass you still, with that caustic, derogatory manner. Please, Jinny, if you care anything at all about me, don't get any ideas about things being different now that you're grown up. Why should I share you with him? He walked out on you. He didn't want you. You're mine. I brought you up, cared for you, was everything to you. You're all I've got, dear heart. Don't let me down." She became a little impassioned in the stuffy, pin-strewn fitting-room.

Virginia had finished dressing and was ready to leave. She did not like to see her mother losing, or pretending to lose, her grip. Loving entreaty sat discrepantly on that hard-shelled face.

"Don't get excited, Helen," she said easily. "I'm not going to see him again. I don't want to."

But did she want to? The last time she had seen her father was when she was twelve, and when she heard that it was the last time, she had not minded. Afterwards, as she grew older, she began to mind a little. It was so arbitrary to be suddenly cut off from one of your parents. It was so unnatural, so unsatisfactory to have a father alive and not to know anything about him. Other girls had fathers. If they did not, their fathers had died, and they accepted that as irrevocable. If their parents were divorced, they saw their fathers occasionally, going on exciting trips to Edinburgh, or Paris, or even, like Martha Broome, to the south of France, where she had been smuggled into the casino under age and had met a prince.

Even the unexciting, awkward trips to the flat would have been better than nothing. At least she could have told her friends at the beginning of the term: "I went to see my father. He gave me a bag." Or a scarf, or a bracelet. Except that Harold Martin had never given her anything, not once on any of the visits she made to him after the divorce. This had disappointed her at the time, but later she had wondered whether he was only trying to be fair to her mother by not bribing Virginia to like him.

She did not like him very much on these visits. He was reasonably familiar to her because he was her father, but he had never tried to get close to her even when they were living in the same house. He was withdrawing rapidly now into a stranger, and Virginia could do nothing but back away too, step for step with him.

He had always behaved at home as if he mistrusted her, irritably waiting for her to say or do the wrong thing. Now when Virginia saw him only rarely, he was as uneasy with her as she was with him. He did not know how to treat her, and so she did not know how to behave.

Sometimes during those difficult afternoons they spent together, she behaved badly, out of embarrassment. She would boast, or use puerile slang expressions from school, or fidget and make faces, and spill her tea on his carpet. She always meant to behave impeccably. She would dream, during the journey to the flat, of the visit turning into a miracle, with she and her father on the top of the world together. When it did not turn out like that, she would find herself doing all the things which irritated him.

Harold Martin was an irritable man, disappointed with the way his life had gone, and with himself for not managing it better. Helen knew him as opinionated and intolerant. She would not have excused that even if she had known that his quickness to find the flaws in other people arose partly from his dislike of the flaws in himself.

He was a tall, colourless man, with hair that receded from a thinning widow's peak, and a loose-skinned face that did not smile enough. Virginia had often wished for a cosy father, with firm cheeks and a curving watch-chain, on to whose knee she could climb at any time. She never climbed on her father's knee, except possibly as a baby, which she could not remember. His knees were not the kind you climbed on. She doubted whether her mother had ever climbed on to them. It would have been better if she had; but if Harold's knees were not scaleable, neither was Helen the kind of woman who climbed on knees.

Once, when Virginia had gone to the flat by the river, dressed in her best by Helen, to show that the female side of the family was prospering, her father was not there. He had forgotten about her. He had gone out, the housekeeper said, and she had taken Virginia down into her own basement flat and given her cocoa and shortbread.

Helen had been furious when Virginia returned home, and had sworn never to let her go again. However, a few days later there was a stilted letter from Harold, apologizing briefly, and offering to take Virginia to the zoo. Virginia did not particularly like the zoo, but she recognized the wish to make amends and went, against her mother's advice.

It was a scorching, airless Sunday. The paths of the zoo were so crowded with heated parents and sticky children that you could hardly get near the animals, and the queue for the rides on the exhausted elephants was so long that Harold said they could not wait. The zoo smelled abominably, and most of the animals were sulking and panting at the back of their cages, so that whatever pleasure you had hoped to take in them was turned to pity.

"Aren't you enjoying it?" Virginia's father had asked. She looked up at him to see what she ought to say. He was so obviously suffering himself that she was honest, and said no.

Their mutual relief at being able to leave brought them a little closer. It was the first time that Virginia could remember them feeling the same way about anything. He bought her an ice cream on the way out, and she spoiled their slightly improved relationship by spilling the melting ice cream down her dress. Both of them, as usual, were relieved when he put her into the taxi to go home.

The next day, Virginia had been sick with a mild form of sunstroke, and her mother had grumbled for a long time about Harold. In the next holidays, he had gone away, and by the time the holidays after that came round, it was somehow tacitly assumed that Virginia would not visit her father any more. Helen did not write to arrange a visit, and Harold did not write to ask when Virginia was coming.

It was considered to be a relief to all parties, and Virginia did not see her father again.

It was only as the years went by without a father that Virginia began to remember a few good things about him. She remembered how he had played the piano, and how, occasionally at the flat, she would sit content for the brief while he consented to play, and watch the red stone in his signet ring catching the light from the lamp, although she was not interested in the kind of music he played.

She remembered, long after she saw him for the last time, something that she had not noticed before. As much as he disliked her mother, and she felt sure that he did, he had never once said anything derogatory about her. Virginia was accustomed to hearing her mother criticize her father, and tell of mean things he had done in the past, but Harold never said anything. He did not praise Helen, but he never blamed her. He did not talk about her.

In the days that followed Virginia's revelation in the fitting-room, Helen talked intermittently about the woman Virginia had seen getting out of the taxi in the snow. She was piqued by the idea that Harold should have the effrontery to be married when she was not, and she was also greatly intrigued by the mysterious woman.

"What was she like?" she kept asking. "You must have seen more of her. There's a street-lamp by the gate. Was she pretty?"

"Honestly, Helen, I told you. I only saw her back. She had on a fur coat, that's all I know."

"What kind of fur?" Helen pounced, hoping to hear that it was rabbit. "How can you be so unobservant? You're simply being sly. Was she plain? Did she look older than I do?"

She was so vexed with curiosity that finally Virginia took pity on her, and restored her peace of mind by telling her that she had seen enough of the woman after all to know that she was dowdy, and much older than her mother.

This mollified Helen considerably, and she dropped the subject, except to ask once: "Did she have red hair? He always hated red hair, and it would serve him right to marry a woman who had it."

Virginia's curiosity was not so easily quenched. She could not forget the couple. When she was a child, she had been willing to put her father out of her life. Now that she was grown up, and had seen him again, she could not forget that he was her father. She must know what had happened to him.

She had finished her daytime course at the college, which had ended with a sad little homily from Mr Deems on the subject of the *Northgate Gazette*. She was waiting now for her interview with the managing editor of *Lady Beautiful*. Having nothing else to do, she took a bus one morning after her mother had left for the office, and walked up the hill to the once familiar house, which had now become a house of mystery.

She did not want to see her father. She had made a promise to Helen, and did not think of breaking it. Virginia wanted to see his wife, and she had devised a plan for getting into the house without revealing who she was.

The hollow sound of her knock on the door, echoing in the high-ceilinged hall, was disturbingly familiar. As Virginia waited for an answer, she found herself hoping intensely that the woman would be nice. The motive which had brought her here was a desire to see the loose ends of her father's story satisfactorily tied up. If she was never to see him again, she wanted to think of him as happy and settled, so that she could without compunction carry on her life without him.

A woman opened the door. The first sight of her was so startling that Virginia almost took a step backwards, but recovered her balance in time. One side of the woman's face was covered from upper lip to hairline with a dark red birthmark, mottled like a bruise. The discoloured skin was shiny and slightly raised. The eye on that side was like a negro's eye, the white more noticeable against the dark background.

The hideous birthmark gave the woman the air of a victim. It did not look as if it had grown with her, but rather as if it had been slapped on from the outside, like a smack in the face.

Virginia's first thought was: How Helen would love to hear about this! She would never tell her. Pity and embarrassment had knocked her prepared opening words from her lips, and she felt herself staring, but she knew that it would be even ruder to look away.

Some women look suspicious when they open the door to a stranger. Some, if they are busy, look cross. Others look completely blank, as if they expected nothing from anyone any more. This woman, however, on seeing Virginia on her doorstep, broke into a welcoming smile that at once lessened the affliction of her face. The birthmark could not be ignored, but it suddenly looked less like an injury, and more like an integral part of her face.

"Mrs Martin?" Virginia asked, her own name sounding strange. She had not expected the woman to contradict her, and so was not taken off her guard when she nodded. She had known as soon as the door was opened that this was her father's wife. She had expected it to be, and in that moment of shock when she saw the disfigured face, she was certain. Everything fell into place. Her father, hypercritical, intolerant of physical or mental defects, had been irritated beyond endurance by Virginia's mother, with her carefully-groomed poise. He had found fault with her appearance even when it was almost perfect. Now he had found himself a woman who was so imperfect that she must be above criticism. There would be no need for intolerance any more.

"Can I help you?" Mrs Martin asked. Her voice was quiet and friendly. She made no attempt to turn her face to one side.

"I represent the Colgate-Palmolive Company," Virginia said, remembering the lines she had rehearsed. "We're conducting a survey on consumer habits. If you wouldn't mind, I would like to know which of our products you use, and why you like them."

"That's nice," the woman said amiably. "I've heard of people being asked things like that, but no one has ever done it to me. The only thing is, I'm not sure which are your products. There are so many different new things, and they all have such attractive names. I buy all sorts of things I see in advertisements, to see if it's as good as they say. They never are. Oh, but I shouldn't say that to you, I suppose."

Virginia had the impression that Mrs Martin was talking to gain time. Her remarks were a little at random, as if there were something else she really wanted to say.

"That's all right," Virginia said. "I'm not in the advertising department. Perhaps if you could let me see your kitchen, I could find out which of our products you have."

It was easier to get into the house than she had expected. The woman stepped aside at once, as if she were glad of the chance to ask her in, and Virginia entered her own house feeling like a stranger.

The house did not look the same. There were more rugs on the floor. The walls, which Helen had kept pale and austere, were covered with a lively paper and hung with intelligible pictures. The dark passage to the kitchen had new lighting. The kitchen itself, which had defeated Tiny and the daily woman with its cheerlessness, was now a place of gay curtains and bright linoleum, with the old yellow dresser painted white and hung with floral china.

Virginia could imagine how her mother would scoff. "Homey," she would say. "Revoltingly snug." Helen had disliked the house so much that she had not bothered to try and make anything of it. If she had redecorated it, it would never have been in this way.

"I was just going to have some coffee," Harold's wife said. "Sit down and I'll pour it." She took an old-fashioned coffee-pot from the back of the stove. Homey again. Virginia could hear the voice of her mother, who would never drink coffee from anything but an electric percolator.

They talked of the weather, and of nothing in particular. Mrs Martin still seemed to have something on her mind, which she was trying to voice. Perhaps she had sensed from the start that Virginia was an imposter. However, since she said nothing, the impersonation must be carried through. Virginia had got into the house. She had seen her father's wife, and the kind of surroundings in which he now lived. It was time to go.

"Well," she said. "I had better get down to business." She

took out the reporter's notebook which she had bought for the *Northgate Gazette*. "If I could just see your soap powders, and polishes, and—and those things."

"Look, my dear." Virginia looked at Mrs Martin and saw that she was blushing. The flush on the unaffected cheek and the deepened red of the birthmark gave her face a fiery look, as if she were standing at a furnace. Her hands were making little nervous pleats in the front of her overall. As Virginia noticed this, she noticed something else. The overall was a smock. Was it possible? The woman looked over forty. Her figure might be naturally bulky.

"Forgive me," Mrs Martin said, standing up, as if this gave her courage, "but please don't pretend any longer. Unless you want to, of course. I think I know who you are. You're Harold's daughter, aren't you? Virginia." She spoke the name as if she enjoyed the sound of it.

Virginia looked so startled that Mrs Martin said in confusion: "Oh, dear, have I made a mistake? I shouldn't have said anything, but I felt so sure."

"It's all right." Virginia closed her notebook and tried to laugh. "I wouldn't have known what soap powder to look for, anyway. How did you know?"

"I saw your picture in the *Tatler*, not long ago, when you were at a dance. It was just like you. I see that now. I kept the picture. I have it upstairs, but I didn't show it to Harold. Perhaps I should, but I thought it was better for him not to know what you looked like than to know that you were beautiful, and he couldn't see you. Have you come to see him?" Her face grew flushed again with eagerness.

Virginia shook her head. "I came to see you. I saw you in the street one night with him, and I wanted to see you again. I think I ought to go," she added uncertainly. "I don't think my mother would like me to be here." She did not normally care what Helen liked or did not like, but she had made a pact with her and she could not go over to the other camp.

Mrs Martin seemed to understand. "I wish Harold could see you," she said, "but if your mother wants it this way, that's her business. Perhaps she's right. I don't know. The whole thing is such a pity. I shan't tell him you came, if that's

64

what is worrying you. Perhaps you could come again, Virginia, if you ever want to. I'm always here. I don't go out much." Her hand touched her discoloured cheek, and she smiled.

When Virginia was leaving, Mrs Martin said: "I wish you had come in the afternoon. You could have seen Andrew when he got back from school."

"Your son?"

"Yes. Perhaps when he is older, you two will meet. And the other one too." She glanced down at her smock. "People think I'm very old to be having a baby, but I'm not really. I'm only thirty-eight. I look older, you see, because of this." She touched her face again. "I always looked quite old, even when I was young. Funny, to think I tried to commit suicide once. Now I don't mind about it at all. There are so many other things."

When she went to the house, Virginia had thought that if she could discover a hint that her father was happy, she would not be troubled by the thought of his existence. Now that she felt sure he was happy, she found that she wanted more than ever to see him again. She walked down the hill away from the house as if she were walking away from home. But as long as she lived with her mother, she could not go back. She could not do that to Helen.

5

ONE evening, when Helen was out at a cocktail party, Felix came up to the flat. Virginia sat down contentedly with Felix, secure in the knowledge that her mother could not join them. She still did not know whether he had taken her mother out on the night when she went to the Benbergs. Helen had not chosen to tell her, and Virginia had not chosen to ask.

Virginia did not know whether Felix had come to see her or her mother. He seemed a little nervous, rubbing his small, clean hands, and glancing round the room, as if he might be wondering where Helen was.

"I'm afraid I've stayed away too long," he said in his soothing bedside voice, "but I've been frightfully busy. Cæsarians at the hospital—emergencies mostly—and half the women in London decided to have babies this week." He leaned back and closed his eyes for a moment. Virginia saw that he looked tired.

"I hope you don't mind my coming," he said, "but Robert and I get on each other's nerves at times, even when he's not working, and I felt the need for a little feminine stimulation."

"Haven't you got a girl friend?" He seemed less nervous now that he had started on a scotch and soda. Virginia felt that she could ask him that.

"Not at the moment. I was engaged once—not long ago, as a matter of fact—but it didn't work out."

"Why not?" Virginia asked with a slight sigh. Here we go again. He wants to talk about his love troubles. Why do they always think the next girl will be interested?

"It sounds absurd," Felix said, "but do you know what it was she finally couldn't bear any longer about me? She didn't like my being a gynæcologist."

"I can understand that in a way. After all, your patients are women. She might have been jealous."

"It wasn't that. She was too conceited to be jealous of anyone else. It was—oh, well, skip it. It was just a neurosis. Women can be very hard to understand."

"You should be able to understand them surely, if anyone can."

"I can understand *patients* all right." He tossed the word aside, as if it signified a lesser breed. "I mean, the women you *know*. The ones you fall in love with. They're quite something else."

He turned on the sofa and looked at Virginia sitting next to him, nursing her cool glass.

"You are very attractive, Virginia," he said gravely. "Even in that black dress, and sitting still, you manage to give the impression of colour and movement."

He said this deliberately and with difficulty, as if he were not in the habit of paying compliments to women, and was more at ease talking to them about their internal than their external appearance.

"Felix," Virginia said, "I have to ask you this before we go any farther. Did you take my mother out on Monday night?"

"Monday?" he said. "Let's see . . . Monday. Heavens, no. I was catching up on a back-log of hysterectomies until after ten o'clock."

"Or any other night?"

"What an odd idea. Your mother would never come out with me. I imagine she can get a far more exciting escort any time she wants."

"That's not the point. Would you ever ask her?" Virginia had to plough on now that she had started.

"I don't see why you and I shouldn't take her out sometimes if she wanted to come," he said, puzzled by Virginia's earnestness. "Of course I wouldn't ask her out alone. I mean, not unless it was sort of—well, in a family way. Hell, I'm going to say something rash. Don't pay any attention. I mean, if she was my mother-in-law."

He looked so scared when he had said this that Virginia

67

burst out laughing. "Who could help paying attention if you suddenly say a thing like that?"

"It sounded like a leading remark. It wasn't meant to. My God, I've only met you a few times. You must think I'm insane. Forget it. I didn't mean it."

"That makes it much better, of course." Virginia looked away.

"No—I mean, dash it, look here, Virginia——" Felix was pitiably confused. "After all, people don't say things like that when they hardly know a girl. I mean, not people like me." The charming, crooked smiles were all gone from his face. He looked defeated, as if he had abandoned whatever campaign he had in mind before it was even started.

Conversation foundered. Neither of them knew how to get back to friendly talk. Irritated by Felix's clumsy approach and retreat, Virginia hoped that he would soon go away. Now that she knew that she and not her mother was the object of his nervous pursuit, she was not sure that she wanted him to catch up with her.

"I'm sorry," Felix said, sensing her sudden boredom. "I talked like a fool. Forgive me."

"Oh, don't be so humble." Virginia stood up and walked away from him. "I'm not surprised that girl broke off the engagement if you went about apologizing for everything you said before you even said it. No, that was mean. I shouldn't have said that. I'm sorry."

"It's all right," Felix said, without rancour. "That was one of her grievances, as a matter of fact." He stood up. "I'd better go. I haven't said what I came to say, though." He picked up the black homburg hat and turned the brim round and round in his fingers. "I wondered if you would care to come home with me for dinner on New Year's Eve. My parents are having a small party. Only family."

"I'm sorry," Virginia said. "I promised to take Helen out to dinner that night."

"Oh." Felix looked at his burnished shoes. "In that case, well—oh, well, I'd better be going." He opened the door of the flat and lingered for a moment wistfully on the top stair. "I'll see you soon, I hope," he said.

"Oh, yes," Virginia said. "I hope so," and brightened her smile to make her words sound less half-hearted.

"You can go in, Jinny," Grace said, putting down the telephone. "Your mother has an American gentleman in there, but she said it was all right for you to go in. In fact," Grace raised her neat eyebrows a fraction, "she seemed very glad to know you were here."

Virginia went into the throne-room, where her mother was talking to a middle-aged man with a heavy face and bushy eyebrows. Things did not look quite right. Her mother was not sitting at her desk in the middle of the room, commanding the situation. She was in one of the armchairs, smoking a cigarette and looking as relaxed as she ever could. The man was sitting by her, his big body perched on the edge of the low chair and his big feet splayed outwards.

He pushed himself out of the chair with difficulty as Virginia came in. He had a teutonic head of dark-grey hair, cut like a stiff brush. His thick eyebrows had been cut at the ends until they were almost square. His mouth was too small for the bulk of his face. It was rosy and a little petulant, the lower lip pushed wetly out like a baby's.

"Spenser," Helen said, without getting up, "this is my daughter, Virginia."

"I've heard so much about you," Spenser said, offering a hand like the butt-end of a ham. His voice was quiet and hoarse, more like a strained whisper; and he wheezed a little when he spoke.

"You have?" Why should Helen talk about her to a business acquaintance?

"Sure." He studied her. "What a fine, tall girl," he said, instantly making Virginia feel oversized and gawky. He was not very tall, and the double-breasted, loosely-cut jacket of his suit was too long for the length of trouser. "Nice girl," he rasped decisively, as if he were not accustomed to having his word challenged. "I like that clean, swept-back look, and the strong, coarse hair. We had a model just your type last year. Did very well in sweaters and slacks."

"This is Mr Eldredge, Jinny," Helen said, with a trace of

69

laughter in her voice. "He is a dress manufacturer from the United States. He's over here looking at material. We met at that show Aubrey had, of his tweeds."

"Surely," Mr Eldredge said, still studying Virginia.

"He has an estate on Long Island," Helen added, "overlooking the sea, with two tennis courts and a nine-hole golf-course."

Virgina was impatient. She had come into the throne-room in a hurry to tell her mother something. She did not want to hear the history of Mr Eldredge. Why the careful explanation from Helen, and why were they both looking at her with half smiles? This must be the new boy-friend. They had certainly not been talking business. Helen always sat at her desk when she talked business, even with her own staff. She would never sit casually in an armchair to put them at their ease.

"Sit down, Jinny," Helen said. "I'll get Grace to bring you some coffee." She seemed to have an unusual amount of time to spare.

"I haven't got time," Virginia said. "I'm meeting Mary for lunch. She's just got engaged, and she wants to tell me about it."

"You ladies," Spenser said, with a wheeze of heavy humour. "You no sooner catch a man than you want to start tearing him to pieces."

Virginia imagined that his line of humour would be full of stale half-truths about women. He would love to make jokes about women changing their minds, or talking too much, or being dangerous at the wheel of a car. She was puzzled by her instinctive aversion to him. He did not look a bad sort of man; but an indefinable smirk in her mother's attitude had put her on her guard.

"Why did you come then, if you are in such a hurry to go?" Helen asked.

"I came to tell you something. I'm afraid you may not like it very much. Perhaps I'd better——" She took a step back towards the door.

"Go ahead, dear heart," her mother said, tapping out ash with a jingle of bracelets. "We're all friends here. Excuse me,

70

Spenser." She flicked a smile at him. "Just a little family matter."

"It isn't," Virginia said. "It's business. I've just come from Mr Owen's office."

"Archie didn't tell me he was seeing you." Helen's voice hardened.

"Why should he? Does he always consult you before he hires anyone? I know he doesn't, because I remember you being so wild when he took on that McCarren girl."

"You mean to calmly tell me he's given you a job?" Helen was unnerved enough to split an infinitive. She did not stand up, but she sat up so alertly in her chair that she was as poised as if she were on her feet.

"I start next week. In the correspondence department. Channelling the mail, you know, and sorting out the readers' letters."

"Yes, yes, I know. You don't have to tell me what my own correspondence department does."

Helen was angry. Virginia had expected that. She had already made it clear that she did not want Virginia in the same office. One of her excuses was that the rest of the staff might feel obliged to favour her. Knowing how most of the staff felt about her mother, Virginia thought that they would be more likely to do the reverse.

Helen tapped her fingers on the side of the chair. "I don't like you going behind my back like that," she began. Then she remembered Spenser, who was standing solidly on the carpet, taking it all in, appraising, with little pushing movements of his moist lower lip.

"But of course," Helen added swiftly, and her body relaxed a little as she decided what line to take, "since it is all settled, I naturally could not be more delighted. I think it's a pity though that you didn't come to me about it. I could have put you into a much better job. One of the girls who helps on the beauty page is leaving. I've filled her place now, but if I had only known you wanted to work here, if you had only told me——" She looked at Spenser with spread hands and raised shoulders, as if to enlist his sympathy for a mother whose daughter never told her anything.

71

"Mom is always the last person to hear anything." Spenser readily answered the call to make one of his favourite jokes.

Virginia did not argue. What was the use? She had got her job, that was all that mattered, and she knew that she had got it by her own initiative, for Mr Owen had no love for her mother, and had helped Virginia in spite of the fact that she was her daughter, not because of it.

If Helen wanted to lie her way out of the situation to save her face with Eldredge, that was all right. Virginia would not spoil any little fling she might be having with him.

The fling, it appeared, was to include a champagne party at the Savoy on the following night, which was New Year's Eve.

"Such fun," Helen said, although Virginia had often heard her say that she detested mass merriment in restaurants. "You're fixed up with a party, of course, Jinny?"

"Not exactly," Virginia had refused Felix's invitation because she had promised to take Helen out to dinner. "But something will turn up, I expect."

"Why don't you come with us?" Spenser asked. Whatever he thought about it, he was too polite, and perhaps kind as well, not to feel compelled to say this. Virginia liked him better, and wondered how she could as politely refuse.

Helen went to her desk, and began to look through papers in a random way. "That's very kind of you, Spenser," she said, bending to look in a drawer, "but perhaps Jinny would rather be out with her own young friends than with us old fogies."

"Oh? Well, that might be so." Spenser took this literally.

"She has dozens of friends. There's sure to be something going on, isn't there, Jinny?"

Returning home after her lunch with Mary, Virginia met Felix hurrying out of his doorway, as if a baby threatened to be born at any minute.

"Happy New Year!" he called to her.

"It isn't New Year's Eve yet."

"It will be. I hope you and your mother enjoy yourselves."

"Helen can't come out with me after all. Something else came up."

"Then you'll come with me? Please do, Virginia. It won't be very exciting, but if you'd care to, my parents would be delighted. My mother will love you."

They always said that hopefully. It was embarrassing then if the mother did not take to you. It looked as though it were your fault.

Felix's mother and father lived staidly, in a fair degree of unimaginative comfort in a large flat in St John's Wood. To say they lived would be extravagant. They existed, rather, in a prison of stagnant respectability more daunting than anything Virginia had imagined. She had guessed that they would not be exhilarating. People's parents were often boring, or conventional, or foolish; but these two had no such recognizable qualities that could be played up to, or forgiven. They were unapproachable, unreal, so cocooned in their own dullness that they were impervious to the advances of a livelier spirit.

Felix was no eccentric, but it was obvious that he was far outside their narrow world, and had long ago given up trying to make contact with them. He was polite almost to deference, but it was the politeness rather of a stranger than of a respectful son.

The mother was tall and stiffly corseted, with harshly-sculpted hair and a long, wooden face. The father was slight and concave, and might have once looked a little like Felix, but his face now had lengthened and blanked out with the inward-turned expression of a bore. Like his son, he was a doctor, a moderately able surgeon, who had lost lives through slowness and lack of flair, but never through lack of caution. Theatre nurses went slowly demented while he muttered over an open abdomen, pondering whether to take something out or leave it in. Young house surgeons fretted themselves into mistakes, desperately holding clamps and artery forceps while Mr Allen peered into the cavity through his sterilized steel spectacles and thought of all the disadvantages of any procedure he might finally take.

He was as deliberate in his speech as he was in his work, weighing his words momentously, even if they were only going to add up to a casual remark.

"How do you do?" he asked Virginia, as seriously as if he were taking her case history. He held her hand for a long time, not from friendliness, but from an inability to let go, and then said: "Yes—Yes," and nodded, as if he had stated an opinion.

"Felix, my boy." He turned slowly and patted Felix on the arm, as if he were trying to familiarize himself by feel.

"How are you, Dad?" Felix spoke a little louder than usual, although his father was not deaf. "Everything all right?"

"Thank you." A pause. "I am well."

"Business good?"

Mr Allen considered this. His cautious eyes wandered round the unhomely drawing-room, where the chairs stood round the walls, in the wrong places for easy conversation. His gaze crept over the pelmet of the curtains, the straight, unrestful sofa, the little table with the glasses and the bottle of sherry and the half-bottle of gin.

When his eyes returned to Felix, he answered: "Satisfactory. And you?"

"I've been very busy." Felix did not talk quickly, but in contrast to his father, it sounded as if he were gabbling. "The days are as hectic as usual, and I've been out most nights. Up all last night, as a matter of fact. A very unusual case. I'd like to hear what you think of it."

Virginia guessed that he always came prepared with some special case in which he might interest his father, to flatter the old man, and give them something to talk about.

Mr Allen insinuated his hands into his trouser pockets, and rocked slowly back and forth from heels to toes. "Tell me," he said.

"Come and sit with me, Miss Martin, if the men are going to talk surgery," Mrs Allen said. Virginia would have liked to hear about the unusual case, but Felix's mother, walking as if she were at the head of a stately procession, led her over

74

to a window, where two hard-backed chairs stood formally in a draught.

"May I offer you a glass of sherry?" she said regally. "Or perhaps you would prefer gin." The way in which she said gin made Virginia answer: "Sherry will be fine, thank you." In any case, she could see nothing on the little table to go with the gin.

Mrs Allen had sat down. She rose all in one piece with a straight back, not using the arms of the chair.

"Please don't trouble. Let me get it," Virginia said.

"Thank you." Mrs Allen sat down again in the same unbending movement, without looking back at the chair. "You may bring me a small glass too, if you will."

Virginia went over to the table, feeling the frigid gaze on her back. She tried to pour the sherry neatly and gracefully, but a few drops spilled on the shiny surface of the table. She mopped it with her finger, and had to wipe the finger on her skirt, because she dared not lick it.

She handed the sherry, sat down, and waited to be talked to. You did not start a conversation with Mrs Allen. If you tried, she answered shortly and changed the subject. She liked to ask the questions, and you had to answer. In a surprisingly short time, and without asking anything inquisitive, or appearing remotely interested, she had managed to find out quite a lot about Virginia.

While he was talking to his father, Felix kept looking at Virginia, wondering how she was faring. She smiled back at him reassuringly, and tried to look gay. It was bad enough for him to have such an uncomfortable mother, without being made aware of how she affected other people.

Felix did not ask for a drink until his father offered him one. They went to the table. Mr Allen accepted a straight gin, and sipped at it deliberately, without flinching.

"Is there any vermouth, or anything, Mother?" Felix asked. "I'm afraid I can't drink like Dad."

"I believe there may be some orange juice in the kitchen," Mrs Allen said vaguely, as if the kitchen were as unattainable as Mars. "No, don't go for it. It's bad for Florence. Ring the bell, please."

75

Felix rang the bell at the side of the fireplace, which housed a simulated log fire with a flickering electric glow, which gave very little heat and bore no resemblance to flames. After a long time, a maid appeared, an elderly woman as rigid as her mistress, who looked as though she had long ago lost whatever interest in life she might once have had.

There was another long wait while she fetched the bottle of orange squash, carrying the tall bottle in on a small tray, a feat which required some skill and a funereal tread.

Felix drank his gin and orange without pleasure. He looked at the small bottle of gin. Virginia knew that he needed another drink, but he did not take one, although he offered Virginia another sherry.

Virginia looked at Mrs Allen. Her glass was almost un-tasted. "No, thank you," she said, despising her cowardice, and wondering how she was going to keep awake.

Felix's brother and his wife were late. Mrs Allen would not start dinner without them, and the wait was interminable. From time to time, the door opened noiselessly, and Florence looked in with mute enquiry. "Keep the roast warm," Mrs Allen would say. "We will wait." She looked as though she could wait indefinitely before she felt anything as stimulating as hunger.

Eventually the brother Edward arrived, puffing apologies for a faulty car, and bringing with him a wife in a blue crêpe dinner dress, who touched cheeks with Mrs Allen as if they had not been in the same family for years. She was a negative, pasty-faced woman, who obviously had dropped no stone into the turgid waters when she married into the Allen family.

Edward was older than Felix, a stout man with bulging eyes and a heavy breath, who would drink nothing and eat scarcely anything, because his life was organized to terror of his heart.

"Nothing the matter with him, actually," Felix whispered to Virginia, while Mr Allen was dissecting the roast beef so slowly that it was cold before Florence handed it to any-one. "He's read too many magazine articles, that's all."

"I've never seen you look better, Eddie," he told his

brother. Edward shook his head unbelievingly, patted his chest, and continued to look askance at the food on the other plates, and at the bottle of Algerian wine, which Florence carried round the table, pouring half a glass to each, well trained in how to make it go round.

After dinner, Mrs Allen took Virginia and Edward's wife into the bedroom, where the dressing-table was covered with little pin-boxes and photographs in silver frames, and on the double bed were laid out the high-necked nightgown and the striped pyjamas, striking a shockingly intimate note.

It was impossible to think of Felix's mother and father undressing and lying down in the same bed. Impossible to think that they could ever have conceived Edward and Felix, and that Mrs Allen had given birth to them. She must have closed her eyes and blanked out her mind.

In the drawing-room, Mrs Allen announced that they would play bridge until it was time to drink the punch at midnight. Virginia looked at the clock with a sinking heart. It was only ten-thirty.

"I'm afraid I don't play bridge," she said.

"Not play bridge?" Mrs Allen's long face was uncomprehending. "How extraordinary, Miss Martin."

"Please call me Virginia," Virginia said for the tenth time. Mrs Allen bowed stiffly and continued to call her Miss Martin.

"If Virginia is not going to play, I won't either," Felix said. His family looked at him, weighing the implication of this remark. "Dad can make up the four. I'm really too tired to play. You don't mind, do you, Dad?"

Mr Allen debated this, and finally admitted that he supposed not. The tables and chairs were set up. Mrs Allen moved at once to a chair and took up the cards avidly, showing enthusiasm for the first time. Bridge was her passion in life, her only passion. She spent every afternoon at a bridge club, and nearly every evening at a bridge table with such people as shared her passion, if not her friendship.

The other three sat down without eagerness or aversion. Mrs Allen shuffled the cards like lightning in her bony hands, and skimmed them round the table. They began to

77

play as grimly as if they were strangers. They did not talk, and discuss, and bicker mildly, as families do when they play bridge. When it was necessary to speak, they spoke in monosyllables. Mr Allen was very slow at the game, re-arranging his fan of cards over and over, deliberating for minutes on end before he made a bid, while the others waited with their eyes on their own cards, not impatiently, but in a vacuum, as if they had suspended thought and action.

Virginia sat on the sofa with Felix, and they looked at copies of the *Illustrated London News* and the *Geographical Magazine*. From the flat next door came faintly the sound of music, and people laughing.

"The Bernsteins are at it again." Mrs Allen nodded significantly to her husband.

"What's that? At what? Oh, yes—yes. The Bernsteins."

"Your bid, Dad," Edward droned. He belched resonantly, but did not beg anyone's pardon. He considered the belch permissible to him as a sufferer. Everyone should find it as welcome as he did.

"I'm sorry, Virginia," Felix said in a low voice. "This is rather dull for you. I'm sure you wish you hadn't come. I'd forgotten how dull it was," he admitted, "until I brought you here. I've got used to it, but you seem to—somehow show it up."

Virginia did not know what to say. She was torn between wanting him to be loyal to his parents, and wanting him to be human enough to chafe at them.

"Don't apologize," she said. "You're always trying to find something to apologize about. Remember? We nearly quarrelled about that the other night."

This little attempt at an intimate joke fell flatly between them, and was lost in the hard-grained cushions of Mrs Allen's sofa. It was difficult to talk responsively in the leaden atmosphere. The air seemed thick with a deadly torpor that forced itself between them and kept them apart.

"I wish I could have taken you out instead," Felix said, "but they would have been so hurt if I hadn't come. New Year's Eve is one of their big nights."

Neither Mr nor Mrs Allen looked sensitive enough to be hurt by anything more subtle than a steam-roller, and if this was a big night, imagination boggled at their ordinary ones; but Virginia said: "Of course. I know what it is with families." She had always regretted not having a family, but now she thought that perhaps she was lucky.

"If I thought we could leave without——" Felix began, but Mrs Allen looked round from the table with a slight frown.

"What are you two whispering about over there?"

"Nothing, Mother. We didn't want to disturb your game."

"Well, please don't whisper like that. It's so common." Mrs Allen made deliberate markings on the score-card, printing the figures as precisely as if it were a bank ledger.

When the telephone rang, Felix got up hopefully.

"Let Florence go," his mother said, without looking up from the game.

"Isn't she in bed?"

"She doesn't go to bed until we do."

"It's probably for me."

"If it is, she will tell you."

Florence stood in the doorway and looked at them all before she said: "It's for you, Mr Felix."

Felix came back into the drawing-room, trying to look regretful. "I'm sorry Mother—Dad. That was the hospital. That ovarian cyst woman doesn't look too good. They think we may have to do a laparotomy."

Virginia panicked. Was he going to leave her here?

"You'd better come too, Virginia," he said. "I'll drop you at a taxi rank."

"Miss Martin can stay here," Mrs Allen said. "Edward and Beryl can take her home."

"No," said Felix, and Virginia could have hugged him for standing up to his mother. "It's out of their way. Get your coat, Virginia. I've got to hurry."

Mrs Allen scarcely looked up from her game to shake Virginia's hand stiffly and offer Felix her cheek. "I'm sorry that you had to spoil the party," she told him, as if she suspected him of inventing the woman with the ovarian cyst.

"Did you invent her?" Virginia asked, when they were outside the door of the flat.

"God, no, though I'm sure she wishes I had, the way she feels. Here, what on earth——?"

Like a bird released from a cage, Virginia had started to run and swoop down the long corridor, jumping up to touch the lights in the low ceiling, running back and making him run too, dragging him with flapping overcoat towards the lift. It was so good to be free! All the stale boredom of the last three hours was bursting within her to be let out, swept away, in great gusts of physical energy.

"Oh, Felix," she said, clutching his arm, as they went out into the raw, clouded night of Finchley Road. "Smell that air! I wish you weren't in a hurry, and we could walk. Oh, doesn't the air smell good!"

"Smells like fog to me," he said a little dourly, as he started the car.

"Don't be offended. I didn't mean it like that. You know I had a lovely time, but oh, it's New Year's Eve, and—look, Felix! Look at those people!"

As they passed the Underground station, a group of revellers burst from the depth in paper hats, waving rattlers, punching each other, shouting and singing their way across the road in a straggling line, ignoring cars. The sight was so invigorating after her three hours in the tomb that Virginia leaned out of the window to laugh and shout at the tipsy people. They shouted back, and one of the men broke away and tried to run after the car. He fell flat on his face and lay in the middle of the road, kicking his legs and trying to raise his paper crown.

"London on New Year's Eve." Virginia drew in her head. "I wouldn't be anywhere else. Oh, I love London. There's nowhere in the world so solid and so crazy at the same time. Look, Felix—look at that taxi! The man's trying to climb on the roof. Look—they're having a party in that house. What a huge room—and thousands of people. It looks such fun from outside, but probably if you were in there, it wouldn't be much fun at all."

It was exciting to drive through London on New Year's

Eve. As they came to Oxford Street and crossed into Regent Street, the excitement increased. There were more people in the streets, all at once a crowd of them, all going the same way in a jostling mob, shouting and cheering as if it were the end of the war all over again.

The traffic became thicker and slowed to a crawl. Men and girls in open cars stood up and screamed at strangers. People threw things, threw laughter at each other, as they were borne along on the tide of hypnotized gaiety towards the magnet which gathers to itself the fervour of London's gala days—Piccadilly Circus, with the policemen part of the comedy, and the bonfires already burning at the corner of the Haymarket.

Felix had driven into the congestion before he realized that he could not get out of it. Traffic was almost at a stand-still. The mass of cars stopped for five minutes, moved for five seconds, then stopped again. Horns blared, but chiefly to make noise. No one was going anywhere. They were out to ride on the roofs of taxis, to lean out of sports cars and squirt each other with syphons, to cheer and add to the hullabaloo of the rowdiest evening of the year.

Felix fretted and peered, and tried to draw out of line to turn into a side-street, but he was solidly wedged. He backed until he struck the bumper of the car behind him, and a man in a yellow cap got out of it and came to shake his fist at Felix through the closed window. Felix spun his wheel, paying no attention, but he still could not get round the car in front. He struck that one too, and the tail-light fell off, for it was very old; but it was full of young men with bottles of beer, who were shaking the car up so much from the inside that they did not feel the bump.

A strange man in a college muffler suddenly climbed into the back of the car, slapped Felix on the back, kissed Virginia clumsily, climbed out of the other door and into the car alongside, where he was received with female shrieks.

They had almost reached Piccadilly Circus now. Virginia could see the people skirmishing round the pedestal of Eros, the turbulent sea of shouting faces, vivid under the neon signs, the young men climbing up the lamp-posts, the policemen with linked arms forming cordons here and there from habit, although in this heaving ocean of equality there was nobody who need be guarded from anyone else.

The cars could go no farther. "It will be midnight in a few minutes." Virginia turned to Felix with shining eyes. "Let's get out and stand with the crowd. They'll sing *Auld Lang Syne.*" Felix would sway with her, pressed close against her, excited, caught up in the boisterous harmony of the people. They would kiss. Everyone kissed in the streets on New Year's Eve.

"Come on." She caught at his arm. She was half-way out of the car when he pulled her back.

"Are you crazy? I'm supposed to be at the hospital. I've got to get out of this. I'd better leave the car and start running."

"I'll run with you."

"You'll have to stay with the car." It was the first time he had ordered her to do anything. She was almost surprised into obeying him, but she did not want to be left alone to play chauffeur to the shiny black car. She saw a policeman and shouted to him. Like all Londoners, she believed that a policeman was the answer to everything.

This one did not disillusion her. There was much calling and waving and shouts of: "Doctor here! Let the doctor through! Easy a bit. Right hand down. Steady as you go!" The policeman got Felix out to the other side of the road, and held back the cars there while he drove up it on the wrong side and turned off.

Virginia hated to leave the crowds, but she had felt important. People had stared at them, and demanded: "What's that fellow doing? Oh, a doctor. Come on, you chaps, what's the matter with you? Let the doctor through. Emergency."

If the woman with the ovarian cyst was still capable of feeling anything, she should feel flattered that the common surge towards midnight in Piccadilly had been held up and disrupted on her behalf.

The streets rapidly grew emptier as they drove away from the lights and noise. Felix drove fast, his face intent. Without looking at her, he put his hand on Virginia's knee.

"Sorry," he said. "Another time. I'll see the New Year in with you next year in Piccadilly Circus, or anywhere you want."

As they crossed Parliament Square, the yellow harvest moon of Big Ben showed that it was nearly the hour. Virginia turned on the wireless. A choir was singing the last hymn of the Watch-Night Service.

Felix stopped the car outside the hospital. "Take the car home," he said. "You'll never get a taxi tonight. I'll get back all right."

"I'll wait for you, if you like."

"No, I might be a long time. But thanks for saying you would." He looked at her with a hesitant smile, and held out his hand. "Virginia, I——"

"Hush. It's midnight." She took his hand, and they heard above and behind them in the sky the first note of Big Ben, coming to them just a fraction of a second after its radio voice boomed out and filled the car.

"Happy New Year," he said. Then his mouth was on hers, and her ears were full of the chimes and the echoes of the chimes overlapping each other in widening circles of pulsating sound.

★ 6 ★

Virginia caught Helen red-handed. A few weeks after she started to work for *Lady Beautiful*, Miss Braithwaite, the department head, allowed her to go home earlier than usual, because she had a headache. Virginia went quickly into the flat, and straight to her bedroom. There, standing at the desk by the window was Helen. She was so startled that she turned round with the letter still in her hand.

Virginia shut the door and leaned against it. "Reading my letters again, Helen?" She knew that her mother was capable of looking through her desk when she thought Virginia was out. That was why she had long ago ceased to keep a diary, and always hid or destroyed any letters that mattered.

"How can you accuse me of that?" Helen cried, her eyes shifting, seeking how to put the blame on Virginia. "What a terrible thing to say to your own mother! I came in here to dust your room, and this letter was lying out on the desk. I just this minute picked it up."

"Where's the duster?" Virginia asked. "Oh, well, never mind. I thought the letter was safe in that little drawer, but I see I shall have to find a new hiding-place."

She threw her coat on the bed, and sat wearily down beside it, pushing back her hair, which the February wind had tumbled. "Since you have obviously read it," she said, "what do you think of it?"

"Of course I haven't read it." Helen threw the letter down. "I'm not interested in your love-letters."

"I don't get so many love-letters that you could guess this was one without reading it," Virginia said patiently.

"Well, of course, I couldn't help seeing one or two phrases, and who it came from. That niggling little signature, with the prim little dots underneath, like a prescription." Helen grasped at something to deride. "And since you ask what I think of it, I think it's quite absurd."

84

"Oh? Poor Felix. I thought it was a charming letter."

Helen gave a little snort. "It would need to be—trying to get a girl half his age to marry him."

"Not quite half his age," Virginia said carefully. "Eighteen years younger, to be exact."

"But that's much too big a gap! He admits that himself, right there in the letter. Oh, Jinny, it's unthinkable. Don't tell me you were even considering it."

"I don't know why not." Virginia lay back on the bed, and talked to the ceiling. "It's the best offer I've had so far. The only one, for that matter."

"But you're barely twenty-one! And I wish you wouldn't put your shoes on the bed. That counterpane was expensive. You shouldn't be thinking of marrying anyone, and certainly not Felix." She pronounced his name with some contempt. She had disliked him ever since she realized that it was Virginia he was pursuing and not her.

"Listen to me, Jinny." She stood by the bed with her arms folded, caressing her sleeves. "You think I don't know anything about what is good for you. No daughter credits her mother with any sense. But allow me to tell you—you know nothing. Nothing, do you hear? You're a child. No doubt you think you're having a very worldly love affair with the great obstetrician, but it's a dream. You don't know what love is."

"Don't I?" Virginia said. "What about Billy? Wasn't I in love with him?"

"Oh—Billy! My dear child, don't be ridiculous. That was only calf love, and the intoxication of the Austrian Alps. You were both pitifully immature."

"How cold it was in the early morning, remember?" Virginia closed her eyes. "And then when the sun came out, you wanted to peel off all your clothes and roll in the snow. But of course, Helen, you hardly ever went out of the hotel."

Long days on the mountain with Billy in that thick white sweater which darkened his bronzed skin. Days of speed, and hilarious falls, and thick pea soup and hard bread in the huts, and the lights from the windows of the village shining softly on the trodden snow as you stacked your skis outside

85

the *gasthof*, and tramped your melting boots inside for the hot spiced wine.

"I didn't feel immature," she said, remembering the entrancement of it, which had faded away like Billy's suntan after they returned to London. "Children of divorced parents are supposed to be more mature, you know. It's the emotional shock."

"Don't throw that up at me." Helen frowned. "It's most unfair to suggest that I have ever done anything but what was best for you. And now you threaten me with this—this *tragedy*."

"Oh, really, Helen." Virginia swung her legs off the bed, and went to the dressing-table.

"Yes, tragedy is what it will be if you marry Felix. The man is settled, set in his ways. His life is half over. Yours is only just beginning. He's successful enough, I grant you. He has got where he wants to, but do you want that? How do you know what you want?"

She talked to Virginia's back, with histrionic gestures, which Virginia could see in the mirror. "Please, Jinny, please; if you have any regard for me, please listen to what I tell you. Can't you see I'm trying to help you?"

Virginia let her talk. She did not say that she had no intention of marrying Felix, and that she had already told him so, and listened in embarrassment to his humiliated apologies for having asked her. Poor Felix. It would be kinder to him to let Helen think that it was she and not Virginia who had put an end to the mild affair.

He had vowed that he would move away from the mews, and never see Virginia again. That was a pity, because Virginia liked him; but if it made him feel better to be dramatic about it, at least that would give Helen the pleasure of thinking that she had driven him away.

"Dear heart." Helen put her hand on Virginia's shoulder. "Don't leave me yet. I need you. Don't leave me for a man who could never make you happy. You and I have been so happy together."

Did she really believe it? She bent forward and laid her cheek alongside her daughter's, and they stared together

86

into the mirror, the young sceptical eyes and the scheming anxious ones.

"You're all I've got, Jinny," Helen said, watching her own lips move sadly. "You're all I've got."

All I've got, indeed! Virginia walked up Endell Street in a fury, slapping her feet on the pavement and swinging her arms.

All I've got. I need you. Don't leave me. I'm only thinking of your happiness. And all the time, she knew—she *knew* what she was planning to do without a thought for how it would affect Virginia.

Cooing there in the bedroom, putting on that fraudulent maternal act. If she had told about it then, the whole conversation could have been different. But no, she had to do it this way. She had to have her big scene, with Virginia nowhere in the picture, Virginia in the background, trying to smile and pretend that everything was wonderful.

It would be a long time before she could forget the scene in Helen's office, the scene from which she was now storming away, trying to cover the hurt with anger.

It had been nearly time to leave the office. Miss Braithwaite had come to Virginia's desk and said: "Your mother wants to see you before you go. You can run along now, if you like. Those few letters will keep until the morning." Miss Braithwaite was very kind. She fussed over the girls in the correspondence department as benevolently as a sitting hen.

"But there will be a whole heap of new ones by the morning." Virginia slit another envelope, and began to read a letter from a lady in Bristol, challenging her mother's last editorial on How to Live Graciously on Three Hundred Pounds a Year.

"I know, dear, I know. If the letters didn't come, that would be the time to start worrying. But tomorrow is another day. Don't let's try to set the world on fire tonight." Miss Braithwaite's kind red face smiled like the setting sun. "Run along to your mother," she said, as if she were a nurse and Virginia a child.

Grace was not in the outer office. She was in the throne-room. So were a lot of other people; all the more senior members of the staff, standing about looking a little uncomfortabale, and keeping an eye on Helen.

"What is this—a party?" Virginia did not go up to her mother. She waited on the outskirts of the ring of people that surrounded the editorial desk.

Helen stood up when she saw her. "There you are, Jinny. We're only waiting for you." She seemed excited, but in complete command of herself and the situation. "I am going to make a tiny speech," she gave a tuneful little laugh, half deprecatory, "if you will all bear with me for the briefest of moments." She clasped her hands at chest level, and looked round her audience with her head poised.

Virginia saw Spenser Eldredge standing behind her. He was wearing a chunky, grey chalk-stripe suit with a white carnation in the buttonhole. He looked serious, as if he were giving someone away at a wedding. A wedding! Virginia came out of her daze and realized what her mother was saying.

"—I thought it better to tell you all together like this. I know how rumours go about in an office, and I want you all to know the truth—and to congratulate me, if you will. I am going to marry Mr Eldredge. I am very happy about it, and I hope that you will be too."

Helen's voice held a theatrical throb. She was enjoying herself enormously. Spenser stood with his head jutting forward, betraying no emotion. What he thought about being exhibited like a prize bull was no more apparent than what the bull thinks.

"Yes, I shall be leaving you all too soon." Dressed in her green Dior for the occasion, with the best jewellery she possessed, Helen floated along with her speech, so word and gesture perfect that it was obvious that she had spent a long time practising before a mirror. "I have been here longer than most of you, longer, perhaps, than any of you, with the exception of my dear Judy." She flung a hand and a smile in the direction of Judy, who stood four-square in the front row, with her feet planted and her arms folded, like a mill-worker at a protest meeting.

88

"I just wanted to take this opportunity of thanking all of you who have worked so hard, and I hope so happily with me to make *Lady Beautiful* what it is. To thank you for giving of your best, for your co-operation and your unfailing loyalty, which has meant so much to me during both good and bad times alike."

"Save us, the same old stuff." Judy looked round to see how the others were taking it, and noticed Virginia. "Sorry, Jinny, I didn't see you." Then she saw Virginia's face. "My God," she whispered, "didn't you *know*? How could she do that? What a way to break it to your daughter!"

"It's all right." Virginia managed to smile. "I knew about it. I knew this was coming."

She had not known. She had not thought of Spenser as anything more than a temporary meal-ticket at the Savoy; and her mother had not given her the smallest hint. She thought of her telephoning sweetly to Miss Braithwaite: "Would you ask Jinny to come along to my office for a moment?" Helen had planned it like this to give Virginia no chance for argument until the announcement was made, her resignation handed in, even the wedding date perhaps already fixed.

All I've got, indeed! Virginia tramped past the Prince's Theatre, avoiding cars and walkers by instinct, not properly seeing them. Why, if Helen had this planned, had she made such a fuss about Felix? It would have been more natural for her to have grasped at the opportunity to have Virginia out of the way. It could not be all jealousy. She did not need Felix now that she had Eldredge and his estate on Long Island, which would be of much more value to her.

Vanity? Perhaps. That too. Helen was the one who was getting married. She was the queen of the hour. She would not have the thunder of her wedding stolen by a pre-sumptuous daughter coming up with a wedding of her own.

Virginia was to remain a daughter, not to become a rival married woman. Helen wanted everything—everything for herself. She wanted Eldredge, but she wanted to keep Virginia too, to drag her off to America, no doubt, as if she were a steamer trunk, labelled: The property of Mrs Spenser Eldredge.

It would serve her mother right if she ran straight back to Felix and said: "Forgive me. I will marry you." But perhaps even Felix would have too much pride to be accepted as an afterthought. If he were humbly grateful for the insult, that would be only one more reason why she could not marry him. How disastrous to tie yourself for life to a man you did not want, because of a moment's pique with your mother.

The moment grew and lasted. As the future became more defined, Virginia liked it less. Her supposition was right. Helen did plan to take her to America. After the wedding, she and Spenser were going on a trip to Europe. They would then take Virginia "home" to the estate on Long Island—how she hated the sound of it already, with its orchid houses, and its fireplace transported stone by stone from a castle in the Black Forest—and Virginia would complete her education by going to college.

"But I don't want to go to college," she argued, over cocktails in the bar of the Savoy grill. "My education was finished long ago. I'm not a schoolgirl. I've got a job now. I'm doing well there. Ask anyone, Helen. Ask Miss Braithwaite. Ask Mr Owen. I'm to be given a chance at subbing next month. I won't be taken away.

"I like that in you, Jinny." Spenser leaned forward, the small table dwarfed to the size of a tray by his bulk. "I like that determined ambition. That's going to get you a long way. But not here, my dear. Over in the States, where I can give you every advantage you—excuse me, Helen—never had. If it's a job you want, though, of course, there's no need for it, I can get you in anywhere you want. But you must go to college. Everyone does. Bryn Mawr, I think, for you. I always planned that for my daughter, only, of course, I didn't have any children. My first wife"—he looked down at his martini—"she didn't care too much for the idea. But now that I have a daughter," he smiled benevolently at Virginia, and laid his heavy hand on hers, "I shall see all my hopes fulfilled."

Spenser was becoming as possessive as Helen. It seemed that he wanted to marry Virginia as well as her mother. She went along as part of the bargain. His kindness towards her and his affection, which was growing alarmingly sentimental, made it more difficult for Virginia to oppose him.

He had eaten all the cheese straws and cashew-nuts while he was talking. He clicked his fingers at the waiter. "Bring some more of these. They never give you enough. And," he circled his fingers over the glasses, "another round, as long as you're coming."

"Jinny doesn't usually have more than one cocktail," Helen said, with the sweet smile she used for Spenser.

"Oh, Helen, I do. What are you talking about? You've let me drink what I like for ages. What is this?" Virginia tried not to sound irritable against the warm family atmosphere the other two seemed bent on creating. "Are you trying to turn me into a juvenile so as to make me do something I don't want?"

"But Jinny, of course you want to go to America. You're just being stubborn. Stubborn and ungrateful." Helen, too, had some difficulty in keeping her voice pleasant. "It's a wonderful opportunity for you. Here is Spenser offering you a chance any girl would jump at. I can't think why you're being so funny about it."

"Girls are funny," Spenser said, diving deep into his second martini, the glass almost invisible in his meaty hand. "A girl is a woman, don't forget, Helen. That means she's illogical, unpredictable. You can't drive her into anything. You have to lead her, on a silk ribbon." He wheezed his laugh, and pushed his pink lips in and out with pleasure at his little quip.

"But you are trying to drive me," Virginia said. "I think you're very kind, honestly, and I like you, and I'm glad you're going to marry Helen, but please take her without me. I'm not ready to go to America yet. I've got too much to do here. I like my job, and I mean to do well at it. Not just staying on the magazine. I want to go on and on. But I want to do it here, where I know what the people are like, and how they think, and what they want to read. Not in another country where I would feel out of place for a long time, and where anything I've learned so far and begun to believe in wouldn't be much use."

"You're talking froth," Helen said. "America is not a cannibal country. The people are just like us. Look at Spenser."

"My ancestors were British," he said eagerly. "I told you that, didn't I? They came from Leicester. See, Helen, I even know how to pronounce it. I made a trip there last time I was over, and looked at all their records. There are some Aldritches listed in the parish archives. Aldritch—Eldredge, you get it? Let's go in and order dinner, what do you say? Virginia will feel better about this whole thing once she's eaten. I know I always do."

"I will never feel better about going away," Virginia said. "I love London. I've lived here all my life, and I need it. I need the—oh, the smells, and the Underground, and the greyness that makes it important when the sun shines . . . and the terrible futility of the people who have money or a title, and the terrible acceptance of the people who have nothing. I couldn't live anywhere else."

"The young are so lyrical." Helen made it a crime to be young. "Be practical, child. Where would you live? You know I'm giving up the flat when we get back from Europe. You can't expect Spenser to make you an allowance just because of this absurd whim. I wouldn't let him."

"I wouldn't take it. I don't need anything. I'm earning, and I can find myself a place to live."

"Not much of a place, on what you are getting," Helen said. "Don't forget I know what the magazine pays you. No, Jinny." She rose, and picked up her furs and bag. "This nonsense has gone on long enough. You are not yet twenty-one. You are my daughter, and you're coming with us. If you want to be ungrateful and cruel about it, that's your affair. No doubt you don't mind how much you hurt me and Spenser." She nodded graciously to the waiter, and led the way to the grill-room.

Virginia followed her unhappily. Why should she feel

like a sinner because she wanted nothing more than to live
her own life?

Spenser walked beside her, breathing heavily. "Please
don't be angry with me," he said. "I don't mean any harm.
I like you so much, and I just want to be a good father to
you."

"I like you too," she said, "but I already have a father."

She had a father. Habit, and loyalty to Helen, had kept
Virginia from going to him, or even wanting to go to him.
She had agreed to make her life with her mother, and that
was the only life she knew. But things were different now.
Helen was going to be married. She was going away. She
had money, security, companionship. She did not need
Virginia.

What was to stop Virginia from going to Harold and his
wife, and throwing in her lot with theirs? Legally, she was
old enough to choose. Very well, she chose her father. She
did not debate her decision with herself. She wanted to take
action, not thought. She wanted to take some assertive step
that would free her from the smothering danger of
becoming the property of Mr and Mrs Spenser Eldredge,
the pride of Bryn Mawr.

It was a wild idea, but she pursued it before her impulse
could slacken, hurrying as if there were no time to waste,
up the hill to the ugly house with the stone wall. What if
her father did not want her? He must. She would not be
afraid of him. His wife would understand.

Virginia pictured Mrs Martin opening the door with that
pleased smile, which instantly ameliorated the blemish of
her face. She would be wearing that flowered smock with
the bow at the neck. No—she might look a little different.
There might already be a baby there, bleating in some
upstairs room, bringing the bleak house to life with its
demands for love and care.

Virginia knocked, and waited a long time for an answer.
Her hope and purpose began to wilt in the anticlimax of
finding nobody at home. What could she do now? Should
she walk up and down, or sit on the steps and wait for Mrs

93

Martin to return? She had said that she seldom went out. She might be only in the High Street. Virginia could look for her there.

She turned back to the door as she heard a shuffling on the other side. Bolts were knocked back and a chain rattled. The door opened slowly, and a woman stood there in carpet slippers, her head tied up in a scarf, and a grey rubber pad bound to each knee, as if she were in a horse-box.

"Mrs Martin?" she repeated. "There's no one of that name here."

"There must be. They live here."

"They do, do they? Well then, you know something I don't know, for it's the first time I've heard of it. Martin? I never heard the name." She sucked a tooth, distending her cheek as if her tongue were a caramel.

"They must have let the house, unless they've sold it. Who lives here now? Can I see them? They would know my—Mr Martin's address."

"No one lives here." The woman kept her hand on the door, ready to close it. "At least, not to say *lives*. It belongs to the National Health, the way I understand it. Being made over into a day nursery, they say. Not that I know. I'm only here to do a bit of scrubbing and washing down."

"Perhaps they could help me at the Town Hall."

"Ah, the Town Hall. Well, they might. I couldn't say. Good day, Miss. I've got to get back to my floor."

She shut the door. Virginia went slowly down the steps, and stood in the muddy garden, looking at the house. The windows were closed and dirty, and all the curtains were gone. She could see into the front room, which had once been her nursery. It was bare, and the fireplace was full of rubbish and sweepings.

At the Town Hall, anyone who could help her was out to lunch. She waited, and finally saw a woman who knew something about the day nursery, and who consented to look at her records. Yes, the house had been purchased from a Mr Harold Martin. No, they had no other address for him. All the business had been completed before he went away.

94

Disheartened, but not wanting to give in without a struggle, Virginia went to see her father's solicitor. She remembered his name, because Helen had made jokes about it at the time of the divorce. Curtis Cowmeadow. She found him in a dim, triangular office in one of the buildings near Saint Paul's that was marked for demolition. He was a gnome of a man, with a big head and lined cheeks. He eyed Virginia carefully through the top half of his bifocals, then tipped his head back and examined her through the bottom half.

"Yes," he said. "I see it. You might be Harold Martin's daughter."

"I am. I've just told you."

"No need to take me up. I'm not doubting your word. I merely meant that you do look a trifle like him, as I remember him."

"Remember him? Haven't you seen him lately? He has just sold his house, and I thought that you must have acted for him."

"Oh, no." Mr Cowmeadow shook his heavy head, which was insecurely balanced on a thin, pulsing neck. "I haven't handled his affairs for quite some time. I have no idea where he might be. There was some bad luck, I believe, a few years ago. Lost his job, was it? Perhaps you know about that."

"I don't know anything. I haven't seen him since I was twelve. I found him quite by chance a few months ago, and now it looks as though I've lost him again."

"Oh, come," Mr Cowmeadow said. "It can't be as bad as that. No one can be lost. There are ways, you know, of tracing people."

"I don't know now that I want to find him," Virginia said flatly. "Perhaps it was all a mistake. I should have let it alone."

She felt suddenly defeated. The little office was airless, and smelled of cigarettes stubbed out in a metal ash-tray. Mr Cowmeadow looked rooted there, as if he had grown up behind his desk like a toadstool, and never known anything of the outside world. She did not want to be involved with him any more.

95

She went down the worn, narrow stairs, and walked aimlessly in the busy street. The excited determination that had sent her hurrying to her old home had all faded away in disappointment. She did not want to look for her father any more. He had deserted her, just as he had deserted her before. He was not the answer. There was no answer except to do what Helen wanted. If her father and his wife had been at the house, it would have been different. Her impulse would have been right, and to find them would have been the logical end of a journey.

People were going in and out of Saint Paul's. Virginia climbed the steps, and went in to that unbroken bubble of peace within the restless city. The organist was practising chords. The cathedral was full of sound and of people walking about, and yet it seemed deserted. Virginia stood isolated at the end of the nave. The quiet groups of sight-seers in the side aisles seemed miles away from her. The organist was in another world. She stood emptily in the tall solitude of space under the vaulting roof, and waited for her angel. Where was he now? Was it not true, after all, that you were never alone?

JOE COLONNA went into the tiny, cluttered kitchen and stirred the spaghetti sauce. It smelled good. He tasted it. It was good, better than the one his father used to make. He crossed the passage into the one room which was his home in the Chelsea basement, and threw some more wood on the fire. He was proud of that fireplace. All the other bed-sitting-rooms in which he had lived had electric fires, or gas stoves which popped and roared and dropped pieces of asbestos into the grate. The combination of a wood fire and an address in Chelsea were of proven value. The street was too far down the King's Road, but it was still in Chelsea, and to be able to say: "I have a place in Chelsea" was very different from saying: "I have a place in Fulham." The wood fire made something romantic out of the shabby basement room, with its covered bed that still looked more like a bed than a divan, and its window half below the pavement, where the feet passing beyond the area railings were on a level with your head.

Joe switched off the ceiling light and lit the lamp on the table by the window, which was laid for four. The leaping firelight made the other end of the room inviting. Derek's girls would like this. Other girls had liked it. "Oh, a wood fire—how lovely!" they cried, and in no time at all they were sitting on the floor with their shoes off, curled up and purring, thinking that they looked as attractive as the girls in films who were made love to in log cabins, with the camera trickily placed behind the flames.

Joe shook up the pillows on the divan, took a last look round the room, then put on his coat and went up the steep area steps to the street. He went into a wine shop in the King's Road, and bought two bottles of cheap red wine and a bottle of whisky. After he had paid for them, he looked again into his wallet. There were no more pound notes in there, and this was only Wednesday. The girls would have to be satisfied with red wine. He must make the whisky last.

Back in his room, he set the wine in front of the fire, and put the whisky in the cupboard under the kitchen sink. When he stood up, he looked at himself in the shaving-mirror. Smooth, the new haircut. Thank God his hair lay back naturally, without having to flatten the wave out of it with grease. Black hair, like his father, and he had given Joe his dark Italian eyes and high ridge of cheek-bone. Of his mother's docile, pallid features there was no trace.

Joe was better-looking now at thirty than he was as a young man. He had been too slight then, too narrow in the face, and the army uniform had at first looked too clumsy for him. But the war, and the first disciplined life he had known had filled him out and toughened him. It had taken the softness from his mouth and the smoothness from his skin. It had weighted his immature shoulders with a man's muscles, and his inexperienced mind with the conviction that for a man who had nothing behind him, there was always a war on, even when the world was at peace.

While he was studying himself in the small circle of mirror, he heard a car door slam in the street above, and then voices on the pavement. Girls' voices. One was giggling. Joe stood at the back of the other room, so that he could not be seen, and watched them coming down the stone steps. Which one belonged to Derek? One of the girls was tall and clean-looking, with a clear, pale skin and very bright lipstick. The other was small, with a froth of short curls. She was the one who was giggling.

She was not Derek's, Joe decided, as they came into the room and took off their coats. The short girl wore a tight, flaming red sweater, and had a small, greedy mouth. Derek went for the safe, amenable girls, who dressed incon-spicuously, and did not demand too much from him.

The other girl though, Virginia—she did not look like Derek's type either. She was sitting on the divan with her long legs crossed and her eyes and her big mouth smiling. She sat easily, as if she were at home, not primly and on her guard, as Derek's other girls would have sat in the den of a strange man, whom Derek had undoubtedly described as dangerous.

Nora, the short girl, was sitting on the floor by the fire, and would take off her shoes any minute now. They drank the first bottle of wine out of the thick, squat tumblers which were the only glasses Joe possessed. Derek, with his fair hair already flopping over his round face, sat on the bed beside Virginia and took her hand. Joe noticed that she immediately asked him for a cigarette, so as to have an excuse to take the hand away.

"Come and sit by me, Joe." Nora pulled another cushion on to the floor, and patted it.

Oh, hell, Joe thought. She's been told she's for me, and she can't even wait until after supper to show that she knows it. Towards the end of the evening, she would make some excuse, if Joe did not do it for her, to get Derek and Virginia out of the place without her. Making love to her would be too easy and too familiar. She was like a hundred other greedy little girls.

"No," he said. "The spaghetti's done. I don't want to spoil it. It's the only thing I can cook."

"You don't need to cook anything else when you can make spaghetti like that," Derek said eagerly. "Wait till you taste it, girls. You never had anything like it."

He admired Joe enormously. He could never quite understand how he had made friends with him, nor how he had managed to keep the friendship. Joe was the racy element in Derek's otherwise trim existence, the spice which peppered his unadventurous life, which was divided between the art department of *Lady Beautiful* and a cosy family circle in Buckhurst Hill.

Derek had been with the magazine for nearly eight years. Joe never seemed to be in the same job for more than two months at a time. He had been running some kind of fly-by-night club when Derek first met him. Derek had drunk ingenuously and passed out. His friends had deserted him. Joe had picked him up, allowed him to spend the night in his own room, and given him kippers for breakfast. It was not this room. Joe had lived in a variety of places since Derek had known him, and he had been in and out of a variety of jobs. Derek was not even sure what Joe was doing now. Something to do with a small theatre club, he thought, but he was not certain. Joe would not always tell you what he was doing.

"Not that it's anything shady," Derek had assured Virginia in the office when he had suggested this party. "There's nothing *wrong* about Joe. He's the salt of the earth; so do come. He said he felt like cooking spaghetti, and he asked me to bring a couple of girls, so of course I thought of you." He squeezed Virginia's hand behind a filing-case. She was working in the editorial office now. "I've asked that little girl, Nora, the new blonde in the reception-room. She looks like Joe's type," he added, making it clear where Virginia stood if the party resolved into pairs.

The spaghetti was a great success. They all ate enormously, and the second bottle of wine was finished so quickly that Joe wished that he had bought another at the expense of his lunch tomorrow. He was pleased with himself about the supper, and strangely exhilarated, as if the rough Algerian wine had been champagne.

The exhilaration was not engendered by Nora, who was back by the fire again, trying to look like a kitten. It was the other girl—Virginia. She was candid and young and a bit too leggy, but there was something about her that was different from other innocent girls who moved like fillies and had skins like flowers. She looked—Joe puzzled to define his impression—she looked wide awake, as if she were waiting for something to happen. She looked as if she were on the brink of life, ready to plunge in.

This made Joe think: I'll bet she looks good in a swimsuit. But the summer was a long way off. She would be gone from him long before that, back to her own clean and probably prosperous world, where people like Joe did not exist.

They played the gramophone and danced on a few square feet of worn carpet. When Joe danced with Nora, still without her shoes to make herself seem very small and cuddly, it was just as he had expected it would be. Her body pressing against his felt almost as familiar as if he were married to it.

When he danced with Virginia, it was different. She danced gracefully, much better than he did. Joe did not like anyone to do anything better than he could, so he stopped dancing with her quite soon; but the feel of her remained with him after they were apart. She had not nestled against him, and she had not held herself back. She had just felt so beautifully alive in his arms that he had a sudden impulse to tense his fingers and hurt her.

He went into the kitchen for the whisky, weakening in his resolve not to bring it out tonight. He needed it, if Nora was going to get what she was looking for.

They drank half the bottle of whisky. Derek was getting a little tight. His hair hung in his eyes like a sheep-dog. He put his arm round Virginia's waist, and she was kind enough, and pleasantly uncaring enough, to let it stay there.

"Let's do hypnotism," Derek said. "Try it on the girls, Joe. You didn't know he was a hypnotist, did you? He is." Derek nodded solemnly. "Best you ever saw. Remember that girl at Alexander's, Joe? Boy, you put her right out. I never saw anything like it."

Nora squealed with delight. "Oh, do let's!" She wriggled on the cushion.

"Oh, I don't know," Joe murmured, lying on the floor with his head in Nora's lap. "Not tonight. I couldn't."

Hypnotizing the half-drunk girl at Alexander's had been a joke. Joe had only pretended to know something about hypnotism, and the fact that the girl had gone off in an intoxicated swoon was nothing to do with him.

"But you must!" Nora pushed his shoulders upright. "Do me first. Hypnotize me. I'll bet you could."

"All right." Joe stood up. It might be amusing, and at least it would focus Virginia's attention on him. "I'll do Jinny," he said. "She's a better subject."

"No, she's not. Do me. Please, please, darling Joey, do me." Nora jumped to her feet and hopped up and down. "You can do her after, if you like. I want to be first." She pouted at him.

Joe said: "O.K.," and pushed her in the chest, so that she sat back in the chair facing the fire.

"I must have a key."

"A key?" Nora wriggled in the chair. "What for? What are you going to do?" She giggled. "Good-bye, all, in case I never come out of the trance."

Joe took Derek's front-door key from him. It was a Yale key, with a hole at the top. Standing in front of Nora, he held the key before his face, and ordered her to shut one eye, and look through the hole of the key into the pupil of his eye.

Virginia laughed. "It looks like a lorgnette."

"Be quiet," Joe said. "It's not supposed to be funny. I can't do it if anyone makes a noise."

Part of the act was the building up of a sinister, staring silence, during which he gazed unblinkingly at Nora, who sat with one eye screwed up, gripping the arms of the chair.

"Look at me," Joe ordered, in a deep, intoning voice. "Look at my eye. You can't look anywhere but into my eye. You are going to sleep . . . to sleep . . . to sleep . . ."

Nora squealed, and kicked her feet up. "Are you there, Jinny?" she asked, still looking at Joe. "Don't go away, anyone. I'm afraid I'm going to be seduced."

"That shouldn't frighten you," Joe said in his normal voice. Then intoning again: "Be quiet now. Be quiet. You are going to sleep . . . to sleep . . . You are asleep. You will do exactly what I tell you. Look at me. Look at my eye. My eye will tell you. You will do exactly what I tell you."

Joe had seen hypnotism acts on the stage, and knew that part of the routine was to repeat a few words over and over again. He did not expect it to have any effect on Nora, although she was eminently suggestible.

The room was very quiet. A log shifted in the rustling flames. Virginia was leaning forward on the divan at Joe's side. He could hear her breathing, and faintly trace her perfume.

"Nora," he said, "Nora. You are asleep. Do what I tell you. Raise your right hand." Nora raised it too quickly. "Stand up." She stood up, tightening her lips against a smile.

"Bark like a dog." Nora's yaps trembled with suppressed giggles.

Joe ordered her to do a few simple things, and then told her to sing *You Do Something To Me*. It was the first song he thought of. It had been running in his head all day.

"I can't." Nora opened her other eye and put her hands on her hips. "I don't know the words."

Joe lowered the key and laughed, shaking his head to relieve the strain of staring.

"Oh, you silly thing," Virginia said. "You weren't hypnotized at all. You were pretending."

"No, no, I wasn't. Honestly I wasn't." Nora was determined to have been hypnotized. "I wasn't trying to do what he said. I just had to. It was the funniest feeling. I feel funny all over. Feel me. I'm trembling." She put out her hand to Joe. "Honestly, darling, you *are*. Fancy you being able to do that. You've got powers. I'd be afraid to be in a dark room with you."

Joe did not take her up on that. He turned to Virginia. "Let me try it with you; I might have more luck. Nora's too jittery. She won't concentrate."

"But I did! How can you say that? I was hypnotized, I really was. It wasn't my fault I didn't know the song. Try me again, Joey. I'll bet you could make me do anything."

"No." He took Virginia's hand, and put her in the chair. "Jinny's turn."

"I'm going to get myself a drink then. I feel funny. My nerves need steadying." Nora went to the table at the other end of the room, and made a great deal of noise with the bottle and glasses, angry at being pushed from the centre of the stage.

"Shut up over there," Joe said. "I must have quiet. Close your eye, Jinny. The left one. Now look at me. Look through the key. Do you see my eye? Look at my eye."

Virginia sat upright and still, staring at him without a sound. "Look at me," Joe said. He was enjoying himself. He felt masterful. "Look at me, and you will go to sleep. You are going to sleep . . . to sleep . . . You can't do anything but look at me. You can't do anything but go to sleep. You are going to sleep. . . . You will do exactly what I tell you. Can you hear me? Can you hear what I am telling you?"

Virginia did not answer.

"Raise your right hand."

Virginia remained perfectly still, only her chest moving gently up and down.

"She's not trying," Derek grumbled. "Don't spoil it, Jinny."

"Ssh!" Joe waved a hand at him. "She's going to sleep. You are going to sleep, Virginia. To sleep . . ." Through the key, his eye saw her eye, brown pupil and green iris, broken by a triangle of light from the fire.

Something had happened. The other eye was open, and both were staring at him, and through him. He lowered the key, and her eyes did not move. She still sat upright, and yet her body was relaxed. Her hands lay limply in her lap. Her ankles were no longer crossed, but turned loosely, with one foot on its side.

God, did he really possess hypnotic powers after all? Joe was thrilled and afraid at the same time. He waved his hands in front of Virginia's frozen face. She did not move.

Virginia was walking down a long, dark passage. At the end of it was a small circle of light, like the hole in a key. It grew larger, and the light brightened. As she drew near to it, she saw that the hole was a little door within a larger door. She stepped over the sill, and was in a garden, in sunshine.

It was evening. The sun was low, shining directly in front of her. She was in a kitchen garden. There was a brick wall all round it, with fruit trees trained in formal shapes against the brick. Little paths with miniature box hedges ran up and down the garden, and in the plots between the paths, lettuces were growing, and raspberry bushes, and in the far corner, roses.

The garden looked neglected. The lettuces were going to seed in dry spires. The raspberries were straggling and tangled. When she walked towards the roses, she saw that the big flower-heads were wilting, and dropping pale petals on to the weeds that covered the ground.

Instead of being desolate in its neglect, the small garden held between its walls a hush of content. She knew that she had come here from a long way away, and that in the corner beyond the overblown roses was what she had come to see. The sun struck over the wall at that corner. It shone full in her face, and as its lower edge reached the bricks, and the shadow of the wall crept out over her feet, she was conscious of a deepening joy. Her happiness grew as the sun sank lower. She was drowning in the well of peace within the garden walls.

The sun had almost disappeared, and she knew that when its burning rim slipped below the wall, in the corner where the peach tree spread its arms, she would see what she was looking for.

She could feel it now, could feel its blessed presence, as the branches of the peach tree spread like wings. It was the answer to everything. It was—— she reached out with a cry, as someone pulled her roughly back by the shoulder, and Derek was shouting in her ear: "Wake up, Jinny! For God's sake, wake up!"

She leaned against the back of the chair and looked at him.

"God," he said, pushing back his hair, "you had me scared. What happened to you?"

"She was faking," Nora said scornfully. "What a silly trick to play. You had the boys all excited. Joe thought he'd started something he couldn't stop."

"No, I didn't," he said. "I knew what I was doing. You really were asleep, weren't you?"

Virginia wanted to cry. She had been within reach of something lovely, and now it was gone. She could hardly remember where she had been. A garden, was it? It was slipping away from her. What was it she was going to see?

She looked round at their faces; Derek still flustered, and sobered with alarm, Nora laughing at her, the strange man Joe leaning against the mantelpiece with his hands in his pockets and something like triumph on his face.

"No," she said. "Nothing happened. I didn't feel anything. I must have dozed off for a moment. I am rather tired. It's late, Derek, I think I'd better go home."

Joe did not say anything. Derek looked a question at Nora. "You two go on," Nora said quickly, "if Jinny wants to. It's early yet. I'll stay a little while so as not to break up Joey's party."

In the days that followed, Virginia could not get the dream out of her mind. Was it a dream? She seemed to have fallen asleep, and yet no dream had ever seemed so real. Real at the time, but faded now beyond recovery. All she could remember was the feeling of reality, and of the deep and drowning peace. Vaguely, there was a garden, rose petals on the ground, the spread branches of a peach tree, and that haunting sense of having been within grasp of something she had travelled all her life to see.

If only she could get back there again! Every night, she tried to recapture the dream, thinking herself back into the garden as she lay in bed; but she could not dream. She could not even fall asleep.

How had it happened? Did that man really have something to do with it—that strange, conceited man with the dark face that kept coming into her mind as she lay awake and struggled to sleep?

She drifted through her work by day, and fretted through the nights, thankful that Helen had gone away, and could not question why Virginia was out of bed making coffee when she should have been asleep.

Joe. Joe Colonna. The last kind of man to be a friend for Derek. The kind of man you met unexpectedly, remembered for a while, but did not meet again. What had he done? What power did he have to open the door into the haunted garden? A garden haunted by content, a garden where it was not impossible to believe that you could see an angel.

It was childishness. It was imagination. It was the wine and the whisky and the wood-smoke in that stuffy basement room. She held out, telling herself these things, for three days. Then she did what she had known all the time that she would do.

Joe had decided that he would wait for a week, and then

telephone Virginia. He would telephone her at the office, where she could not talk freely or for long. She would have to make up her mind quickly, with less time to think of an excuse.

He did not have to wait for a week. A few days after the supper party, a letter came. The handwriting was large and semi-legible. The notepaper was thick and good.

"Please telephone me as soon as possible," she had written. "I want you to do something for me."

Joe allowed her to wait a day, then he rang the number of the magazine.

"Editorial." Her voice sounded business-like. When she knew who it was, she said: "Oh." He heard her take a breath. "I can't talk now," she said quickly. "I wish you had called me at the flat. I'll have to explain when I see you. Can I see you?"

"Why not?" He saw himself grinning in the mirror that was set into the telephone box above the slots for money. "When?"

"Tonight if you can. It's important. There's something I—oh, look, I'll have to ring off."

"I'll be waiting," he said, as he heard her put down the receiver with an agitated clatter.

Joe had lighted the fire again. He had made the room look as it had looked the other night, with the pink lamp on the table, and the other end of the room lit only by the shifting flames.

When Virginia came in, she went straight to the fire, looked into it for a moment, then turned and said with the defiance of nervousness: "I want you to hypnotize me again."

Joe laughed, and came over to her slowly. "That's a good one," he said. "What do you think I am—Svengali?"

"I don't know. I don't know what you are. You'll think I'm idiotic, but something happened the other night, and it wasn't finished. I want to finish it."

"You're right, it wasn't finished," he said, staring at her coolly. "It only just began."

"How do you know?" She frowned. "I don't think you

107

know quite what you did, but somehow it worked, and I want you to do it again." She sat down facing the fire with her head up, gripping the arms of the chair, as if she were going to be electrocuted. "Do it quickly, and let's get it over."

"Get it over? What's the hurry? Let's have a drink and talk. Then if you still want to play games—we'll see."

"I don't want a drink. I had too much the other night. That may have been the trouble. Please do it again. Come over here, in front of the fire. Do what you did before, and see if you can put me to sleep."

"Why do you want me to hypnotize you?" Joe stood in front of her, standing easily, with his hands in his pockets and his well-shaped head on one side. "I didn't think you liked it very much the other night. You looked like death."

"I had a dream. I can't forget it. You see, I was—oh, I can't tell you. It sounds absurd. But I have to get back into the dream again. Haven't you ever come out of a marvellous dream, and fought against waking up, trying to fall back in again? I've tried to get back every night, but nothing happened. I thought perhaps you could do it for me."

Joe shrugged his shoulders. "Funny way to pass an evening, but if you insist, I'll try. I'll need a key though. Mine isn't a Yale."

"Give me my bag." Virginia did not want to move now that she was in the chair. There were two keys to the flat in her purse. She gave one to Joe and settled back in the chair, closing one eye and staring fixedly with the other.

Joe started the same rigmarole which he had acted before. Virginia stared at his eye through the hole in the key, trying to recapture that swooning sense of drifting right away from the room. When it happened before, it had not been a gradual loss of consciousness, like going naturally to sleep. It had been a sudden, obliterating removal from sight into sensation.

Nothing happened. Joe stared at her, and droned obediently on, but Virginia could still see and hear, and feel the worn arms of the chair under her gripping hands. She was still acutely conscious of everything: the fire, the ugly picture on the wall beside it, Joe's glossy black hair, his red, open-necked shirt, and his brown hand holding the key.

She blinked, and shifted her position. "It didn't work. What do we do now?"

"Give it up?"

"Oh, no. Try something else. What other ways do you know?"

"We could try without the light." He went to the other end of the room and turned off the lamp. The fire was burning without flames, and Virginia waited in the faintly-glowing darkness until he stood in front of her again.

"Now I won't be able to see your eye," she said.

"You won't have to. Shut both eyes, and I'll do it with my voice."

She shut her eyes, seeing the shape of him behind the lids. "You are going to sleep . . . to sleep . . ." She had never felt so wide awake. Why didn't it work? She could not get away from the room.

She stiffened herself, trying to think of nothing, trying to force herself into vacancy. Desperately she sought for the garden, but it was nowhere, not behind her eyes, not in his voice, not in the faint whisper and tick of the fire.

She opened her eyes, and saw that he was grinning at her. "I can't——" she began, and then he was on top of her, forcing her against the back of the chair, extinguishing all sensation with the brutality of his mouth.

Her numb resistance was more effective than if she had tried to push him away.

He stood up. "What's the matter?"

Virginia got up quickly and went to the other end of the room to turn on the light. "Where's my coat?" she said. "I want to go."

He stood in front of the fire. "What's up? Isn't that what you came for?" He laughed. "Don't tell me you really thought I could hypnotize you. It was only a joke. I don't know the first thing about it."

"Why didn't you say so? Why did you let me come here?"

"Think it out for yourself."

It was not until she got home and let herself into the flat

that Virginia realized that she had left the second front door key with him.

When he came, several days later, it was almost a relief. She was frightened when she heard the key turn in the lock, but it was an end of the wondering whether he would come, and the wanting him to come, and the dreading that he would.

★ 8 ★

HELEN came back from Europe looking slightly different from when she had gone away as the triumphant bride of Spenser Eldredge. Marriage to a rich and devoted man suited her taste well enough, but it did not suit her looks as well as being an independent woman with a living to earn.

She had only been gone for three months, but already she was a trifle stouter, a trifle less exact in her knowledge of how to look her best. She brought back trunkfuls of new clothes. Some of the Italian ones were too exaggerated, and some of the French ones were too youthful, as if Spenser's idea of her as a girl had hypnotized her into agreeing with him.

As the editor of *Lady Beautiful*, she had always looked finely groomed. Hers was the kind of appearance that makes you aware not so much of the end result as of the effort involved in achieving it. The effort was now even more apparent, and more important to her. She took twice as long to dress now that she had no work to fill her day. She kept Spenser out of the bedroom for twice as long as her night-time toilet had taken when she and Virginia were alone at the flat together. She would not go to any party without first visiting the hairdresser, and if the manicurist painted her nails the wrong colour, her evening was ruined.

She was becoming spoiled, and it showed in her face. There were new lines and a pampered puffiness which Virginia had not seen before. She was extremely impatient of anyone who crossed her desires, and inclined, after her luxury tour of Europe, to find fault with the way things were done in England.

The assistants in the shops were fools. Deliveries were hopeless, because they did not satisfy her instant's whim. She could not get a meal to her satisfaction, and taxi-drivers conspired against her by all having fares when it was raining.

She grumbled at the weather, and at Spenser, who bore it placidly, and at Virginia, who bore it not at all.

After the first meeting, with its natural gladness of reunion, she and Virginia quarrelled more than they ever had before she went away. Virginia's life was a whirlpool which centred round Joe, but she struggled to keep her head above water, and to appear as if she had nothing on her mind. She tried to be pleasant, but Helen was so demanding, so captious, so indifferent to Virginia's interests—even to her interest in the magazine, now that Helen was no longer at the helm of *Lady Beautiful*—that scarcely a day went by without a battle.

Spenser, who craved domestic harmony, tried to referee the battles, but to no purpose. His wife jumped on him if he seemed to be taking Virginia's side; but if he agreed with Helen, she was liable to snub him with: "Why do you always echo everything I say? It's most irritating."

If Helen was already so difficult after only three months of being a rich man's wife, what would she be like in America, as she settled egotistically down into her life of idle luxury? There were many servants in the Long Island house, Virginia knew. There would be parties, clothes, jewellery, furs; everything that Helen wanted, including, Virginia began to imagine, as she noted her mother's frequent failures to appreciate poor Spenser, a possible sycophantic boy-friend or two when Spenser was away on business trips.

"We sail on the eleventh of next month," Helen announced one morning, as she was lying face down on her bed being pummelled by a strong-armed masseuse called Lotta. "The *Elizabeth*, of course. Spenser is seeing to the reservations today. Well, what's the matter?" She turned her head sideways, as Virginia said nothing. "Why do you stand there with that pudding face? It's no shock to you. You knew we were going."

"But not just yet. I didn't know it would be just yet. I'm not ready."

"Well, then, you had better make haste and be ready. Lotta, you're murdering me. You know I can't bear to be touched there. If it's clothes you want, Jinny, Spenser will

112

let you buy anything you want, although you would do much better to wait until we get to the States. There's not a thing in London I would be seen dead in. If I hadn't bought things in Paris and Rome, I wouldn't be able to show myself on the streets."

"Turn please," Lotta said. "On the side. Thank you, madame." She worked on Helen's thickening flesh with a wooden face, as disinterestedly as a baker kneading dough, her mind far away.

"Be careful," Helen said. "This is supposed to be relaxation, not mediæval torture. You'll tell them at the office, of course, Jinny. You had better leave at the end of the month, though I really can't think why you don't leave now."

"I don't want to. I like working for the magazine."

"Everyone to his taste," Helen said, with the air of one who has long outgrown such childish things. "I'm going to pack up the flat as soon as possible, whenever I can get those dreadful people at the warehouse to apply themselves to the job. We'll go to a hotel. The Connaught, probably. It's the only place nowadays. We should have gone straight there when we came back from Europe. It's been dreadful living here cramped up like this."

"Spenser likes it," Virginia said. "He's tired of living in hotels. He likes London, too. I believe he would stay on a bit longer if you encouraged him."

"Oh, what nonsense, of course he can't. He's finished what he came to do over here, and he has to get back. You seem to forget that he's a business man, and a very important one, as you'll find out when we get to the States. So don't think that you can prolong the agony that way, just because you don't want to leave this man you're running to all the time. John, Jack, whatever his name is. I don't like the sound of him. Have you any daughters, Lotta?"

Lotta brought herself back from wherever her mind was, and smiled. "Two, madame."

"Do they ever conduct hole-and-corner affairs with unspeakable men whom they won't bring home to meet their parents?"

"They are only eight and ten years old."

"I see." Helen lost interest in Lotta's family. "Where are you going tonight, Jinny?"

"I don't know. I might meet Joe."

"Well, tell him from me that this is his swan song." She flopped over on to her back as Lotta finished the massage, and lay comfortably on her pillows, softening towards Virginia. "I'm sorry, dear heart," she said. "It was nice for you to have someone to amuse you while I was away, but you're starting a new life now. There will be plenty of young men in America, and one of them, you'll see, will turn out to be a husband. There will be men on the boat, too, there always are. You won't give this Joe creature another thought."

Virginia went down to the theatre club in South Kensington to find Joe. It was an odd little place, a post-war phenomenon born of the price of West End theatre seats, with pretensions to culture that belied the fact that the back room was often used for poker games, and had for a time housed a roulette wheel, until there was a scare about a police raid.

There had been no raid, but the roulette wheel did not come back. William and Henry, who owned the club, were cautious, and they were doing well enough with the tiny, pretentious theatre, and the bar, and the little restaurant where everything was fried in oil and garlic to give the illusion of a continental cuisine. If those who used the club for convenience rather than culture wanted a poker game in the back room, or if Joe wanted to negotiate bets there, that was their own affair.

William and Henry were usually called William and Mary. Mary did not mind. He was an elderly homosexual, who had corrupted a few boys in his time, but was comparatively harmless now. His fangs were drawn, he declared sadly, and was content with looking perverted enough to provide a thrill for those who came to the club half fearfully, like tourists visiting the innocent show-places of Montmartre.

It is true that some of the plays that were performed in the theatre were noticeably salacious, but only because that was

114

the only means the authors knew to achieve dramatic effect. The plays were usually "advanced," which is to say that they were too advanced for any West End manager with an eye on his box-office. How much the audience enjoyed them is hard to say. The more abstruse the play the louder they applauded it, assuming that if they could not understand it, it must be very intellectual indeed, and why did they belong to the club if not to prove that they were intellectuals?

The theatre held about fifty people, on folding chairs that often made more noise than the actors. The performance was sometimes on the level of village hall drama, and sometimes surprisingly talented. It was never certain who was going to produce or act, because no salary was paid for the privilege. It was up to William and Mary to persuade any unemployed talent they could find that a spell at the club was just the experience they needed.

Mary, who had been vaguely on the stage a long time before, performed occasionally, when there was a Restoration play, which allowed him to wear a wig and display the calves of his legs. When he was not acting, he played the piano in a corner of the combined restaurant and bar, the pouches under his eyes shaking gently to the simple rhythm of his grubby little songs.

The customers at the painted tables would stamp their feet and call for their favourites, to show their guests that they were initiates. "Give us *Banana Lil!*" they would shout. "Come on, Mary, good old Mary, do the one about the lamp-lighter."

"Shocking character," they would tell their guests nonchalantly. "Queer as a three-pound note, but he's a lot of fun."

When the show in the theatre was over, many of the audience would come through to the restaurant, eager for beer and inadequately-fried sausages, to mingle rather condescendingly with those club members who did not seek Thespian culture, and to listen to Mary's songs and buy him drinks, until the top of the piano was filled with empty glasses.

Mary provided the club's local colour. William, with gleaming spectacles and a round head of neatly-brushed hair, was a more stable figure in the background. He dressed soberly and kept the accounts straight, and the cook reasonably hygienic, and the barman moderately sober.

Joe had come into the club one night with a friend called Jackson, who was wanted by the police. It was in the days of the roulette wheel. Jackson had disappeared early, after a warning telephone call from one of his scouts, but Joe had stayed on and lost all the money he had with him, and his watch and cuff-links as well.

As he was out of a job at the time, William, who was the kindest of men, put him temporarily on the pay-roll, tolerating Joe's irregular attendance as long as he would do any job that was necessary while he was on the premises.

Sometimes Joe helped the cook. Sometimes he worked behind the scenes of the theatre, or had a walking-on part, or took the money at the door, or was sent out to do the marketing. He was the barman at the moment, since William had failed to prevent the last bartender from pouring part of every cocktail he made into a jug and drinking the mixture in the men's room.

Virginia found Joe behind the bar, reading the evening paper with his feet up on a crate of ginger ale. It was early yet, and there were only a few people in the restaurant, the solitary desperadoes who turned in for a drink on their way home from work. Mary was sitting at a corner table, writing letters with a quill pen. He looked up as Virginia came in, and gave her the smile which could not help being a leer, even when it was only meant to be friendly.

"Joe," he called across the room, in his cracked lisp, "the missus is here."

As Virginia was the first girl who had been seen in Joe's company for so long at a time, it was the club joke that he was as fettered as if he were married.

Joe lowered the paper, but did not put down his feet. "Hullo, Jin," he said, without surprise. She came to the club on most nights when he was working there. It did not matter. She could not be coy and elusive with Joe. That

116

would have bored him. Sometimes she made herself stay away, to prove that she did not need him, but she always came back quite soon. He was pleased to see her, but he would not say that he had missed her.

Sometimes when she came, he would be in the back room, where women were not encouraged to go. Mary would tell her: "Go home. You're wasting your time," but the good-hearted William would interrupt the poker game to tell Joe that Virginia was waiting for him.

Occasionally, when he was winning, Joe came out almost at once. More often Virginia waited in vain, helping William and the half-caste girl Betty to serve the food, so that she would not appear too obviously abandoned, until it grew late, and she had to go away without seeing Joe.

Virginia went behind the bar and began to polish glasses for Joe, who hated to do that. He sat with one arm on the bar and watched her. He was wearing a white shirt without a tie. In the open neck of the shirt, the trunk of his throat was dark and strong.

"Joe," she said, still busy with the cloth, "the missus is going to give you your freedom." She tried to make it sound like a joke, because she did not like saying it.

"Tired of me?" he asked casually, knowing that she was not.

"Helen says we're sailing on the eleventh of May. I shan't be seeing you much longer."

"Just as well for you," he said, getting up to make a drink for a man who had signalled from one of the tables. "Ending this is probably the most sensible thing you've done. You never should have started it."

"I started it?" She followed him to the other end of the bar, where he was bending to get ice. "How can you lie like that?"

"Did I ask you to come back to my room?" He grinned at her over the cocktail shaker. "It was you who came, with your cooked-up tale of wanting to be hypnotized."

"But I did. I've told you a thousand times. You don't understand. You'll never understand about the dream. I don't understand it any more myself. It seems so far away.

117

I begin to wonder if I ever saw—what I thought I saw."

"Lots of people wonder that, after they've seen mice running up the walls. You were tight, my love." It was only occasionally, when he said words like "tight" that his accent was just perceptibly wrong. Virginia did not mind that. She liked the way he talked, unselfconsciously, without precision. "Here," he said, handing her the glass. "Take this to that chap in the corner, and see that he pays for it. His credit's poor."

"Not that I wasn't quite pleased," he said when she returned, "that you had thought of an excuse to come back. Of course I didn't know you were going to behave the way you did."

"I didn't know you were going to kiss me."

"What did you think I would do? How odd you are, Jin. You're worlds apart from me. The only sensible thing about you is that you know it. Don't think I don't know why you've never taken me home since your mother came back. Here, let's have a drink. We'll have one on the house."

"No you won't." Mary came up to the bar, with his quill pen sticking out behind his ear like the plumage of a bedraggled hen. "You'll pay for it, even if the experience is a novelty."

"I can't. I haven't any money."

"I'll pay," Virginia said quickly, opening her bag. "How much is it?" she asked Joe, embarrassed because Mary was looking on.

"Six bob," Joe said, not in the least embarrassed. He swept the money into his palm and dropped it into the cash drawer. He raised his glass. "Your mother," he said. "Here's to her. Not that I want to meet the old girl," he added, mixing a drink for Mary.

"Perhaps she doesn't want to meet you, dear," Mary said, entering cheerfully into the discussion. "Miss Jinny may be smarter than we know. If I were a girl, which rumour has it that I am, I would think twice before I took a lusty boy like you to meet my mother." He put on his debauched face.

"Don't try to seduce me, you dirty old man," Joe said. "I'm not a customer."

118

"I'm sorry. I forgot." Mary took his drink and wandered over to the piano, where he began to pick out a tune with one finger.

"You . . . do . . . something to me," Virginia sang. "That's the tune you tried to make Nora sing. Remember?"

"The silly little bitch didn't know it. I'd been humming it all day, and then you came. Queer that." He listened to the piano for a moment, and then said: "Oh, hell, don't let's get sentimental. I can't stand that. Look, Jin, you'll have to go. I don't want you around tonight. I've got a couple of men coming in to see me on business."

"What kind of business?"

"Nothing to do with you. There might be a little money in it though. If there is, I'll take you out one day soon. Dinner, if you like. Anywhere you want to go. That satisfy you? All right, be a good girl and run along. I'm going to be busy."

That was just the way he was nowadays. He could not understand himself. He had never known a girl like Virginia. She was no use to him, or he to her, and yet he could not shake free of her. Every time he tried to push her off, he found himself offering her something nice, so that she would not be disgusted with him.

Well, she was going away soon, and he would be free again. Damn it, but he was going to miss her. She had no right to make him miss her.

After he had haggled with the two men in the back room over a little deal that involved persuading a disqualified doctor to report knife wounds as dog bites, Joe drank quite a lot that evening. Some of the drinks were paid for by club members. Some he took for himself. He did not care whether William and Mary liked it or not. He would not be here much longer. As soon as Virginia had gone, he was going up to Glasgow to see a man about a job at a greyhound track. Why wait until she had gone? The greyhounds lured him, and Glasgow was a tough, exciting place to be. Better than fiddling away his time here playing flunkey to a lot

119

of highbrows and pansies. But he knew that he would not leave until Virginia left him.

He went away from the club before eleven, leaving William to look after the bar. Joe was nowhere near being intoxicated, but he had drunk enough to feel restless. He could not stand the club and Mary's simpering, smutty songs any longer. He went up to Bloomsbury, and walked into the mews where Virginia lived, with his hands in his pockets, kicking at a stone.

The lights were on in the front room, and the curtains were not drawn. Joe stood in the shallow gutter that ran down the centre of the mews, and looked up, whistling under his breath. Virginia passed across the window in silhouette between him and the light, and he clenched his hands in his pockets, feeling her on the skin of them. Was she alone? The window was closed, and he could hear nothing. He stood there for a few minutes, feeling shut out, feeling like a boy outside a sweet-shop window. Then his fingers touched the key that was still in his pocket, and he pulled it out, pushed open the outside door of the building and went up the stairs.

Outside the flat, he stood in the hall and listened to the voices. When he opened the door, they all stopped talking, and the silence cut across the conversation like a knife.

They were in evening dress. They were all staring at him. For a second, the tableau was motionless, fixed like a stereoscopic picture on Joe's eyes. The big man in the loose dinner jacket, cradling a goblet of brandy. The woman in the fancy green dress, her hand flown up to the pearls at her neck, as if Joe had come to steal them. Virginia sitting on the arm of a chair in a flowing black dress with her hair brushed back from her ears, cool and lovely, his girl—untouchable.

In a moment Virginia had risen and come quickly to him with her hands out, and the frozen tableau was broken up into sound and movement. Virginia stood between him and the other two, smiling at him. Her mother and the man in the dinner jacket were saying something that he could not hear.

"Jin, I haven't even got a tie on." He tried to laugh, aware of her scent, and the softness of the carpet under his feet, and the comfortable feminine decoration of the room. "I didn't know you'd be all dressed up."

"We've been out to dinner. It doesn't matter." She took his hand. "Come in. Don't stand there." She had recovered herself rapidly. "Helen," she said, leading him forward as if he were a dog, "this is Joe Colonna. My mother, Joe, and this is my stepfather, Mr Eldredge."

"How do you do, Mr Colonna?" Virginia's mother said, pronouncing the words meticulously. "Forgive me if I appear boorishly inquisitive, but may I ask how you got in?"

"The door wasn't shut properly," Virginia said quickly. "I came in last, I remember. You know you have to push it hard to catch the lock."

"Do you?" Helen turned her face to Virginia, but continued to look at Joe out of the sides of her eyes.

Having looked Joe over carefully, Mr Eldredge pushed himself out of his chair and held out his hand. "Glad to know you, Mr Colonna," he said huskily. "Nice of you to come and see us. We've heard something about you from Jinny here. Not too much. You know what girls are with their parents, but it's good to have the chance to know you. What can I get you to drink?"

Joe hesitated. What would be the right thing to ask for?

"He'd like a Scotch I expect," Virginia said, knowing that Joe had been drinking whisky.

"Surely." Mr Eldredge ambled to the cabinet by the wall. Virginia smiled at him gratefully, glanced at her mother, who was swinging a foot, and told Joe to sit on the sofa. She sat beside him, not touching him, trying not to look at him. He did not look at her. He took the glass from Mr. Eldredge, accepted an American cigarette, and sat back, hoping he looked at ease.

God, but he wished he had not come! This would be the end of him with Jin, and now that he had seen her with her family, he did not know that he cared. Damn them, why did they have to be all dressed up like this? They might have done it on purpose to make him feel a lout.

His jacket and slacks needed pressing. He had been meaning to have it done for days. His shirt, open at the neck, was not even clean. If it had not been for Virginia, he would not care how he looked, but Jin, she—God, she was a lady, and he could wring her neck for it. These were the kind of people he hated, the people who had things. All the years of his childhood and manhood of having nothing, being no good, caught in his throat and choked him into silence.

He sat there like a dummy. He could see himself. He knew that he was scowling, while Virginia's mother chatted in that high, surprised voice, making conversation, asking him silly questions, like a duchess entertaining a game-keeper.

Virginia put her hand on his knee. Her hand was warm and tender. He knew that she was crying inside for him. What right had she to be sorry for him? He did not want that from her. He wanted nothing from her.

Her stepfather was genial enough, but even his good-humoured talk fed Joe's resentment. The old boy could afford to be genial. He was on the winning side. He was taking Virginia away to a life of college boys and smooth characters with fast cars. Joe was nowhere in the picture. Joe was an unfortunate mishap, who had blown in like a fly, but would soon be swatted away. Mr Eldredge offered him another drink. Joe refused and stood up, saying that he must go.

"But you've only just come!" Virginia's mother smiled, as if to say: Look at him. Isn't he ridiculous? "Do stay a little longer. I want to hear some more about that fantastic club. Jinny never tells us anything."

"No, I have to go. I have a date with a man in Charing Cross Road, just round the corner. That's why I thought I might as well drop in here."

Joe felt more pleased with himself. That was a good excuse for having come, and it got him out without loss of face. "Good night, everybody. Thanks for the drink." Did one shake hands with these bastards? Apparently not. No one moved a hand. He got himself to the door. He had not said much, but at least he had not been rude. Virginia should be proud of him after all.

With her mother's eye on her, he thought that she would say good night to him coolly at the door; but when he opened it, she came out with him and shut the door behind her.

They stood at the top of the stairs, looking at each other. "Oh, God, Jin," he said. "I'm sorry."

"It's all right."

"You'd better go back in," he said. "They'll give you hell."

"No they won't." She laughed and put her arms round his neck. He kissed her as if it was the last time. He knew that it was. Virginia went back into the flat with her head up, not caring that her hair was tumbled and her lipstick smeared.

"It could hardly be worse," Helen said. "Get me a drink, Spenser. I am the most disillusioned woman in town."

"Why disillusioned?" Virginia asked. She saw that she would have to fight this out now, if Helen were determined to attack her right away.

"I am disillusioned because I thought that I had brought you up to certain standards. You have met the right people, been to the right places. I have tried to see that you made the right friends. Thank you, Spenser. That looks very strong. I think I need it.

"The right young men," she continued, "have all been there for you to choose from. You have known, Jinny, what a gentleman is, if you'll pardon an expression that I believe you do not like. That is why I cannot, why I simply cannot understand this—this lapse, this folly, this——" She lifted a hand and let it fall limply on to her knee. "I am at a loss for words."

"What word are you looking for, Helen?" Virginia asked politely. "If you're trying to say that Joe is common, you can think of another word, because he's not."

"I refuse to discuss this with you while you stand there looking like a wanton. Go and fix your hair and lipstick. Then I will talk to you."

"Oh, look, dear," Spenser said. "It's getting late, and I'm tired. You're tired too, or you wouldn't feel so badly. Couldn't we talk about this in the morning, if we must talk about it at all?"

"I want to talk about it now," Helen said. "I want to have this out now. I will talk about it." She sounded like a spoilt child, whining to have its own way.

"In that case," Spenser said, coughing through his fiftieth cigarette of the day, "I think I'll go to bed. This is no place for me."

"Please stay," Virginia said, combing her hair at the mirror on the wall. "I need someone on my side."

"But I don't know that I am on your side, honey. Should I be?"

"I should hope not."

"I hope so."

Helen and Virginia spoke at the same time. Spenser looked helplessly from one to the other, caught between them.

"Must we fight about this?" Virginia turned from the mirror and sat down opposite her mother. "I can't see what all the fuss is about."

"She can't see what the fuss is about," Helen mimicked. "Ever since we came back from Europe, and for heaven knows how long before that, you've been spending most of your spare time with one man. A man you had not the decency—or perhaps I should say the courage—to bring home. Finally, he barges in of his own accord. We see him. Then we know why you wouldn't bring him home."

"What's wrong with him?" Virginia asked, tensing with anger. "What's wrong with Joe? You did your best to make him feel uncomfortable while he was here, and to put him at a disadvantage. How could you expect him to make scintillating conversation?"

"I don't," Helen said. "I'm sure he couldn't. You ask me what is wrong with him. Very well, I'll tell you. You gave me the word yourself just now, don't forget, so don't jump down my throat if I say that he is common."

"What do you mean, dear?" Spenser looked baffled. He could not understand this talk about being common, or not being common. "I didn't see that the man was vulgar in any way."

124

"It's not a question of that. You don't understand. Americans, if you'll forgive me, Spenser, don't understand the difference between being a gentleman and just not being one."

"Oh, don't they?" he said, not taking offence. "That's interesting. I didn't know that."

"Well, forget it right away," Virginia said. "Don't listen to her. She's being ridiculous and snobbish, and she's trying to make you that way too, and you're much nicer as you are. Oh—why are we talking like this? I hate this." She got up and stood with her hands at her sides, holding the skirt of the black dress. "What does it matter, anyway? Even if there was something wrong about Joe, what would it matter? I'm not married to him, am I?" She surprised herself with the word. She had not thought of it.

"But as it happens, there's nothing wrong with him. He may not have such a wonderful education, but that wasn't his fault. His mother died when he was fifteen, and his father —he was Italian—went back to Italy. Joe wouldn't go, so he was left here to fend for himself. He left school to get a job, and then he left that job at the beginning of the war, and lied about his age to get into the army."

"Now you will say, I suppose, that he fought for my life, and I should be grateful to him. Well, I'll surprise you by saying that I am." Helen looked complacent. "Thank you, dear heart, for telling us the life story of Mr—Colonna, is it? Yes, I see. The Italian name. What was his father doing over here?"

"He was a waiter," Virginia said sullenly. "He married an Irish chambermaid who worked at the same hotel. There, now I've told you. You can mock at that."

"I don't choose to mock," Helen said. "I think it's very nice of you to tell me, considering that you imagine, quite mistakenly, that I am snobbish. As for the young man, well, surely it's a very fine thing that he was able to make something of himself with so few advantages. There were many officers in the war who started with even less."

"Oh," said Spenser, blundering into the wrong question, "was he an officer?"

"He could have been," Virginia said. "He was a sergeant, actually, but his commanding officer thought so much of him that he wanted Joe to take an officer's training course. It was only bad luck that he couldn't. Just before he was to go up for selection, his mother was terribly ill. They wouldn't let him go to see her, so he went absent without leave, and of course that lost him his chance."

"I thought you told me that his mother died before the war." Helen's eyes were crafty.

Virginia was flustered, forgetting now exactly how the story went, refusing to doubt that Joe had told her the truth. "Oh, well, I may have got it wrong, but anyway, it was something like that. Let's go to bed. I'm tired of this. Poor Joe, it isn't fair to pull him to pieces as soon as he's out of the room."

"I agree." Spenser got up. "Let's all go to bed."

Helen remained sitting in her chair. "I'm not pulling anyone to pieces," she said. "I am merely showing a perfectly natural interest in someone who—listen, Jinny." She suddenly sounded more sincere. "I've been away for three months, with no idea what you've been doing. A man comes in here, and he has a key to the flat. Don't deny it. I know he did. I heard the lock turn. What conclusions do you think I have to draw?"

"I don't know." Virginia shrugged her shoulders, trying to be calm. "Think what you like."

"I think this." Helen spoke with icy clearness. "I think you are sleeping with him."

"Oh, now look, for heaven's sake——" Spenser was red in the face. "You can't talk to your daughter like that."

"Perhaps *you* should, but if you won't, I must. Tell me the truth, Jinny. Are you?"

Virginia looked her squarely in the face. "No," she said.

Helen looked at her with equal directness. "I don't believe you," she said calmly.

The following evening, Virginia and Helen went with Spenser to a party at the American embassy. Virginia did not want to go. If she did not go to the club tonight, Joe

126

might think that she was angry about his visit to the flat. She wanted to find out whether he was angry with her for the embarrassment it had caused him, and to show him that nothing was changed between them.

Since last night, she had a new feeling about Joe. She felt a responsibility towards him, the beginnings of a stubborn loyalty, which she was afraid would endure long after she had gone away from him for ever.

When she told Spenser that she did not feel well, he was so disappointed that she had to agree to go to the party. Spenser was very proud of knowing the American ambassador. He wanted his family to appreciate the acquaintance. He also wanted to show off to anyone he knew at the party the family he had acquired in England.

He introduced her to several people, but Virginia could not find much to say to any of them. To please Spenser, she was wearing one of his presents to her, a full-skirted white dress, which left her shoulders bare, and accented her young bosom; but she would much rather have been behind the bar of the club in a skirt and sweater.

This was how it would be in America. Dressing up nearly every night in the costly clothes that Spenser would buy for her, making trivial conversation with easy-mannered people for whom she could raise no enthusiasm. Perhaps she would look interestingly sad when she went to America, and people would guess that she had left her heart in England.

She did not think that she was in love with Joe, and yet, what was love, if it were not this compulsory attachment, which she had not sought and could not unloose?

Helen was enjoying herself, in a dress unbecomingly unusual enough to attract attention. She talked fluently to Spenser's friends, and wittily enough to make him proud of her. Virginia stayed close to her mother in the crowd, since she did not know anyone else, but Helen hardly spoke to her.

When Spenser wandered off for a while, Helen worked busily on a man from the United Nations, who talked a lot of charming nonsense, and wore a tartan dinner jacket and tie, like a man in a magazine advertisement. Virginia half listened to their conversation, letting her mind wander.

"I understand," said the man in the tartan tuxedo, "that you're planning to go to the States pretty soon. Mr Eldredge has one of the finest estates on Long Island, I hear."

"I hear that too," Helen said. "You must be sure to come and see us when you get back to New York."

"I will indeed," he said, "but perhaps you and Mr Eldredge and your charming daughter would have dinner with me one night before you sail."

"That's very kind of you, but we're leaving in two days' time."

Virginia's mind came back to the party in an instant. She swung round to look at her mother, but Helen was talking lightly on, as if she had not said anything unusual.

The man from the United Nations went away to get Helen a drink. Helen was turning to talk to someone else, but Virginia grabbed her arm and pulled her round.

"Why did you say that?" she demanded.

"Say what? Oh, dear, have I made a *gaffe*?"

"We're sailing next month. Why did you say we were leaving in two days' time?"

"Didn't I tell you?" Helen said casually. "I meant to. Spenser has changed his mind. He doesn't want to go by sea, and his New York office needs him, so we're flying over on Friday. You'll have to start packing tomorrow."

"I know why you've done this." Virginia kept her voice low, but the words were as vehement as if she had shouted them. "It's because of Joe, isn't it? You want to get me away."

If Helen had denied it, it was possible that Virginia might have believed her. But Helen was so sure of herself, so certain that she could make people do what she wanted, that she said: "What do you think? Of course."

The man in the tartan dinner jacket came back with the drinks, and Helen turned to him with a smile, as if she and Virginia had been discussing no more than the weather.

Virginia moved away from her into the crowd, hurried to get her fur cape, and went out into Grosvenor Square to take a taxi to the club.

Mary gave a wolf whistle when he saw her in the dazzling

white dress. "How lovely you look," William said. "I never knew you were so beautiful." His spectacles gleamed as brightly as the glass he was polishing behind the bar.

"Where's Joe?"

"He isn't in tonight," William said. "I thought he was probably with you, but you look as if you'd been keeping finer company. What's the matter, my dear? You look upset. Is something wrong?"

"No, it's all right," Virginia said breathlessly. "I just want to see him about something."

Mary looked over the top of the piano. "You'll have to go down to Victoria then, if you want to see him," he said, still playing the accompaniment to his song. "I heard him say last night he was going to a wrestling match."

"Where is it, do you know?"

"Yes, but I won't tell you. It's no place for a nice girl like you to go, especially looking like that." He took up the words of the song again.

"You must tell me." Virginia went to the piano. "I have to see him. It's very important."

Mary gave her his lewd smile and continued to sing softly, caressing the suggestive lyric with his slippery lips as if it were great poetry.

"Oh, please," Virginia said across the empty glasses on the top of the piano. Mary shook his head.

Virginia turned back to William. "Do you know?"

"Don't tell her," Mary said. "She shouldn't be chasing after that character. He's no good for her, and if she appears in that den of thieves looking like that, the wrestling won't all be in the ring."

Some of the people sitting at nearby tables had been listening to the conversation. They laughed, enjoying the scene, and Mary winked at them and chuckled.

"Don't laugh at her," William said. "The poor girl is in trouble of some kind, aren't you?"

"Yes, I am. Please help me."

"I thought so." William nodded. "It's not for me to say what you should or shouldn't do. If you really want to find Joe, here——" he was drawing a rough map on a bar chit.

"This is where the place is. I don't say whether Joe will be glad to see you, but that's your affair. And for heaven's sake keep that fur done up round your neck." He was staring at her bosom.

"Oh, yes." Virginia drew her cape round her shoulders. "Thanks so much. You're very kind."

"I try to be," William said. "We are all put into this world to help each other," he added sententiously, and Mary made a rude, sardonic noise.

Virginia took a taxi to Victoria, and then walked behind the station to find the street marked on William's map. She could not bring herself to ask the taxi driver to take her to the door of the Vauxhall Sporting Club.

The side-streets were dark and dirty, with small shuttered shops, and shabby houses hiding their lights behind torn blinds. She passed one or two men who stared at her with their heads down, and three youths arm in arm, who gave her the expected whistle. In the doorway of the club, more youths were lounging. They were not talking. They were apparently not waiting for anything. They were merely leaning against the wall in a vacuum of time, staring at nothing with vacant eyes. As Virginia approached, their eyes turned to her as if they were threaded on one string, followed her to the doorway, and remained staring emptily, while she hesitated, not liking to enter the dim corridor.

The name of the club was written over the door in faded paint, but Virginia asked: "Is this the Vauxhall Sporting Club?" The youths said nothing for a moment. Then one of them nudged another, and he nodded.

"Is it all right if I go in? I mean, do you have to be a member?" This was too much for them. They looked at her as if she were speaking Chinese.

"Oh, well—thank you," Virginia said nervously, and walked into the passage. Behind her, the youths broke out in a volley of guffaws.

As Virginia went down the passage, she could hear a gradually increasing roar of sound. When she reached the thick curtain which hung at the end, she could distinguish individual shouts against the background clamour. It was a bestial noise, mindless, cruel. She had heard it when she went to a boxing match; a male crowd noise, split here and there by women's shrieks, quite different from the more genial open-air crowd noise of a football match.

There was a chair and table at the end of the passage, with a saucer full of cigarette stubs, but no one sat there. The heavy curtain swayed, as if someone knocked against it on the other side. As it parted slightly in the middle, Virginia saw the yellow light fogged with smoke, men's backs, and a Laocoon-like glimpse of a struggling naked torso beyond them.

There was nothing to do but go in. She slipped inside and stood with her back to the dusty curtain, hoping that she would not be noticed before she could see Joe. There were no benches round the ring. The men, and a few women in the front, were standing up, jostling one another, swaying together in surges of excitement, waving their arms, or flinging out a stiffened finger as they shouted instruction or abuse at the wrestlers.

The two men in the ring were squat, vast shouldered and hairy. They circled each other like snarling baboons, then were suddenly locked together, and rolled to the ground in a deliberate motion that looked more like a joint effort than a battle. Their short legs strived and twisted, their arms embraced, their heads beat the ground, and the black hair on their backs was matted with running sweat.

Watching in startled fascination, Virginia forgot for a moment to look for Joe. She caught her breath as one man picked up the other and hurled him to the ground with a thud that made the hoarse crowd yell and stamp their feet. Virginia could not take her eyes from the ring. She was leaning forward with her mouth open, and a little cry escaped her as an arm like the trunk of a small tree was twisted and bent back, while its owner screamed and gnashed his teeth.

The man standing in front of her looked round. He nudged his neighbour, who turned round too.

"What are you doing here, little girl?" the first one said. "Lost the way to the Ritz?" He was a mean-looking man with a face like a knife, and Virginia felt afraid. She stood on tiptoe, searching the crowd for Joe.

"Looking for someone?" the man asked, shifting a match from one corner of his mouth to the other.

"Yes. Joe Colonna. Do you know him?"

"Never heard of him," the man said. "Come and stand here by me. You'll see better." He put out an arm to pull her forward. Virginia twisted out of his grasp, and moved away on the edge of the crowd, peering over heads and between shoulders. She could not see Joe anywhere.

Several men said things to her, or whistled. A woman with hair like a wet black retriever made some joke which Virginia could not hear, but those who could hear it laughed and stared at Virginia as she passed, then lost interest and turned again to hurl their comments at the struggling monsters in the ring.

One of the wrestlers was howling like a dog. Virginia stopped to look between two men. She thought he was being killed. Someone pushed her, and she staggered against a burly man in a tight, shiny blue suit. She clutched at him to avoid falling, and gasped as the wrestler howled again.

The man pushed her upright. "Don't worry about George," he said. "He always does that. It's part of his act. Hullo," he looked at her more closely. "Where did you come from? You shouldn't be here on your own." He frowned, bringing his hairline almost down to his eyebrows. His face was squashed together, as if there were a heavy weight on the top of his head.

"I'm not on my own," Virginia said, clutching the fur cape across her chest. "I'm with someone, only I've lost him for a moment. Do you know him? Joe Colonna."

"Old Joe? Sure," said the man. "Got away from you, has he? He got bored with the fights and went in the office to have a drink with the governor. You won't find him out here." He looked away from Virginia for a moment to shout: "Kill him!" at the ring, and then turned back and said: "Want me to take you in there? Midge don't like strangers barging in."

Virginia followed him as he pushed back through the crowd and sidled round the wall to a door in the far corner. He beat on it with his fist.

"Who is it?" The voice from inside was as high-pitched as a child's.

"It's Terry. Got a friend of Joe's here. Wants to see him."

"O.K."

Terry opened the door and pushed Virginia inside. The door shut behind her, cutting down the clamour of the crowd to a dull roar. Joe was sitting at the table in a yellow sweater, his black hair shining under the naked light which hung from the ceiling. He did not look pleased to see Virginia.

"Jin," he said, without getting up. "What the hell are you doing here?"

"I had to see you. I'm sorry." She felt foolish, standing by the door of the drab little room, with its bare floor and its stained walls hung with pictures of horrible, half-naked wrestlers. Midge was an elephant of a man, in a grey suit like an elephant's baggy skin. He and Joe were staring at her, and she was conscious that her cape had fallen away from the front of her low-cut dress, but it would look more foolish to pull it together again.

"Who is this, Joe?" Midge asked, in his high, unresonant voice. His great flabby head hung slightly forward, as if it were too heavy even for his thick neck. His thighs, crossed one over the other, strained at his trousers. His hand on the table was like a bundle of fat red sausages. There was a bottle and glasses among the litter on the table, and an ash-tray like a dog's dinner bowl, with the last cigarette end still smoking among the other twisted stubs.

"This is Miss Martin," Joe said brusquely, as if her identity were not important. "You shouldn't have come down here, Jin. How on earth did you get through the crowd in that—that nightgown?"

"It's not a nightgown. It's my best dress." Virginia came forward to the table, wishing that one of them would get up and give her a chair. She felt limp and breathless after what she had been through to find Joe. "I was at a party with Helen, but something happened, and I left. Silly, I suppose, but I felt I had to tell you."

"What's happened?" Joe asked irritably. "Tell me what you want, and then you'll have to go. Midge and I are busy." He picked up his glass.

"I can't tell you, when——" Virginia looked uncertainly at Midge.

"You mean you want me to get out?" he asked tractably. "Turned out of my own office, eh?" He cackled softly, and began the ponderous manœuvre of getting to his feet. "Never let it be said that I wouldn't oblige a lady. I'll give you a few minutes, Joe, while I go and see how George is making out, but for God's sake don't let any more of your girl-friends come crashing in here. It disturbs my metabolism." He took a long look at Virginia, his heavy head swaying slightly from side to side, like a bull summing up a toreador. Then he sucked his teeth and said: "Not bad. Not bad at all," and shambled in his tent-like suit to the door.

When he had gone, Joe stood up. "Now listen, Jin," he said. "This is a bit thick. I can't have you trailing me all over London."

"You won't any longer. Helen's just told me we're leaving by plane the day after tomorrow. I came to—well, I just came to say good-bye."

Why had she come? It was not to say good-bye. She had run to Joe, because it was the only thing she could think of in her distress and anger.

Joe came round the corner of the table and pulled the cape off her shoulders. "My God, that dress," he muttered. He stood in front of her, staring at her, gripping her arms painfully. "Why should you say good-bye? We never met. It's finished, forgotten. You don't look like anyone I know."

"You know me better than I know you," she said. "You know I don't want to go away. You can pretend to forget me if you like, but I shan't forget you."

"The old girl—your mother, is she rushing you off because of me?"

Virginia nodded.

The thought elated him. "Don't go then," he said. "Come

134

and live with me. That would give her something to gripe about."

"I couldn't do that. Those things never work. It wouldn't last, and then I'd be left with nothing. No family, no you, no self-respect, nothing. I'll have to go with her. Helen's won this time. I hope she's satisfied."

"Damn her eyes," he said. He moved his hands from her arms to the sides of her face. He pushed back her hair and kissed her, bending her back against the edge of the table. Then he suddenly pulled her upright, turned her round, and stood behind her with his cheek on her hair and his hand over her breast.

"Listen, Jin," he said against her ear, "you're the best thing that ever happened to me. God knows I'm not much good now, but if I lose you, I'll probably end up in the gutter. Let's get married, then no one but me can tell you what to do."

Virginia looked down, and saw her heart beating violently under his hand. "You don't want to marry me," she said shakily. "I thought you said you never wanted to marry."

"I did, but I'm not the man I was. Remember the song— *You Do Something To Me*? Listen, we'll get married tomorrow. That will spike the old lady's guns. God, I would like to see her face!" He chuckled, rubbing his cheek against her hair. "Would you do it?"

She turned round and put her hands on his sweater, stroking them across his chest. "Yes, I would, but we can't, Joe. There isn't time. You can't get married all at once like that."

"I can fix it. I know what to do." He laughed. They were both excited now, their eyes shining, intent on each other. "I know the dodges," he said. "I nearly got married in a hurry once before, only luckily I had the sense to send the girl to a doctor, and found out she was lying."

"You never told me that."

"I never told you a lot of things. I probably never will."

"I don't care."

"You will," he said. He took her hands and pushed her away from him. "Here, put this fur thing on before Midge comes back. No one's going to see my wife half naked. Go home now and pack some things. Be ready to clear out any time I call you. Your mother will only think you're packing to go with her. You needn't tell her anything."

"I must. It would be too unkind. I'll have to leave her a note at least. But where will we go? We can't stay at your place. She'd find us. She'll get the police out. You don't know Helen."

"We won't be there," he said. "Oh, hullo, Midge. Yes, you can come in. We're all through with the drama."

Midge came in, and some men followed him. Outside, the wrestling was over. There was a shuffling, coughing hubbub as the crowd began to leave.

"Where will we be?" Virginia asked Joe, moving closer to him as the room filled up.

"In Glasgow. After last night, I didn't want to stick around. I wired Anderson that I was coming up after the job. You'll come with me."

"This sounds interesting," Midge said. "What's the deal, Joe?"

"We're going to be married." Joe looked round the room defiantly.

"Well," said Midge, sitting down at the table with a thud and a sigh, "now I've heard everything."

★ 9 ★

VIRGINIA spent her wedding night in the night train to Glasgow, sitting up in a carriage with five other people, dozing fitfully, with her head on Joe's shoulder.

Joe slept for long periods, peacefully, with his dark lashes fanned out, and a slight smirk in the corner of his mouth. Virginia, sitting uncomfortably awake, squashed into the corner by his limp weight, would have liked to study him while he slept; but the woman opposite was awake all the time, and never took her eyes off them. When Virginia looked at her, she would shift her gaze slightly, but as soon as Virginia looked away, or closed her eyes, she knew that the woman's eyes were on her again.

They were hooded, censorious eyes, and the woman was solid and masterful, in a creased plastic raincoat, with a handbag like a small portmanteau set firmly on the middle of her lap. What did she think of Joe and Virginia? Did she guess that they were newly married from the way Virginia could not help fingering the thin platinum ring on her finger?

Why did she look so disapprovingly because they lay against one another when they slept? Did she guess that they had eloped? Half dozing into a shallow dream, interwoven with the reality of the railway carriage, like two exposures on one negative, Virginia imagined that the woman knew the whole story, and was sitting there in judgment.

The night was interminable. The dark, sleeping land outside the steamy windows would never grow light and come to life. Joe would not stay awake and talk. He only wanted to sleep. Once, when he stirred and opened his eyes, Virginia said: "How can you sleep like that? I wish I could."

"You'd better," he muttered. "This is the last good night's sleep you'll get for some time." The woman opposite cleared her throat and scraped her stoutly shod feet on the dirty carriage floor, as if she had heard and understood.

The train stopped at a station long enough for them to go out and have tea and sandwiches. Then they got back into the train and Joe went to sleep again, and it was three o'clock in the morning, the dismal slump between night and day.

What have I done? What have I done? Virginia cried to herself as the train rocketed her through the darkness. She had thrown up her mother, her job, her friends, everything she knew, to fly off on this crazy escapade with a stranger.

She must not allow herself to panic. There was nothing to panic about, she told herself, as she watched the grey veil of receding night draw gradually away before the coming dawn. This was no crazy escapade. It was a great adventure, an exciting plunge into living. Joe was not a stranger. He was her husband. They were pledged for ever, and she would not regret it. It would turn out well. Why should her luck change? Things had always turned out well for her as long as she believed that they would.

She would make a success of this, a greater success than anything she had ever hoped to achieve. Joe was clever, attractive, confident. With Virginia behind him, he would get where he ought to be. They would get away from Glasgow; but while he was working there, she would get a job on a newspaper, and they would save money together, and make a good start in London. They would have children, and she and Joe would never quarrel and make them feel in the way, as Virginia often had when she was young.

As morning came up sweetly on the sour Glasgow suburbs, she thought of her father and his wife, and wished that she could tell them she was married. Other men seemed to like Joe. Her father would like him, and be glad for her.

She thought of Helen, baffled and deceived, and felt more guilty than triumphant. Helen would have found the note long ago, yesterday evening when she came back from her round of farewell visits. What had she said? What did her face look like? Had she slept last night, or had she stormed about the flat, keeping Spenser from his bed to listen over and over to the same tirade? Would she accept what Virginia had done, and take the plane with Spenser, or would she stay to search for her and make trouble?

When the train at last panted to a standstill in Glasgow Central, Virginia stumbled out of it, stiff-legged and numb with weariness. She saw a policeman standing near the ticket barrier. He was waiting for her, of course. The trouble was beginning.

"Joe." She pulled at his arm. "Helen's found out somehow. I told you she would. Look at that policeman. Oh, please do something. What shall we do?"

"That dick's not after you. Don't start imagining things. Pick up your feet, you're half asleep. Come on, and we'll see if we can find a bed in this town."

Joe rode back on a lurching Glasgow tram to the back street hotel where he had left Virginia. Well, this was marriage. Coming home to a woman, and knowing that she would be there. Would she nag at him, as other men's wives did, because he had been so long away? It wasn't his fault that he had had to chase all over the town after Anderson. He had done his best. No one could say that he had not tried.

Why prepare excuses? Virginia was not the nagging kind. He thought of her waiting for him in the small square room, which was all bed and dark wallpaper. He smiled, looking about him at the other men riding home on the tram. They were Glasgow men, stunted, grey-skinned, oppressed. None of them was going back to a young wife with a skin like petals, who could have married anybody, but who wanted him. No doubt they were content with their broad-beamed scolds. They could never imagine the triumph of stealing a woman from the enemy, of taking her out of her soft life, and making her live your way.

He walked through the pungent hall of the hotel, and up the worn stair carpet without smelling or seeing anything. He could not remember ever being so excited about a girl.

He would have to watch himself. She was a virgin. He had sometimes joked with her about her name. Rather a feeble joke, but it had pulled him out of his anger at her stubborn determination to stay that way.

Virginia was lying in the high Victorian bed, asleep. She seemed to be half undressed. The strap of her slip had slid down her bare shoulder, and her thick dark hair was spread like a stain on the pillow. Joe shut the door quietly, his eagerness dissolved for a moment into tenderness. God, let him be good to her! Let him not ever be fool enough to chuck all this away. What he had here seemed now like everything he had ever wanted. He went softly to the bed, but Virginia sensed him in the room, woke, and sat up, holding the bedclothes in front of her.

"Hullo, darling," she said. It was the first time she had been sure enough of him to call him that. "You're very late. I waited and waited, but I couldn't keep awake. I think I've slept for hours. I'm starving. What happened to you?"

"I had a bit of trouble running Anderson down." He sat on the bed and pulled down the sheet. He could not take his eyes off her.

"Is it all right about the job?"

"It's a bit vague at the moment. Things have to be worked out. Don't bother now. I'll tell you in the morning."

"Aren't you hungry, Joe? Don't you want to go out and get dinner? I'll get dressed." Her voice was quick and breathless, and her eyes had darkened.

"Don't get dressed," he said. "You fool, don't you know you're on your honeymoon?" He pushed her back on to the pillow, and found that she was warm and eager and readily excited. Her clouded eyes searched his face, and he knew that his desire was written fiercely there.

"Joe," she whispered. "Don't be angry, but I'm afraid."

"Don't be," he said. "It's all right. You're lovely, Jin. Come to me. This is what you were made for. Come to me. I'll show you. . . . I'll show you what it can be like."

He had always said that he had no use for girls who did not know their way around. Now he knew the joyful pride and mastery of awakening desires that were untried, unguessed; of teaching her and leading her, and seeing in her willing response the unending delight that they could find together.

When Virginia woke next morning, her first sensation was of hunger. She remembered that they had not eaten dinner. She remembered a lot of other things, and she was glad when Joe woke and turned to her and wanted her again.

She lay in bed and watched him dress. She had never felt so delightfully indolent. She could imagine that it must be gratifying to be a courtesan and lie languorously in bed every morning after your lover had left you. Joe was shaving at the wash-basin in the corner. He wore only a pair of briefs, and Virginia contemplated the muscles of his back and shoulders with pleasure.

"If only one could spend all the time in bed," she said lazily. "How easy life would be."

"You're right there." He turned round, rubbing his face with a towel. "But you can't try it today. You've got to get up and catch a train. We're going back to London."

"What about the job?" Virginia sat up.

Joe threw the towel on the floor, and pulled his shirt over his head. "No deal. Anderson doesn't keep his promises, it seems. Of course, he said he'd remember me if anything came up, but I know just how much that means. Luckily, I'd told the Mortimers not to get rid of the room until they heard from me, so at least we've somewhere to go."

"But what will we live on? I've only got a little money in the bank. That wouldn't last long, and what they pay you at the club is chicken feed. What will you——"

"Stop fussing, Jin, for God's sake. You've had a nice trip to Glasgow. What are you crabbing about? Everything will be all right. Just leave it to me. You haven't a thing to worry about."

When they got back to London, Virginia telephoned the airport to find out whether Helen had left on the plane for New York. She was told that Mr and Mrs Spenser Eldredge had left on flight No. 453, Pan-American Clipper for New York, on Friday morning.

She ran from the telephone box on the corner back to the basement room, where she had left Joe lying on the bed reading a newspaper. She had given him his breakfast in bed, and the dirty cup and plates were strewn beside him on the floor.

"It's all right," she said. "They're gone. She can't do anything to me now."

"She never could have," he said. "You're twenty-one, and you're married to me. So what? If she doesn't like it, she can do the other thing."

"But it would have been so awful. There would have been a row, and we all would have said terrible things. Or she might have been hurt and pleading, and I would have felt worse than I do already for playing her such a dirty trick."

"I'm the dirty trick, I suppose. Thanks."

"You know I didn't mean that. But it is a dirty trick, from a mother's point of view, to get married without her approval. I hope my daughter never does it."

"Oh? Are we going to have kids?"

"I hope so. Do you mind?"

"Don't know," he said, reading the newspaper. "I'll find out."

"Joe, I wish you wouldn't smoke in bed. It's dangerous. Here, let me get you an ash-tray. That's better than flicking the ash at that plate and missing it. Shall I ever cure you of being so untidy?"

"You'd better not try, my love."

"They'll be in New York by now," Virginia said, moving about the room to pick up the clothes he had scattered the night before. "I wonder how Helen feels. After all, we did live together all those years, and I know she loves me, though she didn't always show it. I love her too, in spite of everything. I'm sorry that I had to do this to her. I know you can't stand her, but you can understand how I feel. Think if it was your mother."

He lowered the paper. "My mother was lovely in every way," he said. "I wouldn't have done it. Wouldn't have had to. She left me alone, and anyone that I liked, she liked too."

142

"Would she have liked me?"

"You bet. She was a funny little woman. All eyes, you know, at the end, when she was dying, only no one knew she was dying, because she went on working. I saw her dead. They shouldn't let a boy do that." He stared in front of him and flicked his cigarette ash at the plate on the floor. "I took up her hand. They'd crossed them on her chest, you know, like they do. It was rough. It felt like a cold steel file."

"I'm sorry, Joe. I wish I had the kind of mother who would be—well, a mother for you too. But Helen will come round in time, you'll see. She'll be nice to you."

"Like hell she will." He leaned over and ground out his cigarette on the egg-smeared plate. "The old girl hates my guts."

"Not really. Wait until they next come over. She will have got over being upset about all this. She'll feel quite differently when she sees how happy I am."

"Are you happy, Jin?" He looked at her seriously.

"Deliriously." She bent to kiss him. "I'm going up to the flat now that I know Helen's gone, to get the rest of my things. Heaven knows where I'll put them," she looked round the room, "but we'll manage. Are you going to stay here?"

"Why? Why do you want to know what I'm going to do?" There was an edge of resentment in his voice.

"I'd just like to know that you'll be here when I get back, that's all."

"Afraid I'll get away from you? Don't worry. You're stuck." He raised his arms above his head and yawned. "I believe I'm going to like marriage, if you'll give me breakfast in bed every day."

As Virginia went up the stone steps to the pavement, he looked out of the window and called after her: "If Spenser's left any whisky behind, bring it."

A moving-van blocked almost the whole width of the mews. Upstairs in the flat, two men were busy with crates and shavings and labels, packing up the contents of the drawing-room.

143

"What are you doing with that?" Virginia asked, as the younger of the men wrapped the china figure of a dancer in a newspaper and stowed it in a barrel. "That belongs to me."

"None of my business," the young man said. "Better ask Mr Fiske." He jerked his head to where the older, stouter man was kneeling by the fireplace, trying to persuade the fire-irons into a neat bundle.

"You can't take away my things," Virginia told him. "I have a place of my own now. I need them."

"I was told to take everything to storage," Mr Fiske said. "Only following my orders." He sat back on his heels, curling up the crêpe soles of his shoes. "I never heard anything about separating the knick-knacks. It's a bit late now. We're pretty near done. What do you expect me to do, miss—unpack all the boxes?"

"Could you?" She wanted to have her possessions round her in Joe's room. They would make it seem like her room too.

"Be a lot to ask." He shook his head and glanced at the younger man, who had paused with a clock in one hand and a piece of newspaper in the other, disturbed at the turn of the conversation.

"In any case," Mr Fiske said, standing up and cradling the fire-irons over to a box, "I don't know who you are, miss, do I? It might be worth my job to let you take anything."

"But I used to live here! I lived here for years. Naturally a lot of the things are mine. I'm Mrs Eldredge's daughter—Miss Martin. Mrs Colonna, rather." She laughed. "It's hard to get used to. I just got married."

Mr Fiske's face broadened into a beam of delight. "Well, well! Isn't that wonderful, miss—pardon me—madam, I should say." He threw the fire-irons into the box with a noise like Agincourt, and came forward with his hand out. "Allow me to offer my heartiest congratulations. I hope you will be very happy."

"I'm sure I shall. Thank you very much. Now, about my things——"

"Geoffrey, come here, and shake hands with the young

lady, and offer your congratulations." Mr Fiske was not ready to be brought back to business.

The young man set down the clock, palmed his trousers, and shook hands damply. "Best respects, I'm sure."

"What a happy, happy time for you," Mr Fiske said, his eyes glazed with sentiment. "A time to remember all your life, believe me. The wife and I often look back on our first days together. We were at Sydenham then, of course. I've never forgotten it."

"I'm sure you haven't." Virginia fidgeted. "That's nice, but could you please tell me what I'm——"

"Ah, happy days, happy days!" Mr Fiske sat down on a nailed-up crate, and beat his hands gently on his knees. "As I always tell Gwennie—that's my daughter, you know, and a high spirited one if you like—there's many fathers are not best pleased when their girls decide to fly the nest, but I'm not like that. I'll be the happiest man in Her Majesty's kingdom—God bless her sweet face—to see my girl settled down with the fellow of her choice. You be careful with that clock, Geoffrey. I know an antique when I see it."

He got up. "Well, back to work. This won't buy the baby new clothes. If you'll pardon the expression, madam, being newly married. All the best to you, my dear, and to the lucky man."

He took nails in his mouth, and began to hammer down the lid of the barrel which held Virginia's dancing figure, and probably many other things that belonged to her. He softly whistled a romantic tune between the nails that splayed out between his teeth. Virginia abandoned the hope of getting him to unpack anything. She could always go to the warehouse later on when she and Joe found a larger place. You could have things unpacked there if you paid for it.

She went into her bedroom. All the furniture was gone. The suitcases which she had packed and left behind when she fled breathlessly to meet Joe were stacked in one corner and labelled with storage tags.

She went back to Mr Fiske. "Did my mother tell you to take those cases in the small bedroom?"

145

"Everything to go was what she said."

"Well, you can't. They're my clothes. You may get away with my china, but you're not getting away with my clothes."

"My dear young lady," Mr Fiske stopped work again. "I'm not trying to get away with anything. I'm merely following my orders."

"I'm taking those cases away with me now, as soon as I call a taxi."

"Phone's cut off," Geoffrey said.

"I'll go out and get one then. Don't you dare put those cases in the van before I get back."

"No call to get worked up," Mr Fiske said. "Gently does it. I know how it is, when you're just married. All the excitement, and the novelty and that. You're not yourself, I expect."

"I am perfectly myself, and the fact that I've just got married has nothing to do with wanting my clothes."

"All right, all right." Mr Fiske continued to soothe her paternally, as if she were the high-spirited Gwennie. "I haven't said you couldn't take them, have I? Just to prove my good intentions, I'll carry them down for you myself."

"I can manage." Virginia rejected his coals of fire. "You've got your work to do."

"I must say we did want to get finished by dinner-time, reckoning without interruptions. That's why we're hurrying along, see?" said Mr Fiske, who did not look as if he could hurry along from a fire. He sat down again and lit his pipe. Virginia went back to the bedroom. She had closed the door when she came out before, and now she saw that there was an envelope pinned to the top panel. On the envelope was written: "Mrs Joe Colonna."

For a moment, Virginia thought that it was a parting shot from Helen, or, less likely, a gesture of reconciliation; but it was not Helen's handwriting. She took down the envelope. It was large and thick. Inside was a bundle of folded five-pound notes, stiff and new. There was a note with them. It said:

146

Dearest Jinny,

Forgive an old man who only wants to be a father to you, but I couldn't go away without giving a present to the bride. I'm taking a chance that you will come back to get your things, but if someone else finds this first, I hope it brings them lots of luck too. Be happy. I cannot imagine you as an unhappy person.

Your affectionate stepfather,
Spenser Eldredge

Virginia counted the notes. Spenser's wedding gift was a hundred pounds. Her eyes filled with tears, and one fell on to the suitcase as she bent to open it and stuff the money inside. Darling Spenser. Perhaps what she had done was worse for him than it was for Helen. He had wanted so much to take her to America.

She blew her nose, and went into the kitchen to look in the cupboard of the dresser. It seemed a shame to take his whisky, but Joe had asked her to bring it, and if she did not take it, Mr Fiske would. She took the two bottles of whisky, half a bottle of brandy, and all the tins of food and soup that remained on the shelves. She had a feeling that she and Joe were going to need them.

Joe looked out of the window, and saw the taxi-driver helping Virginia to pull the suitcases on to the pavement. He ran up the steps and paid the taxi. Luckily he had some change in his pocket. It made him feel good to do that.

"Loot," he said, when he carried the cases down into the room. "What have you got?"

"All my clothes, and some food, and yes, there was some whisky left behind. There, in that one."

"Wonderful. We'll have a celebration tonight. A sort of house warming, what do you say? I had thought of taking you out, but it would be more fun to have our party here."

"Oh, yes, darling." She came into his arms eagerly. She was splendid to kiss, so warm and full of life, and he still got that dangerous, exhilarated feeling of wanting to grab her too fiercely and hurt her.

147

He raised his head. "The old hypnotism still work?"

"Do you think it was only that?" She always looked worried when she spoke of that peculiar evening, as if she were trying to puzzle something out. "I did feel that night that you had some power over me. Was it only—this kind of power?"

"I don't know. I told you, I had no idea what I was doing. I only knew I wanted you terribly."

"Why did you let Nora stay on after I'd gone?"

"Why look a gift horse in the mouth? The poor girl didn't have much fun though. My heart wasn't in it."

"She looked very smug next day."

"That was for your benefit. You're not sore about that after all this time, are you?"

"Perhaps I should be, but I don't care. I don't care about anything you've done, as long as it's all in the past."

"It is, my love, it is." He hugged her, swaying from side to side. "I'll never look at another woman. Do you believe that?" He believed it himself. He could not remember ever being so happy, and he knew that she was perfectly happy too as long as he held her, and shut out the conflictions of her old life beyond the barrier of his arms.

"What have you got in the gunnysack?" he asked. "I'll open all the tins and cook you something you never had before. Did you bring that white dress—the one with all the vital parts missing? Wear it. Wear it for me, will you? Let's make a big night of it."

"Joe." She held back a little from him, and he saw that clear candid look in her eyes, that searching for truth that made him look away when he could not tell it to her. "Aren't you going to the club tonight? Can't you still have your job there?"

Here it came. Sooner than he had planned, and just when things were going so well. She was not so different from other women after all, with her uncanny ability to ask the awkward question at the wrong moment.

He walked away from her. "I'm not going back there," he said. "I chucked up that miserable job for good before we went to Glasgow."

148

"They'd take you back, though. William's kind. He likes you too."

"He can find another mug to be kind to. Get this into your head. I'm not going back there. I can't think how I stuck it so long."

"What will you do, then? Have you thought of something else? I hate to be sordid, but we must have some money coming in from somewhere. How are we going to live?"

"You've got a job, haven't you, on that fancy magazine? We can get by on that for a start." He looked at her to see how she was taking it. She was pale, but she was taking it all right. You could say that for Jin; she would never let you knock her cold.

She said quite calmly, measuring her gaze to his: "I haven't got the job any more. I told them I wasn't coming back."

"Go back and tell them you've changed your mind."

"I can't. They probably wouldn't even take me after I walked out on them like that. You don't call up an editor one day and say: 'I'm not coming in any more. I'm going to be married,' and then waltz in a few days later, and say: 'Turn that woman out of my chair. My husband says I'm to go on working here.' What a funny man you are, Joe. You see things all upside down sometimes."

"Only by your standard." He resented her tone of light rebuke. "Why shouldn't the editor take you on again, if you were getting on as well as you said you were? Listen, you don't *mind* do you?" He wanted to make it impossible for her to mind. "You always said you loved working there. If I stopped you doing it, you'd say I was ruining your career. What's wrong in giving you the chance to go ahead with it?"

"You don't see, do you?" Virginia picked up the suitcase that held the tinned food and the whisky and went into the kitchen. Joe followed her. They were close together in the tiny kitchen, which was scarcely more than a large cupboard.

"Why are you being so difficult about this?" he asked. "I thought you would jump at the chance."

"I'm not being difficult." She shook back her hair, and tried

149

to smile. "I'd be glad to go back to the magazine. I hated leaving, but I thought I had to, if we were going to Glasgow. It's just that—don't you see, Joe? I would have liked to be the one to suggest it."

She bent down to open the case. He took her arm and pulled her up again. "Well, you weren't," he said roughly. "And if you're trying to take me over, you can stop it right away. You'll do what I tell you. We're married now, don't forget that." He felt her arm quivering under his grasp. Was it excitement or fear? Did she like this kind of treatment, or did she hate him for it? He had been too rough, but she had it coming to her. If she was going to start taking offence at everything he said, she had got to be straightened out right away.

"Let go of me," she said quietly, and he loosened his grasp.

"I didn't mean to be like that. I'm sorry, Jin," he said with difficulty. He hated apologies. He had never cared what people thought of him, but he cared what Virginia thought. It was a new sensation; painful, and a little humiliating.

"I'm sorry too. I didn't mean anything." She knelt down and began to take tins out of the suitcase and stack them on the floor. "Of course I'll be glad to go back to the magazine. It will give me something to do, while you——" She sat back on her heels, and asked without looking at him: "Are you going to get a job too?"

"I may. I'll have to look around. I thought I might start on the book I've been wanting to write." He had not thought of that for some time. Now it seemed like a fine idea. He felt sure that he could bring it off.

"There's money in it, Jin, I'm certain of that. I've got some first-class dope. Never been written before, as far as I know. I'll be famous. I'll make you rich. Listen to me! Listen——" He knelt on the floor beside her, scattering the tins. "Don't turn away like that. What's the matter with you? You think I'm too dumb to write a book, is that it?" This time she gasped as he took her arm, and he knew that he had hurt her.

He pulled her against him, and forced her head back.

Her mouth was closed and rigid. He forced it open, and felt her shudder as she relaxed against him.

"Yoo-hoo! Anybody home?" There was a clatter of heels on the stairway from the house above, and Mrs Mortimer appeared in the doorway before they had time to get to their feet. "Excuse *me*," she said. "Do I intrude? Don't mind me, Jo-Jo. I know what young love is. I just came down to pay my respects to the bride.

She was a shrill, sparse woman like a quail plucked for the oven, with the fixed eye of a bore, and a thin red nose that had rejected the pale powder which clung patchily to the rest of her face. As Virginia and Joe scrambled to their feet among the rolling tins of soup, she came into the kitchen, holding out two hands, ugly with bitten hang nails.

She embraced Virginia. "Welcome to the ancestral home. I hope you'll like it here. Jo-Jo always grumbled about it, but in my opinion, he's lucky to get a place as nice as this. He's not the best of tenants, but I dare say you'll straighten him out."

"Don't worry, Mollie," Joe said, trying to laugh off his resentment at the intrusion. "She's already got me where she wants me. Why didn't you bring Paul? Let 'em all come. We're having open house."

"She did bring me," Paul said from the passage. "No room for me in the kitchen. Sorry to intrude on you like this."

"Glad to have you." Joe took Virginia out to meet their landlord. He was a tall, ungainly man, with a long stiff neck like a giraffe, and some trouble with his feet, which necessitated his wearing carpet slippers all the time he was in the house.

He gave Virginia a cold, shaky hand, and said: "Congratulations, my dear. You look as if you were much too good for Joe, but there again, you don't look as if you would have married him if you thought so. If you see what I mean. I'm a bit fogged today. I hope you'll be very happy." Then he slapped Joe on the shoulder, and said vaguely: "Good boy, good boy."

They all went into the other room. Mollie exclaimed at the way Virginia had already tidied it. "It always looked a shambles, in my opinion," she said. Her opinion was the mainspring of her life. She gave it at the slightest opportunity, and believed that everything she said must be true, because she had said it.

"No man has the slightest idea of keeping house," she declared, trying a chair with her hand before sitting on it. "I always told Joe: You've made a pigsty of this place, I always told him. Not," she added, catching Joe's quick glance towards Virginia, "that I was ever down here more than a few times, to give messages, or a parcel. I believe in leaving the tenants alone, although the one we had before Joe, the schoolmistress, she used to beg and beg me to come down at night and keep her company. The poor soul was desperate with loneliness."

"So desperate that you eventually drove her away to find a place where she could get some peace and quiet," Paul said, and his long body shook with silent laughter. He folded himself gratefully into a chair, and rubbed his feet.

"How can you say that when you know it's not true? Don't mind him," Mollie told Virginia. "He's a dreadful man. In my opinion, he's the most dreadful man I ever met."

Joe could see that Virginia was still a little shaken from the crude interruption of her emotions, but she had recovered enough self-possession to be conscious of her position as hostess. In that easy, well-mannered way, which Joe would never openly admit to admiring, she asked: "What can I get you, Mrs Mortimer? Some tea or coffee? You're our first visitor. You must have something."

Like all self-centred people, Mollie could hear a question, and then answer it with something else from her own train of thought. "I must say," she announced, "Jo-Jo is the last person I would ever expect to get married. You could have knocked me down with a feather when he told me. I said so to Paul, didn't I, Paul? Wake up there, old-timer, you can't go to sleep when you're paying a visit. The last man on earth, I said. I never was so surprised."

"Why is it so strange?" Virginia asked, narrowing her eyes at Mollie. Joe could imagine these two women getting into a fight some day.

"Well, my dear," Mollie shrugged her shoulders, as if it were obvious, "because he's not the marrying kind, that's all."

"Mollie, you don't say that kind of thing to a girl who's just got married," Joe said uneasily.

"Well, I'm sorry. I have to say what I think. You must take me as you find me."

Virginia certainly knew how to behave herself. Most of the girls Joe had known would have put their claws out and scratched back. He would not have thought any worse of them, but he thought all the more of Virginia for ignoring it, and renewing her offers of hospitality.

"Which shall it be?" she asked smilingly. "Tea or coffee? It won't take me a minute to make either."

"I don't care for anything," Mollie said. "Thank you—what is your name again? I can't call you Mrs Colonna. Virginia. Good. I shall call you Virgie."

"No one ever calls her that," Joe said.

"All the more reason then why I should. Virgie and I are going to be very *special* friends, I know. It will be nice for me to have another woman in the house again. Paul is the quiet type. He doesn't always feel like talking."

"Don't forget what happened with the schoolmistress, Mollie," Paul said, blinking and stretching his eyes to keep himself awake.

"There you go again, being perfectly dreadful. Of course I wouldn't dream of gate-crashing the love nest. I know when people want to be alone." She made the harmless remark sound offensively lewd. "I just want Virgie to feel free to come up and chat with me whenever she likes. No man is ever such a good confidante as another woman, in my opinion."

"Don't expect Virginia to run up and cry on your shoulder every time we have a row," Joe said. "She's not that kind."

"And we don't have rows," Virginia added. "Joe, why don't you get Mr and Mrs Mortimer a drink? They must have something, now that they're here. We've only got whisky, I'm afraid, but nobody has drunk to our health yet. You can be the first."

She sounded wistful, and Joe had a sudden vivid picture of what her wedding would have been like if she had married the kind of man her mother expected. White lace, and yards of that flimsy stuff they hung over the heads of brides to make them look like virgins, and champagne, and people making speeches, and Virginia radiant as a queen. She had looked radiant enough in her plain blue dress in the registry office, but not like a queen, more like an excited child.

He put his arm round her. "You shouldn't have said that," he whispered.

At the word whisky, Paul's eyelids had flown up like shutters, and he had leaned forward in his chair. Mollie had stood up and gone to him, holding out her hand to help him to his feet.

"We'll have to be running along," she said. "It was so nice meeting you, Virgie. I hope we'll see a lot more of you."

"I hope so too. I'm sorry you won't stay to drink our health, Mrs Mortimer."

"Mollie to you, I insist. We don't drink, dear. Thank you all the same." She departed quickly, hustling Paul's stumbling feet up the stairs, and leaving the smell of stale lavender water in the air behind her.

"What's the matter with her?" Virginia asked. "I tried to be as nice as I could, though I don't think she likes me. Did I say something wrong?"

"You did, but it wasn't your fault. It was the whisky that sent her scuttling off like a scared rabbit. Paul's an alcoholic."

"Oh dear."

"No harm in him. He manages to get the stuff, when he can get away from her, but he's perfectly respectable about it. You just won't see him around for two or three days sometimes, but he'll come out of it looking as innocent as a baby. It all goes to his feet. I can't think how he does it. The only time I was ever on a real bender, I ended up in hospital. Scared the pants off me. Don't look so alarmed. I won't do it again."

"I hope not. It must be dreadful for Mollie, but I dare say she drives him to it."

"She's not so bad, compared to some of the landladies I've

154

had. We'll have to keep in with her in case we ever can't pay the rent, but I hope she doesn't come crashing down here every time we—where were we, Jin?"

"In the kitchen. You were kissing me. Like this." She put her arms round his neck and kissed him lightly.

"Not quite like that."

"Don't, Joe. I want to hang out that white dress if I'm going to wear it tonight. Put that case on the bed for me, will you?"

He lifted the case, and opened it for her. Virginia came quickly across the room. "Don't bother. I'll do it." She shut down the lid so swiftly that she grazed the back of his hand.

"What's the matter? What's in there that I can't see?"

"Nothing. What would there be? It's just that it's a mess. I packed in a hurry. I don't want you to think your wife is untidy."

She spoke quickly. She was covering something up. Well, let it go. He would find out what she was hiding. Perhaps it was a present for him, or the picture of some old boy-friend she couldn't bear to leave behind. Old love letters. They would have some fun with those. After he had read them, he would scrounge some wood from Mollie, and they would light a fire, and have a ceremonial burning. The death of Virginia Martin. The birth of Joe Colonna's wife, rising like Phœnix from the ashes.

Who said he couldn't write a book? He would buy a type-writer next week. You could get one with only a small down payment.

What instinct had prompted Virginia not to tell Joe about Spenser's wedding gift? When she had found the money at the flat, she did not think of hiding it from him. Then when she had seen Joe swinging the suitcases jauntily down the basement steps, so pleased with himself because he had given the taxi-driver a lordly tip out of the last small change in his pocket, Virginia had known that she would not tell him that he was carrying a bundle of five-pound notes.

Some instinct had warned her to be cautious, and after their disturbing talk in the kitchen, she was thankful that she had obeyed it. Even if he were going to write a book and make hundreds of pounds from it, as he believed, they would have to be careful, if he was not going to look for a job meanwhile. The two of them could only just live on her earnings from the magazine. They must save the hundred pounds for emergencies, and Virginia did not think that Joe knew how to save.

She did not blame him for that. It was part of his nature which he could not help, because it came from never having enough money. Poverty made one type of person over-cautious. The other type, Joe's type, were made reckless by poverty. If money came to them, they wanted the immediate enjoyment of spending it without fear of what they would do when it was gone. They had been poor once; they could be poor again.

Virginia did not mind that Joe was like that. She had known it before she married him. She did not mind any more that he had given up his job at the club and was disinclined to look for another. Minding about it would not change him, so she had decided not to let herself mind, any more than she would let herself mind that he took it for granted that she would be glad to work for both of them.

She was glad to get back to the magazine office. She knew that as soon as she stepped into the splendid antechamber of *Lady Beautiful*, and was greeted with the full-lipped, toothy smiles of the girls who decorated it.

One of the girls was Nora, in a new poodle haircut and a cotton dress with a boned, pushed-up bodice. "Is it true you got married, Jinny?" she asked at once.

"How do you know?"

"Didn't you think it would be all round the office? What's he like? We're all dying of curiosity. Why didn't you tell us about it?"

"I didn't know myself until just before it happened."

"I wouldn't have thought you were such a fast worker," Nora said admiringly. "Or else he was. What's his name?"

"Joe Colonna." Nora would have to know sooner or later.

156

"Do I know him?" Nora's eyes were startled, but she affected not to recognize the name.

"You ought to. You spent the evening at his flat. Oh—with me and Derek, of course." Virginia smiled. "But perhaps you and he never got as far as exchanging names."

"No." Nora patted her hair and spoke distantly. "No, I don't recall that we did." She watched Virginia slyly, wondering how much Virginia knew, and how much she minded about what she knew.

Virginia would have liked to say: "I know you spent the night there, but I'm prepared to forget it, if you are." However, even without the avid interest of the other two girls in the office, she could not say it to Nora. Nora's immorality was conventional. She would think it the worst of taste. She would be more shocked at Virginia for saying it, than Virginia was shocked at Nora for having stayed with Joe.

"Well," Nora said grudgingly, "congratulations, old kid. I hope you know what you're doing. What are you doing here, for a start? I thought you'd chucked the job."

"Just another office rumour," Virginia said. "Of course I haven't. People can get married and go on working, can't they?"

"Oh, surely, surely," Nora said. "Most of them have to these days, if they want to eat."

Virginia said coldly: "I'm not starving, thank you. I just like working here."

She pushed open the wide polished door, and walked down the passage past the office doors with their glimpses of activity, past the door through which, with any luck, she would soon be going in and out again, belonging as much as anyone.

She felt at home here. She had trained and worked for this. If only one of them was going to have a job, it was sensible that it should be her. She had a better chance than Joe. He did not seem to be trained for anything in particular. He had never stayed long enough in any one job to learn it properly. He could do many things sketchily, but none well. Perhaps writing would be his craft, and this book the stepping stone to achievement. She would do all she could to encourage and help him.

Miss Adelaide Small, the editor who had replaced Virginia's mother, was a dry, business-like woman who wasted no words, and no sympathy on anyone who made a mistake. She told people what she thought of them concisely, whether what she thought was good or bad. The staff much preferred this to Helen's elaborate speeches, which had wasted their time, and had come in the end to the same thing as Miss Small's brisk pronouncements. Either you were right, or you were wrong.

"So you want your job back?" she shot at Virginia, as soon as Grace had closed the door by her usual scrupulous method of hanging on to the handle on the other side, so that not even the click of the lock should disturb the editorial muse. "Well, you can't have it. Frances is in your place on editorial. I've been waiting for a chance to move her up."

"Oh." Virginia stood before the great desk, feeling like a schoolgirl at the mercy of a headmistress. "I'm sorry, Miss Small. I know I shouldn't have gone off like that without even coming in to explain."

"You left a lot of work unfinished, if you remember." Miss Small's handsome face was not stern. It was merely impassive, as if it were too well-organized to betray her thoughts by any change of expression.

"I know. I'm sorry. Perhaps I shouldn't even ask you to let me come back. I'll understand if you haven't a place for me."

"Who said I hadn't? Don't put words into my mouth, Virginia. It's a bad habit. It sometimes makes people change their minds about being nice."

Virginia said nothing. Miss Small studied her for a few moments. Then she tightened her mouth into her controlled version of a smile, and said: "So you ran away to get married."

"I got married, yes, but I didn't run away," Virginia said quickly. There was no reason why anyone at the office should know that.

"Yes, you did. I'm not criticizing you. It's none of my

158

business. That's what I told your mother when she wanted to waste my time discussing it over the telephone."

"My mother rang you up?"

"Last Friday morning. She wanted to know if I knew where you were. I told her that I presumed you were on your honeymoon, in which case it was immaterial where you were. The poor woman had some wild idea of rescuing you 'before it was too late.' I don't remember her exact words, but it was all depressingly reminiscent of the kind of women's magazines that used to be published before things like L.B. were thought of."

"How could she tell you all that? She hardly knows you."

"Had to tell someone, I suppose. You know what women are," Miss Small said, as if she were discussing another sex. "I had to call Grace on the other phone, and ask her to cut in with a long-distance call. Callous, but, after all, I am your editor, not your spiritual mentor."

"You mean you were my editor."

"No, no." Adelaide Small's face crumpled into kindness, the lines deeply etched. "Don't be so proud. I'll take you on again. I like your work. You can't have your old job," her face was once more business-like, "but I'll fit you in under the beauty editor. She's short of assistants. I take it your mother has gone to America, or you wouldn't be in London."

"Yes. I called the airport. She must have left soon after she talked to you."

"Then I have not lived in vain," Miss Small said with satisfaction. "I told her to go. You were married by that time, so I told her not to make a fool of herself, but to go and get on with her own marriage, and leave yours alone."

"Oh, poor Helen. She doesn't like to be talked to like that." Virginia thought that her mother must have been very desperate even to have listened to that kind of talk. Normally, if anyone told her that she was wrong, she either walked out of the room, or hung up the telephone.

"I don't care if she likes it or not. Excuse me, it's your mother, of course. But if I got involved in the private lives of all my staff, I should be greyer than I am already, which would make me snow white. Well——" she slapped a notepad down on the desk, and stood up, needle thin in her dark linen suit. "Do you want to work with Jane Stuart, or don't you?"

"Of course I do. I can't thank you enough for giving me another job."

"You'll need it," Miss Small said grimly, "if your husband is as feckless as your mother says he is."

"How can she say that? She doesn't even know him. He's wonderful, Miss Small, and——"

"They all say that."

"And," pursued Virginia, who was determined to say this, "I'm not working because I have to, but because I want to."

"Mm-hm." Adelaide Small accepted this without cynicism or disbelief. "Go and explain yourself to Jane. I have another appointment."

As Virginia went to the door, Miss Small called after her: "That's a nasty bruise on your arm, Virginia. You ought to put some witch-hazel on it."

Virginia looked down at the discoloured marks of Joe's hand which showed on her upper arm below the short sleeve of her dress.

"I knocked it," she said.

"I didn't ask you how you did it. I said look after it. If it swells, you won't be able to type."

Virginia wore long sleeves to work until the bruise had faded. If anyone but Miss Small had noticed it, it would be all round the office that her husband was knocking her about. The unmarried girls were jealous of the ones who were married, and lost no opportunity for gossip. If you listened to them, you could hardly believe that there was a married woman on the staff who was not on the verge of divorce.

Jane Stuart actually was on the verge. She was separated from her husband, a commercial artist working at home, who resented her being out of the house all day on affairs of her own. Jane dreaded the domestic rut, and would not give up her career. According to office legend, there had been a furious battle, in the course of which Mr Stuart had said:

"You can choose between me and the job." Jane had chosen the job.

She did not appear to regret the choice. She was supremely happy with her beauty page, and her readers' letters, and her little excursions to salons and shops to find out what was new in the entrancing business of making women feel that they looked better than they did.

She passed on the news in phrases of ardent sincerity to her readers, who believed, with each new discovery, that they were going to be transformed into raving beauties overnight. When they were not, they did not abandon hope. They took notepaper, and confided to Jane Stuart all the problems of pimples, pallor, broken veins, big noses, small eyes, lank hair and peeling finger-nails that were burdening their lives.

Virginia's job was to read the letters, and make a preliminary decision on which should be answered by mail, and which were of enough interest to other readers to be answered in the magazine itself. After a week with the letters, she began to wonder if there was a woman in the land whose life was not made hideous by some physical defect. Like a doctor who begins to imagine that he suffers from the diseases of his patients, Virginia found herself searching in the mirror to see whether she had whiteheads or blackheads or swollen ear lobes, or a lipstick that turned blue in the evening.

She worked on the letters in the mornings. In the afternoons, she took down Miss Stuart's dictated answers. If the beauty editor had given as much care to her marriage as she did to her readers' complexions, she would not now be working towards a lonely middle age. Her dictation was as conscientious as if she were giving advice on how to invest thousands of pounds, and she would often keep Virginia working late to answer the letters with the religious fidelity she considered was due to the readers for their belief in her.

"They trust me," she would say. "It's a great responsibility. If I told them to shave their heads and put bacon fat on their faces at night, I believe they would do it. Come,

Virginia, I know it's long after six, but we must put this poor lady in Tunbridge Wells out of her misery. How would you feel if you were waiting to be told how to close your open pores? You wouldn't want to wait another day for an answer just because the typist was newly married and wanted to hurry home. I'll make up your time another day," she would say, adjusting her spectacles, whose frames were decorated with gilt whorls, and which she took off and put on a hundred times a day, making as much play with them as a barrister in court.

She never remembered to make up Virginia's time, and Virginia, trying to keep her attention on the dermal problems of women in Kent, would bite her pencil and fret about getting home late. She did not worry about what Joe would think. He seldom knew what time it was. He would sometimes be asleep when she got home, or sometimes out, and surprised when he returned to find her there before him.

She worried for herself. Before she was married, the working day had never seemed too long. Now it was an endless interruption in her life with Joe. All afternoon, she would feel building up in her the excitement of seeing him again. After she had cleared away the office tea tray, it was difficult to think of anything but hurrying back to the room in the basement, where she was no longer a tired typist, but a woman with a man of her own.

The other girls in the beauty department alternately pitied and envied Virginia because she was married. Sheila would come in with a tale of some wonderful man who had taken her out, and pause in her recital of the evening's thrills to look sadly at Virginia and say: "It must be awful in a way to have all that behind you."

Christine, who grumbled at everything connected with the magazine, including its readers, would run her hands through her thin, pale hair and sigh: "God, I'm fed up with this life. You're a lucky devil, Jinny, to be married and know that you could get out of it any time. I can't think why you stay here when you could be at home running the vacuum cleaner."

Virginia did not tell her that she had neither a vacuum

cleaner nor more than one room to clean with it. No one knew where she lived. No one knew that her husband was out of work.

It was natural that Derek should come in from the art department to discuss illustrations with Jane, but Virginia thought that since she had come to this office, he visited it more frequently than necessary. Often when he came in, he would have nothing particular to say to Jane, and would drift over to Virginia's desk and perch on the edge, fiddling with pencils and erasers, and trying to think of things to say that would make her stop working and talk to him.

Derek's attitude towards Virginia had changed slightly since her marriage. Before, he had been admiring, but diffident. Now he was admiring, but vaguely solicitous, as if Virginia's marriage were a form of ill health. He kept asking her if she was all right. He frequently tried to persuade her to go to lunch with him, offering her a good meal, as if he thought she needed it.

Although he never dared to say anything against Joe, it was plain that he was nervous about the marriage, and that he saw himself in the role of the trusted friend, ready to leap into the breach at the first sign of trouble.

Once, late in the evening, when the other girls had gone home, and Jane Stuart was with Miss Small, Derek came and leaned over Virginia's typewriter, and said very solemnly: "I want you to know, Jinny, that I am always there if you need me."

"Why should I need you?" Virginia went on typing, struggling for accuracy. Miss Stuart always read through letters before she signed them, and was aghast at mistakes.

"Oh, of course not." Derek stood up and came behind her, resting his soft hand lightly on her shoulder. "I didn't mean anything. I just wanted you to feel that you could always tell me anything. Your mother's gone now. I know how I would feel if I didn't have my mother to rely on. Everyone needs somebody to talk to."

"I've got Joe to talk to, thank you." Virginia typed: *"With sincere good wishes,"* which was how Jane liked to end her letters, and pulled the paper out of the machine with a snap. "I wish you'd stop this, Derek, this—hinting that I've made a mistake in marrying Joe." She swung round to look at him. "I know you don't think much of him, although you've hung around him for ages, but I think the world of him. I'm perfectly happy, and I intend to stay that way for the rest of my life."

"Of course, my dear, of course." Derek pushed back his sheepdog hair. "I wouldn't want anything else for you."

"Well, then, stop hanging about like a ghoul, waiting to see me come in with swollen eyes. Please leave me alone. Joe wouldn't like it if I told him."

"There's nothing to tell him," Derek said nervously. "I don't know what you mean. Why should you tell Joe?"

He looked so scared that Virginia laughed and said: "Of course I wouldn't. There's nothing to tell." She was often tempted to laugh with Joe about Derek behaving like a sheepdog as well as looking like one, but after she had told him about Felix, and seen his sullenly jealous reaction to the idea of a man in her past, she did not want him to start imagining about men in her present.

"Why don't you go home?" she asked, starting another letter. "It's late."

"I thought I might go part of the way home with you. It's raining. I've got an umbrella."

"So have I."

"Oh, well, I just thought—if you're ready to leave, we could go along together."

"I'm not finished. Don't wait for me."

"I'm afraid you're working too hard," he said anxiously. "You don't look as well as you used to. Are you sure you feel all right?"

"Want something, Derek?" Jane Stuart came into the room and waved her glasses at him.

"I just came to bring you back those beach pictures." He looked once more hopefully at Virginia, and seeing her put another page in the typewriter, he left the room.

Virginia waited until she thought that he had left the building. She did not want to hurt Derek's feelings, but she did not want his company on the bus. She wanted to sit and relax, so that she would not seem tired to Joe when she got home. He did not like her to be tired. He liked her to be lively and ready for anything he wanted, whether it was a meal, or the cinema, or a tour of his favourite bars, or some childish jokes and fooling, or the passionate love-making in which she never wanted to disappoint him.

Virginia was glad to see the light in the basement window. When Joe was out, she seldom knew where he was. He rarely told her in the morning what his plans were for the day, and he would not always tell her at night where he had been.

When she went into the room, he was sitting at the table by the window with his back to her. He greeted her briefly without turning round, and said: "Don't disturb me. I'm working."

There was a new typewriter on the table, two thick packets of typing paper, an assortment of shiny note-books, and half a bottle of whisky. Virginia kissed the back of Joe's neck where the black hair grew out of the smooth brown skin. He quickly put his hands over the paper in the machine, and said: "Run away for a bit, there's a good girl. Go and cook something. I'm starving. I'm an author."

In the kitchen, Virginia found a steak bleeding through its wrapping paper, a camembert cheese, a pound of the best bacon, and several other items of food of the kind she could not afford to buy nowadays. She looked in the cupboard under the sink, and saw two bottles of whisky that had not been there in the morning.

She went into the other room, and waited until he paused in his erratic typing to light a cigarette and pour himself a drink.

"Want one?" he asked, holding up the bottle.

"Not just now. Tell me something, darling. Where did you get the typewriter?" She tried to sound casual.

"I didn't steal it, if that's what you mean."

"I didn't mean that. I just asked where you got it."

"From a man I know. I bought it wholesale. Twelve per cent reduction. Real bargain." He began to type again, stabbing at the keys with one finger of each hand.

"You'll think I'm inquisitive, but what did you use for money?"

"All right." He pushed back his chair and turned to face her. "Now I'll ask you one. Why didn't you tell me you had a hundred pounds hidden away?"

Virginia had hidden the money in a small handbag, which she had put inside a larger bag and locked in a suitcase. She had the key. Joe must have picked the lock.

When she asked him, he said: "Why not? I don't like to have locked bags lying around my place unless I know what's in them. Where did you get the money?"

"It was Spenser's wedding present to me."

"Why didn't you tell me?" He pushed out his lower lip and slumped in his chair, scowling at her.

"Why should I?" She decided not to be intimidated. "It's my money."

"Your money!" He laughed. "Don't kid yourself, Jin. You never heard of With all my worldly goods I thee endow?"

"I wasn't going to spend it on myself. I wanted to save it for something important. I didn't want us to fritter it away on things we don't really need."

"Don't you think I need this typewriter? How do you expect me to write a book without one? My God, you should be glad I've started on it. I thought that was what you wanted. I got down to it as soon as I got this thing home." He patted the typewriter. "You've no idea what a grind it is. I've suffered agonies all day. I thought you'd be so pleased with me, but all you do is accuse me of robbing you." He pulled a face of childish self pity. "I've a damn good mind to chuck the whole thing up and sell this gadget back to the bloke I bought it from."

Virginia kissed his hair. "Don't do that," she said. "I'm terribly glad you found the money if it has got you started on your book. What's it about? Can I see?"

"Not a chance." He pulled out the paper and slapped it face down on the small pile beside the typewriter. "And don't ever go prying when I'm not here, or I'll wring your neck. Now go and cook that steak."

"All right." She went to the door. "Where have you put the rest of the money?"

"I left it in the case. It's as safe there as anywhere. I don't think old Mollie is a thief, whatever else she is."

Virginia went to the cupboard under the stairs, where they had stacked the suitcases. "What are you doing?" Joe called, as she pulled out the case with the broken lock. "Counting your hoard? I'll save you the trouble. I spent twenty-five pounds. Not bad, considering what I got for it."

Virginia came back to the doorway. "Joe, promise me this —please. Don't take any more. We must save it. We can manage all right on my salary, if we're careful, but we can't save on it. We must keep that money, in case anything goes wrong."

"I know that," he said. "I'm not a child. Why don't you hide your precious money again, if you don't trust me? Only find a better place next time."

That made it impossible for her to hide the money. She knew that he would look in the suitcase to see if she had taken it away. She could only pray that he did not become so thrilled with himself as an author that he felt obliged to buy a dictaphone.

It was going to be a hot summer. Already by the end of June, London was losing her spring freshness. Pavements roasted the feet, and the fumes from buses and cars shimmered like oil above the sticky roads.

The open windows in the office let in more grime than air. The atmosphere was oppressive with fretful, perspiring women. Thinking of holidays, the girls began to lose the lively interest in their work that Jane Stuart demanded. Virginia was not thinking of holidays. She and Joe could not afford to go away. She had not lost interest even in the routine seasonal work of telling readers how to tan without peeling, and how to get sea water out of their hair. She was still intrigued by every facet of the process that brought a glossy magazine from the conference room to the bookstalls; but she was tired, and she was losing weight.

Jane Stuart was as enthusiastic as ever, and the vitality

with which she attacked each new problem challenged Virginia's store of nervous energy, and spurred her to a hectic activity, which carried her on wires through the day's work, and left her unable to relax and recuperate at the end of it.

It was impossible to relax with Joe, in any case. When he worked on his book, which was more often than Virginia expected, his alternating author's moods of exuberance and despair demanded a correspondingly exaggerated reaction from her. They lived at high pitch, arguing, laughing, making love. The bones of Virginia's face grew more clearly defined, her eyes were more brilliant, her movements quicker, yet more controlled. She thought that at last she looked entirely grown up, with no dreamy trace of adolescence.

Adelaide Small sent for her. "What's the matter?" she asked, without beating about the bush.

"Nothing," Virginia said in surprise. "Everything is wonderful."

"You're too thin," Miss Small objected, although she herself was like a rail. "You didn't look like that when I took over from your mother. Jane is working you too hard. However, I'm going to work you harder. Stick the beauty page for another two weeks, and you can come back to editorial. I feel like economizing. You can do two people's work. No, don't thank me. I'm not being nice; I need you there. Joan's had a better offer from Fleet Street, and Sonia is leaving to get married. She's got more sense than you. She's not going to try and live two lives. It isn't easy, I know. I've seen plenty of girls before you wear themselves out trying to run a home and a job."

"I'm not tired, Miss Small."

"Yes, you are. Don't argue with me." She looked at Virginia as if she knew about the unmade bed and the untidy room and the dirty dishes in the sink, all waiting to be dealt with when Virginia came home from the office. As if she knew about having to run out again before the grocer in the King's Road closed, because Joe had forgotten the things he had promised to buy. As if she knew about having to be gay and lively for him and always ready to listen when he wanted to talk, and being sometimes kept up half the night if he felt like a party, or being kept awake half the night when he felt like making love.

"If I move you up," Miss Small said, "you'll have to get in on time. I gather you've been late too often. That's bad."

"I know. The buses are frightful," Virginia said hopefully. "The traffic gets worse every day."

"Leave home earlier then."

It was not as simple as that. Often, Joe would not let her get away in time to be punctual for work. He would think of everything to detain her. He would demand bacon and eggs at the last minute. He would ask her to iron a shirt. Sometimes, when she was almost dressed, he would pull her back to bed and undress her.

Afterwards, he would lie in bed smoking, and laugh at her worrying and hurrying, and tell her that she was an idiot to fuss about giving her employers their moneysworth.

He was beginning to resent her job on the magazine. Although they were both dependent on it, it irked him that she should stay away from him every day in this other world that meant so much to her and so little to him. When she wanted to talk about her work, he would change the subject, or at best listen condescendingly, as if she were a child telling of school excitements. He began to ask questions about Derek. He would not believe that Derek had been no more than a casual office friend when Virginia came with him to the spaghetti supper.

"I don't trust that rat," he said one morning. "I don't like you working with him."

"I'm not. I've told you hundreds of times, I'm in a different department."

"But you see him all the time."

"Of course he has to come into our office."

"To see you, no doubt. If he ever makes a pass at you, I'll wring his neck."

The idea of Derek making a serious pass at anyone made Virginia grin. "I shan't tell you then," she said, "if he does."

"You won't have to. I'll know it. I know everything about you, whether you like it or not."

"I do like it." She smiled at her reflection in the mirror on the wall.

"Come here, then."

"Not now. I daren't be late again after what Miss Small said."

"—— Miss Small. Come here, I said. Who comes first, the job or me?"

Virginia did not go to him that time. She finished combing her hair quickly, and left the room without kissing him good-bye.

He was still cross when she came home that night. He was typing, and he would not do more than grunt at her and go on working for another hour, while she made the bed and cleaned the room and began to cook something for their supper.

When she told him that the food was ready, he went on writing, although she knew from the way he stared for long intervals into space, and pecked half-heartedly at the typewriter that he was only fiddling with the book, and had long ago lost interest in it for the day. When he finally gathered up his papers and locked them in the table drawer and put the key in his pocket, the lamb chops were dried up, and the cabbage was a sodden waste.

"Throw it away," he said. "Let's go out and get something to eat."

"How can you be so extravagant? Anyone would think you'd been brought up on millions."

"I've been brought up to know what I want to eat and what I don't," he said. "I'm not hungry, anyway. Forget supper. Let's go out and get a drink."

"You go if you want to. I'm tired. I'd rather stay here and eat the chops." As a novice cook, she had an uncritical regard for anything she had achieved on the small, rusty stove.

"You're tired! What do you think I am?" he asked petulantly. "You never tried to write a book. You can't imagine the torture. You're always shoving it down my throat that you're the one with the job, but it's not so wonderful. I'm working far harder than you."

"I know, darling. I know. I'll come out with you, if you like."

"No." He often gave in to her, if she gave in to him first. "Give me some cash, and I'll nip out and get a bottle."

When he came back, Virginia was reading a sheet of his typescript that she had found on the floor under the table.

"Give that to me." He snatched it away. "I told you you couldn't read it until it's finished. The whole thing stinks. I'm going to rewrite it."

"Don't. It's very good. This bit, anyway. It's alive. I wish you'd let me read some more."

"Shut up about it." He turned to get the corkscrew.

"How do you know about that—the warders listening to the prisoner talking to his girl through the glass screen?"

"How do you think I know?" He pulled the cork and banged the bottle on to the table. "I spent nine months in jail. That's what the book's about."

They stood and looked at each other. His fists were clenched. She wondered whether, when she opened her mouth, any sound would come.

"What for?" she whispered.

"Attempted armed robbery." He laughed without smiling. "I came out of the army with a gun and no job. No one wanted me. All right—what did they expect me to do? I used the gun."

"You shot someone?"

"I'd still be in jail if I had. No, the gun wasn't loaded. I wasn't fool enough for that. That can get you life. I just used it to scare the old man, but he was too quick for me. He got out the back door of the shop, and ran slap into a rozzer."

Virginia did not say anything. Joe fetched a glass and poured himself a drink. "All right," he said, raising the glass with a small swagger. "So now you know. What are you going to do about it?"

"What should I do? It doesn't make any difference."

He drank the neat whisky and shuddered. "Funny girl," he said, not coming closer to her. "Aren't you afraid of me?"

She shook her head.

"Most women would scream and run—women of your kind, I mean. What was all that stuff you told me once? About having an angel looking out for you. Is that what makes you so damn cocksure?"

"I don't know." It was a shock to hear him talk of angels with that set, rebellious face. "I haven't thought about that for ages. Perhaps you're right."

"Do you think angels are bullet proof? I've got another gun, you know. I'd never be without one, after I saw the look on that old man's face."

"What are you trying to do, Joe?" She walked towards him, smiling. "I don't care what you've done. I told you that long ago. You can't frighten me. I love you."

"You've never said that." He did not touch her. She put her arms round him, feeling suddenly stronger than him, and strangely elated.

"Oh God, Jin." He buried his face in her neck. "I'll never hurt you. I swear I'll never hurt you."

★ 10 ★

THINGS were going quite well for Joe and Virginia. Joe met a man called Peter Sykes, whom he had known in the army, and Peter was now working in a publisher's office. Encouraged by a few drinks at Peter's expense, Joe told him that he was writing a book.

Peter sighed, as if too many acquaintances had told him that they were writing a book, or had written a book, or were going to write a book, but he asked politely what it was about.

"Prison," Joe said morosely, wishing that he had not mentioned it.

"A novel, is it? My god, of course. I remember. You've been in yourself, haven't you?" Peter was debonair enough to be neither shocked nor sympathetic. "I saw the story in the papers at the time, with a picture of you. Not very flattering. Is the book about your own time in prison?"

Joe nodded. "We thought the army was tough, but it was paradise compared to that place where they put me away. I saw things there, Pete, that a nice boy like you wouldn't believe. I'm writing it all down. Nobody knows what it's like. It's time someone told them."

Peter was interested. He told the publisher, who read the few chapters that Joe had written, and promised to consider it when it was finished. Joe was so elated that he did no more work on the book for several weeks. He was an author. His stuff was going to be printed. People would know his name. Joe Colonna, they would say, and everyone would know who they were talking about. Plenty of time to finish the book. Peter and his lot could wait, since they thought that much of it.

Virginia was moved into the editorial office, and was given a small increase in salary. It was not much, but it came in time to meet Mrs Mortimer's unexpected demand for higher

173

rent. The rates had gone up, Mollie said, and in her opinion it was only fair that Joe and Virginia should help, considering her kindness in not even charging them what the flat was worth. She always called it a flat, although it was no more than one room and a hole in the wall to cook and wash in.

Virginia did not believe the story about the rates, nor did she believe that the rent could be raised without a court order, but it was better to agree than to risk trouble by having a battle with Mollie.

Mollie was leaving them alone. She seldom came yoo-hooing down the stairs, but Virginia occasionally felt obliged to go up and pay her a visit. Mollie did not seem to like her very much, but it was ridiculous to be living in the same house with someone you never saw.

Once or twice when Mollie was out, Mr Mortimer shuffled down to the basement to see if Joe had any whisky, but Virginia could never persuade Joe to go upstairs for a visit with her. She did not blame him. The ground floor of the house smelled so badly of cats, and Mollie's conversation was so boring, and so spiked with thinly veiled contumely that Virginia always regretted her neighbourly impulse, and told Joe that she was not going upstairs again, except to take a bath, which was permitted to her and Joe three times a week under the terms of their rent.

One Saturday, however, Joe heard through some local source that Paul Mortimer had been on a three-day drunk, and had been brought home by a policeman and put to bed, whence, according to Joe's version, it was doubtful whether he would ever rise again. Virginia had never seen Joe completely drunk, but she had seen him near enough to it to make her feel sorry for Mollie.

"I'm going up to see her," she said.

"Stay away, if you know what's good for you. She'll only think you're spying."

"No she won't. She must feel dreadful, alone up there with that soaked log. I don't think she has any friends. She's talked them all away, except that sanctimonious sister of hers, and she wouldn't want her at a time like this.

She'd start quoting the Old Testament. I'm going up."

She knocked on the door which led to the hall outside the Mortimers' kitchen. Nobody heard, so she went through into the house. At the sound of her feet on the clotted linoleum of the hall, Mollie came flying down the stairs, her nose bright red, and her creased cotton housecoat buttoned up wrong down the front.

"How dare you come in here as if you owned the place?" she called out in her high, grating voice. "What do you want? I can't see anyone now."

"I'm sorry, Mollie. I heard that Paul wasn't well, and I wondered if there was anything I could do to help."

"Thank you, Virgie," Mollie said more calmly, descending the stairs. "Yes, Paul is ill, very ill indeed." She glanced upwards. "But he'll pull out of it. He has these spells, you know. He's never been strong." She paused with her hand on the banister post, and looked at Virginia with her unblinking, bird-like eye, to see if she would accept this.

Virginia could not help admiring her for keeping up the pretence. The whole neighbourhood knew that Paul was an alcoholic, and Mollie must know that Virginia knew. Virginia felt sure that if Joe were in a drunken stupor, and somebody came to try to be nice to her, she would break down and confide all her misery.

Mollie kicked away a cat which came to rub itself against her white drumstick legs. She did not like the cats, which overran the house like cockroaches, and yet she never got rid of any of them.

"You don't look very well yourself, Virgie," she said, taking the attack. "You're losing weight. You'd better be careful. In my opinion, this craze for slimming is most unbecoming."

Virginia wished that she had brushed her hair and renewed her lipstick before coming up here. Mollie never lost an opportunity to tell you when you were not looking your best. "I'm not slimming," she said, and then, less curtly: "Look, Mollie. Are you sure there's nothing I can do to help?"

"You can't do anything for Paul, if that's what you mean.

You can't go upstairs." Mollie moved quickly between Virginia and the staircase. "He's much too ill. Nobody but me can nurse him. I'm the only person he will have near him. It's a fact, Virgie, I don't know what he would do without me when he has these spells. Why, I can't even go out of the house in case he calls for me."

Virginia could understand that she dared not leave the house for fear of what Paul might do. Although Joe had assured her that he was harmless, he had later told her that Paul had once become violent enough to be put into a strait-waistcoat. The doctor had sent a male nurse, but Mollie had been so nasty to the nurse that he had packed up his white coats and his soft shoes and his paper-backed thrillers and walked out of the house, leaving only the strait-waistcoat.

"If you can't go out, perhaps I could do your shopping for you," Virginia suggested.

"You can if you like," Mollie said, as if she were conferring a favour. "I'll give you a list. There isn't much I need." Kicking aside the cats, she went to the kitchen table, and wrote out a shopping list as long as her arm. She searched in a tooled leather handbag, and gave Virginia two pound notes. "Keep it separate from your own money," she said sharply. "Then you won't get muddled with the change."

Virginia felt sure that she knew exactly the price of everything on the list, and would count the change to the last halfpenny when she returned.

She went out of the front door. It seemed strange to walk down the shallow chequered steps to the street instead of up the steep stone steps from the basement. The whole street looked different from this angle, as it would look if Virginia were a lady with a houseful of rooms of her own, and no need to go below pavement level unless she wanted to scold the cook.

The items on Mollie's list were not large, but they involved going to several different shops. Some of them, like the box of chocolates and the lavender bath salts, seemed unnecessary at a time of crisis, as if Mollie had deliberately added them to the list to give Virginia as much trouble as possible. It was late in the afternoon when she got back to the house and handed over the shopping bags and the handful of change, which Mollie spread on the kitchen table to count.

As Virginia went towards the door which led to the basement, she heard a bellow from one of the rooms upstairs. It was a weird sound, neither human nor animal. It seemed to hang on the air like a balloon, having its own substance. Mollie looked at Virginia sharply. Virginia pretended that she had not heard and opened the door quickly as another tormented cry from upstairs set the hair bristling on the back of the scarred tortoise-shell cat, and its tail flicking straight up in the air.

"Joe, it's awful. He's making a terrible noise. I never knew drunk people sounded like that." Virginia was into the room and talking before she realized that Joe was not alone.

"They don't usually," Joe said. "But this one's got D.T.s. Jin, this is Ed Morris, a business friend of mine."

"Pleased to meet you, my dear." Mr Morris, who was a short, rubbery man in a pink shirt and pale trousers, sprang out of the chair and grasped Virginia's hand, hurting her fingers with his large jewelled ring. "Bit late to offer my felicitations, but I haven't had the pleasure of meeting you before. Now I see why Joe keeps you away from his friends." His eyes bulged a little as he looked at her.

"Don't trust a one of you," Joe said easily. He put his hands on Virginia's waist and spun her round. "Isn't she something?"

Virginia felt like a prize heifer in an auction ring. "Joe," she said uncomfortably, "I think you ought to go up and see if Mollie needs you. She shouldn't be alone with Paul when he's like that."

"Landlord got 'em again?" Ed Morris said, rubbing his hands cheerfully. "I know how to deal with that. Let's all go up. Make a party of it."

"Gentlemen are requested to wear strait-jackets." Joe laughed, and he and Ed Morris, enjoying their own wit, encouraged each other to make some more crude jokes about Paul. Ed's accent was fairly rough, and Virginia noticed that Joe slipped with him into a more careless way of speech.

177

"Don't laugh about it," she said, frowning at Joe. "It isn't funny to Mollie, I promise you. I wish you'd go up. She may need a man to help her with Paul."

"She needs a man all right, but not for that." Joe winked at Ed. "Don't worry about old Mollie. She can cope with it. She's had enough practice."

"Aren't you going up, then?"

"Of course not. Don't panic, Jin. This is just routine stuff. Happens all the time."

Virginia took a book and sat by the table to read until Mr Morris left. He and Joe were talking about things that meant nothing to her, and about people she did not know.

"Who was that man?" she asked, when Mr Morris had gone, blowing her a kiss, and hopping up the steps as if his legs were springs. "Why were you trying to show off?"

"I wasn't. Don't get nasty with me, just because you did your girl guide act, and I wouldn't play boy scout. Ed and I were just having a bit of fun, that's all. Since when have you got so serious?" He sat on the bed and swung his feet up on to the cover which attempted to make it look like a divan. "God, I'm tired. I haven't done a thing all day, and I'm as tired as a dog." He put a cushion under his head, punched it and settled down. "Ed's a good chap," he said with his eyes half closed. "You'll like him when you know him better."

"Do you see him often? What did you mean, he was a business friend? What business? Don't tell me he's anything to do with that publisher."

"He's in a much better racket than that. He's a bookie. He's the man I work for on and off, taking bets on commission."

"Oh, I see."

"Well, don't make that face about it. You knew I was doing that at the club. I never made a secret of it."

"I didn't know you were still doing it."

"Can't afford not to, when I get the chance. We're not millionaires."

Virginia pulled down her mouth. "Don't I know it? Joe,

178

don't mind me asking this, but do you—do you ever make any bets yourself?"

"I take bets. Take them for people who want to put money on with Ed."

"You know what I mean. Do you ever put any money on a horse yourself?"

"I'm not such a mug. Unless of course it's a dead cert." He closed his eyes and turned his face to the wall, as if he were going to sleep.

Virginia went to the cupboard under the stairs and pulled out the suitcase with the broken lock, not caring how much noise she made. They had not touched any of Spenser's money since Joe bought the typewriter. No need to count it really. She counted it. Six of the five-pound notes were gone. There was only forty-five pounds left.

She went back into the room and stood by the bed. "Joe," she said, "wake up, if you're asleep. If you're shamming, open your eyes."

"What's the matter?" He looked up at her with clear, wide eyes, but she knew that he had heard her go to the cupboard.

"You know what. How could you do it, Joe? How could you do it, when we need the money so badly?"

"I was going to double it for you." He looked away. "I would have done more than that. Got some amazing odds at the last minute. But the wrong horse won. It wasn't my fault."

Virginia sat on the bed beside him and put her face in her hands. "Not your fault, not your fault. . . . How can you be such a child?"

He sat up and took her hands from her face. She was not crying. She was too defeated for tears.

"I couldn't help it," he said, holding her wrists and pulling her towards him so that her head was against his shoulder. "I shouldn't have taken the money, I know, but I couldn't help it when I got a chance like that, I was only trying to do the best thing with it."

"We can't go on like this," she said. "The money's nearly all gone. Pretty soon we'll have nothing, except what I get. It's hateful to be so poor."

179

"You wouldn't have to be," he said hopefully, "if only you'd take my advice and write to that stepfather of yours."

"Don't say that. You know I never would. I've told you, it's the last thing I would ever do."

"I know, my love, I know." He stroked her hair. "You're proud and good and brave, and I'm a swine. I let you down every time. I'm sorry," he kept murmuring. "I'm sorry."

Then he put his arms round her and held her tightly. They sat without speaking. They were very close. There was no excitement in the contact of their bodies, only a great tenderness between them, born of her hopeless pity for his folly, and his shame at having failed her.

The next day, Joe went out to look for a job. He found work in a factory, drilling identical holes in endless strips of steel. He hated the long journey to Croydon, he hated the work, he hated the food in the canteen, and most of all he hated the foreman, a lugubrious old hand with an instinctive grudge against all newcomers.

"Don't mind old Frank," the men in the machine-shop told Joe. "He never throws you a decent word till you've been in the place a couple of weeks. You make a mistake in answering him back though, mate. He doesn't like that, old Frank doesn't. Just take it easy. He'll soon lay off you then."

Joe, however, continued to answer back every time the foreman criticized his work, or told him he was taking too long at the tea break, or caught him knocking off two minutes early. Other men knocked off early and got away with it. Joe was always the one who got pulled up on the way to the washroom, and sent back to his machine. By the time he got there, the whistle would blow, and the other men who had been quietly edging towards the washroom door would be at the basins before him.

It seemed that Frank was always picking on him. He would appear at Joe's side with his gloomy moustache hanging over his lip and his faded eyes mournful. "Get a move on, Joe. You're making a bottleneck. Look at all the work piled up behind you. I never had a man who was so slow on this drill."

Joe, who had never done this work before, was proud of the way he had picked it up. No one could tell him he was slow. He could do anything as fast as anybody. "Lay off me, Mr Fuller, for Christ's sake," he snapped. "I'm doing my work. I'm not going to get my hands caught in this bloody machine for you or anyone else."

"You watch your language," Frank said in his creaking, sorrowful voice, "or I'll have you in the office. Don't think they wouldn't fire you on my say so. We can get a dozen better than you any day of the week."

Joe bit his lip and said no more for a while. As much as he disliked the job, he did not want to lose it yet. Virginia was proud of him because of it. When he first came back from the employment office and said that he had found work, and watched her spreading beam of delight, he had been half afraid that he would wipe the wide smile off her face when he told her what the job was. She might not like to be the wife of a factory hand; but to his surprise, she took it in her stride as if it were the most natural thing in the world for him to tell her. She accepted it as easily as if she had lived in a mill town all her life, and appeared to take pride and pleasure in washing out his overalls and getting up early to feed him and get him off for the train.

He was earning more than she was too. That was the way it should be, although she still insisted on paying the rent and the housekeeping expenses out of her own salary. She had never asked for his pay-packet. He knew that many of the men had to hand theirs over as soon as they came home on Friday, and woe betide them if the seal was not intact. But Virginia was not like that. She did not even ask him how much he was earning.

She came to him sometimes and asked him for money to buy extra food, or stockings for herself, or stuff to put on her face. It was flattering when she did that. Joe enjoyed putting his hand in his pocket and pulling out the wad of notes, and peeling one off. It made him feel like somebody. He had not felt like somebody for a long time, not since the publisher had written so encouragingly about the book, which had somehow come unstuck since then, and had lain untouched in its drawer for weeks.

Perhaps there was something in this idea of being a respectable husband with a steady job. Who would have thought that he would end up like this? Joe marvelled sometimes at the picture of himself as a solid breadwinner, trudging off to the station in the yellow morning light.

What was Virginia trying to do to him? No, be fair to her. It was his doing. He cared enough about her to want to make her happy. This job on the drill was a dead loss, and he was going to black Frank's eye for him some day, but he would stick to it until he found something better. It was worth it to have Jin so pleased with him, and making so much fuss of him when he came home, treating him like the lord and master he should be if this marriage was going to amount to anything more than a lot of glorious tumbles in bed.

Almost worth it. When Joe had been at the factory for six weeks, Frank told him dolefully that it was time he learned to use a drill properly, and Joe struck him full in his wet moustache and walked out.

How was he going to tell Virginia? She would be disappointed. He would tell her that the factory was laying people off, but she would still be disappointed. Well, let her be. It wasn't his fault. No man could be expected to take that kind of stuff day after day from an old man who would have been laid off long ago if he had not toadied to the management.

The job was nothing, anyway. Miles below what he could get if he chose. He would never have taken it if Virginia had not pushed him into it after he lost that bet. Joe worked himself round to thinking that it was Virginia's fault that he had ever gone into a factory. Thus he did not mind so much telling her that he had got himself out of it.

He told her belligerently, prepared to shut her up if she made a fuss about it. She did not make a fuss. He should have known that she would not. Her eyes opened wide, and she looked at him in silence for a moment, as was her habit when coping with any shock he threw at her. Then she smiled and said: "Well, that's no tragedy. It's not the only factory in London, and you never liked the work they put you on. There are lots of other places. You'll get something better next time." She spread the evening paper on the table. "Come on, let's have a look and see what else there is."

Joe pulled the paper from under her hands and crumpled it up. "Forget it," he said. "I'm not getting another factory job. I've had that. Do you think that's the best I can do? I thought you were so ambitious for me."

"I am, darling. I know you can get anywhere you want to. But in the meantime—well, I didn't think you minded the work so much, and we were so happy, both with our jobs, and not having to worry about money. I thought you——"

"You think too much about what's good for me and what isn't," Joe said sulkily. "And about money too. That's because you've never wanted for it. Why do you worry all the time about money? There's always some around if you know how to pick it up. You worried yourself sick when that apology for a horse lost some of your savings, but didn't I go out next day and start earning ten quid a week? I could do it again, any day I want, but I'm not going to kill myself for it next time. I'll look around for a while and see what turns up."

"I'm not worrying," Virginia said cheerfully. "I'm glad about it in a way, because it will give you more time to get on with your book. The publishers sounded a bit impatient in their last letter. You ought to send them something more in case they lose interest. How much more have you done? You never tell me anything about it. How is it coming?"

"Oh hell, Jin, don't nag me about it. You can't drive an author to work. I'll get down to it when I've had a bit of rest. I haven't been in the mood lately, even if I'd had the time. It'll get done, if you'll only leave me alone."

It was all there in the locked drawer, waiting for him to take up the story again. He could pick it up any time, and once he got over that sticky bit, he could probably finish it in three weeks, if he kept at it and had enough whisky on hand. No hurry. He might start on it after Sandown. The meeting was next week, and he could go along with Ed. Good thing he had had the sense to smack poor old Frank in the face before Sandown.

Virginia was trying to make Joe go with her to a party which was being given by *Lady Beautiful*. It was to be a large party, with dinner and dancing in a private ballroom at a smart hotel. All the office staff would be there, together with outside contributors, advertisers, artists, fashion designers, hairdressers, beauty experts—what a crew! Joe could not see himself there. He had not got a dinner jacket.

"That's no excuse," Virginia said. "You can hire one. Lots of people do."

"Not those sort of people. It wouldn't fit me, and they'd say: 'There goes Virginia's husband in a rented tuxedo. Poor girl. Isn't it sad for her?'"

"Not nearly as sad as if you don't come." Virginia was sitting on his knee, trying to coax him out of his antipathy towards the party and everything connected with the magazine. "Everyone wants to meet you. They keep asking me about you. They couldn't understand why you didn't come to the cocktail party for Archie's birthday."

"Straight from Croydon in a pair of oily dungarees. That would have been charming."

"They'll begin to think I haven't got a husband," Virginia said sadly, stroking the hard line of his jaw. "The other women's husbands will all be there. I've seen most of them, and there's not one as attractive as you. I'll be so proud of you. Come with me, Joe. I don't want to go alone."

He shook his head. He had taken his stand, and he was not going to be persuaded to change his mind. He did not want to have anything to do with this other world into which Virginia fitted so well. He did not want to see her there, belonging with that group, belonging with people who had money and jobs and sophistication. She would go away from him, chattering brightly, and he would be left stranded with some supercilious cow, and not the faintest idea what to say to her.

"I'll hate it without you," Virginia said.

184

"Don't go then."

"You know I must. I've told you. Everyone has to go. But they will all have somebody. Most of the unmarried girls are taking boy-friends. Who will I dance with?"

"Derek?"

"Derek can't dance." Virginia jumped off his knee. "All right, I'll dance with Derek. All evening. And probably kiss him behind a pillar. Now will you come?"

"No. But I'll wait outside and shoot Derek."

Virginia put on the topless white dress to go to the party. "Take that off," Joe said. "You're not wearing that."

"Why not? It's the only decent dress I've got."

"It's my dress. You only wear it for me." He began to pull at the zip fastener, swearing because the bodice was so tight that the fastener would not slide easily.

"Stop that, Joe." Virginia pushed his hand away and pulled the fastener up. "I'm going to wear this. I haven't anything else. If you had agreed to come with me, you would have seen me in it. You've spoiled my evening by not coming. You're not going to make it worse by letting me go there looking like a tramp."

"That's a good word to use," he said, "even if you didn't mean it that way. You will look like a tramp, tarting round there trying to pick up any man who'll take a good look down your front."

He had been drinking most of the afternoon. He did not like Virginia going alone to the party. In the morning, he had begun to wish that he had agreed to go. But it was too late now. He could not go without the right clothes. Damn them, they had to make it a dress-up party just to make a fool out of him. He went to a public-house for his lunch, and came home with a bottle of whisky. He had drunk half of it. He would put himself to sleep with the other half, and be snoring when Virginia came home flushed and girlish and eager for romance.

He would not go out to get a taxi for Virginia, so she had to go upstairs to use Mollie's telephone. That would give poor old Paul a thrill, but what would Mollie think of her going out without Joe, and looking like that? She would be certain to look out of the window when the taxi came, and would see Virginia go off alone.

When Virginia left, Joe could not help going to the window to stare up at her as she crossed the pavement. She had some kind of glittering thing in her hair, holding back the heavy wave that liked to flop over her forehead. She looked like girls he had seen in films and magazine pictures, and never dreamed of having for his own. He tortured himself with the sight of her long legs as she raised her skirt to step into the taxi, and then he went back to the whisky bottle.

He was not drunk when Mollie came down, but he was in a state of suspended animation, dreaming muddled thoughts. Mollie tapped on the door and poked her head round it.

"All alone?" she asked, feigning surprise. "Where's the better half?"

"Gone to a party," Joe said. "I wasn't invited."

"Isn't that a shame? She shouldn't have gone without you. I'm sure I would never go anywhere they didn't think Paul was good enough to come with me. Did I disturb you, Jo-Jo? I just felt like popping down for a visit, but since Virgie——"

"Come in, anyway," Joe said. "Have a drink."

"You know I don't."

"I know you do when no one's looking." He poured a drink for her, and tipped the last of the bottle into his own glass.

Mollie glanced round at the chairs and then sat down on the bed. "You don't mind?" She put her head on one side and crossed her bony legs. "In my opinion, this is the only comfortable piece of furniture in the room. I've always meant to get new chairs, but is it worth it, with tenants the way they are? Excuse me, Jo-Jo. I didn't mean you." Joe did not like the way she smiled at him.

"Happy days." Mollie raised her glass, and swallowed half of the whisky and water in a surprisingly short time for a woman who did not drink. "It's a long time since we had one of our little chats, isn't it?"

Joe grunted. Stretched out in the chair with his chin on

his chest, he looked at her, then lowered his lids and looked away. The poor old girl had floured her face with that white powder, and smeared on some lipstick. Some of it had come off on her teeth.

Mollie talked nervously, leaning forward and finishing her drink in quick sips, as if she were perched on the edge of a bird-bath. She put down her glass and patted the bed. "Come and sit here, Jo-Jo. You'll be more comfortable."

"I'm O.K."

Mollie got up and came to sit on the arm of his chair, pulling her tight skirt down over her knees. Or was she trying to pull it farther up?

"How about a little kiss for old times' sake?" she murmured.

Joe did not move. Although she revolted him, he could not help feeling sorry for her. The poor old thing was starved for it. And after all, in the old days, she had let him off an occasional week's rent for the sake of a kiss and a mild fumble. He moistened his lips. They felt dry and swollen. If he could only have another drink, he would feel much better.

"Well, how about it?" Mollie said. "You needn't be shy with me, you know. You never used to be."

"Sorry, Moll," he said thickly. "It's different now. I'm married."

"Oh, pooh," she said, resting her claw-like hand on the top of his hair. "In my opinion, it's the feeblest apology for a marriage I ever saw. How long do you think that girl is going to stick to you? I've seen it happen like this dozens of times. First it's wanting to go off and have a job of her own. Then it's going to parties on her own—like tonight. Don't you know she thinks she's much too good for you?"

"Shut up," Joe said angrily. "That isn't true. Get away from me." He pushed away her hand as it slipped from his hair to his cheek, and got up from the chair, swaying a little on the hearthrug, and rubbing his hand roughly over his face, as if he were trying to rub away the words that Mollie had spoken, and the mocking sound of them in his head. *She thinks she's much too good for you.*

The slam of a taxi door cut sharply across his clouded thoughts. "Clear out, Mollie," Joe said. "That must be her coming back."

"Why should I? Why shouldn't I come down for a visit in my own house?"

Joe heard only the shrill complaint of her voice, without hearing what she said. He was listening to the voices on the pavement. Virginia's voice, and a man's.

Virginia came in alone, and stopped just inside the door when she saw Mollie. "Oh—hullo," she said vaguely. "Been keeping Joe company?"

"That's right," Mollie said, folding her hands smugly. "We had a nice little chat. You're back very early from your party. I'm sure Joe didn't expect you back yet."

"I didn't feel well," Virginia said shortly. "I'm sorry, Mollie, but I'll have to ask you to go. I want to go straight to bed."

"Oh, certainly," Mollie said, in her grandest voice. "I know when I'm not wanted. Good night then, Jo-Jo. Thanks for the visit."

Joe felt her hand brush his arm as she passed him, but he did not see her go. He was watching Virginia. She looked pale, and she moved more slowly than usual. He watched her as she went to put away her evening bag, bending to open the drawer. Her smooth young back grew out of the white gown's embrace like a flower from its calyx.

"Come here," he said.

She turned to look at him. "You're drunk," she said, not critically, but as a statement of fact.

"Not too drunk to be fooled. I mean, not to be fooled. I mean, what do you think I think? I mean, how do you— what am I——" His speech could not cope with the words that were tumbling in his head.

"I don't know what you mean." Virginia frowned. "What was Mollie doing here? I don't like her being here."

"Never mind that. What I——"

"But I do mind. She looked as if she was after something."

"Of course she was." He grinned. "The poor old soul has been trying to make me ever since I came here."

"She has?" Virginia suddenly became animated, as if his words had switched away the veil of tiredness. "You mean even after I came? That woman's got a nerve. Just let me get my hands on her!" She picked up her skirts and moved fast. Joe grabbed at her, lurching forward, but she ran to the door and slammed through it. He heard her feet hurrying up the stairs, and then the slam of the other door into the house.

"That's torn it," Joe said aloud. He sat down again and beat his fist slowly on his knee, waiting for her to come back.

When Virginia came down again she was flushed, and her eyes were shining. She looked invigorated, as if she had been for a walk in the fresh air.

"Well, I did it!" she said triumphantly. "I didn't know I had it in me. I've never had a real slanging match with a woman before. I told her what I thought of her, and she told me what she thought of me. Didn't you hear us shouting? Poor Paul put his head under the bedclothes. That creature . . . of all the nerve . . . that vile woman . . ." She prowled round the room like an angry leopard, too aroused to keep still.

Joe caught hold of her and swung her round to face him. "Who came with you in the taxi?" he asked. His voice was more controlled now.

"Only Derek." She blinked in surprise at being jerked out of her furious concentration on Mollie. "I tried to make him come in for a drink, but he wouldn't. He's a bit scared of you, I think."

"He'd better be."

"Oh, don't be silly," Virginia said. "He was only being kind. For some reason, I suddenly felt faint after dinner, and I wanted to come home. Derek wouldn't let me come alone." She laughed. "I think he thought I was pregnant."

"Are you?"

"Of course not. You know that. But poor Derek was quite worried. He kept talking to me in a soothing voice, as if he—Joe, what *is* the matter? Why are you looking like that? Surely you can't mind if a simple creature like Derek brings me home?"

"Why shouldn't I mind? I've taken just about all I can stand from dear, simple, kind Derek, and all the rest of that fancy crowd you run around with, for that matter. I don't want you to go back to that office."

"That's nonsense. How can you be so childish? You're drunk. You'll forget all about it in the morning." She turned away, but he grabbed her arm and pulled her round again.

"I said you're not going back!"

"Don't shout at me. I heard you. And you heard me say it was nonsense. I'm not going to lose my job just because you choose to sit here with a whisky bottle and sulk yourself into a state of pointless jealousy." She stood in front of him, with her cool, smooth shoulders and her cool, defiant face.

"I said you're not going back." Joe did not shout it this time. He could not. The pounding in his head was in his throat too, robbing him of breath, filling his ears with the sound of Mollie's mocking voice. *Don't you know she thinks she's much too good for you?*

Virginia smiled. "I'll do what I like." The smile disappeared under his hand as her head jerked backwards and she stumbled to the floor.

It was the first time he had ever hit her. Even as his hand touched her mouth, he had the terrible feeling that now that he had done it once, it would be more easy to do it again.

When the door opened, Virginia was still sitting on the floor with her hand to her mouth and her head hanging forward, the sparkling clip swinging on the end of her heavy lock of hair. She was half hidden behind a chair, and Joe went quickly to the door, so that Mollie should not come into the room and see her.

"You can clear out," Mollie was shouting, her head jerking on her scrawny neck, and her eyes staring hatred. "You can clear out of my house—or be put out! People like you should be thrown on the street, that's what I'm telling you, thrown on the street!"

"Look here, Mollie, what on earth——?"

"Don't Mollie me, you lout. Don't think I'm going to listen to anything from you after the things your wife said to me. If Paul was half a man, he'd come down here and kick your teeth in. As it is, I'm kicking you out. No one can speak to me like that and get away with it. A month's notice, that's the law. If you haven't found anyone before that who's fool enough to take you in, you can go and sleep on the Embankment for all I care. I'll not have that—that—that—woman in my house!" Mollie's voice rose to a shrill stutter. "I don't need people like you. I don't have to put up with this from every common girl who wants to move in here and sleep with you. Married, you call yourselves. Well, I'm lady enough never to have asked any questions about that, but in my opinion——"

"Shut up," Joe said, and she jerked up her hands as he took a step towards her. "Shut up talking like that. We're married. We'll get out all right, the sooner the better. You can keep your stinking basement."

Mollie slammed the door in his face. Joe turned back into the room as Virginia got to her feet, pulling herself up by the arm of the chair. What would he say to her? What would she say to him? What did a woman say after you had knocked her down?

Virginia pushed back her hair. "Thanks," she said. "Thanks for not letting her see me on the floor. That would have been too much of a triumph for her."

"Go on," Joe said. "Say it. Say what you think of me, and let's get it over. I knocked you down. What are you going to say about that?"

"I don't know." Virginia rubbed the side of her mouth thoughtfully. "I never was knocked down before. I don't know what to say, except don't do it again." She looked at him candidly. "It hurts."

Joe went to the bed and flung himself on it face downwards. That was the worst of getting drunk. One minute you wanted to hit out. The next minute you wanted to cry.

When Virginia got out of bed the next morning, Joe woke up, groaned, begged feebly for water, and rolled over on his side again. Virginia dressed, and made the best she could of her face, although the swollen side of her mouth and the small slit in her lip could not be disguised. She wondered if the girls would believe that she had run into a gate-post in the dark.

As she went to the door, Joe turned over and sat up, feeling the sides of his head. His hair was on end and his chin was black with stubble, but the brown skin was stretched so firmly over the prominent bones of his face that a hangover did not make him bloated and puffy. He looked rather appealingly gaunt and deep-eyed, like a starving Mediterranean poet.

"Where are you going?" he asked.

"To work, of course."

"I told you you weren't going back there."

"That was last night. You didn't mean it. Look, I must go. I'm late already. I didn't think you would want breakfast."

"God forbid." He made a face. "All right, you'll have to go there, I suppose, to give in your notice, and work out whatever time you owe them. But that's all. You're through with it, understand? You're through as a career girl. You can get down to being Mrs Joe Colonna."

"That's fine," Virginia said. "And what will Mr and Mrs Colonna live on?"

"Don't worry. I've something in mind. Don't think I have to be kept by you. What do you think I am—a pimp?"

"It isn't a question of keeping you. Whether you get a job or not—Joe, I can't give up mine now! I'm beginning to get somewhere. It's what I've worked for, done my training for. If I stay on and get some more experience, I'll be able to get something better on a newspaper, or another magazine. It's what I want. You can't stop me doing it because of some stupid jealousy about Derek."

"It isn't only Derek." He was sitting hunched in the bed, with his arms round his knees. "Though I hate his guts. I hate the whole set-up. I don't like you being a journalist. You're too damn independent. They call you Miss Martin. I know they do. I don't like that."

"But don't you see it's best for both of us that I should get ahead?"

"If anyone gets ahead in this family, it's going to be me."

"Why not both of us? Why not me too?"

"Don't ask me why. It's just the way I feel. Of course, if you don't care about how I feel, go ahead and live your own life. Plenty of marriages have been successfully broken up that way."

"Don't talk like that. It doesn't make any difference to our marriage. If you would only be sensible——" Virginia was going to argue, but then she suddenly hated the argument, and the sickening chain of arguments and jealousy and battles that lay before them if she chose to go her own way.

She sighed, and away with the breath of her sigh went all the things for which she had worked and planned. "All right then, darling." She could smile now, secure in her surrender. "If it makes you happy, of course I'll give it up."

"Promise?"

"I promise."

"Good girl." He lay back on the pillow. "That's my girl," he murmured, and closed his eyes to sleep again. He had no idea of how much Virginia had just surrendered.

Was she right or wrong? What did it matter? She had done it. There was no going back on her promise. She had promised herself out of a job, and last night she had talked herself out of a home. What now?

Virginia was only twenty-one, and she needed someone to talk to. There was no one. In her absorption with Joe, and the completely different circumstances in which she lived with him, she had lost touch with all her friends, except the people in the office, and there was no one there in whom she could confide. Even the married ones would not understand. They did not have husbands like Joe. Jane Stuart's husband had the same ideas as Joe, but Jane would not understand. She had dealt with her husband's ideas by leaving him.

Adelaide Small was the only one who knew that Virginia had made a runaway marriage. Could she tell Miss Small the truth about why she had to leave the magazine? Miss

Small was wise and honest. Would she be the one to whom Virginia could talk?

When Virginia went to the editor's office, she was sandwiched in by Grace at the last minute, between two other interviews. Miss Small was very busy. She seemed preoccupied, scarcely looking at Virginia as she stood before the massive desk, and scarcely hearing the careful story that Virginia had prepared to explain her resignation. If she had queried it, or shown any interest, Virginia might have told her the truth. But Miss Small merely looked a little vexed, and said: "I'm to take it, I suppose, that you know your own mind this time, and won't be turning up again looking for your job?"

She dismissed Virginia briskly as Marigold came in, with a smile for Virginia that changed to a questioning look as she saw her disappointed face.

"Virginia is leaving us," Miss Small said, without looking up.

"Oh? I'm sorry. Is it true then—the good news that Derek's been spreading around?" Marigold's eyes dropped instinctively from Virginia's face to her figure.

Virginia shook her head. "No. It's . . . other things." She could not embark again on the story she had given to Miss Small. She might not tell it right. As she left the office, Adelaide Small was already discussing with Marigold who should be moved into the editorial office in Virginia's place.

Virginia walked part of the way home that evening, along the Mall, and round the Palace into Eaton Square. It was too warm to be shut up with a crowd on a bus. There were a lot of people walking to Victoria through St James's Park. Many of them walked as though the paths were rails of habit, hurrying straight ahead without seeing the grass or the shining lake, where the waterfowl rode burnished in the slanting light.

Virginia too had walked this way many times in the summer, but tonight she did not feel that she belonged with the workday crowd. She had another week to work at the office, but already she did not seem to belong there any more. People had been kindly disappointed to hear that

194

she was leaving, and momentarily curious about her plans, but their thoughts could not follow her beyond the bounds of the magazine.

How useless to rely on getting help or advice from Miss Small, or anyone else. People could be allies and even cronies when you worked together, but as soon as you went outside their world, they lost interest. There was no one to rely on but yourself. You were the only one who could decide what should happen to you. Advice was only of value to support your own decisions. You did not take it if it was not what you wanted to do, so where was the purpose of seeking it?

It was just that she wanted someone to talk to. The long terraces of Eaton Square would not have seemed so long if she were walking with someone, discussing her thoughts with someone who would abandon their own thoughts for long enough to listen to hers. There were so many things she could not talk to Joe about, and the chief of them was Joe himself.

It was like that at the beginning of all marriages, Virginia supposed. That was why wives clung to their old girl-friends, or made new ones among the new neighbours, or irritated their husbands by continually wanting to run to their parents. If Helen had been in London, Virginia would not have run to her; but if she only knew where her father was, she would go to him.

She had thought about him many times since that unexpected, tantalizing moment of seeing him outside the old house on the hill. What had happened to him? Where had he gone, with his dear, disfigured wife and the little boy, and the baby? Had he really been in difficulties, as the solicitor had said, and if so, how had he got out of them?

The more Virginia had thought of him after her rebellion against Helen, the more she understood how much she had missed in growing up without her father. She had found him for a moment, for just long enough to realize that she needed him, and then he was almost immediately lost to her; but the need remained. She did not need advice or money from him. He probably would have been able to give neither; but he would have been someone to talk to.

195

If it was only money she needed, she could write to Spenser, and he would send it at once, probably double what she asked; but Virginia had promised herself never to ask him. She would not give Helen the satisfaction of seeing her disparaging predictions fulfilled.

On the surface, Helen was reconciled with Virginia. After Virginia had written to her three times, Helen had at last replied, and they now exchanged letters fairly regularly, dispassionate letters that were not like those between a mother and daughter. Helen wrote about all the parties, and the travelling, and the clothes and the people and the theatres, but she never mentioned Virginia's marriage. Virginia wrote about people and events at the office, and things that were happening in London, but she never mentioned Joe.

At Sloane Square, Virginia took a bus to the turning off the King's Road that led to home. Soon it would not be home any longer. She was out of a job and out of a home, and now —it seemed that everything was happening at once—on the floor of the passage where Mollie had thrown it downstairs, was a telegram from Tiny's sister, saying that the old nurse was dying, and asking Virginia to come at once.

"Bit late to start out for Epsom," Joe said. "Go tomorrow. I'm taking you out to dinner tonight, to make up for what I did to you yesterday." He touched Virginia's mouth with his fingers. The lip was still swollen. "You should put ice on it," he said, as detachedly as if he had not caused the damage himself.

"It's all right. And you don't have to take me out to dinner to make me forget about it." The bruised lip made her smile crooked. "I've forgotten. But I'll take the dinner anyway. Tomorrow. I must go to Tiny tonight. She must be very ill for her sister to send a wire. They're both of them frightened of things like telegrams. Tomorrow might be too late."

"If she's as ill as all that, she won't know you, so what's the point of going?"

"I must. She was my nanny. She was wonderful to me. You don't understand about nannies, because you never had one. But people who've had nannies never forget them, not all

196

their lives. When you're little, it's like having something—well, not better than a mother. but something more your own than a mother. Mothers have husbands. They have friends. They go out to parties, or to a job, like Helen. Nannies never go anywhere. The old ones, like Tiny, have no interests except you. You take everything from them, greedily, because you adore them. They're safe and comfortable and always the same, but you don't stay the same. You grow up, and suddenly you're not their baby any more. That's a nanny's tragedy."

She found Tiny in the bed that was so much too wide and high for the little room under the roof of her sister's cottage. Tiny was conscious, but drowsy. Virginia kissed her, feeling the familiar creased velvet of her skin, and held her dry, crooked hand for a time while the old woman talked quite sensibly, asking her why she was out so late, and whether she had had her dinner, and why she was so thin.

After a while, she mumbled herself into a doze. Virginia went downstairs. Hilda, the sister, was in the low front room, looking sceptically at a television set which Tiny had bought with her savings, although for a long time she had been too feeble to come downstairs and watch it.

"She doesn't seem so bad," Virginia said. "I thought she would be much more ill than this."

"Well, she rallies now and then, dear. Bother that thing!" Hilda jumped up to turn off the television. She was even smaller than Tiny, but more active and wiry, her fingers always moving, her head constantly nodding, so that she had to have a little chain on her pince-nez to catch them when they slipped off her short nose. "I hate these clever plays. That B.B.C. will clever itself right out of existence one of these days. So Rosa talked to you? I thought she'd be able for it. She picked up quite a bit when I told her I'd sent the telegram. She knew you would come."

"Should you have told her? She ought not to know how bad she is."

"You don't have to tell her. She knows all right. Bless you, Rosa's not afraid of dying. She's always asking the doctor how long she's got, just as if she had a train to catch. It's quite a joke between them."

"Is she really dying?"

Hilda raised her hands and let them plop on to her knees. "Who knows? Who can say when any one of us will go? Except our dear Lord Himself." She looked at the picture above the mantelpiece, a large and crudely-coloured painting of the Sacred Heart. "But the doctor told me this morning she hasn't long to last. That's why I sent for you. I knew you'd never forgive me if you didn't see her before——" For the first time, her small, tight face trembled, and Virginia knew how lonely she would be without the burden of an invalid sister to care for. Then she drew her mouth into a busy smile and said: "And nor would Rosa either. She'd come back and tell me what she thought about it. When I told her this morning I was going to send the wire, she said: 'You do that, Hilda. You get my Jinny here, and then you can send for Father O'Hagan. I'm not ready for him and his holy water until I've seen my Jinny.'"

When Virginia went upstairs again, bending her head to go into the bedroom, Tiny was still asleep. She lay propped on the pillows with her mouth open and her knees drawn up. Her small, humped figure did not reach more than half-way down the big bed, which had been Hilda's marriage bed until her husband died.

The sheets were clean, the pillow-cases were beautifully embroidered, and a silk counterpane, laundered out of all colour, was spread over the blanket, with the corners precisely turned. Tiny herself looked as clean as a newly-bathed child, her frail skin luminous, her scalp showing pink through her soft white hair. The little room was fresh and neat, with the furniture polished and exactly in place on the bright rug, starched doileys under every ornament, and a stiff white runner under a row of photographs on the dressing-table.

There were photographs everywhere. What little wall space there was below the sloping ceiling was as closely covered with pictures as an Italian votive chapel. Helen as a schoolgirl, sharp-eyed and imperious; Helen's parents, faded to sepia; Helen's brother, who had died of pneumonia when he was a child; Helen's wedding to Harold, with Helen in a low-waisted dress and corrugated hair, and Harold lean and grim.

There was a picture of the red-brick Chiswick house where Tiny had nursed Helen, and one of the ugly house on the hill, leaning at an odd angle against the dark sky, its stone wall blotting out the foreground. There were pictures of Virginia at every stage from babyhood, and all the photographs that Virginia had sent since Tiny left them.

The last one was of herself and Joe, taken at a race-meeting. The wind was blowing Virginia's hair sideways. She was clutching her coat and laughing. Joe had his arm through hers, with his head up and his white teeth showing in an exuberant smile. Virginia went over to look at the picture. There was a crowd moving in the background, and one woman had seen Joe's friend with the camera, and had stopped to make a doltish face at it. Virginia and Joe looked very gay against the bovine, preoccupied crowd. It had been a happy day, carefree and loving, one of the days when Virginia and Joe both felt that there was nothing in the world they wanted more than each other.

A movement of the bedclothes made her look round. Tiny was awake, moistening her dry lips with a little munching movement, blinking her misted eyes.

"You still here?" she said. "I shouldn't have dozed off. Mustn't waste your time."

"I've been looking at the pictures," Virginia said. "How did you like this one?"

"Nice." Tiny nodded her head. "I said to Hilda, I always knew you'd marry someone with a bit of life in him."

"I'll have to bring Joe down to see you," Virginia said, doubting that she could ever persuade Joe to come.

"No time now." Tiny moved her head gently from side to side on the pillow. "That doctor knows. He won't tell me, but he knows."

Virginia went to the bed and took Tiny's hand. The fingers were bent into the palm like a claw. "Don't go yet, Tiny. I thought you were going to stay and look after my children."

"No, thank you. I don't want no more babies. I've stayed long enough to see you settled and happy. That's enough. Are you happy, dearie?" She turned her moist, loose-lidded eyes without moving her head.

"Very happy." Virginia squeezed the crumpled hand.

"That old angel still looking out for you?" Tiny said more sharply, as if she were ready to tell the angel his business if he were negligent.

"The angel?" Virginia looked blank. How could he be looking out for her when everything was going wrong?

"It's ups and downs," Tiny said. "I know what life is. Just don't forget he's there, that's all."

Virginia was a little girl again, in bed in the dark nursery, afraid of nightmares. The comfort of Tiny's simple belief was calming her, lightening the haunted darkness with the promise that everything would be all right.

"Where's your angel, Tiny?" She smiled to find herself talking as she and Tiny used to when she was a child, and the angels were accepted facts.

"Over there by the washstand," Tiny said comfortably. "Waiting for me."

II

"No, THANK you," said the stout woman with the face of a bulldog. "If I can't take it home to try it on, I don't want it. I don't feel like taking my clothes off today."

"I'm sorry, madam," Virginia said, and Miss Sunderland paused in her sorting of brassières, and listened without looking, her underslung jaw slightly agape. "We never send anything out on approval."

Miss Sunderland nodded, and closed her jaw.

"Peter Robinson's do," the woman snapped.

"This isn't Peter Robinson's."

The woman looked at Virginia to see if she were trying to be rude, then pushed out her chin at the rest of the shop, and said: "That's all too evident," and went out.

Virginia folded the corset, replaced it in its long, narrow box, and put it back in place on the shelf. Although she had lost the sale, she could not help feeling relieved that the stout woman had not felt like removing her clothes in the small stuffy fitting-room at the far end of the shop. Quite often they wanted you to hook them up, or scoop them into brassières, or help them struggle their soft, fat hips into girdles a size too small. Virginia was beginning to feel a revulsion for all female flesh.

Miss Sunderland, who was in charge of the corset counter, did not seem to mind these things. To her, corsetry was an art, and she was never so spry as when she had successfully moulded some flabby woman into a one-piece boned foundation, which left her scarcely able to walk, but actually looking all one piece, instead of two slack masses of flesh connected by a dubious waistline.

Miss Sunderland was a plank of a woman with a long face, and snuff-coloured hair parted in the middle and looped back at the sides like dusty curtains. She had stiff, shapeless legs and long, flat feet, and a skittish manner which fitted ill with her appearance. When she was excited, she would jump up and down and clap her hands, the tape measure round her neck bobbing, and her great slabs of feet striking the floor with springless thuds.

She was excited when she sold an expensive corset, or when Mr Jacobs gave her her holiday, or when someone said that there was a chance of the Queen driving down Edgware Road, because they had seen the gates of the Marble Arch open at lunch-time. The many years which she had spent working for a firm of corset manufacturers seemed to have arrested her emotional maturity. Most of her adult life had been dedicated to whalebone and rubber and embossed pink satin. "I know corsets, you see," she would say. "I know my corsets." But that was about all she did know.

After her years at the corset factory, it was quite a come-down for her to be working in the lingerie shop off the Edgware Road, where the corset department was only a counter and a bank of shelves and drawers half-way down on one side. The shop also sold underwear, nightdresses, stockings, blouses, dressing-gowns, bed-jackets, and everything for the boudoir except the things that customers expected it to have.

Women were always dashing in and asking for elastic or buttons or ribbon. If Mr Jacobs was not spying sideways through the glass door for custom, the first person they encountered was Stella, slab-faced at the stocking counter. "Oh, no, we don't stock *those*," Stella would say, as if they had asked for firearms; and the customer would halt in her tracks dumbfounded, because it looked just the kind of shop where you would find elastic and buttons and ribbon.

But—"Don't give me haberdashery," Mr Jacobs would say to Miss Snelling at the cash desk. "I never want to get into that line." And so women continued to turn in hopefully for pins and crochet needles and glove stretchers, and to be phlegmatically turned away by Stella. Sometimes their eye was caught as they turned by a lacy pair of briefs or a ribboned camisole on the opposite counter, and they would stay to turn their fruitless visit into acquisition.

Virginia had been one of the women who came for buttons

and stayed for something else. She had been on one of her
disheartening excursions round the smaller estate agents
and the glass cases in front of newsagents, looking for a
cheap flat or rooms where she and Joe could live. On that
morning, she was more disheartened than ever, because Joe
had gone to Sandown Park with Ed Morris, instead of to an
interview at a bakery, and if he did not get a job soon, it
would be a question not only of where they were going to
live, but what were they going to live on?

When she passed the lingerie shop, sandwiched between
a chemist and a café in a side street off the Edgware Road,
Virginia remembered that she needed buttons for Joe's shirts.
This was just the place to get small white buttons. She went
in, was repulsed by Stella, walked out again in surprise,
and saw in a corner of the window by a spreading fan of
nylon stockings, a card which announced a vacancy for a
Young Lady Assistant.

Without thinking twice, Virginia turned and went back
into the shop and talked Mr Jacobs into giving her the
job.

It was not difficult to pick up the work on the corset
counter. Miss Sunderland knew everything there was to
know, and was hungrily delighted to instruct. At the corset
factory, she had trained many young girls. Here in Etta Lee's,
which was what Mr Jacobs' shop was called, the girls did
not want to learn about corsetry. Stella, Miss Sunderland's
last assistant, would not be told anything, and had become
so aggressive when Miss Sunderland tried to explain about
inflatable brassières that she had been moved away to hosiery
and the sentry post by the door.

After two weeks at Etta Lee's, Virginia felt as though she
had been selling suspender belts and panty girdles all her
life, and was doomed to spend the rest of life doing it. Miss
Sunderland was delighted with her progress. "I never saw
anyone to pick it up so quickly!" she said, crowing like a
baby with a daisy chain after Virginia had found the one
garment in the shop that would fit a woman whose hips stood
out almost at right angles to her waist. "You really are a
clever one, Ginger." She had called Virginia this as soon

as she heard her name, and the rest of the staff adopted it. "I expect it's because you're educated," Miss Sunderland added, lowering her voice and glancing round the shop, as if it were indelicate. "I never had much schooling myself, but it doesn't matter, you see, if you specialize. I know my corsets. That I will say. I know my corsets."

Miss Sunderland told Mr Jacobs that Virginia was getting on so well that she should not be counted as an apprentice any longer; but Mr Jacobs, who would never admit to a profit, said: "No use talking to me about raises. Business is terrible. I don't know where we shall end at this rate."

Apart from being suspicious of the sound of Mr Jacobs, who had once brought Virginia home as far as Sloane Square in his black Austin, with the rail at the back for dressing-gowns, Joe raised no objection to her job. He could not afford to. He was still hanging around with Ed Morris, making a pound here and there, doing no work on his book, convincing himself that he was looking for a job, but putting off the moment of finding it.

After the bulldog woman had tramped out of the shop, so obviously, from her back view, in need of a new corset that Miss Sunderland sorrowed more for her loss than for Mr Jacobs', it was time for Virginia to go to lunch. Betty from the stockroom went with her.

"Found a place yet, Ginger?" she asked, when they were perched at a counter with sandwiches.

"I don't know what we're going to do," Virginia said. "We have to get out of the Chelsea place in another week, and there doesn't seem to be anywhere. Now that I'm working, there's so little time to look."

"You shouldn't have took the job until you'd found somewhere," Betty said. She was a washed-out blonde, with a peering frown persistently cutting her white forehead, as if she had picked up someone else's spectacles in mistake for her own.

"If I hadn't," Virginia said, "we couldn't have lived anywhere."

"Your young man doesn't seem much help," Betty said, peering to see if Virginia's sandwiches looked better than hers. She had a tactless tongue, but it came from an honest heart, not from a desire to do mischief.

"It's not his fault," Virginia said defensively. "Jobs aren't so easy to find these days. Anyway, he's writing a book. That's much more important."

"I dare say, if anyone publishes it."

"They will. They've promised to." Virginia would not allow herself to give up hope that Joe would ever finish the book. He did not talk about it any more, and she did not ask him about it, although she was distressed by the sight of the expensive typewriter collecting dust on the top of the cupboard.

"I just thought," Betty said, with her mouth full of dry sandwich that was only buttered on one side. "I wonder if they ever rented my sister's flat. She moved out last week. Gone to Stockton, her and her husband. My mother could find out for you. She knows the man who lets. It's not much, mind," she added, as Virginia began to get excited. "Not what you've been used to, I dare say, but it would be handy for the shop, and it's cheap, and the building's not too bad, though I wouldn't say as much for the neighbourhood."

"What's the matter with the neighbourhood?" Virginia asked. "Not that I mind. I think I'd take it even if it was in a slum."

"Well, it is really," Betty said. "Very poor." She wrinkled her nose. "I wouldn't live there, mind, but my sister didn't care. She's a bit slummy herself."

Virginia understood what Betty meant when she saw the flat. It was two tiny rooms at the corner of a blackened building, with a kitchen even smaller than the one in the Chelsea basement. Betty's sister had left it in a state of indescribable filth, and Virginia did not attempt to describe it to Joe. She merely took him there, and stood in the doorway between the two rooms, watching him while he looked round, making a face at the smell.

"We can't live here, Jin," he said. "This is awful."

"We must, until we can find something better. Mollie will turn us out. It's no good imagining she won't, just by not thinking about it. She doesn't even speak to me any more if I meet her in the street. We've got to live somewhere. We'll be happy here, darling. We'll be together. That's all that matters." She put her arms round him, and tried to rub the despondency from his mouth with her cheek. "I'll clean it up. I'll come every evening after work, and wash and scrub. I'll soon get rid of the smell and all this foulness." She kicked at the sea of dirty paper and rags and old tins which surged about their feet. "You can do some painting. You told me you'd worked with a painter once. It would be fun working on it together."

"The landlord ought to paint it," Joe said. "Tell him we won't take it unless he redecorates it."

"How can you say that? Anyone would think I was the one who had been poor, not you. You don't say those things to those kind of people; not about places like this, and at the rent he's asking. We're lucky to get it, don't you see? We can't make a fuss about it."

"I do make a fuss." Joe went to the grease-stained alcove which was the kitchen, and lifted up one of the burner rings, which was caked half an inch thick with blackened food. "I hate this place."

"You won't," Virginia said. "I'm going to cable Helen and ask her to cable the warehouse to let me take out some of the furniture. She won't mind. She's much mellower now. She's been put on the New York Social Register. We can have my bed, and as much of my bedroom furniture as will go into that rabbit hutch." She looked through the doorway at the bedroom, with its small dirty window and its walls scribbled over by Betty's sister's baby. "And we'll take some rugs and the kitchen table and some chairs—oh, it will be fine. It will be our own. We'll be by ourselves. No Mollie coming down all the time to make trouble, and no Paul getting drunk."

"The neighbours will do that," Joe said, "from what I've seen of them."

"Let them. We shan't care. This will be our own place. The basement was always Mollie's. This will be our first real home. We'll be happy." She found that she was clenching her fists, insisting on their happiness, willing him to believe in it.

Joe looked out of the window at the street full of children, at the house opposite, one of a tenement row, where a woman in a scarlet wrapper sat at an upstairs window, doing nothing, and another woman with her head tied up in a scarf furiously whitened steps, and screamed at one of the children.

"How can you be happy with me?" He put his hands in his pockets and sat limply on the cracked and peeling window-sill. "I'm a washout. You never should have married me."

"Oh, stop it." Virginia pulled him to his feet and pulled his hands out of his pockets. She hated to see him slouching and despondent. She liked to see him upright and pleased with himself, which was the way nature meant him to be. "I married you because I loved you. Do you hear? I love you."

"God help you," he said, looking round the filthy room. "Look where it's got you."

"I like it," she lied. "It's ours. Let's have a baby, Joe. There would be room. Betty's sister had one—six, I should think, judging by the mess. We'll have a baby."

"My God," he said, "what next?" But he began to grin, tickled by the idea of himself and Virginia and a baby in the tiny flat above the raucous street. He laughed aloud. "You're a wonderful girl, Jin." He hugged her with his old exuberance, tightening his grip until he could make her squeal. "Don't leave me."

Leave him? The thought had never entered her head. It disturbed her now, but he was making a joke of it, and so she said lightly, as he freed her: "Let me have a baby, then I won't. I don't want another child growing up without its father." That was true, but it was not the reason why she would never leave him. She had staked everything on the adventure of this marriage. There was no turning back.

Weston House, which held Joe and Virginia's flat and thirty others, was a squat fortress of stone slabs rising from the criss-cross of narrow streets between Edgware Road and Lisson Grove. It was about fifty years old, and like every other building for acres round, it was indelibly marked by the sooty brand of Paddington and Marylebone stations. The stone slabs might once have been grey, or even white. Now they were pitted and black with a coating of grime that rubbed off on the clothes of scuffling children who knocked against its walls.

Some of the tenants pugnaciously cleaned the inside and outside of the windows; some, making a pact with the railway, cleaned only the inside; some surrendered completely and cleaned neither side. The windows of the Ropers' flat on the ground floor had rude words written in the grime outside, which Mrs Roper could read back to front as she sat and rocked the baby, and let the hours slide by with no work done.

Virginia, attacking the squalid legacy of Betty's sister with energy, cleaned the inside of her windows on the third floor, and made Joe clean the outside. He sat on the sill with the window pushed into his stomach to hold him, and swabbed sketchily at the glass, making faces through it at Virginia, while the woman in the scarlet wrapper watched from her window in the house opposite.

Her name was Mrs Baggott. She was a widow, who lived alone with a parrot. That much was known, although no one could remember Mr Baggott, and no one could remember seeing or hearing the parrot. She spent most of her days and a great part of the night by the window, uncurtained, but closed both in summer and winter. It was said that she knew everything that went on in the street, and once when the American Military Police were looking for a deserter, they went to Mrs Baggott, and either she or the parrot or chance directed them to the room where the coloured soldier was hiding.

It was a Saturday afternoon when the moving-van brought Virginia's furniture, and not only Mrs Baggott, but most of her neighbours on that side of the street were at their windows or on their steps to see the few pieces of furniture carried out of the van, and up the stone steps which wound like a dark entrail up the middle of Weston House.

There were faces at the windows of the flats too, some

leaning blatantly over the sill, some lurking behind the sooted panes. While the two men were trying to get the bed through the narrow front door of the flat, other front doors opened along the passage. Heads looked out, stared, and were withdrawn as they saw Virginia outside the flat in a pair of slacks, pushing and giving advice and hindering, while Joe shouted impractical directions from the other side.

There was a great deal of curiosity about them at first. Virginia did not think that she looked different from the other young women who went in and out of the flats, to and from the shops, or their jobs. She did not think that Joe looked very different from the other men of his age, except that he was better-looking and wore his clothes with a better grace, even when it was only a sweater and an old pair of slacks. Nevertheless, they were newcomers, and therefore queer enough to be stared at.

People stared at Virginia when she met them on the stairs, and if two women were talking in the street when she went by, they would stop talking and stare until she had passed. When she and Joe went out together, there always seemed to be someone watching. Defiantly, she would take Joe's arm and press closer to him, because she had noticed that although the courting pairs walked entwined, the married couples walked a little distance apart, as if they had quarrelled, or were shy of their relationship.

After a while, Virginia began to say "Hullo" to anyone who stared. She wanted to get to know them. It felt wrong to be living among them, and to see them every day and know their clothes and their habits, and to hear through the thin walls of the flats all the noises they made, without knowing who they were.

Some of the people did not answer. Their stare changed from curiosity to surprise, as if a word was the last thing they expected to hear coming from Virginia's mouth. Some of them answered grudgingly, and hurried away, unwilling to commit themselves too far with this stranger. Only Mrs Batey was friendly right from the start. She lived on the same floor as Virginia, in one of the larger flats at the end of the passage. Although she had five children to keep her busy, she usually managed to be looking out of her door when Virginia left for work in the morning, or returned in the evening.

She was a flushed, sloppy woman, with turned-over feet and a figure which Miss Sunderland would have given her eyes to corset. She had a large, loose smile, with many teeth missing, and a cheerful voice which was never much less than a shout. In the evening, she would yell a greeting down the echoing stone passage, and if Virginia went closer to stop her yelling, she would often find herself scooped into the Batey's dishevelled flat and set down at the kitchen table with tea and buns before she could find a way out.

The Batey children were all table high and grinning, except the baby, who was permanently in an uncushioned perambulator in the middle of the kitchen floor, tied in by a chewed dog leash. When Virginia could not eat the buns, she fed them to the children, who begged round her like shameless little dogs. When the baby screamed and strained at the leash to make the pram rock, one of the children would pick a piece of bun off the floor and cram it into his mouth like a comforter.

The children were all fat and filthy and surprisingly healthy. Virginia was clean and thin, and therefore, by Mrs Batey's standards, unhealthy. She treated her like an extra child, and tried to fill her out on starches. Scarcely an evening went by without Mrs Batey's thunderous knock on Virginia's door, and Mrs Batey's exuberant entrance, sure of her welcome, with a plate of cakes or biscuits, or a paper full of home-made toffee.

If a curtain wanted altering, Mrs Batey would tear it off its hooks and take it away to her own flat to shorten it with a crooked hem, which Virginia would have to unpick late at night when there was no fear of Mrs Batey coming in and catching her. If she saw a pile of clothes waiting to be ironed, Mrs Batey would scoop them up too, and bear them off to the devastation of her flat-irons, sprinkling them so enthusiastically that they often returned damper than when they left home.

If she did not like the look or sound of the old gas stove,

Mrs Batey would bring in her husband, who was a gas-fitter, driving him before her like a hostage, and standing over him while he took the stove to pieces before Virginia had a chance to cook supper, and left it dismantled overnight until he could bring a spare part.

Since Mrs Batey was the only friend she had in the flats, Virginia put up no defence against her ministrations, but Joe began to mutter under his breath as soon as her shining red face appeared round the door. Mrs Batey took no notice. She was used to men, and had long ago discounted them, except as the begetters of children. Women were what mattered. Women were the ones who made the wheels go round. If she had her way, there would be only women in the government. "Then you'd see the price of bacon come down!"

Unlike most mothers, she favoured her daughters over her sons, and when she was in Virginia's flat, she gave her conversation and the warmth of her heart only to Virginia, and ignored Joe, except to push him aside if he was in her way when she was heading for something that needed tackling.

She was a great one for tackling. She would tackle anything. "I'll tackle it," she would say, if a window needed putty, or a broken sugar basin needed glue. She took far more pride in Virginia's flat than she did in her own, which had lapsed beyond redemption.

"Nosey old bitch," Joe said, when she had gone away with his socks to darn. "Why can't you keep her out of here? She only comes in out of curiosity, to see what we're up to. Why are you so nice to her, Jin? You weren't half as nice to Mollie, and she wasn't half as much nuisance."

"She wasn't half as nice. Mrs Batey is friendly. I like her. She's the only one who has tried to be friendly. The other people all look so suspicious. They look at me as if I didn't belong here."

"You don't," Joe said. "Not yet. I've lived in this sort of place before. When you first come, you're a stranger for weeks, sometimes for ever, if they don't like you. You can't expect to jump right in and make friends with everyone right away. They don't trust you. Why should they?"

"Wouldn't you, if you lived here, and I moved in as a new tenant?"

"I'd be hammering on your door with my tongue hanging out," he said, "but that's different. Making a woman doesn't take as long as making friends, not in a place like this. Or anywhere, for that matter. But in this place, it takes longer to make friends. Why worry about it? We'll be out of here long before these people give themselves a chance to find out what they're missing."

He was wrong. The weeks went by into winter, and it was very cold in the flat, with only a small gas fire in the sitting-room and no heating in the bedroom, but Virginia and Joe stayed on.

What else could they do? The rent was low, but it was all they could afford. Joe had been in and out of two or three temporary jobs, but he was no nearer to being the success Virginia had promised herself he should be. He had sold the typewriter to pay a debt, and, as far as she knew, he had destroyed what he had written of the book. When she asked him about it, he said: "If it was published, everyone would know I'd been in prison, and how would you like that?"

"You could use another name."

"Don't be silly. Why should I sweat my guts out to write a book if nobody's going to know I wrote it?"

Virginia accepted this, just as she accepted the realization that Etta Lee's and the flat at Weston House were no longer a stop-gap until something better came along, but a regular pattern of life. A different pattern to any she had known, but one to which her rugged youth enabled her to adapt herself without discouragement. Weston House was dirty and tawdry and lacking in all the refinements and many of the essentials of comfort. The street was alive with poverty—but it was alive. Shame and tragedy and failure were here, but so was courage; and the easy, unsubtle humour that relished the sound of a laugh; and the insidious, gossiping fellowship of women caught in the same boat, with small hope of leaving it for something better. Virginia was in the same boat, and the women began to accept her. The women's tongues ruled the neighbourhood. They could make or break a character. The men merely lived there, and took little part in the dramas and intrigues and confidences with which the women painted some colour into life.

Gradually, Virginia began to know her neighbours. She was no longer a stranger. Other new tenants came and were stared at, and Virginia, from her vantage point of resident, found that she was just as curious about them as people had been about her. Imperceptibly she became part of the life of the flats, belonging to it just as surely as the Bateys and old Mr McElligott and the Ropers and the flashy Dales and poor Miss Few, and all the other couples and families and widows and spinsters and lonely old men who made up the population of Weston House.

She began to know some of the people who lived across the street, although in winter there was not the same pavement and doorstep camaraderie that the summer brought forth. She never got to know Mrs Baggott. Nobody did, because Mrs Baggott never came down from her eyrie to speak to anyone. She had not been seen for years, except dimly from the waist up, as she kept watch in her shapeless red garment at the window. No one was ever allowed into the two top-floor rooms she shared with the legendary parrot, who was reputed to talk like a human, although how he had acquired this reputation no one could say, since no one had ever heard him.

Mrs Fagg, who lived on the ground floor of the same house, and was the only woman on the street who whitened her steps every day in rain, sun or fog, bought Mrs Baggott's groceries, leaving them outside her door, and picking up the money that Mrs Baggott left there. Jacky, the Ropers' eldest boy, who had a newspaper round, took up the paper and the milk; but he had never seen Mrs Baggott, except once when he looked through the keyhole and saw her glaucous eye looking into his from the other side.

The speculations about Mrs Baggott were part of the neighbourhood folk-lore. Some said that she had a disfiguring disease, which would terrify anyone who saw her face. Some said that the disease was leprosy, and talked darkly of calling in the authorities. Others said that she had her dead husband still up there, or a hoard of precious jewels, or that she was in communication with the powers of darkness, through the parrot. Children were brought up on fables about Mrs Baggott, and threatened with her when they were naughty.

The American military policeman who had tramped up the stairs in his dazzling white belt and gaiters was the only person who had spoken to Mrs Baggott within memory. When he came down again, the crowd waiting for him outside Mrs Fagg's house had planned to ask him what the old lady was like; but he looked so unapproachable under his severe white helmet, and his belt and gaiters were so inhumanly white, that they let him drive away in his shining Jeep without daring to ask him anything.

These things and many others Virginia came to know as the winter went by and the noisy, dirty neighbourhood became part of her life. She knew about the railway accident that had killed Mrs Fagg's husband, and word for word what Mrs Fagg had said when she was taken into the waiting-room of the little country station to identify him. She knew that Amy Lewis, who lived next door to Mrs Fagg, was in love with a married man. She had heard Amy's side of it, a tearful rush of confidences one evening when Joe was out. She had heard, and so had most of the street, Amy's father's side of it, when he shouted after his daughter as she went out in her best dress to meet her lover.

Virginia knew that old Mrs Bugle's children were trying to get her into an institution, that Mrs Pickett had been longer under an anæsthetic than anyone else at St Mary's hospital, and that Mrs Roper often spent her evenings in the Five Horseshoes, leaving her children alone. The eldest Roper girl would sometimes carry the baby up the stairs, looking for someone who could stop it crying. Virginia had taken it in once or twice, but she could not quiet it or feed it, although it looked half starved, so she had taken it across to Mrs Batey, who could do anything with any baby, except keep it clean. Her own baby had his underwear taken off once a week in winter and then only just long enough to rush on a new set of vests and binders and petticoats, before the air could get at him.

Virginia knew that Ronnie Dale was in trouble over the payments on his flamboyant new motor cycle, and that his wife was eating her heart out for a beaver coat. She had seen the medal that Mr McElligott won in the war for pulling a man two stone heavier than himself from under a toppling wall. She had seen the photographs of Miss Few's family, stately people, with an impressive house in the background. She had listened to Miss Few's moist-eyed tales of the days when she had her own lady's maid; although everyone knew, and had taken care to tell Virginia, that she had been the lady's maid, and the stately people her employers.

Virginia knew every detail of Mrs Batey's life history, peppered with confinements, and with the rousing battles which broke out periodically between her and Mr Batey, who was normally under her thumb, but could turn like a worm when he had taken drink, and had once been before the magistrates for trying to wrap his wife round a lamp-post.

"Just like Edgar," Mrs Batey said cheerfully, "to do it when a copper was looking. That one never had any sense. I don't know where he'd be without me to look after him. The magistrate said as much. 'Mrs Batey,' he said, 'if you hadn't come to court and spoken for him, I'd have given him ten days.' 'Big help that would be to me, your honour,' I said, 'with four kids to feed.' "

All these things Virginia learned as the winter went by, and the end of the old year was swallowed up by the boisterous festivities of Christmas and of a very different New Year's Eve from the one which had found her in Felix's prosperous car, listening to the midnight stroke of Big Ben. The neighbourhood became her part of London. The people at Weston House became her friends, and even the dark, uncomfortable little flat on the third floor, where she fought to keep happiness as well as passion in her marriage to Joe, became dear to her, because it was home.

Joe never accepted Weston House as philosophically as Virginia did. He still grumbled and talked about getting away from it, although he would not do anything to make that possible. He found some objection to all the jobs Virginia suggested he might try, and such jobs as he did have from time to time barely kept him in drink and cigarettes.

He was not particularly affable to the neighbours, although they were the kind of people among whom he was brought up. But he had grown away from them, and he did not want to go back to their narrow, needy world. He had made friends with some of the men. Not the Mr Bateys and the Mr McElligotts and the colourless, compliant men who made up the majority, but the rebellious few, the vagabonds, who were either not tied down by a wife and family, like the smooth-tongued Jack Corelli, who would get on a box at Speakers' Corner for anyone who paid him, or who were tied so loosely that they never felt the pull, like the roving Will Roper, who worked with a circus, and came home unexpectedly about four times a year, usually in the middle of the night.

Joe and Jack Corelli had brave schemes for making big money quickly. They never came to anything. They were doomed from the start by lack of funds or enterprise, but they kept Joe's enthusiasm alive, and so Virginia did not discourage them. She neither liked nor trusted Jack Corelli, but she bore with him when he came to the flat with his violent shirts and his bombastic talk, just as Joe had to bear with Mrs Batey and the screaming Roper baby and Miss Few's endless tales of dead grandeur. His method of bearing with them was usually to remove himself to the Five Horseshoes.

The Five Horseshoes, two corners down from Weston House, was a very respectable public house, with a décor of grained mustard paint and old port wine advertisements as depressing as any of its kind in London. Virginia did not object to it as a haunt of vice, but she soon became tired of going there herself, and she wished that Joe would get tired of it too.

The Five Horseshoes yielded him a little business for Ed Morris, and he was down there nearly every night, and part of the day too as far as Virginia knew. She walked to the shop in the morning to save the bus fare, and walked wearily back at night, and often, as in the days when she had worked at *Lady Beautiful,* she had no idea where Joe had been while she was away. But in those days he was not drinking so much. When he came home, he was usually sober, and avid to see her. Now he was not always sober. Although there were many times when his desire for her was as fierce as ever, and as powerful as ever to awaken her answering desire, there were times too when he came home only to pick a quarrel with her, as if he resented the fact that she was always there, waiting for him.

Yet, if she had not been there, he would have gone to look for her. Once when she had stayed late at the shop to help with the inventory, Joe had gone down to Etta Lee's and found her in the stockroom with Mr Jacobs. She was standing on a step-ladder to reach the top shelf, and Joe had said that Mr Jacobs had only sent her up there for what he could see.

Fortunately for Virginia's job, he had not said it in front of Mr Jacobs, who was a family man of propriety, and easily shocked. He had said it when they got home, and that was one of the times when he hit her. He hit her again two weeks later, for no better reason than that he was half drunk and discouraged, and infuriated by her refusal to be discouraged with him.

"Why are you so damned long suffering?" he flung at her. "Why don't you pack up and get out of here? You don't belong here. Why don't you go back where you belong?"

"I don't belong anywhere but here," she said. He called her a bloody liar, and as if he were trying to make her a liar by treating her like one, he hit out at her and left her.

Virginia was sitting in a chair feeling sick when Mrs Batey came in. Joe had not shut the flat door properly, and Mrs Batey hurried through it with a green coat over her nightdress, because she had heard Joe's angry voice, and the slam of the door, and the clatter of his feet on the stone stairs.

"Go away, please." Virginia took her head out of her hands and looked up. "Please, Mrs Batey, if you're nice to me, I shall cry."

"And why shouldn't you cry, darling?" Mrs Batey swooped on her and gathered Virginia into her arms, kneeling on the floor beside the chair, with the flannelette nightgown billowing round her legs. With a sigh that was an abandonment of stoicism, Virginia leaned her throbbing head against Mrs Batey's soft, loose front, and they rocked slowly together, while Virginia wept for pain and shame, and Mrs Batey grieved gently for the sorrows of women.

After Joe had slammed out without looking to see how much he had hurt her, Virginia had only wanted to be alone. She was glad that Joe had gone. She did not want anyone there until she had got over this. If the door had been closed, she would not have let Mrs Batey in, but now that she had shuffled in unimpeded in the black quilted slippers with the pompoms hanging by a thread, her enveloping presence was strangely comforting.

Helen had never held Virginia in this protective way and murmured the small sounds of comfort. On the rare occasions of Virginia's childhood tears, Helen had tried to brisk her out of them. Only Tiny had ever hugged her like this and let her cry in peace.

Mrs Batey knew why she was crying without having to ask. She knew what a shouting husband and a weeping wife meant. To her, it was not shocking that Joe had hit Virginia. It was just one of those things about men which a woman must bear with, and which another woman could help her to bear, with sympathy, but without surprise or acrimony.

After a while, Mrs Batey got up, her knees cracking like walnuts, and went to make tea. Virginia stayed in the chair, because her head still hurt, and she did not trust her legs.

"I'm sorry," she said to the back view of Mrs Batey, standing by the stove with her greasy hair hanging down her back and tied with a knot of old bandage. "I shouldn't have done that. I never cry."

"No harm done," Mrs Batey said. "Is this the first time he's treated you rough?" When Virginia did not answer, she said serenely: "I dare say not. He looks a violent one. That's why you went with him in the first place, I wouldn't wonder."

"Not really." Virginia thought for a moment, back to the night when Joe had hypnotized her, back to the night when he had walked into the flat, and the night when she had gone in the white dress to find him in the little room behind the wrestling-hall. "It was—I think I fell in love with him."

"Oh—*love*." Mrs Batey tossed back her straggling hair and turned round with a cup of dark tea in each hand. "I don't take much account of that, although they talk a lot about it. What is love, when you think of it? It's not much more than wanting to lie down with a man. Drink this, darling. It will do you good."

"It's much more than that," Virginia said. "Perhaps you haven't been in love, Mrs Batey?"

"Not with Edgar, if that's what you mean." Mrs Batey pursed her chapped lips to sip the hot tea. "Good thing I wasn't, or I'd have shot myself from disappointment long ago. I've had my moments, though. Don't think I haven't. Don't try to tell me I don't know what love is."

Virginia tried to look beyond the coarse, shining features and the spread flesh to see Mrs Batey as a girl, fresh and ardent and appealing.

"It was in Wales," Mrs Batey said, her eyes softening. "I shall always think kindly of Wales. That's why I voted Labour last time—though Edgar dared me to—because of Mr Bevan."

When she had finished her tea and cursorily inspected the pattern of the leaves, she set down the cup and said: "I'd better clear out before your man comes back. Are you sure you'll be all right now? You want to take it easy, mind, in your condition."

"I never told you about that," Virginia said quickly. "I haven't told anyone yet."

"You don't need to, darling. You can't be that way as often as I've been without you can spot it right off in another woman. Good luck to you, sweetheart, but you tell that villain who fathered it to keep his hands off you for a while. There's things can go wrong. I know. And how would he like to be responsible for *that*?" Mrs Batey gathered the green coat about her and went out, rejoicing in the triumph of maternity over the brute male.

When Virginia told Joe about the baby, he scarcely knew what to think. Although she swore that she felt well, he was overcome by a great wave of anxious tenderness, and wanted to do something for her, to show her how he felt. Then almost immediately he began to wonder how it would all end. It was dramatic and touching with the baby inside Virginia, but what about after it was born? What would life be like then?

A baby? Well, he had done it this time all right. His baby. A son. Another Joe Colonna, dark haired, with big brown eyes. But how would they keep it, when they could barely keep themselves? Virginia was so confident, so sure that everything would go well, but, my God, when people started having babies, it was the beginning of the downhill drag to slumminess. Look at the Bateys. Look at the Ropers. And some of the families in that rabbit-warren across the street. Kids everywhere. Noise and mess and no place for a man about the house. No wonder Will Roper cleared out as often as he could, and only came home for long enough to knock another one out.

Then Joe's misgivings were replaced by tenderness again, and a wondering pride in the thing that had happened to Virginia. He did not go out for several evenings after she had told him. He stayed at home and cooked the supper, and waited on her, using the deft mannerisms with which he remembered his father had sometimes delighted his mother, putting a napkin over his arm at home, and behaving as if he were still at the restaurant. He tried to do her ironing, struggling with shirts and blouses and refusing to take advice from Virginia. She would have been happy to let him go on with it, but Mrs Batey marched in and swept the mangled clothes away from him with cries of horror.

Joe found himself watching Virginia more closely in the days after she told him about the baby. Lately, he had not taken much notice of her, and all the time this thing had happened to her and he had not known it. Why had she waited for two months to tell him? Was she afraid of him? She did not behave as if she was. He had been brutal to her, but she did not flinch from him. When he was rough with her, she would often fight him back, if she could get her hands free.

Joe watched her and wondered about her, and saw for the first time how thin her face had become, how large her eyes and brilliant her mouth against the fine white skin. Her arms and legs were thinner, too, and there were shadows under her collar-bones that had not been there when her shoulders bloomed so smoothly out of the exciting white dress. She looked somehow whittled down, stripped for action against whatever contingency life might bring. And now when Joe watched her more carefully, because she was carrying his baby, he saw that she was nearly always in an apron and with her sleeves rolled up, doggedly tackling the wretched flat as if she had never known any other kind of life. She had got into the habit of standing with her arms folded, resting one hip; the stance of the work-toughened women who gossiped on their doorsteps across the road.

It was her birthday. She was twenty-two, and Joe wanted to do something extravagant and wildly luxurious for her. He wanted to buy her jewels, champagne, an exotic dress in which she would not roll up her sleeves and fold her arms. He bought her a gaily-coloured silk scarf. It was all he could afford.

"It's real silk," he said nervously. "The best they had in the shop."

"It's beautiful." She stroked the scarf and smiled at him with shining eyes. The present was much more than just a thirty-shilling scarf to her, because she thought he had forgotten her birthday. "You shouldn't have spent so much, darling."

"I've saved a bit these last few days by not going to the pub," he said, trying to sound casual. "You know how it is. Now that I'm a father—respectable chap, and all that." He laughed self-consciously. He seldom felt embarrassed with her, but her shining pleasure in the birthday present had thrown him out of his stride and made him feel ashamed that it was so little.

"Oh, Jin!" He suddenly threw his arms round her and held her fiercely against him. "I wish I could have given you something tremendous. I wish I could give you what you want most in the world."

They were both very much in love that night. It was like the first days of their marriage, when they could not be together in a room without touching each other constantly, and when they went without supper because they began to make love before the supper was cooked, and rose at midnight to eat whatever they could find, sitting close together and talking their thoughts with the complete mental abandonment that is possible after complete physical abandonment.

All next day, Joe could not get Virginia out of his mind. He kept seeing the picture she made in her bright red coat, with her hair blown back by the wind that whipped up the dingy street as he leaned out of the window to watch her go. Before she reached the corner, she had turned to look up at the flats. Why had she done that? On other mornings he was never out of bed to wave to her. Did she guess that he would wave today, or did she look back every morning in case he was at the window?

"I wish I could give you what you want most in the world," he had said last night, and he meant it. What did she want most in the world? Well, there was one thing he could do for her. Joe dressed quickly, ate all the eggs he could find in the cupboard to give himself strength, ran whistling down the stone stairs, touched his hat impertinently to Mrs Baggott, and found himself a job in a snack bar in the Edgware Road.

"I'll say this much for your husband," Betty said, as she watched Joe deftly slapping a sandwich together. "He certainly knows his job."

"He's done this sort of work before," Virginia said. "He's rather good at messing about with food."

"Mm-hm." Betty squinted at Joe's back through her thick glasses. "I should have thought he could have found something a bit better."

Betty's fiancé was an undersized but brainy boy who was apprenticed to a solicitor. Her candid comparisons between the law and a snack bar made Virginia wish that she did not have to take Betty to the place where Joe worked. But she liked to go there herself in her lunch hour, and it was impossible to shake Betty out of the tacit assumption that since they went to lunch at the same time, they must eat their lunch together.

"Let's go somewhere else," Betty sometimes said. "I'm tired of everything they serve at the Excelsior."

"I'd rather go there," Virginia would say. "But you needn't come if you don't want to."

"Oh, I'll come with you, Ginger, even if it means the Excelsior. But I wonder Joe doesn't think it a bit funny that you go there every day."

"Why should he? He would think it funny if I didn't go."

"Oh, well. I just thought." Betty wandered up the Edgware Road, maddeningly slow in the cold wind, knocking into people as she veered short-sightedly off her course. "I just thought he might not like to feel that you were checking up on him."

"But I'm not"

Or was she? It was natural for her to go to the Excelsior for lunch. She was glad that Joe worked in a place where she could go every day; but she had to admit that she was glad not only because it gave her a chance to see him, but because she could reassure herself that he had not yet walked out of the job, as he had walked impatiently out of so many others.

He did not seem to mind this job as much as some of the others he had tried. He liked to make sandwiches and cut wedges of pie, and wear the white jacket and the little square white hat which sat so jauntily on the back of his glossy head. He was much more cheerful than he had been at other times when he was working. Most men are at odds with themselves when they are out of work. Joe was usually at odds with himself when he was tied down to the routine of a job.

The cheerfulness was partly due to a new scheme that he was concocting with Jack Corelli. Jack was speaking for the Communists at the moment, and although his impassioned oratory against the evils of capitalism drew big crowds at Marble Arch, and kept a policeman hovering near, he had never been more capitalistically minded himself. He had his eye on a little restaurant in St John's Wood that was going cheap. He and Joe were going to buy it, work up a tremendous business among the residents of the neighbouring flats, sell out at a profit, and start a showier place nearby, to which they would lure away the customers from the restaurant they had sold.

The only thing that was hindering the plan at the moment was that they did not have the money to buy the little restaurant.

"To think of that stepfather of yours with all those dollars," Joe said wistfully. "You'd think he could spare us a few."

"He probably would, if I asked him," Virginia said.

"Why don't you then?" asked Jack, fitting a cigarette into a chromium holder. "It's not very charitable of you, my dear Virginia, to keep all that money to yourself."

"But I haven't got any of it! And I don't want it. I'll never ask Spenser for help. I've told Joe that hundreds of times. You can't understand that, because you don't know the whole story, and anyway, you've got no principles. So you keep out of this, Jack. It's none of your business."

"Sorry, sorry." Jack removed the long cigarette-holder from his mouth with a flourish, and funnelled two jets of smoke down his nose. "Very sorry, I'm sure," he said in the affected voice with which he thought he was imitating the way Virginia spoke. "We're only trying to help you. Doing our best for the little woman, so she can be in the chips. It seems strange that you wouldn't want to help our honest effort."

"Oh, leave her alone," Joe said. "I know how she feels about it. She's got scruples. You and I don't understand that. We've never been able to afford them. We'll get the money all right. I've got a hunch something big is going to come up for me soon." He winked at Jack. Jack frowned, and just perceptibly shook his narrow, lizard-like head, and Virginia guessed with apprehension that they were up to something.

One evening when she went to the Excelsior on her way home from work to see if it was one of Joe's nights to leave early, she found him talking to a cadaverous man in a tightly-belted raincoat. Joe was wiping down the counter in front of the man, and making the casual remarks he might have made to any customer, but there was something about the way the man looked at Joe that made Virginia think that this was not an ordinary exchange of pleasantries.

When Joe saw her, he came at once to the end of the counter where she sat. "You didn't need to come tonight, Jin," he said, not smiling as he usually did when he saw her perching there. "You know it isn't my early night."

"You didn't tell me. You were asleep when I left this morning. I came on the chance that we could go to a cinema and have some supper out."

"Not tonight. I'm not off till eight-thirty. You go home and get some rest. Sweetheart," he added, because she looked disappointed. "And don't wait up for me, because I might be a bit late. I've got a date after work. Business."

"Something for Ed? I wish you'd stop that, Joe. You don't need to be mixed up with him now that you're working here."

"I'll choose who I'm mixed up with," he said, leaning forward on the counter as he lowered his voice. "It happens to be nothing to do with Ed, but you keep your nose out of it, anyway."

The woman who had come to take the empty stool next to Virginia heard this last remark and looked interested, so Joe stood upright and nodded to Virginia, and went to take an order at the other end of the counter.

Another day, when Virginia and Betty went to the Excelsior at lunch-time, the cadaverous man was there again. He was not talking to Joe, who was busy with the noon-time rush. He was drinking a milk shake and reading a newspaper.

He was there again another day, and although he was again reading a newspaper, Virginia still had the impression that he was watching Joe.

"Who is that man?" she asked that night. "That man who's always at the Excelsior, drinking milk shakes."

"What man?" he said. "Dozens of people come there nearly every day, and dozens of them have milk shakes."

"I know, but this man looks as if he knew you. And I've seen you talking to him."

"Since when can't I talk to customers? I talk to the women too. How do you like that?" Joe had been edgy these last few days. He seemed to have something on his mind besides the plans for the restaurant. The restaurant, in fact, was seldom discussed. Jack had not come swaggering into the flat for many days, and if he and Joe were on the street at the same time they walked on opposite sides. It seemed as if they were trying to avoid being seen together.

"Joe, you know who I mean. The man in the raincoat. His hair is cut very short, and he has a long jaw. His head looks like a skull."

"No doubt he has a skull under his head, like most people," Joe said. "I've no idea who you're talking about."

"All right. I'm fanciful, I expect. Mrs Batey says you get fanciful when you're pregnant." She dropped the subject of the cadaverous man, but she still worried about him. She saw him again in the Excelsior at lunch-time, and Betty asked in her loud, clear voice: "Why do you keep looking at that man over there? Do you know him?"

Joe told Virginia that he had been given a Saturday off, and was going to a race-meeting in the Midlands. She asked if she could go with him.

"How could you? You couldn't get off."

"I might, if I ask Mr Jacobs. He's very kind. He treats me almost as if I were sacred now."

"Well, you can't come. It would be too tiring for you, the journey and everything. I didn't know you liked going to the races all that much, anyway."

"I don't particularly. I just felt I didn't want to spend the week-end here alone."

"Alone! My God, no one could be alone in this tower of Babel. You'll be all right. You know everybody here. If you're scared at night, go across the passage. The gas-fitter will defend your honour."

Joe was going to be away two nights. He said that he was going with Ed Morris on Friday evening. Ed would put him up at a hotel, and they would be back on Sunday. On Friday morning, Virginia said suddenly: "Please don't go."

"Don't be silly, darling. I've promised Ed. He doesn't like driving alone. Besides, I have a feeling I'm going to make some money this trip. There's a couple of horses that can't miss."

When Virginia came home that evening, he had already gone. His coat was not behind the door, and when she went down to look in the basement storeroom she saw that her small suitcase was not there.

All Sunday she waited in the flat, but he did not come. In the evening she roasted a piece of beef, because she thought he would be hungry when he came back. Joe was always hungry when he came home from anywhere. She kept the food warming for him until after midnight, and then she turned off the oven and went to bed. It was the first time they had ever been apart. It was cold in the bed without Joe, and Virginia got up again to put on a sweater and a pair of his socks.

When she went to the shop on Monday morning, she left a note on the table to welcome him home. When she got back that night, the note was still there, untouched.

He could not telephone her at the flat, but he knew that the Dales had a telephone and would give her a message. Or he could have sent a telegram. How could he not let her know what he was doing? Even Joe could not be as casual as that. Unless there had been an accident. Her mind went over all the possibilities, and by the end of the evening she had Joe laid out on a mortuary slab and herself creeping in to identify him, just as Mrs Fagg had crept into the station waiting-room to identify what was left of Mr Fagg.

She was too worried to go across the passage for Mrs Batey's comfort. Mrs Batey would click her teeth and say that it was all you could expect from a man, which would be no comfort at all. She would tell her that no news was good news, and that if there had been an accident, she would have heard about it all too soon. That would be no comfort either. Virginia knew all that, but if she could not make herself believe it, Mrs Batey was never going to convince her.

On Tuesday night, she decided to call the police. She would have to go out to a telephone box. If she rang the police from the Dales' flat, the news would run through Weston House like a stab of lightning that Joe Colonna was in trouble of some kind.

In trouble? The spectres of Jack Corelli and the man with a head like a skull danced at the back of her brain as they had ever since she began to worry about Joe. She went down one flight of stairs and along the passage to the flat where Jack lived with a woman who was not his wife. The woman opened the door with a scowl, her dry, bleached hair hanging in her puffy eyes. She had been asleep. Jack was out of town, she said. What did Virginia want with him? She shut the door in Virginia's face before she could answer.

There could be many reasons why Jack was out of town. There could be many quite innocent reasons why Joe had not come back. But Virginia decided not to call the police.

"What's the matter with our Ginger today?" Miss Sunderland asked on Wednesday morning. "You are in the dumps, and no mistake. What's the matter, dear? Don't you feel well?"

"I'm fine. Just a bit tired, that's all."

"Tired is the word all right. You're only half alive this morning. Shake a leg now, Ginger, there's a good sort. There's all that pile of uplifts to be priced, and you know it's my half day. I'm going to meet my sister at Barker's, and she won't half give me stick if I'm delayed."

Miss Sunderland sang under her breath for most of the morning. She always sang when it was her half day, although she never went anywhere more exciting than to Kensington High Street with her sister. Worried and irritable, alternately sick with anxiety about Joe, and furious with him for doing this to her, Virginia could not stand the sound of *I saw a peaceful old valley,* crooned over and over in Miss Sunderland's cracked monotone. Miss Sunderland was always several years behind with her songs. Her favourites now were the songs that had been popular during the war, and when she had worn the peaceful old valley to death, she began to hum *Roll out the barrel* while she stamped price-tags and clipped them on, and even while she accompanied customers to and from the fitting-room, which was inadvertently insulting.

"Must you keep on singing that?" Virginia said finally, and immediately was sorry, for Miss Sunderland's face fell like a stone.

"Excuse *me*," she said, her eyes daunted, her large hands hanging helplessly. "I had no idea I was getting on your nerves."

"No, you're not. I——" Virginia began hastily.

"Oh, yes I am." Miss Sunderland's face was screwed into contrition. "No, no, don't tell me you haven't got any nerves. I know you must have, in your condition. Don't think I don't know, just because I'm a silly old maid." She had an embarrassing way of belittling herself that made you feel that you had said the insulting things, and not she. "Why, my sister, when she was that way, she couldn't bear to hear a door creak. Her husband had to go round with an oil can at all hours of the night, and for some reason, she couldn't stand the sight of the milkman. "He gets on my nerves," she'd say. Very awkward, it was. They had to train him to go to the front door, so that she couldn't see him through the window when she was in the kitchen. Nerves! I ought to know what nerves are. And here am I, silly old fool that I am"—she beat her head with the palm of her hand—"upsetting you and making you jumpy, just when everything should be peace and glory for you."

"I get on Ginger's nerves," she told Mr Jacobs ingenuously, as he came up to the counter. "Isn't that terrible? Wouldn't you think I'd know better at my age?"

Mr Jacobs murmured something soothing. He had his eyes beyond the door where he could see a woman vacillating at the shop-window. Virginia kept repeating that it was all right, and even found herself begging Miss Sunderland to start singing again, but Miss Sunderland was quite distraught. She handed over the next customer to Virginia, and stood back against the shelves, sucking her finger and looking humble. When it was time for her to go, she plodded out of the shop with her long neck bent, and none of the adventurous bounce with which she usually set out for Kensington High Street.

"What's the matter with *her*?" Stella poked her thick chin towards the door, after Miss Sunderland had closed it gently and stood looking nervously up and down the pavement before she struck out for the bus-stop, as if she were afraid of being followed.

"She's all right." Virginia went past Stella to the window to recorset a pink torso with one of the black mesh girdles that had just come in.

"You don't look so hot yourself," Stella said. "Feeling queer today? My mother always says it's a living hell the whole nine months."

Virginia's baby was an inexhaustible subject of conversation for the whole staff of Etta Lee's. Everyone had something to contribute. Rose, who was married to a traveller, had the advantage of two similar experiences of her own to recount. Mr Jacobs had four children at home, and had delivered the last one himself, and everyone else had a relation or friend on whose pregnancy they could draw for comment. Virginia often wished that she had kept the baby a secret. She had intended to, but Miss Sunderland was too figure-conscious not to notice the first fractional thickening of Virginia's slender waist.

"I'm all right," she said shortly to Stella, and stepped into the window with the black girdle. As she fitted it on to the slippery torso, so much narrower than any woman would be who bought the girdle, Virginia looked out at the street, where people hurried through the rain on their own affairs. One or two of them glanced at Virginia, their eye caught by movement in the window. A man in a soft green hat stopped and looked into the window for a few moments, and Virginia was not sure whether he was looking at her or at the lingerie. He lifted his hat and walked away. The gesture was comically social. Virginia thought after he had gone that she should have smiled and nodded. How funny they would have looked, exchanging civilities through the plate-glass window, with the headless dummy in its brassière and girdle for chaperone. It would be like the prisoner and his girl in Joe's book, talking through the thick glass screen while the warder pretended not to listen.

Why did she have to think of prison now?

"What's on your mind?" Mr Jacobs asked kindly as she stepped down from the window into the shop. "You look as if you were full of troubled thoughts."

"It's the weather, I expect." Virginia manufactured a smile. "This rain is depressing."

"Well, you must keep a gay heart," he said. "That's what I always tell my wife. A gay heart makes a gay baby."

What a good thing that was not true, Virginia thought. If her child were born with this present load of worry indelibly on its mind, it would not have much chance. Perhaps it was only because of the child that she was worrying. She was fanciful, just as Mrs Batey said she would be. There was no real cause for worry. When she got home tonight, Joe would be there with a reasonable excuse. He and Ed Morris had gone to another race-meeting. Ed's car had broken down. They had met friends and stayed with them. Joe had telephoned the Dales, and they had forgotten to give the message. Joe had sent a telegram and it had not been delivered.

She hurried home, and felt her heart beating more quickly as she went up the stairs. She could hardly bring herself to open the door of the flat. As she did, she hastily made her face bright for his greeting. Her mouth was even open to speak to him.

Her mouth remained open as she stood in the room and looked at her note, still lying flat in the middle of the table with the sugar-bowl to keep it down.

Listlessly, Virginia took off her coat. The thought of another evening of waiting and wondering alone in the flat was unbearable. She could not go to any of her neighbours for company, because they would ask her where Joe was. Ever ready for scandal, they would see through any explanation she might give.

She was reaching to hang her coat on the peg behind the door, when she suddenly took it down again and held it for a moment, thinking. Well, why not? She had not seen the Benbergs for more than a year. It was odd that she should suddenly think of them now, but they would not think it strange if she went to see them. They were not the kind of people to forget you, even if you seemed to have forgotten them.

She put on her coat again, and looked to see if she had money for the long bus ride. She left the note where it was on the table. It would be just like life if Joe were to come back when she was out after she had waited in three anxious evenings for him. Well, let him wait and worry for a change. She had had enough of it.

"But my darling, my darling," Mrs Benberg cried, even before Virginia was properly into the house, "what in the name of mercy has happened to you? You are a perfect skeleton."

"Hardly." Virginia took off her coat and saw Mrs Benberg's eyes widen. Since her baby had begun to be apparent, she had grown so used to that quick dropping of eyes from her face to her figure and then hastily up again, that it did not embarrass her any more.

Mrs Benberg's chocolate-brown eyes leaped back to Virginia's face, and they were shining with enthusiasm. "So you're married!" she cried. She flung her arms round Virginia and hugged her. "Oh, splendid, splendid! If only I'd known, I would have come and cheered outside the church. Who is the happy fellow?"

"A man called Joe. Joe Colonna."

"Why didn't you bring him with you? You haven't left him outside, have you? I've known women to do that." Before Virginia could answer, Mrs Benberg darted to the door, opened it and slammed it shut again with a crash that shook the flimsy little house.

"Father!" she called. "Come and see who's here!"

The noise of his wife's welcome had already drawn Mr Benberg from his desk. As she called him, he opened the door of his little writing-room at the end of the hall, pressing a finger and thumb into his eyes with the gesture of a tired author.

"Well, well." He came forward, rubbing his hands, his mouth jerking with pleasure. "This is a delightful surprise. How are you, my dear Miss Martin? How are you indeed?"

"No need to ask her how she is," Mrs Benberg said, leading the way into the sitting-room with her loose woollen skirt trailing at the back and a massive ornamental chain clanking at her neck. "Just look at her. She's monstrously frail. And don't call her Miss Martin. She's married."

Mr Benberg continued to rub his hands and murmur, Well, well, while Mrs Benberg rushed at the fire, which was burning sulkily, and attacked it with poker and bellows until it roared towards the chimney. "Sit down, darling girl," she said. "Sit down and tell us everything. You've left it much too long to come back to us, but come you did, as I knew you would, so now that you're here, tell us all about it. Leave nothing out."

She stood in front of Virginia's chair with her hands on her ample hips, the metallic necklace swinging out and down over her bulky chest, her hair piled up heedlessly, her strong, impetuous face alight with interest.

"There's nothing much to tell." Virginia smiled to see that Mrs Benberg was just as she remembered her. She had thought sometimes that the impression she had carried away from her first visit must be too excessive; but here was Mrs Benberg just as excessive as she had pictured her, filling the room with that same dynamic exuberance which threatened to burst the walls and lift the little house right off its foundations.

"I've been married for almost a year," Virginia went on, "and I'm going to have a baby."

"Happy?" Mrs Benberg shot it at her.

"Yes, very."

Mr Benberg, who had slipped into the chair on the other side of the leaping fire, smiled and rubbed his knees and nodded his narrow head.

"Then why do you look like that?" Mrs Benberg put her head on one side challengingly, and swung the chain necklace back and forth as if it were a censer.

"Like what?" Virginia met her eye defensively. "My face is a bit thinner, but the rest of me is rapidly making up for that."

"A bit thinner! Childie, childie, you're all bones. Are you starving in a garret with a struggling painter?"

"Nothing like that." Virginia laughed. "We have a nice flat, and Joe has quite a good job." She had not come here to complain. She had come to enjoy the company of friendly people.

"Well, you don't look it," Mrs Benberg said shortly. "I'm going to get some cake. We've had our meal. Father has high tea when he's writing, but he's never said no to cake yet, and I don't suppose he'll start tonight."

While she was out making a great clatter in the kitchen, Virginia asked Mr Benberg about his books. He told her that he had completed another novel since her last visit. His weak eyes shone softly as he spoke of it.

"Have you sent it to a publisher?"

"Oh, no. I don't send them anywhere any more. It isn't any use. And I don't see why I should let them discourage me with their rejection slips. One day, the publishers will come to me. Until then, I go on writing so that I shall have as much as possible to give the world when the world is ready to listen."

He leaned back in his chair and crossed his legs, swinging a slipper from the end of one foot. He looked completely satisfied with the situation. "Of course, it may not come until after I'm dead," he was saying, as Mrs Benberg came into the room with plates and mugs and a huge cake like a castle on a scarred tin tray.

"Who's talking about death?" she asked. "Your time hasn't come yet, my friend. Don't forget I've drawn your horoscope. I'll draw yours if you like," she told Virginia, setting the tray down on the floor, since there was no table uncluttered enough to hold it. "I've made cocoa," she went on, kneeling on the floor to cut the cake into vast wedges. "There's nothing like a mug of cocoa when you're feeding two. There," she said, as Virginia leaned forward to take the plate and mug from her. "Go on, eat. There's plenty more when you've put that away."

Virginia ate as much as she could of the cake, which was rich with fruit, soggy and undercooked. It was like trying to force your way through a wedge of cold Christmas pudding. Mrs Benberg remained on the floor, sitting with her thick legs stretched straight out like a child, and her skirt in a limp pile, feeding the little brown dog with lumps of cake, and prodding at the fire from time to time with a poker as big as a pitchfork.

Mr Benberg finished his cake with ease. There was no knowing where he put it inside his concave frame. When he passed his plate down for more, Mrs Benberg said: "Ladies first. Give me your plate, Virginia. Oh, come, you've eaten nothing. Are you ill?" Illness was the only reason she could envisage for lack of appetite. "I'll stake my whole fortune that you haven't had your supper. Have you?"

"Well—no. When I got home from work, I came straight out here to see you."

"Why in such a hurry?" Mrs Benberg drew down her thick, untidy brows and narrowed her eyes suspiciously. "Why?" she repeated, as Virginia did not answer.

"I just felt I wanted to see someone. Joe wasn't home, you see. He's been away for three days. Five days, actually. He went to a race-meeting on Friday, and he—he was supposed to come back on Sunday." She could not keep her voice casual. She finished quickly, with a little urgent gasp: "I'm terribly worried about him."

"Of course you are! No need to tell me that. Great heavens, child, don't you think I could see something was wrong as soon as you came over my doorstep? I love you, Virginia. You probably think I'm mad as a hatter, but Father and I—it doesn't take us long to make up our minds about someone, and we've loved you ever since he brought you here that night. Remember the snow? You looked so pretty going off through the snow, and you were so young and hopeful. You're young and hopeful still. I see that. But I see, too, that you're having quite a fight to keep your hopes. Want to talk about it?" She gazed into the fire, winding the heavy necklace round her fingers.

As Virginia was silent, wondering what to say, Mr Benberg cleared his throat and said gently: "Perhaps Miss—Mrs— perhaps Virginia doesn't want to tell us anything."

Mrs Benberg circled an arm backwards at him. "Of course she does. Everyone needs to share their troubles, and she's told us her mother is in America, so who better to share them with than us, who care about her?" She turned to Virginia, and said briskly: "So your boy has disappeared, has he? Well, men have done that before now, but they always come rolling home when they're hungry. I wouldn't worry too much about *that*."

"I think you're too liberal, my dear." Mr Benberg leaned forward, blinking and earnest. "A man shouldn't go off without telling his wife where he is, especially when she——" His lip twitched down. He looked away shyly.

"Liberal be damned! What else can you be with men? They're not in captivity, just because they're married." Mrs Benberg struggled to her feet, shaking her skirt free of crumbs, which the dog picked neatly off the carpet. "I tell you what, my darling girl." She stood with her back to the fire, and wagged her finger at Virginia. "If you nag at him this time when he does come back, next time he may not come back at all."

"I do try not to nag Joe," Virginia said. "He can't stand it."

"Who can? Who can?" Mrs Benberg lifted her skirt a little to warm the back of her legs. "This girl's got sense, Father. We don't need to tell her her business. If it was Jim now," she nodded at the photograph of her cheery son, "he hasn't a ha'p'orth of sense where his love-life is concerned. He's broken his heart three times already, but he always comes up smiling, with not a lesson learned."

"I don't think I've got much sense," Virginia said. "I

meant to do so much for Joe, but I don't seem to have done anything."

"Who says that? You've stuck to this rascal, haven't you? And you don't have to tell me he's made it tough for you, because it's written all over your face. Don't tell me the details, because I don't want to hear."

"I wasn't going to," Virginia said. "There's nothing to tell."

"Oh, yes, there is. I know all about this young man without clapping an eye on him. But, heigh-ho! we can't change him, so we must make the best of it. What's done can't be undone, no use crying over spilt milk, two wrongs don't make a right, and all the other old saws that spring to my mind at the drop of a hat. So cheer up, love, and I'll get the ginger wine. Things will come out all right for you. I told you that before, didn't I, so why worry? God helps those who help themselves, if you want another old saw, from B. Franklin, who wrote most of 'em."

She scrabbled in a cupboard full of old gramophone records and tarnished silver, and brought out a sticky bottle and three glasses that looked as if they had once held jam.

"But I can't help worrying," Virginia said. "I shouldn't tell you this, but I've no one else to tell. People gossip so where I live."

"Why tell the people where you live?" Mrs Benberg demanded. "The last people, always."

"They are the only people I know," Virginia said. "I've lost touch with everyone else. If you knew where I lived, you would understand."

"What is it you want to tell?" Mrs Benberg asked more gently.

"Just that I'm afraid Joe is in some sort of trouble."

"What sort? Women? Money? Police?"

"Police," Virginia said bleakly. She told them about Jack Corelli and the cadaverous man in the raincoat. She even told them that Joe had once been in prison. But that seemed unfair to him, and so she said quickly: "No, don't count that. It makes him sound bad, and he isn't. I love him."

"Well, I should hope you do!" Mrs Benberg tipped back

her head to get the last oily drops of the sweet ginger wine. "Why else would you marry this villain? But whether you love him has no bearing on whether he's good or bad. Whoever heard of a woman being in love with any of the saints?"

"I think," Mr Benberg said quietly, rolling the wine round the sides of the jam-jar, "I think that he has behaved very badly. Virginia doesn't owe as much to him as she thinks she does. A man like that doesn't deserve to keep a good wife."

Virginia was going to speak, but Mrs Benberg jumped in fiercely. "Don't say such a terrible thing! She's married to him, isn't she? She owes him everything, by which I mean herself. And as for leaving him, that's a lot of subversive bilge I never expected to hear coming out of your head. Suppose you had gone off the rails—do you think it would have made any difference to me? Suppose Virginia's boy has been in prison, and suppose he has made a big enough ass of himself this time to put him there again—what difference is that going to make to her?"

"Oh, no, of course. No, no," Mr Benberg said, recanting immediately under her fire. "No difference at all."

"Could one really be as tough as that?" Virginia said. "It wouldn't be very easy, with everyone knowing about it, and Mrs Batey—she's the woman who lives opposite—trying to cheer me up by telling me how her husband nearly got ten days for brawling with her in Chapel Street. As if you could possibly draw a comparison between Joe and her dingy little man. How would I bear it? Going to see Joe every week. Watching him grow bitter, or surly, or defeated. What do you do with a man when he comes out of prison? How do you help him to start again? There's a woman across the street whose husband did two years. He's never had a job since. He doesn't look at people properly any more. He looks humiliated, as if everything had been taken away from him for ever. How would I bear it?"

"What else could you do?" Mrs Benberg asked, clutching the chain necklace with both hands, as if she were holding a banner. "Of course you would bear it. You might conceivably leave a man who was successful and independent of you, but you don't leave a man who needs you. People shouldn't get married if they don't know that elementary principle."

"You expect a lot of Virginia," Mr Benberg said.

"Of course I do." Mrs Benberg's voice drowned his murmur. "Because I know she has got it to give. That's why it will all be given back to her, good measure, pressed down, and shaken together, and running over. . . . Why do I always get Biblical when I'm worked up?" She shook herself like a large mongrel coming out of a pond. "Let's not get excited. We're all talking as if this poor man was already languishing in a cell with a cannon-ball chained to his leg. Instead of which, he is probably at home beating his head on the wall because he thinks his wife has walked out on him. Run home, my dearest girl, and tell him what you told us."

"What I told you?" Virginia stood up.

"That you love him. He'll be there. I see it. Don't forget I see these things. I'm never wrong, am I, Father?"

"Oh, no, my dear. Oh, no, no. The day you are wrong, the stars will fall from their courses."

Mrs Benberg looked at him sharply to see if he was mocking her, but he had left the room with his wet-weather limp to get Virginia's coat, and she could not see his face.

The stars did not fall. Mrs Benberg was right again. When Virginia got back to the flat, Joe was lying on the bed with his clothes on, fast asleep.

"Darling?" Virginia put her hand on his shoulder. He hunched the shoulder up towards his ear, and twitched his cheek fretfully, as if a fly were disturbing his sleep.

"No, darling," Virginia said to his sleeping, innocent face. "This is too much. I'm not going to wait until morning to hear what you've been up to." She turned him on to his back and sat down on the bed beside him. "Please wake up," she said loudly. "I want to talk to you."

"For God's sake——" Joe mumbled himself half out of sleep, opened his eyes and closed them again and rolled over. "Leave me alone. I need sleep." He flung an arm across his face, but Virginia pulled it away, and turned him back to face her.

"Tell me where you've been. Then you can sleep," she said.

He smiled dreamily up at her, and raised his hand to stroke the inside of her arm. "Pretty girl," he said. "Come to bed now. We'll talk in the morning."

"We'll talk now. You're not getting away with it like that." Don't nag at him, Mrs Benberg had said, but Mrs Benberg did not know that he would try to take refuge in sleep or caresses. "Three days and three nights," Virginia said, "I've waited here for you, with no idea where you were. How about giving me some sort of explanation?"

Joe looked at her calmly. "You weren't waiting tonight," he said. "How about giving me an explanation of that?"

"That's easy. I went to see some friends. How was I to know you would come back tonight? For all I knew you were never coming back."

"Big loss that would have been."

"Don't make silly jokes. This is serious. How do you think I felt, waiting here night after night, thinking of all the worst things that could have happened to you?"

"Why, you're angry," he said wonderingly.

"Of course I'm angry. You always get angry after you've been anxious. First you are relieved, like I was when I saw you on the bed. Then you get angry, like I am now. Not about you staying away longer than you said. That's nothing. I'm angry because you didn't take the trouble to let me know."

"I couldn't." Joe turned his head slightly, so that he was not looking at her. "I didn't want to give them the chance of tracing me here, in case they were on to me."

"They? Who's they?" Virginia knew, but she had to hear him say it.

"If you must know, Jin, the Warwickshire constabulary."

Virginia sighed. "Yes," she said flatly. "Yes. That's what I was afraid of." She was not angry any more. She was disheartened and suddenly very tired.

"There was nothing I could do. After they got Jack, I didn't dare to come straight home. I came a roundabout way, moving about, you see, until I was sure they weren't on to me. You understand?"

"All but one small detail. What had Jack done?"

"Nothing really. It was what he tried to do. But this damn fool girl at the cinema got panicky and gave him the all-clear too soon. The cashier only had to let out one peep and the whole place was swarming with people."

"Joe——" She gripped his arm and searched his eyes, leaning forward so that her hair fell over her face. "Are you mixed up in this?"

"Oh, lord, no, sweetheart." He spoke too easily. His smile was too casual. "I just happened to meet Jack at the races. I had no idea he was going, of course, but I was afraid we might have been seen together. That's why I had to watch myself. There, I've told you all about it, and there's nothing more to worry about. Now let's get some sleep. I haven't had much these last few nights."

Virginia's mind was seething with questions, but she knew that it was useless to ask them. He was not going to tell her the truth. "All right," she said, "there's nothing more to worry about." He closed his eyes and dug his cheek into the pillow as she got up from the bed. She watched him as she undressed. In a few minutes, he was either asleep, or pretending it. Did he really think that she was satisfied with his unconvincing story? Did he think her such a fool, or was it that he did not trust her with the truth?

It was useless to try to get the truth from him. Almost immediately, the whole neighbourhood knew that Jack Corelli was awaiting trial for an attempted hold-up. Joe joined casually in the gossip and speculation when it came his way, but he would never discuss with Virginia his ill-fated trip to the races.

He was restless and a little nervous for a few days, but he soon regained his spirits. He did not seem to be worrying any more about his own part—whatever his part had been—in the foolish, bungled crime. Virginia did all the worrying. She went to the window constantly, staring across the road at Mrs Baggott in her window, trying to determine whether the mysterious old lady was watching their flat. Had she seen Joe and Jack go off together? Did she know that Joe had been away all those days? Virginia had lived long enough in Weston House to be half credulous of the fable that Mrs Baggott knew everything, saw everything, and was an informer in the pay of both Satan and the police.

Every day Virginia expected to see a police car stop outside Mrs Fagg's house. Every day she expected to hear the authoritative knock on her own front door. Virginia had never been afraid of the police before, and the sensation was not pleasant. She realized for the first time how broad was the gap between the law-abiding and the lawless.

Gradually, as the weeks went by, and spring crept unheralded by any growing green into the awakening street, her anxiety began to fade. Mrs Fagg hung all her flattened rugs out on the railings and beat at them with a bamboo stick. Gloria Dale came out in a new turquoise suit. Like a moulting animal, Miss Few shed the mangy hearthrug which was her winter fur coat. Windows that had been closed for months were opened with difficulty. The women across the street began to stand on their doorsteps again, and bronchial children were let out without the layers of clothing which had covered everything but their bony knees. The year was turning towards summer, and still the police car had not come for Joe, and Virginia began to relax and to forget her fears and to drift back towards the ranks of those to whom policemen are allies.

She had something else to worry about now. When Joe came back from Warwickshire, his job at the Excelsior was gone. He was now back at his usual game of "looking around." There was no knowing what he would do. He might get a job tomorrow. He might stay out of work for weeks, and Virginia's doctor had told her that if she did not want to lose her baby, she must give up working at Etta Lee's.

She still had fifteen pounds of Spenser's money. That was all. There was nothing left now but to ask Helen for help.

12

As IF to confirm Virginia's decision to relax the struggle for independence, there came a letter from Helen to say that she and Spenser were flying to England for a short visit.

> *I wish we could stay long enough,* Helen wrote, *for me to be there when the baby is born, but Spenser is too busy to be away from the office for very long. In any case, I hope to persuade you to fly back with us and have your baby in America. The hospitals and doctors are so much better here.*

It was plain that Helen was almost completely Americanized. English people tend to react in one of two ways when they first visit the United States. They either embrace it wholesale because it is different from England, or they reject it out of hand because it is not like England. Helen had embraced the country with both arms, and there was never a letter from her which did not draw some invidious comparison between the old world and the new.

"She's softening me up, you see," Virginia said, showing Joe the latest letter, "so that I will be amenable by the time she gets here."

"Will you be? Would you like to go?"

"How can you ask that? I would never go without you, and I know you wouldn't want to."

"Oh, I don't know," Joe said lazily. "I wouldn't mind. There might be better opportunities for me over there, especially with a rich father-in-law."

"No," Virginia said firmly. "We're staying here. You and I are Londoners. We would never be happy anywhere else."

"We're not so deliriously happy now, if it comes to that—are we?" Joe was sitting by the window in the slanting sun which found its way to their side of the street in the late afternoon. He spoke without looking at Virginia, staring expressionlessly down at the street, where some children were scrabbling with a puppy.

"Aren't we?" Virginia asked. "I thought we were. Things are a bit rough now, I know, but we'll get on our feet again, if Helen will help us. We'll pay her back. It won't stop us being independent."

"I'm not worrying about that," Joe said. "I'll be happy to take anything the old girl will give us, and Lord knows she must have plenty to give. It's just that—well, I don't know. I thought you were fed up with me."

"You know I'm not." Virginia came to the window and stood beside him, looking across at the featureless blur that was Mrs Baggott's face behind her dusty window.

"You should be. Most women would be fed up with living in this hole, if they'd ever known anything better."

"I don't mind it nearly as much as you do. I've got used to it. In any case, what difference does this place make to you and me? What difference does it make whether we have money or we haven't? We've never had any money. We've always only had each other. Isn't that good enough for you? It is for me. I'm not complaining."

"No," he said dourly. "That's the trouble with you. You never complain."

"What do you want me to do? Throw the furniture about, or go for you with a kitchen knife, like Mrs Roper did with Will?"

"At least that would put you in the wrong for a change. It's always me who's the louse, and honestly, Jin, you're so God damn forbearing and unselfish that sometimes it's enough to drive a man mad."

"Well, I'm sorry," she said stiffly. "I'll try not to be in the future. Remind me to be selfish." She walked away from him. "I think I'll go down to the shops. I'm not doing much good here."

She went into the bedroom to get the loose-fitting coat which she had to wear now. Her eyes were blurred, and when she looked into the mirror, she saw that the corners of her mouth were turned down. She hated the sound of the nasty little conversation, which was still vividly in her ears. When Joe said things which hurt her, she always remembered them word perfectly for a long time.

When she came out of the bedroom, Joe said quite cheerfully, as if the conversation had never taken place: "Bring us in a pint of whisky, will you?"

"If I do, I won't be able to buy the meat."

"Forget the meat then. We'll have all we can stuff into ourselves once Mrs Rockerfeller gets here."

Virginia was hungry. She had been trying to fill herself up for too long with bread and cheap buns. She craved for meat, but what would Joe say if she took him at his word and retorted that she needed meat more than he needed whisky? He would not compliment her for being selfish. He would shout at her to get the whisky and shut up about it.

Virginia had no idea how Helen would behave towards Joe. Her mother never referred to him in her letters, and she had given no hint of how she felt about the marriage. Virginia was also uncertain of how Joe would behave towards Helen. He had only met her once, and then at a disadvantage, which had made him unusually diffident. Now that he was married to Virginia, he would be more cocky.

It might be a little difficult. She saw them bristling at each other like two irreconcilable dogs, with herself caught in the middle, trying to keep peace with both sides.

Joe was not in the flat when Helen came. Helen had not announced the date of her arrival, and she took Virginia by surprise by arriving at Weston House in a taxi and manifesting herself suddenly outside Virginia's door with a face of incredulous horror.

Virginia drew her into the flat and embraced her, feeling unusually tall. She had forgotten how short Helen was, short and decidedly stocky now, her figure plumped out, and not flattered by the expensive blackberry-coloured suit with the cuffed hem of the jacket standing out from her hips.

Her kiss was somewhat perfunctory for a mother who had not seen her daughter for a year. The kissing and the welcome were quickly brushed aside in her impatience to speak.

"Jinny!" she cried, as soon as Virginia removed her arms. "This isn't where you live! Just tell me it isn't true. That's all I want to know."

"Of course it's true." Virginia was amused by the definite American inflection in her mother's voice. "What's wrong with it? Look." She waved her hand. "We have two rooms. The last place we lived, we didn't even have a bedroom."

"But honey, it's terrible! When the taxi brought me down that street, and slowed down, I couldn't believe it. 'Go on, driver,' I said. 'I told you Weston House.' 'This is Weston House,' he said. They don't call you Madam any more, I notice. And he pointed to this—this filthy *gaol* building. My hands were shaking so that I could hardly count out the fare, and how I got up those stairs, I'll never know. You shouldn't be climbing all those flights in your condition." She looked at Virginia, sharply assessing her increased size.

"Nonsense, Helen," Virginia said. "Exercise is good for you. Look, don't let's spend all our first time together crabbing about the flat. Sit down. Let me look at you. Tell me all about yourself and Spenser and your house and everything."

"I will in good time. Right now, I'm only interested in getting you out of this pigsty. Why didn't you tell me about it? When you told me you had a flat, and the address, well, I never thought—I mean, Weston House, and the postal district—it sounded perfectly respectable. I knew you couldn't be anywhere very grand, but this—this—why, Jinny, it's a slum!"

She sat down and looked round the room with a face of grim disgust. Her face fell into the lines of displeasure as naturally as if that were its most frequent expression. The luxury of marriage to Spenser, which had eased her life, had not eased or smoothed out the ageing lines of her face. The increased plumpness had not filled out the lines. It had chiselled them deeper below the puffy contours of her cheeks and chin. She was still smart, well-groomed and very upright, but her smartness was too ostentatious. The blackberry suit was not simple enough. The glittering white-and-gold hat was too young for her. She wore too much heavy

jewellery. Her gloves were too elaborately embroidered for
the daytime.

Virginia was amazed at the difference that a year had made
in her. Admirably turned out as the editor of *Lady Beautiful*,
a successful career-woman with a snap and a sparkle to her
manner, she now looked like a rich, idle woman, for ever
wanting something, for ever dissatisfied with it when she
got it.

"Let's see." She was making plans busily, while Virginia
boiled water for coffee. "We could have them unlock the
door between our suite and the bedroom next to it. I'll help
you pack, and you can move into the Savoy tonight.
Tomorrow, we'll go out and buy clothes for you. Is that
dreadful smock thing the only maternity garment you
have?"

"I have other things. I don't need clothes." Virginia came
out of the greasy alcove which housed the stove and the
cracked sink. "And I'm not moving out, Helen, thank you
all the same. Don't let's have a quarrel the minute you come,
but I could tell by your voice that the door you are going
to have unlocked is the door to a single bedroom. I'm not
going anywhere without Joe. Or with him, for that matter.
This is my home. I'm quite satisfied with it. If you can't bear
it, I'll come and see you at the hotel. Joe and I will come
and see you. You've got to understand that I'm married."

"We'll talk about that later." Helen tightened her mouth.
"Don't give me any coffee," she said, having watched
Virginia make it. "I'll have to drink tea while I'm over here.
I can't stand English coffee any more. Where is—Joe?" She
had some difficulty in bringing out his name. "What is his
job now?"

A pounding on the door saved Virginia from answering.
Mrs Batey, with one of Edgar's old shirts tied round her
waist by the sleeves to make an apron, had brought a plate
of gingerbread.

"I was making a batch, dear," she said, "so I made extra
for you. I know you need it. It's the sweetness, see. Enriches
the blood. Oh, excuse me." She came right into the room and
confronted Helen. "I didn't know you had company."

"This is my mother," Virginia said. "She's just come over from America. Helen, this is Mrs Batey."

"Your mum!" Mrs Batey wiped her hand on Edgar's shirt and seized Helen's hand, which was still gloved. "Well, this is a treat, I must say." She stood flushed and beaming, taking in every detail of Helen's clothes and jewellery, for retailing to the rest of the women in the flats.

Helen glanced nervously at her glove. "I'm glad to know you, Mrs Batey," she said, too condescendingly. "My daughter has told me in her letters that you have been kind to her."

"Well, of course." Mrs Batey squirmed with pleasure, and pushed back her disordered hair. "I've done what I can. I always believe in helping the young ones when they're starting out. And as I say, we're all in this world to help each other. Virginia is a lovely girl, Mrs—er, and since she didn't have a mother's care, I've treated her like my own, and glad to do it. Especially now that she's carrying. I'll be here to help her when her time comes. Don't worry about that."

"Thank you," Helen said, "but Virginia is coming away with me. She won't be here more than a few days at the most."

"Yes, I will——" Virginia began, but Helen silenced her with a look, and Virginia realized that they could not have an argument in front of Mrs Batey.

Mrs Batey's shining face had fallen. She looked from one to the other in undisguised disappointment. "Well, that is bad news," she said. "There's many here that will be sorry to see her go, but I dare say it's all for the best for her to have everything nice, and what she should have. Not that there's anything wrong with these flats, mind, but this would be a pokey place to start a family. Of course, I have a much larger place," she said grandly. "One of the better flats."

"Mum!" screamed a voice outside the door. "Baby's done a puddle again."

"Oh, dear, I'll have to go," Mrs Batey said equably. "No peace for the wicked, they say. Bring the plate back any time, love, and good-bye, Mrs—er. Step across the way any time you feel like it." Mrs Batey opened the door, and shooed

248

away the dirty child who tried to peer round her legs to look at Helen.

"Who," Helen said faintly, "who was that woman?"

"I told you. Mrs Batey. She's my friend. She's been nicer to me than any friend I ever had, so don't be witty about her, please."

"Oh, my God," Helen said. "I didn't know you'd become a Socialist, on top of everything else. Don't be bitter with me, honey." She did not call Virginia Dear Heart any more. That was too English. "You're a little warped, I expect, because of your condition."

"Don't drag that in," Virginia said. "It makes no difference to the way I feel. As soon as you get pregnant, everyone starts to make that an excuse for everything you do. Why should they? It doesn't make you a different person, just because you are temporarily two people."

"You haven't changed," Helen said. "You look ghastly— ten years older, but that's beside the point. You haven't changed. Right now I'm going to take you back to the Savoy and feed you two people the biggest dinner you have probably had since I went away. Some sort of cream soup, I think. Steak, very rare, then perhaps a *creme aux marrons,* if they still do that well. What do you say?"

Virginia could feel the juices beginning to flow in her mouth. The thought of sitting down in the comfort of the Savoy Grill and eating that food made her almost faint with desire.

"Change into something you can be seen in," Helen said, "and call a taxi."

"We haven't got a telephone," Virginia said.

"I'll get a taxi for you. Who wants a taxi? Anyone want to leave?" Joe came into the flat. He had apparently been listening outside the door. He came forward a little unsteadily, with a wide grin on his face, held out his hand to Helen, then changed his mind and bent to kiss her.

Helen moved a step away. "You've been drinking," she said.

"Sure. Know any law against it?"

Virginia's heart sank. So he was going to be difficult. He

249

was going to be defiant, trying to show that he was as good as anybody, and succeeding only in being insolent. Now it would all start again—the antagonism and the disparagement and the unpleasantness, just when Virginia had hoped that she could reconcile her mother to her husband.

"It's damned hot in here." Joe took off his jacket. He was wearing a faded blue shirt without a tie. He threw the jacket at a chair. It missed the chair and slid on to the floor.

Virginia picked it up. Because Helen was watching her, she spent a little time hanging the coat over the back of a straight chair, smoothing it out, tweaking up the shoulders. It was an old tweed jacket, rubbed at the edges and with a button missing. Virginia had been meaning to replace the button for weeks, but she decided to do it now.

Helen watched in silence while Virginia took out her sewing-basket, sat down with it and began to look for a suitable button; then she burst out impatiently: "For heaven's sake, Jinny! Do you have to start being domestic now? Spenser is waiting for us."

"First things first," Joe said. "She has to sew on my button first. You didn't know what a good little wife your daughter was, did you, Helen?"

He managed to make the name sound fairly natural, but Virginia knew his voice well enough to guess that he was forcing it out because he had made up his mind to be casual with Helen. If he had been sober, it would have sounded only casual. As it was, it sounded somehow mocking and insolent, especially as he was standing with his hands in his pockets, rocking back on his heels and looking Helen up and down as if he were undressing her.

"Of course I knew," Helen said coldly. "I didn't expect her to be anything else."

"But you didn't expect her to waste it on a bum, eh?" Joe continued to stare at her with a twisted grin.

"Joe, please," Virginia said uneasily, bending her head over her sewing.

"Joe, please what? What have I done now?" He went over to Virginia.

She broke off the thread and looked up at him, holding the

jacket in her lap. "Don't be like this, darling," she murmured. "You're making everything worse."

"Don't be like what?" he echoed loudly. "Here, I'll take that." He snatched the jacket roughly away from Virginia. "I'm going out again, since I seem to be making a mess of myself here."

"Don't go," Virginia said. "Helen has asked us to go and have dinner at the Savoy."

She looked challengingly at her mother. Helen could only say: "Yes, of course, the invitation includes your husband if he would care to come." She said it stiffly. The way in which she said "your husband" made it impossible to imagine her ever addressing him as Joe.

"No, thanks," Joe said. "Not tonight. Some other time."

"Please come, Joe," Virginia said, "I'm hungry."

"Well, go ahead," Joe said airily. "You go ahead. Don't worry about me. I'll find a piece of bread and cheese or something." He made it sound as if Virginia were deserting him.

"I'd much rather you came." Virginia felt that if he did not come now, and meet Spenser, and have dinner as one of the family, the ice might never be broken. Joe would never abandon his childish defiance. Helen would take it as an accepted thing that she saw Virginia without him. "Please come," she said again.

"I told you, no. I told you to go ahead." Joe sat down in the chair by the window, stuck out his legs and took up a newspaper.

"If you two are going to spend all evening fighting about it," Helen said, "nobody will get any dinner. I must say, Jinny, I didn't expect to be mixed up in a brawl as soon as I saw you."

"It's not a brawl."

"It sounds like one to me. Go and change your clothes," she ordered, as if Virginia were a child again, "and let's get started. If your husband doesn't want to come, that's quite all right. At least, you can't say I didn't ask him."

"You didn't," Virginia said. "I did." Joe did not look up from the paper. Virginia shrugged her shoulders and went into the bedroom. She changed her dress hastily, listening for voices from the other room. The only sound was the rustle as Joe turned the pages of the newspaper.

When she came out, Helen was still standing near the door with an aloof face, and Joe was still sitting in the same position, gazing intently at the newspaper which Virginia knew he had already read.

Virginia wore a red silk dress that had once been effective, but was now much too tight for her. She had covered the split at the waist with a broad belt, which emphasized her shape.

Helen looked at her. "Aren't you going to wear a coat?" she asked.

"Will I need one? It's warm."

"You will need one." Helen shut her mouth tightly and looked away, as if the sight of Virginia in the tight red dress was too much for her.

Virginia put on the shapeless coat which she detested, and went to kiss Joe. He lifted his sulky face to her, but he did not return her kiss. Virginia could not risk asking him to get a taxi, in case he refused.

"Let's walk, Helen," she said, opening the door of the flat. "We can pick up a taxi in Edgware Road. Or we can go by bus, if you like. You'd probably enjoy going on a bus after all this time."

"Thank you," Helen said, "but if I never go on another London bus it will be too soon."

She did not say good-bye to Joe, and he did not get up. Helen and Virginia went out of the flat. As Virginia was closing the door, she glanced back and saw that Joe was looking after her with a lost unhappiness that she had never seen on his face. Almost she ran back into the flat to say she would not go, but Helen tweaked impatiently at her arm, and she shut the door and followed her mother obediently down the dim passage to the stair-well.

Virginia waited until after dinner to say what she had to say to Helen. Spenser's delight in seeing her, his friendly, easy-going conversation, the pleasure of eating a first-class meal politely served, combined to produce in her an un-accustomed well-being which she did not want to spoil.

After the brandy, which Helen said Virginia should not have, but which Spenser declared was medicinal, Virginia went up to Helen's suite. She was glad that Spenser stayed downstairs to read the stock-market tape. She would have felt embarrassed and grasping saying what she had to say in front of him. It was embarrassing enough to have to say it to Helen, although the fact that the money was not strictly Helen's made it somehow easier to ask for it from her than from Spenser.

The sitting-room of the suite, with its thick carpet and handsome furniture, made Virginia feel like a stranger from another world. There were flowers everywhere, flowers which must have cost more than she earned in a week at Etta Lee's. The bedroom was larger than the whole of Virginia's flat in Weston House, and the bathroom made her want to tear off her clothes and lie for hours in scented hot water. At the public baths, where she and Joe went twice a week, there was a time-limit, and a limit to the amount of hot water you could use. Putting on your clothes afterwards and going straight out into the street was not the same as wrapping yourself in a bath-robe and falling on to a bed, sodden and dizzy with steam.

While Helen was attending to her face, Virginia sat down on one of the soft beds, and said to the back of her mother's lacquered head: "Helen, I want to ask you something."

"Go ahead." Helen's voice came distortedly through a mouth stretched to receive lipstick.

Virginia looked at the floor and said with great difficulty: "I need your help. Do you think you could lend me some money?"

Helen kept her waiting while she finished with the lipstick. Virginia sat and stared at her feet, and knew the humiliating anxiety of the beggar.

Helen put the lipstick back into its case, returned it to a drawer, tidied the top of the dressing-table, and patted her hair before she turned round. Her face was cautious, but before she turned, Virginia had glanced up and caught the flicker of triumph on Helen's reflection in the mirror.

"I can't lend you money," Helen said, "but I will be glad to give you anything you need."

"I don't want that. I'll pay you back. It might take a little time, but I couldn't take anything from you unless I paid it back."

"Why so proud? What is a mother for, after all?"

"But this is different. I ran away from you to marry someone you didn't like. That doesn't give me the right to expect help from you."

"I'm only surprised that you haven't asked for it before. Do you think I'm so vindictive? I would have helped you any time, and of course I'll help you now. On one condition."

"What's that?" Virginia asked, although she knew what her mother was going to say.

"That you come back to the States with me. As you know, I had planned for you to have your baby over there, and now that I've seen—what I've seen, my mind is completely made up. I'm not leaving you here."

"I'm staying, Helen. My mind is made up too." Virginia stood up, and they confronted each other warily, each watching the other's face for a sign of surrender. "I'm not going to make bargains with you. All I want is for you to lend us some money, just enough to tide us over the baby, until I can get about and start earning again. Mrs Batey will look after the baby while I'm working. I'll get another job. We'll be perfectly independent again, and eventually we'll be able to pay you back, and we won't have to bother you again."

"And while you are farming your baby out on that unspeakable woman, and working your fingers into a condition even worse than they are now"—Virginia put her hands behind her back—"what will your charming husband be doing, if one may ask?"

"He'll be working, too, of course."

"Is he working now?" Again that fleeting look of triumph passed across Helen's face, as if she thought she had Virginia trapped.

"Well—not at the moment. He's had some bad luck. That's

why I had to come to you. But he'll find something soon. We'll be all right, only we'll both have to work if we're going to pay you back."

"Don't keep saying that!" Helen stamped her foot lightly. "I've never asked you to pay me back. I don't want that. I want you to accept my help as a gift, but on my terms, Jinny. After all, it's my money. I think you're being a little presumptuous in trying to tell me what to do with it."

"What are your terms then—that Joe and I should trail meekly with you to America and live on your charity?"

"Joe and you! You must be crazy. Nothing would induce me to have that man living in my house. Apart from my dislike of him—which I gather from his attitude is mutual —I would be ashamed to introduce him to people as my son-in-law."

"Stop that, Helen," Virginia said heatedly. "There's nothing wrong with Joe. I won't let you talk like that. He's my husband, and I love him."

"Oh—love him!" Helen flung up her hands. "What will the child say next? How can you love a man who treats you like that? Why, it's degrading. There's something almost masochistic about it."

"You don't know anything about the way Joe treats me."

"I can tell. He's tried to drag you down to his level. He's tried to break you, and dominate you. I can tell by the way he speaks to you, by the way he looks at you, even. I know his type. I wouldn't be surprised at anything I heard about him. Has he ever hit you?"

"No." Often in the past, Virginia had been rashly honest with Helen, and regretted it. She was more cautious now, and Helen invited lies by her egotistic failure to be tolerant of the truth.

"He will," Helen said smugly. "I told you, I know the type. If you go on with him, Jinny, you're headed for disaster. Leave him. Come back to me, and I'll help you. I'll give you everything you want—even a house of your own on the estate, if you want it that way. Spenser can get you the best lawyer. There should be no difficulty about a divorce."

"There'll be no divorce," Virginia said. "I'm not leaving Joe, and you can't make me."

"All right then, I'm not giving you any money. Why should I support that drunken tramp, who hasn't the guts to do anything for his wife and family?"

"It isn't like that at all," Virginia lied angrily. "Joe is only out of work for the moment. He'll get something very soon, but you've no idea how difficult it is in London now. Good jobs are hard to find. You have to take what you can get, and it isn't enough while I'm like this. Helen, you must help us." She was ashamed of the appeal in her voice. "I hate asking you. I wouldn't do it if I wasn't pretty desperate."

"Leave him, and then I will help you."

"I can't leave him. Don't you understand that?"

"As far as understanding it goes," Helen said lightly, walking over to a table to get a cigarette, "you might as well be talking a foreign language." She lit the cigarette and sat down, taking an ash-tray on to her knee, as if she were prepared to fight this out in a long session. "You say that you are desperate. That is no surprise to me, now that I've seen what your marriage has done for you. You've made your mistake. Have the grace to admit it, and get out while the getting is good. I've shown you the way. For God's sake, child, have some sense and take it."

"Walking out on your husband isn't the way." Virginia began to move restlessly about the room, unpleasantly conscious of her shape in the tight red dress. She saw herself in a mirror. I look awful, she thought. Pregnant and sullen. Pregnant women should have beautiful, serene expressions, if they're going to carry it off.

She continued to look sullen. "Do you think my father did the right thing by walking out on you?" she demanded, stopping in front of Helen. "I don't believe you minded too much. I believe it was harder in the end on him than it was on you. I know that you and he weren't happy together, but leaving you didn't make him any happier. I know. I saw him after he was alone. You didn't. I didn't realize how things were for him then, but I do now."

"Don't let's drag poor Harold into it," Helen said with a

sigh. "He has nothing to do with it, though no doubt if he knew what was going on, he would feel the same as I do."

"He wouldn't. No one who has made the mistake of breaking up their marriage would ever advise anyone else to do it."

"But there is really no comparison, you see." As Virginia's voice grew more vehement, Helen's became more airy. "Harold left a perfectly good wife. You are leaving a perfectly worthless husband."

"Can't you understand that I'm not leaving him? It's no use sitting there trying to talk me into it as calmly as if we were discussing whether to send back a hat that didn't suit me. No one could talk me into it, but you would be the last person. You're prejudiced and snobbish, and you don't care two straws for people's happiness, as long as they do what you want them to do."

"Thank you," Helen said. "Thank you for such a delightful description of your mother."

"I'm sorry. I didn't mean to say that." Virginia picked up her coat from the bed. "I think I'll go before I say anything else. Forget about the money. We'll manage. Other people do."

"I know," Helen said. "I saw plenty of them in the street where you live." She stood up. Virginia looked at her, and suddenly they both smiled. The battle was over. Neither had won, but they smiled as if they had reached some unspoken agreement not to fight any more.

Helen helped Virginia with her coat. "Wait, honey," she said. "I've got a hat that will look just darling on you. I want you to have it." She searched among tissue paper and reached up to place on Virginia's head a little red hat with a turned-up brim that immediately transformed Virginia and the sloppy coat and the tight dress into an object of charm and assurance. As Virginia looked at herself in the mirror, her smile widened. All was not lost. She could still look attractive in the right clothes, and she made up her mind in that moment that one day, if she died in the attempt, she would have them again.

"Thanks, Helen." She kissed her mother. "You've done

more than you know by giving me that hat. You've made me want to get myself out of the slums."

"Then you'll come?" Helen clasped her hands. "You'll come home with me and start a fresh life?"

"Oh, no." Virginia shook her head, still smiling. "I'll come for a visit, perhaps, when Joe and I can pay our own fares. But I'll never come without him. You'll never understand that, Helen. I don't believe you understand what marriage is at all."

"Ha!" Helen gave a short, but affable laugh. "At twenty-two, you tell me that. My heavens, the young are arrogant."

"Sure they are." Spenser came through from the sitting-room, his heavy feet making dents in the thick carpet. "The older you get, the less you know, and the less sure you are of what you know. That's a cute hat, Jinny. Say——" He looked closer. "Isn't it that John Fredericks hat I gave you, Helen?"

"You don't mind," Helen said, a statement rather than a question. "I never looked very well in it, and look what it does for Jinny."

"I'm glad for her to have it. She's beautiful, anyway, but in that hat she's a knock-out. What have you two been doing? Talking about hats all the time, I'll bet. I know what you women are when you get in a bedroom. You either discuss your husbands or your hats." His husky laugh and the coughing spell which followed it covered the fact that no one else laughed.

Helen and Virginia looked at each other for a moment. Opposed as they were, they were still mother and daughter, and they could still agree by a silent glance to keep something to themselves.

"Well, we've not been talking about husbands," Helen said, "so I guess it must have been hats."

Spenser went with Virginia down the corridor to the lift. "Get that young man of yours to come along tomorrow," he said. "We won't eat him."

"It's not that," Virginia said quickly. "He couldn't come tonight. He——"

"Your old stepfather knows more than you think." Spenser squeezed her arm. "I've been making some enquiries on the

258

side. I have my spies, you know. That's one thing money can do for you. So don't think I don't know the way things are with you."

"We're all right." The bravery of the words was hollow. Saying them made Virginia realize how far from the truth they were. But she would never tell Spenser that she had asked her mother for help and had been refused.

She pressed the call-button for the lift. "I'll have to hurry," Spenser said. "I don't want to say this in front of the elevator-boy, and I didn't dare say it in front of my wife, because I haven't told her yet, and she likes to be the first to know things. I'm going to help you, Jinny."

"No, thank you. We don't need any help."

"That's my girl. I knew you'd say that," Spenser said with satisfaction. "You're just as stubborn as your mother. That's why I'm not going to talk to you. I'm going to talk to Joe. Send him round here tomorrow. Noon will do. We'll have lunch," he said, in the tone of a man accustomed to having his summonses obeyed. "I know he's not working, so he can't make that an excuse."

The doors slid back and Virginia stepped into the lift. She could not promise to send Joe to see Spenser. She did not know whether he would go. But even with this doubt, her mind was looking anxiously over his meagre wardrobe, deciding what he could wear to make the best impression.

13

THE Olive Branch was one of the most attractive public-houses in that part of London which lies between Portman Square and Cavendish Square. Pleasantly situated in a quiet cul-de-sac of neat, expensive houses, it was convenient both for the commercial folk of Marylebone High Street, and for the professional medical men who flew their small brass flags of success in the neighbouring streets and squares.

The clientele had once been heterogeneous, but since the war the unassuming little tavern had become increasingly fashionable among the kind of people who liked to refer in a sporty way to Going Round to the Local, and who treated the Olive Branch as a kind of club, so that a labourer who turned in casually for a half pint of bitter might turn quickly out again to seek the more democratic air of the Swan in the High Street.

The Olive Branch was not old, but it was constructed in a cottagey style, with cream-washed walls and a tiled roof, that gave it the air of a village inn in the heart of London. A firm of brewers had built it before the war as a public-house, but it somehow managed to give the informal impression of an ordinary house turned into a pub, like one of those country cottages which have a window pushed out at one side of the porch to turn the parlour into a sweet-shop.

The public and saloon bars were on opposite sides of the flagged entrance passage, and both of them looked like parlours turned into bar-rooms. The windows were small, with small panes and wide sills where tankards could be set down among the geraniums. The walls were panelled half-way up and whitewashed above. Oak beams ran across the low ceilings, and the bars themselves were made of darkened oak, with surfaces deliberately full of splits and knot-holes to give the impression of years of use.

Behind the two front-rooms were a kitchen and a storeroom and upstairs were three small but charming rooms for the landlord. Behind the house was a tiny walled courtyard, with seats made out of beer casks for customers who wished to drink outside in the summer, and an ivy-covered woodshed to supply the mellowed brick fireplaces which added to the cosiness of the two bar-rooms.

It was a snug little berth all right, and Joe congratulated himself that it was his. Well—his and Virginia's, of course. It was her stepfather who had got them the job of managing it for the brewery, but if Joe had not put on such a good show for the old man, he might not have pulled it off.

"Very man to man, I was," he told Virginia. " 'You must realize, my boy,' the old duck kept saying, 'that you are a family man now, with all the responsibility that entails.'

" 'Of course, sir,' I said. I kept calling him sir. He liked that. 'All I want to do is to make a good home for my wife and baby.' I cleared my throat. A little emotional, I was, when I talked about the baby. He seemed to like that too. Then I looked him in the eye, and put on my sincere face."

"What is your sincere face?" Virginia asked.

"Like this." He opened his dark eyes very wide and set his mouth in a straight line. Virginia laughed, and they laughed together, and he hugged and kissed her in the saloon bar, paying no attention to Lennie, who was rubbing up the fireplace with red brick polish.

Lennie was their assistant, a thin, red-haired boy with a face like a freckled wedge, small wondering eyes, and a shortened leg from the infantile paralysis which had condemned him to spend most of his childhood in irons. Barman, pot-boy, maid of all work, he had worked in the Olive Branch since he left school. It meant more to him than his own home, and he knew its working inside out, and knew the names and affairs of all the regular customers, and could advise Joe on who should be tactfully denied credit. Everyone knew him, and knew his name, and gave him presents at Christmas, and tried to buy him drinks, although he was a teetotaller; a broadminded one, however, with an expert's æsthetic appreciation of bottles and shining glasses, which allowed him to be tolerant of those who drank from them.

261

The last landlord, a genial clown, who was largely responsible for developing the popularity of the Olive Branch, had
taught Lennie everything he knew, except how to drink a
quart of beer in one swallow, before he died of a heart attack
half-way between the woodshed and the public bar, carrying
a load of wood on Lennie's day off.

Lennie had loved him. He mourned him deeply, never
ceasing to blame himself for having taken the day off, or for
not having filled the wood-baskets before he took his day
off. Since he had to love the person for whom he worked, he
attached his affection to Virginia. He would do anything for
her, and although he was resentful of Joe, because he could
not forget the jolly, fat man who had died, he tolerated him
because he was Virginia's husband, and helped him in every
way with the running of the public-house.

Joe was a little sickened by the way the boy tagged after
Virginia, with those innocent eyes following her every move.
When she went shopping, he limped after her to carry home
the groceries. If she picked up anything, he took it from her.
If she rested in the daytime, Lennie went dot and carry up
the stairs with cups of tea and vivid sugar cakes from the
bakery on the corner. He called Joe Mr Colonna, but he
called Virginia, more familiarly, Mrs. C., and referred to
the coming baby as Our Baby.

If Joe found Lennie upstairs, bringing sustenance on a
bar-room tray, or asking Virginia if he could run any errands
for her, he shooed him down to his own part of the house.
He did not consider Lennie a man, but he did not want even
the runty, hobbling boy hanging round his wife, and he kept
a sharp eye on the men in the bar if they joked too familiarly
with Virginia.

He had never known that it was possible to feel so
possessive about a woman. With other girls, he had not
cared too much whether they cheated him or not. With most
of them, it was a relief when another man took them off his
hands. It was more fun to look for a new one than to tag
along with the same girl after the first excitement had
degenerated into habit.

With Virginia, however, it was different. The excitement

had never worn off. Even now that she was swollen and clumsy, she still had the power to move him uncontrollably. He would never let her go. No one else must have any part of her, and he was thankful that her mother and stepfather had gone away again and removed the danger of even the slight influence they might have with her. She belonged to him, to Joe Colonna, who had never before owned anything worth having. His desire to possess her utterly made him love her and hurt her at the same time. She was passionate, obedient, faithful, and yet he knew that there was something at the heart of her which he would never possess and master, and it was that tormenting knowledge which compelled him at times to abuse her.

Now that they were at the Olive Branch, they hardly ever fought. Life had suddenly become so good that there was nothing to fight about, except when Joe thought that she was pampering Lennie, or being too familiar with him. Virginia was happy. Joe knew that. Her kitchen and her three sunny rooms upstairs were a palace to her after the dingy little flat. She was preparing for the baby as if it were the only one that had ever been born. As if it were Jesus Christ himself, Joe sometimes told her, but she did not like him to say that.

That was one of the things he could not understand about her. She did not go to church, and she told him that she had never been taught any religion, and yet she believed in things like the Bible, and all the useless fairy-tales about Christmas and Easter, and once he had caught her by the bed saying her prayers. She had scrambled quickly to her feet, bulky in the thin nightdress. When he had asked her what she was praying for, since she now had everything that any girl could want, she had said that she was repeating something her nurse had taught her. *Angel of God, my Guardian dear,* it went. That angel again. Well, it had brought them together in the first place. He must admit that, although it irritated him that it was still roaming about in the corners of her mind. With bloody great wings, no doubt, and a plate on the back of its head, like the ones on the statues in the big Catholic church round the corner, where Joe had wandered in once at the tail-end of a crowd to see somebody getting married.

At first, Virginia helped Joe and Lennie to serve in the bar. She enjoyed that, and Joe was proud of the way she looked and the way she knew how to talk to the classiest customers on their own level. Nevertheless he watched her. Let her never forget which side of the bar she was on. She was on Joe's side. She was in Joe's world, not theirs.

After a while, when the time for the baby drew near, Virginia did not want to show herself any more. "You're too big to get behind the bar, anyway. You're as big as a house," Joe said. He said it in front of Lennie, who cast down his eyes and hurried out of the room. Lennie did not like to hear that kind of talk.

Virginia stayed upstairs and sewed and waited, and packed and unpacked and packed again her bag for the hospital. Joe kept Lennie in the public bar, and ran the saloon bar himself. Not that it made much difference, since the customers wandered from one to the other, but Joe felt that it was only right that the landlord should be in the saloon. Besides, there was that woman, the wife of the man with the hawthorn-hedge moustache, who drove racing cars. She always came into the saloon bar. Ella, her name was. She usually wore pants, and Joe was prepared to stake his life that they were hot ones. Joe looked at her. She looked at him. She did not talk much, but in the old days, he would have taken her up on that look.

Meanwhile, he joked with her husband, and got on the right side of him . . . just in case. No harm to Virginia; but Joe had been faithful to her ever since they were married. If he did not break out some time or other, he would begin to think he was getting queer.

Ella's husband was jovial and friendly. All the people who came into the Olive Branch, unlike the morose beer-suckers in some public-houses, were friendly, accustomed to being on good terms with whoever was behind the bar, ready to buy you a drink if you kept them amused. And you could buy yourself a drink any time of the day, whenever you felt like it, and even fiddle one now and then off the record, if you were careful. It was a good life. It was the first time that Joe had been his own master, or been paid for doing work that he enjoyed. He was happy, confident, and once more full of the old bravado that had been knocked out of him by the squalid, penny-pinching months at Weston House.

When the baby was born, Joe stood drinks on the house for everyone in the bar. The people in the public bar came across the passage to see what the noise was about, and they got free drinks too. Joe was in his element, the centre of attraction, congratulations, and crude masculine jokes. He had not meant the baby to be a girl, but there it was. He decided then and there in the bar to call her Jenny, his mother's name, and he became very sentimental thinking about it. This was a great night for sentiment. People began to buy him drinks, and he leaned his elbow on the bar and thought tenderly of Virginia with her big, exhausted eyes, and her dark hair on her shoulders, clutching the dark, shrivelled baby to her, and begging the nurse not to take it away.

Ella was in the bar without her husband. She seemed amused by the occasion. At closing-time she was still there, looking at Joe, and he knew that it would have been easy to take her upstairs after Lennie had gone. But tonight he was sentimental. Tonight he was the husband and father to end all husbands and fathers, and Ella shrugged her bony shoulders and went out with the rest of the people into the little street that was so quiet until the Olive Branch let out its customers into the warm night.

For a while after Virginia came home, Joe was tender and considerate, delighted with Virginia, and proud of the tiny living thing he had created. Presently his delight in Virginia's achievement was tempered by his realization of the baby's demands on her. His pride in his daughter was less intense when he discovered what it was like to have a new-born baby in the house.

From the start, Jenny was a nervous, difficult baby. She cried a lot, and did not want her feeds, and was always awake when she should have been asleep. Virginia worried about her all the time, and expected Joe to do the same, but after a while he did not want to listen to her worries any more.

"It's bad enough," he said, "to have the kid crying half the night, and you jumping in and out of bed, without having to talk about it all the time. The doctor said there was nothing wrong with her. Why don't you believe that, and stop fussing? You used to be such good fun, Jin. Now you're degenerating into just a mother, like all the rest."

"I am a mother," Virginia said, and it still sounded odd to say it. "How can I help worrying? If she just wouldn't cry so much, it wouldn't be so bad."

"You're telling me," Joe said bitterly. The baby's crying was increasingly on his nerves. Sometimes when he was in the bar, he would listen to the piteous, penetrating sound from above for as long as he could stand, and then he would run up the stairs and shout angrily at Virginia: "For God's sake, can't you keep that child quiet? You'll drive everybody out of here before you're done with it!"

People in the bar would make jokes about the child's crying, which could plainly be heard when there was not a noisy crowd. "Safety-pin trouble?" they would ask, raising their eyes to the ceiling, or: "Why don't you go up and slap the poor little brute on the back?"—manufacturing a belch.

"The kid's all right," Joe would say curtly. Although these were the same people to whom he had boasted when Jenny was born, he now resented their domestic allusions, which seemed to minimize him into the figure of a henpecked father, pacing the floor in the small hours with a yelling baby.

Before the baby was born, Virginia was always waiting quietly for him to come upstairs after the bar closed. Now she nearly always seemed to be busy with the baby. Sometimes when he was upstairs after closing-time, he would grow so irritated by the sight of Virginia anxiously trying to make the baby feed at her breast, that he would fling off downstairs and go out to a club, or spend the rest of the evening drinking by himself in the bar.

Weighing the baby to see how much she had taken, mixing the bottle to supplement the unsuccessful breast-feeding, Virginia would try to puzzle out why Joe felt like that. She had always understood that a man liked to see his wife feeding his baby. Joe hated to see it. He thought that Virginia would spoil her figure. He wanted her body to be all for him, not shared even with their baby. Although the conception of Jenny had satisfied his creative pride, he had never really wanted her. Virginia knew that. Now that Jenny was here, he was jealous of her because she had turned Virginia into part wife, part mother, instead of all wife and lover.

Understanding this, Virginia tried to be extra loving to Joe, so that he should not feel left out of this mysterious, unimagined intimacy between herself and Jenny. She had never known anything like the tenderness she felt towards the restless, difficult child, with the fuzz of black hair and the speck of nose and the mouth that folded so sweetly in slumber, and protested so violently much of the time she was awake. When Virginia held her in her arms, and the tiny, groping hands clutched at her, it seemed almost as though, by the very fact of her beloved existence, the baby were protecting her, instead of she protecting the baby.

Since she could not discuss the baby's ups and downs with Joe, Virginia discussed them with Lennie, who was always ready to listen. If Joe went out during the day, Lennie would often stump up the stairs to hang over the crib and gaze with wonder at the tiny child. He bought impossible presents for her, and would nearly break his heart trying to make the feeble hand grasp a tin trumpet or a golliwog. When Virginia let him pick Jenny up, he would sit motionless on the low chair, his feet carefully planted, his short leg trembling a little, his pointed, freckled face absorbed, holding his breath in tenderness and wonder at the feeling it gave him to have the baby in his arms.

Joe came home one afternoon and found him holding the baby like this while Virginia was downstairs in the kitchen. Jenny had been quiet, staring at Lennie with calmly unfocused eyes. When Virginia heard her cry, she ran upstairs to find that Joe had snatched her away, and was holding her awkwardly, while he snapped at Lennie to get downstairs where he belonged.

Virginia took the baby from him. "Just when we had got

her quiet," she said. "I wish you wouldn't be so rough with her."

"If I can't even hold my own kid," Joe said, "I'd better go downstairs and let this pet nursemaid of yours move in up here."

"Don't talk like that." Virginia frowned at him. Lennie was looking from one to the other, fidgeting and embarrassed. "You'd better go down," Virginia told him. "Thanks for helping me."

Lennie looked at the sobbing baby, and made a little hopeless gesture towards her, as if his hands longed to hold her again. She would often stop crying for him when she would not stop for Virginia.

"Do what you're told," Joe said curtly. "Get downstairs and stay there. I don't want you up here again."

"Yes, Mr Colonna." Lennie did not look at him. "How about the milk then, Mrs C.?" he asked. "You didn't bring it up. Shall I——"

"Get out, I told you!" Joe looked as though he would hit him. "You're working for me, not my wife. Now get downstairs and do your work, before you find yourself out of a job."

Lennie took one last anxious look at Virginia and the baby, and scuttled out of the room.

"You shouldn't be so rough with him," Virginia said, as they heard the irregular thump of Lennie's feet hurrying down the steep stairs. "You scare him when you're like that."

"I'll do more than scare him before I'm through," Joe said. "He drives me crazy always toadying round you. I won't have him coming up here any more—understand?"

"You've said that before," Virginia said, rocking the baby and looking at Joe calmly over the top of the soft, wispy hair, "but I can't stop him coming up here. He's been so good to me, and he does love Jenny."

"Let him have a baby of his own and love that, and leave mine alone," Joe said.

"Oh, he will. He's engaged to a girl called Nancy, didn't you know that? They're going to be married as soon as

Nancy can pluck up the courage to tell her parents. Apparently they don't like poor Lennie."

"Well, neither do I. I don't trust that little weasel. He's the only fly in the ointment around here, as far as I'm concerned."

"You would never have learned to run this place without him," Virginia said.

"Who says I wouldn't? Nothing to it. I can run this pub with one hand tied behind my back. I don't need that snivelling cripple to tell me my business. It was different for the chap before. He wasn't married, but you and I could do this place on our own. You could do the cleaning and the glasses, and you could manage the Public all right."

"But I couldn't leave Jenny for so long." It was the first thing that Virginia thought of, but she knew, even as she said it, that it would annoy him.

"Always the damn baby! Who are you married to—the baby or me? Listen, if I want you downstairs, you'll come downstairs, and if I want to get rid of young Lennie, I'll get rid of him. I'm going to speak to the chap from the brewery next time he comes."

"Joe—you couldn't do that! Why, Lennie would die if he couldn't work here. The Olive Branch is his life."

"Well, keep him downstairs then, or I swear I'll get him fired."

"You couldn't be so mean."

"I could. You've no idea how mean I could be to anyone who starts messing about with my wife."

"Messing about—how ridiculous. As if poor Lennie would ever think of anything like that."

"That's what they all say. He's just a poor, simple boy. He wouldn't think of anything like that. And then one day you come home, and the poor simple boy's pants are on the floor, and the poor, simple boy is in bed with——"

"Oh, stop it," Virginia said wearily. The baby was quiet now, and she went to the crib and laid her down. Instantly, Jenny began to cry again. "Why do you have to be like this?" she asked, with her back to him, leaning over the crib. "We're so happy here, and everything has turned out so

269

well. We've got our chance at last. Why do you have to spoil it by picking quarrels about nothing?"

"God knows." Virginia turned, and saw that his face was not angry any more, but a little sad. "It's just that I see red when I think anyone is trying to muscle in on my property."

"Lennie isn't trying to muscle. He's fond of me, I know, but only as if I was his mother. His mother isn't very nice to him."

"I've heard that one before, too," Joe said, with a grin. "'He loves me like a son,' and the first thing you know, there's incest brewing. Keep him downstairs, Jin," he said, more seriously. "He can stay, if that keeps you happy; but he must stay downstairs."

"All right," she said, "if that's what you want. I want to keep you happy too, you see. I hate it when you're so belligerent."

"You don't hate *it*. You hate me. Isn't that more like it?"

"No, darling." Virginia went to him, and stood close to him. "I love you. You know that."

"Yes." He let out his breath on a long sigh. "If I thought you didn't, I'd kill you." He kissed her fiercely, while the baby whimpered and fretted in the crib behind them.

"That child will never stand the winter," Mrs Batey said, crossing her arms in front of her, lifting up her bosom and letting it drop again. She had come to visit Virginia, bringing with her a huge, cracked leather shopping bag in case she saw any bargains in Marylebone High Street. Mrs Batey never went on an expedition without taking the bag for possible booty. Even the short trip from Weston House to the Olive Branch was an expedition, and might yield a cut-price cauliflower or a set of pig's feet.

In the bag was a dented sponge-cake with the jam oozing out, which she had made for Virginia. "Not that you need it as much as you used, love," she said, looking round the little upstairs room with its bright curtains and pink walls and gay nursery rugs on the floor. "My stars, you have fallen on your feet, and no mistake. A bit different to dear old Weston House. Not that I grudge it to you, love. You deserve it, every bit of it, and perhaps that husband of yours deserves his luck too, if any man ever deserves anything. Running a pub! Edgar will eat his heart out with envy when I tell him about it. 'Wouldn't do for you,' I'll tell him. 'You'd drink up all the profits before a week was out.' "

Jenny had been sleeping when Mrs Batey came, but the raucous laugh induced by the thought of Edgar running a public-house woke her up, and as so often, she announced her awakening by a fretful cry.

Mrs Batey tiptoed weightily to the crib, and leaned over it for a long time making chirping and sucking sounds, before she straightened herself up and announced in the voice of an expert: "That child will never stand the winter."

She did not mean it unkindly. She did not mean to frighten Virginia. It was just a piece of news that was worth giving out because it was sensational.

"What nonsense," Viriginia said, trying not to mind. "There's nothing wrong with her. She has a cold now, that's why she looks so pale."

"Well, you watch her, that's all," Mrs Batey said. "I've seen them come, and I've seen them go, and they sometimes go quicker than they come, that's where it is. I lost my first, you know, at four months. That's a bad time for the little ones, with winter coming on."

"Jenny isn't much more than four months old," Virginia said. "Please don't talk like that, Mrs Batey. I don't like it."

"Have I upset you?" Mrs Batey was amazed. "I wouldn't do that for the world. Don't take it to heart so, love," she said, as Virginia picked up the baby and cuddled her, caressing the back of her neck. "I just said what came into my head, and there I go again, putting my foot in it as usual. Edgar says I'll rise up out of my box at the funeral and speak out of turn to the preacher." Her laugh made Jenny jump and quiver a little in Virginia's arms.

"Let me hold her," Mrs Batey said. She took Jenny and sat down with her, making a wide lap, and settling the baby into the crook of her arm as naturally as a violinist tucks his fiddle under his chin. She ducked her head and clucked her tongue and made hideous grimaces, which Jenny accepted passively.

"You see, she's all right," Virginia said nervously. "She's not crying now. I'm sure she's all right."

Mrs Batey pursed her lips and shook her head. "Not strong," she whispered out of the side of her mouth, as if Jenny could understand.

"The doctor said I would have to be careful of her this winter, keeping her warm, and out of draughts, and that sort of thing, but he would have told me if there was anything wrong with her."

"Doctors tell what suits them," Mrs Batey said with a sniff. "Don't they, little love?" she enquired of Jenny. "She's a little love, that's what she is." She began to cluck and grimace again. "Looks just like my poor little Maurice though. He fell away to nothing at the end."

Virginia changed the subject, asking Mrs Batey about the people at Weston House. She was worried enough already about Jenny, without having her anxiety fed by Mrs Batey's tales of horror. Mrs Batey gossiped happily and slanderously on for an hour, until Joe came up from the storeroom, where he had been stocktaking with Lennie. He greeted Mrs Batey civilly enough, and asked her what she thought of Jenny.

"She's a little beauty," Mrs Batey said, "just like her mother. Frail though. My stars, she's frail. I've been telling Virginia, she's got to watch her now that the raw weather is settling in."

"Don't go filling her up with that stuff," Joe said impatiently. "She fusses enough as it is. There's nothing wrong with the baby. She's as strong as a horse. Got my constitution." He never would admit that Jenny was in anything but the rudest of health.

As if to contradict him, Jenny coughed, a dry, painful cough that pushed her body forward in Mrs Batey's arms.

"That doesn't sound too good," Mrs Batey said sharply.

"That's nothing," Joe said. "She's got a cold. Everyone coughs when they have a cold."

Virginia said nothing. Jenny had been coughing like that for two days. Each time the tiny chest jerked, she felt a

272

constriction in her own chest, and sometimes she even found herself clearing her throat, as if she could relieve the child herself. She fetched the bottle from the pan of hot water and taking the baby from Mrs Batey, sat down and tried to make Jenny take her milk. At the first suck, Jenny began to cough again. Virginia sat her up until the spasm ceased, but when she laid her back and put the bottle to her mouth, the choking cough started again.

"Sounds croupy," Mrs Batey said. "I don't like it. You'd ought to get the doctor to her."

"I thought about it," Virginia looked at Joe, remembering the morning's argument, "but I don't like to bother him for nothing."

"That's his funeral," Mrs Batey said. "What's a doctor for? Not to sit all day filling out forms for the National Health."

"And not to be pestered by hysterical women," Joe said. "Jenny's greedy, that's all. You women love to make a fuss about nothing. If I went for my beer like a baby goes for its bottle, I'd choke too, only no one would fuss about me. Look here, Mrs Batey, I wish you'd stop trying to put the wind up Virginia."

Mrs Batey tucked some descending hair back under her hat, buttoned up her coat, which gaped in the middle where there was no button, picked up the shopping-bag and said: "That child is ill, young man, and if you can't see it, you're blinder than I thought you were."

She snapped her mouth shut at him, rattling her false teeth. She had never liked Joe. In the days when she had darned his socks and ironed his shirts, she had only done it for Virginia, and Virginia had often imagined how much pleasure it must have given her to rip her murderous flat-iron through one of his shirt buttons and split it in two.

"Must you go? Too bad you can't stay and see the child die in convulsions," Joe said sarcastically.

Mrs Batey ignored him and went to clap Virginia on the shoulder with her work-grained hand. "I must be running along," she said. "I've got some shopping to do. I promised the kids I'd try and pick up a rabbit. Bye-bye for now, love.

Come back and see us soon. We often talk about you at the flats."

"You'll have plenty to tell them now, won't you?" Joe said, opening the door to hasten her out.

Mrs Batey walked to the door, stopped in front of him in her shapeless hat and her worn, gaping coat, and looked at him as disdainfully as if she were a queen. "I'll tell them that your wife is worried sick, and that you haven't the sense or the decency to help her, if you like," she said, and swept out, trailing the shopping-bag thump, thump after her down the stairs.

The next day, Jenny's cough was worse. "I'm going to call the doctor," Virginia said, starting downstairs for the bar.

Joe followed her. "You've let that old trout scare you," he said. "Sickness and death are her favourite subjects. Why do you listen to her?"

"She ought to know about babies. She's had five—six with the one that died. But it isn't only Mrs Batey. I can see that Jenny isn't well, even though I haven't had six babies. You only need one to be a mother. Please go back and stay with her, Joe, while I telephone. She's breathing so badly, I don't think she ought to be left."

"For God's sake." He leaned against the doorway of the saloon bar, while Virginia went behind the bar to the telephone. "Nothing is going to happen in five minutes."

"I keep remembering what Mrs Batey said. They sometimes go quicker than they come. I can't get it out of my mind. Please, Joe—think I'm silly if you like—but please go up to her."

"I'll go if you like." Lennie came into the passage from the other bar with a broom in his hand. "Nothing wrong with our baby, is there?"

His anxious face looked past Joe through the doorway, but Joe pushed him back and said: "Nothing's wrong. You keep out of this."

"Can I just run upstairs and see her?" Lennie asked.

"No."

"But I can hear her coughing. That little cough does something to me, Mr Colonna——"

274

"Oh, shut up." To silence him, Joe went upstairs, shutting the door of the room with such a loud bang that Virginia had to ask the doctor to repeat what he was saying.

When she finished telephoning, Lennie had crept up to the other side of the bar. He leaned his arms on it, stringy and thin with the sleeves rolled up. He twisted his fingers. "Mrs C.——" he began, not looking at her.

"What is it, Lennie? Don't worry about Jenny. She'll be all right."

"Oh, I hope so. I pray for her every night," he said. "Honest. I pray for you too, Mrs C." He raised his eyes.

"Well—that's nice," Virginia said uncomfortably, "but I don't really need praying for."

"Oh, yes, you do," Lennie said earnestly. "But that's not what I wanted to say. I wanted to ask you"—he dropped his eyes again—"Nancy's people are coming to town tomorrow night. She lives with her aunt, you know. They're coming to see her, just for the one night. After that, they'll be off back to Chelmsford, because they can't leave the shop."

He paused. Virginia could hear Joe walking about upstairs. What was he doing? Was something wrong? She could not wait to get back to Jenny.

"It's like this." Lennie took a deep breath. "They're not in favour of me and Nancy going together, as I told you. We want to get engaged. Not secret, like we are now, but right out in front of everyone, so Nancy can wear the ring and that. She wears it round her neck now." He paused again, thinking tenderly of Nancy's neck. "They don't really know me, you see. They've got no call to object, but it's just that they don't know anything about me. I wondered, could you—could you—oh, no." He took his arms off the bar and turned away dispiritedly. "Of course you couldn't."

"Couldn't what?" Virginia came round the end of the bar and took his arm. "What do you want me to do, Lennie? You want me to go and speak to Nancy's parents—is that it?"

"Oh, Mrs C., you are clever." Lennie's eyes combed her

with admiration. "How did you guess it? That's exactly it. What do you think of it, eh?"

"Tomorrow." Virginia hesitated. "I don't see how I could leave Jenny."

"We thought of that, Nancy and I. I mean, even when we didn't know she was poorly, but knowing how much you thought of her and that. You could go after closing-time, we thought, when Mr Colonna was free to be with the baby. Best to go after supper, anyway. People are always more reasonable then."

"I don't know, Lennie." Virginia struggled with herself. Of course, Jenny would be all right with Joe, but suppose . . . suppose . . . a dozen suppositions raced through her mind as she stood looking at Lennie in his yellowed white shirt with the long apron tied twice about his meagre waist. She had never left the baby with Joe for longer than it took her to hurry to the shops. Perhaps that was her mistake. Perhaps now, when Jenny needed care, was the time to start letting him be a father.

If it were any time but now! But Lennie had said it was now or never, and his eyes were on her, ready to light up in hope, or turn away in defeat.

"All right," she said, and saw his eyes light up. "I'll try for you. How will I find the place?"

"It isn't far. Just up Euston way. Nancy can come round here and fetch you," Lennie said, talking more confidently. "And she'll see you home. We've got it all worked out. We've talked it over and over. Nancy said you'd never do it. 'You don't know Mrs C.,' I said. 'She'll do it.' And"—his eyes were big with the wonderment of being proved right—"you've gone and said you would."

Virginia went back upstairs to wait for the doctor. When he came, he said that Jenny had pneumonia, and after he had said it and left, as if his words had dealt her a blow, Jenny began to get worse. By the following day she was very pale, and her lips were dusky. Her breathing was quick and distressed, with a queer guttural sound at the end of each expiration.

"Respiratory grunt. That's perfectly normal," the cheerful

young doctor said, too cheerful, too impersonal to calm Virginia's fears. "She'll do for now. We'll see how she goes. Don't worry."

Don't worry! Virginia stood at the top of the stairs and watched him run briskly down, clap on his hat, a smaller, more becoming version of Felix's black homburg, and swing out through the front door. How could he tell her not to worry? Didn't he know it was her baby?

She went back to look at Jenny. Even in the few moments when Virginia had been saying good-bye to the doctor, the baby's breathing seemed to have become more laboured. As well as the little grunting expiration, there was now an occasional gasp as she drew in her shallow breaths, as if the effort to get enough air were becoming more painful.

All day Virginia watched her baby fighting its lonely, preoccupied battle for oxygen. Jenny's lips were blue, and her skin like wax. Her tiny little face was pinched and sucked in at the cheeks, and from time to time she wrung Virginia's heart with a gasping, struggling cry, as if she were pleading for help in her pitiful fight for air.

Joe called the doctor three times, and when he came at last, the baby had grown suddenly better. She was sleeping. Her breathing was easier, and her face was growing flushed under the damp black hair, matted closely to her perspiring head.

"Don't worry," the doctor said again, and Virginia felt that he did not believe her description of how bad the day had been. Once more she watched him skipping down the stairs, always in a hurry to get on to the next patient. Once more she turned back into the room where Jenny lay, and went straight to the crib to reassure herself that the baby was still asleep, because she knew now how quickly the changes could come.

Joe was standing on the other side of the crib, his hands in his pockets, his face gentle with a tenderness she had never seen there before for Jenny. "Poor little devil," he said. "You don't realize how you feel about them until they're sick."

Virginia had heard people say that about dogs. It was

not much for a father to say, but coming from Joe, it was enough for her.

When evening came, she had to decide what she was going to do about Lennie. She heard his footstep on the stair, so different from Joe's springy tread, and she went out on to the little landing to stop him coming up. Jenny was still asleep. She did not want Joe shouting up the stairs after Lennie tonight.

Lennie stood below her, leaning forward with one hand on the stair-rail and the other on the wall, looking up at her with anxious eyes. "How about it, Mrs C.?" he asked in a raucous whisper.

"She's still sleeping," Virginia said. "I don't know what I ought to do."

"I shouldn't ask you to go out, should I? Oh, well, it doesn't matter." He took his hand from the rail, and with his back against the wall, dropped one foot disconsolately down to the stair below. "Nancy's here already," he said. "She didn't want to be late. But I'll tell her to go home." He dropped down another stair, sliding his shoulders against the wall. His head was forward and his eyes looked at nothing. Virginia was stricken by the thought that she might be ruining his whole life.

"No—wait," she said. "I'll go with Nancy. I promised you, didn't I? I'm not going back on that."

Lennie's head jerked quickly up towards her. "But the baby?"

"She'll be all right with my husband. She'll sleep, I think," Virginia said, more to convince herself than him.

"I'll go and tell Nancy to wait." Lennie turned and hobbled swiftly down the stairs, looking up when he reached the bottom to flash up at Virginia a vast, adoring grin.

Virginia went down to tell Joe that she had decided to go out and plead for Lennie. When she had told him about it before, he had not liked it. He would not like it any better now. "I thought you were so worried about the baby," he would say, and she would never be able to explain to him how much she hated to go, but how clearly she knew that she must go.

278

Joe was talking to the girl in slacks with the long, straight, blonde hair. Ella, her name was. Her husband was in the other room. Virginia could hear his penetrating, inane laugh. Ella stood by herself at the bar, turning a glass round and round in her predatory hands and talking quietly to Joe.

Virginia went behind the bar. "What is it?" Joe asked impatiently.

Virginia looked at Ella. Ella did not move, so she drew Joe away and talked to him in a low voice. Joe protested, as she knew he would: "I thought you were so worried about the baby."

"I am, but she seems all right now, and this may be Lennie's last chance."

"Lennie, Lennie," he grumbled. "I swear you care more about that simpleton than your own child."

Virginia tried to make him understand, while Ella looked at them out of the corner of her long eyes, with a smile flickering at the corner of her unchaste mouth. Joe was argumentative and a little excited, as if he had been drinking. Ella had probably been buying him drinks. Virginia knew that she did, just as she knew that Ella came to the Olive Branch to see Joe; but there was nothing Virginia could do about it, except hope for the best.

If the best did not happen, she was prepared to fight Ella, just as she had fought Mollie Mortimer, and been thrown out of the Chelsea house for doing it. She would not fight Joe. If he could find it possible to be unfaithful to her, their whole relationship would disintegrate into pieces that could never be put together; but she would fight any woman who tried to make that happen.

After Virginia had gone out, hurrying round the corner with the square, florid girl who looked much too robust for Lennie, Joe sat upstairs for a while listening to the baby's quick, shallow breathing. From time to time he glanced into the crib. Jenny was not so flushed any more. She looked washed out, as if she had been through an exhausting ordeal.

Poor little devil. When she was older, Joe would tell her

about this, and how he had watched over her hour after hour. Well—he looked at the clock—actually only half an hour, but it felt like hours. Hours since he had had a drink. No harm in going down to the bar for a little while. He had promised Virginia that he would not leave the room, but Virginia was hysterical about the baby, and much too nervous. He had never known her like this.

After the argument in the bar, Ella had said, smiling to herself: "She's really got you where she wants you, hasn't she?"

"Don't you believe it," Joe had said, pressing his hands on the bar with a gesture that showed the strength of his arms. "It's quite the other way about."

"Oh——" Ella nodded seriously, although you could never tell whether she was serious, or laughing at you. "Big he-man stuff. I see." She continued to gaze at him reflectively while he poured her a drink, and poured one for himself at her suggestion.

That drink had been the last of several he had had in the bar that evening. The sensation was wearing off. It was necessary to recapture it by going down to the bar and taking up where he had left off. He looked at the baby again. She seemed to be all right. He put his hand into the crib, and the tiny clammy hand closed weakly round his finger.

His Jenny. What was it Virginia had said? *They sometimes go quicker than they come.* Joe picked up the child with the blanket wrapped round her and carried her downstairs. In the saloon bar, he put two cushions on the high-backed settee by the fire, prodded and fed the fire into a blaze, and sat down at the other side of the fireplace with a bottle of whisky to muse and drink and watch over his tiny daughter. Jenny woke once and cried a little, and coughed feebly, as if her chest muscles were too tired to cough properly. Joe took a drop of whisky on his finger and put it in her mouth. She sucked, swallowed, opening her eyes in surprise, then moved her lips in and out like a querulous old woman, and fell asleep again.

The wooden pendulum clock on the wall behind the bar struck the half hour, and Joe tipped the end of the bottle into his glass, drank it, and stood up. He had not realized how late it was. He must get the baby upstairs before Virginia came back. She would find him dozing in a chair in the baby's room. When she kissed him, as she always did when she left home or came back, she would know that he had been drinking—but so what? Jenny would be safely asleep in her crib, and if a man could not have a drink in his own home, things were, as Ella had implied, coming to a pretty pass.

He picked up the baby bundled in the blanket, and hurried to the door. How light and helpless she felt, sleeping like that in his arms. Perhaps there was something to be said for tiny babies after all. Like puppies, they were so hopelessly dependent that they made you feel—what was it he felt for Jenny? Could you love a creature like this who could not love you back? As he started up the stairs, he glanced down at the crumpled face, missed his step, stumbled, clutched at the stair-rail, and felt the baby slip from his arms.

Like a doll, she fell to the bottom step, rolled to the floor and lay in a bundle on the stone flags.

Cold with panic, Joe picked her up and looked at her. She did not look any different. Her eyes were still closed, and she was not crying. How much could a baby take, for God's sake?

Not that much. Not being dropped down a staircase on to a stone floor. When Virginia came home and ran to the crib, the baby was dead.

14

"I HAVEN'T been here for months," the man in the dark grey overcoat was saying as he came into the bar. "There used to be an amusing chap who ran it, but he died. Now, I believe —Virginia!"

Virginia turned round with a bottle of brandy in her hand, and saw Felix standing with another man on the other side of the bar. Felix looked as if he had been hit in the stomach. It took a moment before he could recover enough to say: "What are you doing here?"

"I work here." Virginia was surprised to see Felix, but she did not know whether she was pleased to see him or not. The last few weeks had exhausted all emotion. Tired and inert, half stupefied sometimes from lack of sleep, she was not capable of finding pleasure or displeasure in anything. "What can I get you to drink?" she asked.

"Never mind that for a moment. Tell me—oh, excuse me, Chris. You want a sherry, don't you?"

While Virginia poured it, Felix introduced the other man, who was tubby and polished, with clean hands and a good haircut, like Felix. "Not Miss Martin," Virginia said. "Mrs. Colonna. My husband and I run this place. Joe is in the other bar tonight. You must meet him, Felix."

"Oh, yes," Felix said quickly, sounding too eager in his effort not to appear dismayed. "Yes, I'd like that very much. I didn't know you were married. Congratulations, Virginia." His mouth twisted into his charming, crooked smile, but his eyes stared at Virginia unhappily. Chris looked at Felix, shrugged his fleshy shoulders, and took his sherry over to the fire, where he picked up a newspaper and turned his back.

It was early in the evening. There were only two other people in the bar, talking at a table by the window. Virginia and Felix were left facing each other, trying to think what to say. "Do you want a gin and french?" Virginia asked.

"Pretty good memory." His crooked smile was more natural this time, and a little rueful. "I'm glad there's one thing you haven't forgotten about me."

"I haven't forgotten anything about you." Virginia made her words brisk, because with Joe across the passage, she did not like the sentiment in Felix's voice. "It's good to see you again. I thought I might, because I knew you had a consulting-room somewhere round here."

"I don't go to pubs much," Felix said, watching her while she mixed his drink. "I only came in tonight because Chris wanted to. Lucky chance for me, but perhaps"—how well she remembered that hopeful, humble look—"perhaps you'd rather I didn't come in again."

"Heavens, no, why shouldn't you? What difference does it make? I'm married."

"You don't have to rub it in."

"Do you mind?" Virginia felt a little irritated. He had no right to mind. Just because he had once wanted to marry her, he could not expect her not to marry anyone else.

"Of course I mind. What do you expect? Do you think that when I went away from the mews and we agreed not to meet that I ever forgot about you for one minute? I'm sorry, Virginia. I shouldn't have said that. I'm sorry."

"There you go again," Virginia said, trying to relieve the situation with a shaky joke, "apologizing. Remember how I used to jump on you for apologizing before you'd ever said anything?"

"Yes. You didn't like that." He smiled, and looked more at ease. "I'm sorry. I mean, I'm sorry I said I was sorry. You still don't like it. You haven't changed at all."

"Yes, I have. I'm quite different. Let me get you another drink." He had finished the first one quickly, drinking it in nervous sips. "Here, have this one on the house."

"It sounds so funny to hear you say that. I can't get used to you on that side of the bar."

"I'm used to it. We've been here some time. I like to work in the bar. It gives me something to do." Something to pass the time. Opening and closing hours to mark the passage of the day. People to talk to automatically, talking without thought, scarcely hearing what they said, or what she said to them, managing somehow to talk normally, and even to make jokes, to keep the misery that pressed always at the back of her brain from crowding forward and engulfing her.

"What's the matter?" Felix asked quietly, looking at her over his glass. "Is something the matter?"

"Of course not." She was afraid of succumbing to the sympathy in his voice. "Why should there be?"

"I'm sorry," he said, "if you don't want to talk about it."

"There's nothing to talk about." Virginia turned away to serve the man who came over with two glasses from the table by the window.

When he had gone, Felix said: "Even if I weren't a doctor, I know you well enough to tell that you're in pretty poor shape. You're still lovely, Virginia. You'll always be that to me, but I'm not so blind that I can't see how bad you look."

"Thanks. That's very flattering."

"Don't take it that way. I said you were lovely, though I probably shouldn't, with your husband in the next room." He glanced behind him, as if he expected to see an irate husband come storming in with his sleeves rolled up. "But lovely or not, you're ill, my dear."

"No. I'm not sleeping very well just now, that's all."

"Why not?"

"Don't cross-examine me. I'm not in your consulting-room." But suddenly, it seemed as if she were, and as if Felix were more a doctor than a rejected suitor. He was looking at her with his head lowered and his eyes raised and steady, one eyebrow slightly lifted as he said again: "Why aren't you sleeping?" and waited for her answer.

Virginia looked at Chris. He was reading on the seat by the fire with his short legs stuck out and his polished toe-caps turned up. "Felix," she said, "I lost my baby. I had a baby, and she died."

Her hands were lying on the top of the bar. Felix reached across and put his hands on hers for a moment. He did not say anything. She was grateful for that. She did not want him to talk. She wanted him to listen. "It was pneumonia," she went on, finding it easier to talk now that the first words

284

were out and she had managed them without tears. "She was very bad. Then she got better. One night, I had to go out. She was sleeping when I left, and when I got back, she was dead. She died of pneumonia. That's what the doctor said. He said it could happen suddenly like that."

Felix nodded, and waited to see if she was going to say any more. Then he said: "There's no need to tell me how you feel. When a woman loses her baby, and especially her first—I know what it does to her. There will be other babies though, Virginia. You're so young."

"I don't know. I don't think Joe wants any more. We haven't talked about it, but I think that's how he feels. He won't talk about Jenny, even. That's one of the worst things. We—there isn't much to talk about, if we can't talk about her, because she's what we're both thinking about."

Felix let this pass. He did not want to hear about Virginia's husband. "You're not sleeping, you say?" He slipped easily into a clinical manner. "Headaches? Mm-hm. Nausea at times? No appetite? Yes ... yes. ... That can all come with not sleeping, plus, of course, your state of mind. You haven't seen a doctor, I suppose? No, I thought not. That's just like you—try to battle it out on your own. But you've seen one now, my dear, whether you like it or not, and he can help you. He can help you to sleep, at any rate. That's what you need. How useless to think you can fight a tragedy like that without sleep. Women are the devil. They drive themselves stubbornly into breakdowns, and then come running to the doctor for help when it's much too late."

"I didn't come running to you," Virginia said. "You came to me. You can save the lectures for your rich hypochondriacs. But I'll take the sleeping pills."

"I think I've got something in my car. Wait just a minute."

Virginia hoped that Joe would not come into the bar before Felix returned. There would have to be introductions. Joe would size Felix up, put two and two together, and realize that this was the doctor Virginia had told him about, the one who had wanted to marry her. Afterwards there would be questions, explanations, possibly a quarrel. There had been more quarrels since Jenny died. Joe was edgy, often

285

morose, ready to take offence at nothing, sullenly defensive at any mention of the baby's death, as if it could possibly have been his fault.

Could it have been his fault? She must never think that. How could it have been his fault? That was better. It could have happened even if Virginia had not gone out. The doctor had said that. And yet she knew that she would never forgive herself for leaving the baby with Joe.

"Phenobarbital," Felix said, coming back with a package. "Take one tablet. If that's not enough, it's all right to take two. Don't take the lot though." He grinned, to show her that was a joke, but the grin was an anxious one, betraying what was in his mind.

For a moment, Virginia examined the idea of taking the whole box of pills. It was such an impossible idea that it was possible to allow herself to think of it. You heard of women doing it. Almost every day you could read in the newspaper of unhappy women taking an overdose of sleeping pills, and you always wondered why they did not realize that that was not the solution. If everything else had been taken from you, how illogical it was to destroy the one thing you had left—yourself.

That night she slept badly, as usual. The next day, when the Olive Branch closed after lunch, Joe went out and Virginia decided to take the phenobarbital and sleep all afternoon.

She lay down on the bed without bothering to take off her dress, swallowed the tablet, and waited for the mercy of oblivion. After a while, her head ceased to ache. She felt more peaceful, but she was nowhere near sleep. She closed her eyes, but to keep them closed was an effort, when it should have been an effort to keep them open, if the pill was doing any good. She took another—Felix had said it was all right— and when she found herself still staring miserably at the opposite wall, she reached over for another tablet, then lay back again and let her thoughts wander, hoping that they would wander her away into unconsciousness.

Her thoughts were all of Jenny. All the time, it was only Jenny—coughing so pitifully, struggling for breath with those pinched cheeks and that anguished little cry, sleeping finally in damp exhaustion, with the thin, dark hair plastered on the veined skull. The picture of the sleeping baby was so vivid that Virginia almost got up and went into the next room to look into the crib.

But the crib was not there any more. She remembered Joe carrying it down the stairs. What had they done with it? They had given it to somebody's sister, who was going to have a baby. There was always somebody's sister. Betty's sister, who had left all the tins and rags and paper in the flat at Weston House. . . . Tiny's sister, watching the television. . . . Miss Sunderland's sister, waiting in Kensington High Street . . . always somebody's sister, to take away the crib. The crib had gone. She saw in her mind the place where it had stood on the pink-and-white rug, and without it, she could not recapture the picture of the sleeping baby. Other pictures were in the way, fleeting impressions that came and went in Virginia's heavy head, wavering, unreal, punctuated by words that were as loud as if they were shouted, yet as fantastic as if they had never been spoken.

Mrs Batey's face, affectionate, coarse, the pores like orange-peel. *"They go quicker than they come."* Who had said that? Was it Joe? Joe, standing at the side of the crib in that familiar position with his hands in his pockets and his chin thrust forward. *"They go quicker than they come,"* he said, in Mrs Batey's voice.

Why was Joe laughing? Why was he grinning like that, with his teeth so white and his eyes so gay? He looked like a faun. Now he was gone, spinning away in her spinning head that was spinning her down, down into the bed—what bed? What room? This wasn't Weston House. The walls receded as she fell down into the bed, through the bed into the wheeling dreams of space, while the voices beat their echoes into her ears.

The echoes of Big Ben striking New Year's Eve . . . bong . . . bong. . . . *"I'm sorry,"* Felix said, as he took his mouth from hers. No, it was the doctor. His little moustache was brown and close-clipped, like a new doormat. *"I'm sorry,"* he said. *"I'll have to take her away."* He was holding Jenny. He

287

had her wrapped up so that Virginia could not see her face. Let me see! Let me see! she called out, but she could not hear her voice. The doctor could not hear. He carried Jenny away without turning round. The stripes on his coat met exactly in the back seam as he went away, hiding Jenny with his broad back.

Where had he taken her? Virginia struggled to remember. Joe was holding her back to keep her from following. He was pulling at her shoulders. She must go quickly before it was too late. Let me go! She broke free and sat up. No one was holding her. She was alone in the room, shivering on the bed.

She threw off the blanket and put her feet down to the floor. Her legs were as unreal as if she had been in bed for months. Her mouth was dry and her head was light and empty. She went to the door with her hands out to feel where the door was. Down the stairs carefully, holding the rail with both hands, her feet dropping from step to step without feeling where she trod.

Where was she going? Out into the street. The air was cold on her bare arms. It stung her into purpose. She was going to get Jenny, who was out here somewhere, waiting to be found.

Virginia ran down the street with her hair flying, crossed through traffic, dreamily aware that cars were close. She ran into a man, staggered, pushed him out of the way and went on. Into the High Street, turn to the left. This was the way she always took Jenny in her pram. She must have gone home without her. How careless. Jenny would be crying, waiting in her pram, and it was cold. Which shop? Which shop had she been to? They all looked familiar, but uncannily familiar, like places glimpsed once in a dream.

She hurried desperately up the High Street with the wind whipping at her dress and her hands turning to ice. People looked at her, and a woman spoke to her, but Virginia ran on, leaving them far behind.

She stopped suddenly, and let out her breath with a gasp of relief. There was the pram, just as she knew it would be, outside the post office. No time to wheel it home. Too cold.

She must get home. She must get Jenny home before she coughed again. With a little crooning cry of love, she picked up the baby and hurried home with it across the road, away from the crowd, into the quiet street and quickly through her own front door. Was it the right door? Yes, here was Lennie, coming into the passage in his long apron, with his eyes full of wonder and his mouth agape.

Virginia went towards the fire and sat down. The baby was asleep. She hugged it to her, her arms relieved at last of the long ache of holding nothing. She laid her cheek on the woollen shawl which covered its tiny head, and was at peace.

Lennie was standing in front of her. "You see?" Virginia smiled up at him. "I did find her. I told you I would."

"Where did you get that baby?" Lennie . . . Lennie? Virginia frowned at him, narrowing her eyes to try to bring him into focus. It was not like Lennie to speak so sharply.

"Where did you get that baby?"

Why couldn't he leave her alone? "In the street," she said vaguely. She felt suddenly too tired to talk or move any more. "Please go away." She closed her eyes. She would sit here by the fire with the baby, just holding her like this until the heavy, clouded feeling left her and it was safe to go upstairs.

"Mrs C.—what's the matter? You're not well." Why was Lennie's voice so high and squeaky? Virginia opened her eyes, and saw that his narrow jaw was trembling and his eyes as round as marbles. He was holding out his hands. "Give me the baby," he said, in that queer, high voice. Then he swallowed and said quietly, soothing her as if she were an idiot: "Please let me hold the baby. I'll mind her for a bit. You stay there and keep quiet, while I—oh, crumbs," he said. "Oh, crumbs."

"I do feel very tired," Virginia mumbled. She put her head against the hard, high back of the seat and scarcely felt it when Lennie took the baby from her arms. "Look after her, won't you, Lennie?" Her voice was thick and clumsy. She was not even sure if she had said the words right.

"You bet, Mrs C." His face blurred and wavered in front of her. Was he leaning forward to look at her, or was she peering at him? He held Jenny nicely. Cosily, like a mother. She drifted away from him into sleep.

Joe was shaking her. She struggled out of sleep with a splitting headache, and blinked at him, feeling the seat with the palms of her hands. What was she doing here? She sat up slowly and winced. Her back and shoulders were stiff, and one of her legs was numb. She leaned forward to rub it. "I must have dozed off," she said. "What time is it?"

"Five o'clock. I've just got back. How long have you been here?"

"I don't know. I went to sleep. I'm still not awake, I think."

Joe pulled her to his feet. She stood limply in his arms, leaning against him, savouring his strength and the familiar smell of his skin. "Come up to bed," he said. "You're fagged out. Come up and I'll put you to bed. Lennie and I can manage without you tonight."

Lennie? As Joe helped her up the stairs, she saw a picture of Lennie holding a baby, his long apron hanging down under the bundle of baby as if he were a nurse. She sat down on the bed and looked at her hands. How extraordinary that her hands could remember so clearly the soft, warm feel of wool. A woollen shawl wrapped round a baby.

She looked up at Joe. "I had a dream," she said. "I dreamed I found Jenny. I was holding her—then Lennie was. It was quite vivid."

"Forget it," he said briefly. He laid her down on the bed, and pulled the covers over her.

"How can I?" She lay on her back and looked up at him. I've had dreams like that before, but never so real. It must have been the dope. I don't even remember going down-stairs."

"What dope?"

"A doctor gave me some."

The box was on the table. Joe put it in his pocket. "No more of that," he said, "if you're going to sleep-walk all over the pub. I didn't know you'd been to see a doctor."

"I haven't. It was just that—oh, never mind." She turned her head to one side. "I want to go to sleep."

Joe stood and looked at her for a moment. "Lucky devil," he said, "wallowing in bed, while I have to go down and work all evening. Women have it easy all the way."

Virginia did not answer. She was falling into sleep. She was not sure whether Joe had said that, or whether she had dreamed it, but it sounded so exactly like Joe that he must have said it.

When she went downstairs much later to find something to eat, Lennie was in the kitchen, washing glasses. He turned from the sink and wiped his bony, freckled hands on his apron.

"Feeling better, Mrs C.?" he asked. "Are you all right?"

"I've been asleep, that's all. I wasn't ill."

"Weren't you?" He stared at her. "Yes, you were. You were ever so queer, Mrs C. Don't you remember?"

"Remember what? Did something happen, Lennie?"

"Did something happen!" He swallowed, opened his mouth for a moment while he sought for words, and then stumblingly, apologetically, he told her what she had done.

At first she could not believe it, and then she began to remember. So it was not a dream about the woollen shawl, and holding the baby. She remembered being in the street, and being so cold. "Did I really do that? It's impossible. It's the kind of thing crazy women do—not women like me. Lennie, how could I—Lennie!" She clutched his arm. "Where is the baby? What did you do with the baby? We must take it to the police. The poor mother must be frantic. My God, what will they do to me? Will they put me in gaol?"

"Don't worry." Lennie cocked his head proudly on his stringy neck. "You won't go to gaol. I fixed it up. I didn't let you down, Mrs C. I guessed what must have happened, knowing how low in your mind you were. I saw in a film once where a girl did something like that. So I took the baby round to the Catholic church, and said I'd found it in a telephone box. I gave it to one of the priests there. He knows me. I've passed the time of day with him on the street. You know the way they'll talk to anybody. He took the baby quite natural, just like he was going to christen it, or something. Didn't ask no questions. He wasn't even surprised. They're used to things like that, you see."

"Does my husband know?"

"Not him. I wouldn't tell him," Lennie said scornfully. "No, this is just a secret between you and me. No one will ever know."

"Thank you," Virginia said. "I don't know how to thank you."

"Don't mention it, Mrs C." Lennie picked up a glass and began to polish it, holding it up to the light to see it shine back into his proudly shining eyes. "You done something pretty big for me and Nancy. Now at last I've been able to do something for you."

∗ 15 ∗

SINCE the death of the baby, Joe was drinking more heavily. He was morose, sometimes violent, brutally passionate at times, at others ignoring Virginia, and wanting only to be left alone.

He became unpredictable with the customers. They did not like that. Some of them had never liked him particularly, but now even the ones who liked him were growing irritated by never knowing whether they were going to find him sober. A landlord who drinks and is convivial is one thing. A landlord who drinks and may gratuitously insult you or your guests is quite another.

People began to stay away from the Olive Branch. Some of the regulars were missing for days on end, and when they did come in, they would eye Joe warily to see what kind of a mood he was in. Ella did not come any more, although her husband sometimes rolled cheerily in without her. This should have been a relief to Virginia, but it was not, because she thought she knew why Ella did not come. Joe stayed out all one night, and it was after that that there was no more Ella with her curtain of blonde hair and her long, sly eyes. She had got what she wanted. There was no need to come seeking it any more.

Desolate as she was in the loss of Jenny, Virginia now had to contend with her increasing anxiety about Joe. She had no idea what to do with him. When he was drunk, she could do nothing with him. She could not reason with him and she could not control him. He either laughed at her or swore at her. His drinking pushed him away from her into a separate life, whose only contact with her was to fight her or make love to her, either of which usually ended for her in pain or humiliation.

When he was sober, she could do nothing, because she dared not jeopardize whatever was normal in their relationship by giving him the chance to quarrel. She wanted to show him what was happening to their marriage, so that between them they could stop it before it was too late. She wanted to show him that he was losing customers, and that they would lose their chances of staying at the Olive Branch if he went on like this. She knew that he was not paying for all the drinks he took. He might be clever enough with the book-keeping to disguise it for a time, but sooner or later their employers would find out, and it would be the end. But if she ever tried to tell him these things, he would leap into a quarrel, and a quarrel had only one ending for Joe nowadays. No loving reconciliations or sweet repentance; only the sour and deceitful consolation of the whisky bottle.

Virginia could only wait and hope that time would bring him back to her. Each time they quarrelled, each time he was drunk or violent, she thought that she could not endure it any more. But she had to endure it. There was nothing else to do. Whatever Joe did, whatever he was, she was committed to him, and by something more than duty. There were times when she did not know whether she loved him any more, and yet this bond that held her to him was incomprehensible if it was not love. She had to stay with him. She had to endure this bad time, because she knew that somehow, some day it would get better. It was not possible to believe that it could go on like this.

Felix came to the Olive Branch again, as she had feared that he would. Joe was in the saloon bar with Virginia, and she had to introduce Felix. Joe grunted, and considered Felix for a moment, chewing his upper lip, then moved to the end of the bar to serve some people who were waiting.

"Your husband doesn't seem to like me," Felix said mildly, with an eyebrow raised.

"Why shouldn't he? You're imagining things." It was a busy night, and Virginia had to talk to Felix in snatches, between pouring drinks and going out to the tables to take orders. Felix was alone. He leaned in the corner between the end of the bar and the wall and watched Virginia moving among the people in the room, greeting them, exchanging a few words, playing the part of landlord's amiable wife that she had learned and practised since she and Joe came to the Olive Branch.

"I thought I would find you looking better," Felix said when she came back, "but you don't. You look worse. Didn't the pills help?"

"I couldn't go on taking them. They—they didn't agree with me."

"I'll give you something else."

"No. I'm all right." Virginia glanced at Joe, and saw that he was looking at them.

"I wish there was something I could do to help, Virginia." She was afraid of the tenderness in his voice. She said again: "I'm all right," but she wanted to say: "If you want to help, please go away. Go away and leave me alone, before you start another quarrel."

Felix asked her a question, but she could not hear it, because someone with a louder voice spoke to her. "I'm sorry, Felix," she said, with a touch of impatience. "I can't talk to you tonight. We're very busy." But Felix would not go away. He waited, drinking slowly, always watching her, and sometimes watching Joe, and Virginia thought he saw how roughly Joe pushed her out of the way when she knocked his arm, reaching for the same shelf.

When all the people were gone, and Virginia was wiping down the bar, Joe folded his arms and said: "Well, go on. Tell me about him."

"Who?"

"The natty little chap who stayed in the corner all the time and gazed at you like an idiot."

"Oh, Felix." Virginia continued to polish, although the bar was spotless. "He's a doctor I used to know."

"The one who gave you the sleeping pills, I suppose? Very cosy. Also the one you told me about ages ago, when you were still telling me things, the one who tried to make you. He's still at his old game, I see."

"Don't be ridiculous, Joe. He only came tonight to see if I was all right."

"Why shouldn't you be all right? What's wrong with

you?" Joe took her hands off the bar and held her wrists tightly.

"You're hurting me. He knew I wasn't sleeping well. Don't be so violent about Felix. He was only trying to help me."

"Felix—my God, what a name. You don't need help." Joe dropped her wrists, pushing them away. "You're just neurotic. Sleeping pills! That's a line I haven't met before. If he comes round here again with his sleeping-pills, I swear I'll punch him in the nose, if I don't shoot him first. Don't forget I've got my gun in that drawer."

"It's not loaded."

"How do you know? How does Felix know? I'd only have to point it at him and say Bang, bang, and the little twerp would pass out cold from fright."

Felix was ill-advised enough to come in again. He came at lunch-time, harmlessly, mildly. Except for a greeting and an enquiry after her health, he did not talk to Virginia, but Joe had been drinking since eleven o'clock, and he told Felix to get out of the Olive Branch and never come back if he knew what was good for him.

"I beg your pardon?" Felix asked politely, leaning forward as if he had not heard correctly.

"You heard me. Stay away from here. I don't want you hanging round my wife."

"I assure you, Mr Colonna, I had no intention——" Felix looked discreetly surprised. Joe was excited and breathing heavily, but Felix remained calm and poised, with his umbrella over his arm and his hat and neatly-folded newspaper on the bar in front of him.

Virginia was bitterly ashamed that Joe should show himself like this in front of Felix, and terrified that the other people in the bar would hear, and stop talking to watch the scene.

"Well?" Joe stuck out his jaw. "Are you going, or do I have to chuck you out?"

"Joe—please!" Virginia pulled at his arm, and he pushed her roughly away.

"It's all right." Felix did not look at Joe. He looked at Virginia, and his eyes were filled with concern. "I'll go. I don't want to cause any trouble. God knows I didn't come here for that." He took his hat and newspaper off the bar. "Good-bye, Virginia. You know where to find me if you need me."

"Don't flatter yourself," Joe said. "She won't need you. She never did." But Felix had already turned and was walking out of the bar, putting on the stiff black hat, which came down too low on his ears and immediately made him look a lesser man, subordinated to the hat.

Virginia could not bear to watch him walk through the door with the hat spoiling his dignity. She turned away and went into the kitchen through the door behind the bar. It was nearly closing-time, and she began to make sandwiches for lunch. She heard Joe close and lock the front door. She heard him stop in the bar to pour himself another drink, which he brought into the kitchen. He sat down at the table and leaned his elbows on it, watching her while she moved about the room. She saw that he had half a tumbler of neat whisky between his hands.

"You shouldn't drink so much in the middle of the day," Virginia said.

"Why not? I'll sleep it off this afternoon. You should be glad if I can drink myself to sleep. Gives you a chance to run round the corner and meet your boy-friend."

Virginia did not answer. "I said, it gives you a chance to run out and meet your boy-friend," Joe repeated, irritated that he could not goad her.

"Oh, stop it," she said. "You've made a big enough fool of yourself for one day. Felix won't come back here again. You can give yourself marks for that—if you like losing customers—but you can't give yourself any marks for sense."

Joe took a drink of whisky and made a face. He was at the stage when alcohol is repulsive and essential at the same time. He banged the glass down on the table. "I've got enough sense to see when a man is trying to make my wife," he said surlily, "and when my wife is making it easy for him."

"That's a lie." Virginia faced him across the table. "I don't think anything about Felix. He's been kind to me, that's all, and I've known him for quite a long time. You don't just throw away your friends because your husband is unreasonably jealous."

"You would if you cared anything about how your husband felt. That's the hell of it." Joe gazed moodily into space, his eyes black and empty.

"Not that again. I can't argue with you when you're like that, because you won't listen to the truth."

"How do I know when you're telling me the truth? I tell you, it's a hell of a situation."

"I've always told you the truth. You know that. And I'm telling it now. I don't care a thing for Felix. I never did. I've never cared for anyone but you."

"I notice you don't use the word love any more," Joe said cunningly, shifting his eyes to look at her without moving his head.

"It means the same thing. Here"—Virginia pushed a plate in front of him—"eat your sandwiches, and I'll make some coffee. That will do you much more good than the whisky. Give me the glass and I'll pour it away."

"The hell you will." Joe grabbed the glass as she reached for it, swallowed the rest of the drink and stood up. "Come here," he said. "No, nearer. I want to talk to you."

When she was standing in front of him, he stared at her, trying to focus his eyes, swaying a little on his feet. "Tell me the truth then," he said. "Now that you've seen that guy again, and now that you've been married to me for nearly two years, during which I've—how did your charming mother put it?—dragged you with me into the gutter, weren't you wishing out there in the bar that you were married to him instead of me?"

"No." Virginia shook her head. She could say it honestly, because she had not thought of it. Now, the idea passed through her mind. Marriage to Felix . . . safe, dull, gentle. A comfortable home, children, security, friends, graceful, polite parties . . . so very different from this, and she herself a very different person. A little dull herself by now probably, securely undemanding, content never to know what her body was capable of, never to guess at the passion or the pain. . . .

"What are you thinking?" Joe was watching her.

She brought her eyes back to his face and said honestly: "I was thinking what it would have been like being married to Felix. It wouldn't——"

"You dirty bitch!" Joe lurched forward and struck her in the face. She staggered, clutching at the table, and ducked her head as he aimed another wild blow at her.

"Oh, crumbs, Mrs C.—oh, crumbs!" Lennie had come running into the room when Joe shouted. He pushed Virginia out of the way and stood, pathetically courageous, between her and Joe, squaring his elbows and doubling his fists, his voice trembling up to a squeak. "You leave her alone, you brute, do you hear me? I'll get the police. You lay a hand on her, and I'll get the police to you!"

Joe put his hands on his hips and roared with laughter. "I'll get the police to you!" he mimicked. "What's the matter—can't you fight it out yourself? Put your hands up, big boy, and let's see who's boss around here."

Joe raised his fists, feinting at Lennie with a leering grin. The boy flailed his weak arms like drumsticks. For a moment, Virginia thought that Joe was going to hit him. His arm shot out, and he picked up Lennie by the collar and set him neatly aside. "All right, you sickly little bastard," he said. "You keep out of my way, if you don't want what's coming to you."

"You leave her alone then," Lennie gibbered, "or I'll——"

"Oh, shut your trap, you little rat," Joe pushed him aside and slouched towards the back door.

"Where are you going?" Virginia asked. "Don't you want your lunch?" What a silly thing to say. Just the sort of futile thing one did say after a crisis.

Joe turned at the door. "Lunch?" he said vaguely, as if the word meant nothing to him. "God, no. I'm not hungry. I'm going to get some air. I feel like hell." He brushed the back of his hand across his forehead. His face was pale and sticky with sweat. "I think I'll go and chop some firewood. Do me good. I'll pretend I've got Lennie's neck under the hatchet." He gave a short, brutal laugh, fumbled with the door-handle and went out into the little courtyard.

Virginia sat down and tried to smile at Lennie. The side of her face was flushed and burning. "It's all right, Lennie," she said. "Don't look so upset."

"I am," he said. "Proper upset. It's not right, Mrs C. He's getting so he's not safe any more when he's been drinking. He'll chop his hand off out there, the state he's in," he added, not without satisfaction. "I tell you what it is. I reckon he's drinking so bad these days because he can't forget what he did to our baby."

"What do you mean?" Virginia frowned. "It wasn't his fault. She could have died even if I had been there."

"Didn't you know then?" Lennie poked his head forward to search her face with incredulous eyes. "Didn't he ever tell you?"

"Tell me what? What are you trying to say?"

"He dropped her on the stairs. He'd been down with her in the bar, drinking, see. He wasn't too steady on his legs and he dropped her. Out there on the stone. I saw her laying there, just before he picked her up. I'd been in the storeroom, see, waiting for Nancy. He didn't know I was there, but when I heard him slip and curse, I came into the Public, and I saw it, although he never seen me. He just picked up the baby and run upstairs. Oh, crumbs, Mrs C.," he said, watching Virginia's face. "I'm ever so sorry. I made sure he'd have told you."

Virginia was surprised to hear herself speaking in a normal voice. She sat with her hands on the edge of the table, propping herself up, because she felt so faint. "It doesn't make any difference," she said. "Jenny is dead now. It doesn't make any difference."

"If that's the way you want to look at it." Lennie fumbled with his shirt-collar, which Joe had pulled out of place. "Do you feel all right now, Mrs C.? If you don't need me, I think I'll pop out and get my lunch. This little upset has made me a bit peckish."

"Of course," Virginia said flatly. "Go and get your lunch."

"You sure you'll be all right?" Lennie hesitated, glancing towards the back door, where erratic sounds of chopping could be heard. "Oh, well," he said, as Virginia nodded.

"I'll say bye-bye for now. I shan't be more than a few minutes."

When he had gone, Virginia tried to think. Her mind was numb. The thoughts would not come. There was only a picture, a picture of Jenny, lying in a tiny heap on the cold stone at the foot of the stairs. Dead? Perhaps she had been dead already when Joe put her back in the crib, and he had not had the courage to tell her.

The back door burst open and Joe came in, cursing. "Nicked myself," he said, holding up a bleeding finger. "Moral—always sober up before you use a chopper." He flung the hatchet down on the table and went to the sink to hold his finger under the tap.

"Joe," Virginia said quietly, sitting with her head down, not looking at him, "why didn't you tell me you dropped Jenny on the stairs the night she died?"

Joe wheeled round. "Who says I did?"

"Lennie. He was in the public bar. He saw it."

"Oh." Joe came towards her, sucking his finger. He had not turned the tap off tightly, and it dripped with a steady musical patter into the sink behind him. "Well—what are you going to do about it?"

"Nothing, except to say that you should have told me. Why didn't you, Joe? Were you afraid?"

"Afraid?" He tossed back his hair. "I'm not afraid of anyone."

"It explains so much. The doctor took it for granted, I suppose, that it was pneumonia, because he knew she had it, but I've never been able to understand how she could have been better, and then suddenly snuffed out like that."

"Now you know. I killed her."

"Don't say that." Virginia got up quickly and went to him. Her head was aching from the blow of his hand. She felt dizzy and uncertain of herself, but she knew that she had to straighten this out now, because they could not go on with the bitterness of it between them. "It wasn't your fault. Joe, please don't look like that. Don't be wretched about it. I can see what you must have been through, thinking it was your fault, but it could have happened to anybody."

"If they were drunk enough," he said bitterly. "Stop making excuses for me. Of course it was my fault. I probably broke the poor little beggar's neck, only that lousy doctor was too sure of himself to notice it. You can tell the police that. Oh, yes, you'll have to tell them. They'll get me for murder—manslaughter at the best. Have poor little Jenny dug up and argued over. You read about it in the papers. 'Baby exhumed. Father charged.'" He laughed bleakly. "Make a lovely little scandal, won't it? Hellish good for trade. This will be the only pub in London."

"How could you think I would ever tell anyone? This is between you and me, Joe, and I'll never talk about it even to you, if you don't want. Talking about it won't bring Jenny back. It's best forgotten."

She held out her hand, but he pushed her away. "Grow up," he said. "Stop forgiving me. Stop being so bloody noble, and talk like a human being. Curse me. Accuse me, as you'll accuse me all your life. Every time you look at me, you'll think: That man killed my baby! That's what I think of myself every time I look in the glass. How do you think I like living with that? How will you like living with me now that you know?"

He was breathless and shaking. He clenched and unclenched his hands, and his eyes were dark pits of anguish. He stood looking at her for a moment while the tap dripped unconcernedly into the silence. Then suddenly he sagged, his arms hung limply, and his face crumpled. "Jin——" he said, and she thought that he was going to cry. "You'll go on with me, won't you? This isn't the end? I can't live with myself if you don't go on with me." He reached out for her. His drunken face was weak and quivering, his hands clutched at the air. She could not touch him when he looked like that.

"Of course I'll go on with you," she said. The words sounded empty and hopeless.

"Come here." He lurched towards her. "Come here when I tell you. Don't back away like that, damn you—come here! You belong to me. You're my wife, that's all you'll ever be. God damn you, don't look so disgusted. You think you're too good for me, don't you. I could kill you when you look at me like that, you damn ladylike——" He grabbed the hatchet and threw it at her.

In a split second she saw it coming, and raised her hands too late. She felt no pain as it struck her. She fell across a chair and rolled to the floor, and as she lay there with her arm tangled in the overturned chair, she felt the warm blood tickling her face like a feather. The blood was in her eyes and she could not see, but she heard Joe stumble past her, and heard the shot and the crashing bottles. Then silence, until Lennie's screams brought people running, and the Olive Branch was full of noise and voices.

16

IT WAS the kind of story that makes the front page of the newspapers: a one-day sensation, read with pleasurable horror and easily forgotten. After Mrs Benberg read the story, she had spent all the following days at the hospital, making a nuisance of herself until she was allowed to see Virginia. She continued to make herself a nuisance to the hospital staff, coming at all the wrong times, with vast quantities of unsuitable food, until she was finally allowed to take Virginia home with her.

"Don't tell my mother. Please don't let anyone tell my mother what's happened," Virginia had begged. "I don't want to see her . . . and listen to her. Not yet." That was the only thing she had asked. For the rest, she had submitted without protest to everything that was arranged for her, and she now lay listlessly on the narrow, humpy bed, among the boyish relics of Jim's schooldays in the small front bedroom of Mrs Benberg's house.

Life had stopped. Whatever future there might be was indiscernible, hidden round a corner which she had not the energy to negotiate. She might as well be here as anywhere else. The meaningless days and nights ran into each other, and although the doctor said that she could get up, it did not seem to matter whether she got out of bed again or not.

Jim was home on leave, relegated to the downstairs settee and perfectly happy about it. Like his mother and father, he could not do enough for Virginia. He was in and out of her room all day with a joke, or a present, or flowers, or an armful of magazines. "Something to cheer you up," he would say, darting his chubby, beaming face round the door, with his curly hair on end and his cheeks on fire from the wind in the street.

He could not cheer her up, but at least he could give her his bedroom. He was proud of that. "Think nothing of it," he said, when Virginia apologized for keeping him out of his bed. "Of course you're not spoiling my leave. As a matter of fact, it's simply made this leave for me, having you here. I'm falling in love with you," he said cheerfully. "I never met a girl like you, and I don't suppose I ever shall again, so I might as well make the most of having you here."

Like his parents, he was devotedly eager to help Virginia, and took as much pleasure as they did in doing it. Disaster brought out all that was best in the Benbergs. They rallied unswervingly to the challenge as if it were a crusade, and subordinated all their other interests to Virginia, around whose bed the life of the flimsy little house now revolved. For Jim, she was a sensational figure, unattainable, but an object of dazzled worship because she had taken part in the kind of drama for which his own cheery life would never be the stage.

When she heard Jim's breezy tattoo on the door, Virginia always turned her face aside, and kept the right side against the pillow while she talked to him. She was ashamed of the hideous raw scar which ran from her temple almost to the angle of her jaw. She had looked at herself once in a mirror, and then she had asked Mrs Benberg to take the mirror away, so that she could not see the appalling stigma which she bore in memory of Joe.

She had wept when she looked in the mirror, but not only for her ruined face, and because the doctor would not predict how well the wound would heal. When she wept, weakly, hopelessly among the china animals and the schoolboy books and photographs in Jim's room, her tears were for Joe, and for the terrible way his life had ended.

She knew that her mother would say that she was well out of it, because of what he had done to her. That was why she could not bear to see Helen. Even Spenser might say that. It was what everyone would say. Only Mrs Benberg understood that her marriage to Joe had held the enchantment of a dream as well as the horror of a nightmare, and that the awakening was not merciful, but bitterly sad.

Mrs Benberg was a tireless and enthusiastic nurse. She scoured the neighbouring shops for delicacies. Her spirited

305

step on the stairs rattled the little house countless times a day as she ran up to see what she could do to make Virginia comfortable. Unlike Jim, who was always trying to tease a laugh out of Virginia, Mrs Benberg did not try to cheer her up. "What's the percentage?" she said. "You're wretched now. You wouldn't be human if you weren't, so it's no use my trying to bully you into being happy. That will come later, and no doubt you'll bully yourself into it without any help from me."

Two or three times in the night, she would tiptoe heavily into Virginia's room to see whether she was asleep. Often Virginia was awake, and Mrs Benberg would shuffle downstairs in her voluminous wrapper and furry slippers to heat some milk, and would sit in the frayed wicker armchair and talk about anything that came into her head until she had talked Virginia into drowsiness.

"Shall I ever sleep well again, do you think?" Virginia asked one night. "I haven't slept properly since Jenny died."

"Don't be neurotic," Mrs Benberg said. "Of course you will. You've had the peace knocked out of you for a while, but it will return in due season, like the income-tax demand."

"I can't believe that anything will come back for me the way it was," Virginia said. "It's all changed. I always thought I was so lucky. You always said that things would go well for me."

"So they have, in a way." Mrs Benberg shifted in the chair, which creaked protestingly at every movement of her large body. "You're alive, aren't you? Isn't that something? Most people would have been killed, but not you. You're too tough."

"I used to think I was. I'm not so sure now. I'm not sure of anything. You always think you're immune, and that things like this only happen to other people. Then when they happen to you, it knocks the bottom out of your confidence. Tiny—my old nurse—she used to teach me that there was an angel looking out for me. I used to believe that. I don't any more."

"Oh—angels." Mrs Benberg heaved herself out of the creaking chair and stood by the bed, vast as the Statue of

Liberty in her long, faded wrapper. "Papist stuff. But I've an open mind. I've nothing against angels, for those who want to put their trust in them. If you believe in them, that makes them believable. If you don't, not. It's as simple as that. I can't imagine that angels are so foolhardy as to waste their time fussing over people who don't believe in them."

"I don't believe in anything," Virginia said. "I feel as if there was nothing left to depend on. I don't know what is going to happen to me."

"I do," Mrs Benberg said cheerfully. "I see it all. But I'm not telling. You'll find it out for yourself in your own good time. At this moment, I see that you'll go to sleep if I take my loud tongue and my big carcass out of here, and let you get some rest. I put something in your milk. Not poison. Something the doctor gave me." She winked at Virginia, then bent to kiss her, her heavy, untidily braided hair swinging over her shoulders like hunks of rope.

She turned off the light, and Virginia lay in the dark and waited for sleep. A street lamp shone into the room through the gap in the curtains which did not meet because Mrs Benberg had shrunk them by too many drastic washings with boiling water and soda. The lamp threw a broken patch of light into the corner of the room, just as the lamp outside the house on the hill had sent its patch of light into the corner of the room where she slept as a child. That was the corner towards which Tiny used to nod before she left the room. "You look after my Jinny now," she would adjure the angel, which she had summoned as an antidote to nightmares.

Poor old Tiny. Had she been disappointed not to find her angel waiting for her outside the gate of Heaven when she climbed wearily up there at last? But if Tiny had found Heaven and a gate, and Saint Peter with a big golden key like the ones with which Royalty opened new buildings, and all the other things that Tiny had believed, then there would be an angel too. Everything or nothing, and Mrs Benberg had said that as long as you believed in things, that made them true for you. Was that what she had said? Something like that. . . .

Virginia felt dreamy and confused. The street lamp had

sent her back into the memory of her old bedroom, and she could almost hear Tiny's hobbling step in the passage outside, coming to listen whether Virginia was asleep. No, that was a firm, heavy step. Mrs Benberg listening at the door to reassure herself once more before she rolled into the big double bed alongside the snoring ridge that was Mr Benberg.

He was snoring now. Virginia could hear him across the passage. Her father had never snored like that. But his bedroom was on the floor below; she would not have heard him. Yet sometimes, long after she had gone to bed, she had been able to hear his voice and her mother's raised in argument. That was when they still shared a bedroom. When they went into separate bedrooms, Virginia used to hear first one door bang, then the other, then silence in the chill, unhappy house. Silence while she lay and watched the patch of lamplight and fought against sleep because she was afraid of nightmares.

She put her hand to her cheek and touched the tender, raised flesh. That nightmare was a reality, a million years away from childish dreams and fears. When she was a child, lying in bed wanting sleep and fearing sleep, she used to say to herself: *Angel of God, my guardian dear, to whom His love commits me here, ever this night be at my side, to light and guard, to rule and guide.* She said it like a parrot, without finding any meaning in the words. There was just the impression of an angel, and those soft, white wings like a swan.

Angel of God. . . . She stared at the patch of yellow light, and the light was the evening sun, and the corner was a wall, the wall of the garden where the tangled roses dropped their petals like tears on to the weeds. The peach tree waited with its arms outspread. The quiet garden waited with Virginia, as the tide of contentment flowed gently over her and the last piercing rays of the sun bathed her face with the light that held behind it the promise she had come so far to seek.

As the sun sank, the bright light mellowed, and was diffused into an atmosphere through which, with an instant's clearness, she saw her angel smiling before her. The smile . . . the face. . . . With a lifting of the heart as if she were swept forward on wings, she reached out with a cry and became one with the vision.

The door flew open and the light snapped on. Mrs Benberg stood dishevelled in the doorway. Virginia was sitting up in bed with her arms flung out on the quilt in front of her. "What happened?" she asked, staring at Mrs Benberg.

"You called out. You must have been dreaming."

"No. I don't know. Yes . . . a dream." But how could a mere dream leave you with this warmth and peace, this assurance of a quiet word spoken to dispel anxiety for ever?

"I saw it," she said. "I saw the angel."

"Yes, dearie," Mrs Benberg said soothingly. "Sweet dreams. Lie down now and dream again. You're not awake even now." She came forward to settle Virginia back on the pillows, but Virginia said: "I'm quite awake," and remained sitting upright, drawing up her knees and clasping her arms tightly round them.

"I must tell you something," she said. "You'll think I am insane, but I must tell you."

"Carry on." Mrs Benberg folded her arms. "I'm half insane myself, I often think, so you won't surprise me."

"The angel . . . perhaps it was a dream, but how could I have dreamed it like that? You see"—she searched the shadowless corner where the lamp had shone before the electric light conquered it, but the faded wallpaper kept its secret. "You see, the face——" She looked up wonderingly. "It had my face."

Mrs Benberg blinked her eyes several times, then raised her thick eyebrows, and lowered them again in thought.

"An angel with your face," she said, as practically as if Virginia had described a common or garden sight. "That's interesting. Most interesting. I would have never have thought of that, but now that you mention it—yes, yes, I see."

"See what? What did it mean?"

"Why," said Mrs Benberg, as if it were the most obvious thing in the world, "it means that you are your own angel. Too simple."

"You think it means that there is no one to help you—no one but yourself? But that's a terrible thought."

"No, it's wonderful. Simply superb. It fits, don't you see?

It fits!" Mrs Benberg glowed with enthusiasm. She shifted her heavy weight from foot to foot, clasping her hands. "Oh, you remarkable girl, to dream something as true as that. It's what I always knew, but I never thought of seeing it in terms of angels."

"What fits? I don't understand."

"You don't know your Saint Luke, that's the trouble with you. 'The kingdom of God is within you.' That's what fits," Mrs Benberg said triumphantly. "Some people think that Christ simply meant that He was standing among the Pharisees—within their company, so to speak. But more likely He meant that He was within their minds, and *ergo*, the minds of all who had gone before, and who were to come after. That's you, my precious. That's why you are your own angel, because Christ can only work through you. He can only help you through your own will to help yourself. How do you think you have made such a good showing with your life so far? You thought you had a guardian angel. Well, you did, only you were looking for him in the wrong place. People pray to the wrong place most of the time. They get down on their creaking knees and they pray to an old man with a beard, somewhere away off in the sky. There's nothing in the sky to pray to, except the Martians, and I don't see why they should listen. What you pray to is inside your own self. That's where God is. Now do you see what it means—about the angel?"

"Perhaps." Virginia lay back. "An angel with my own face. I think——"

"Think no more," Mrs Benberg said briskly. "You're half-doped. I don't trust these doctors with their innocent-looking potions. Think no more tonight. We'll think about it tomorrow. An angel with your face!" She chuckled. "You like the idea?"

Virginia nodded. Her eyes were closing. "If you could believe that, you wouldn't ever have to give up, whatever happened. In the garden . . ." she murmured, "the angel didn't have a scar."

"Of course not! Nor lipstick nor powder either. Heavens, how material you are. When will I make you see?" Mrs

Benberg fussed, drawing her wrapper round her, and clicking her teeth. "Joe did his best to destroy you, and I don't mean only at the end. I can say that to you, because you know it too. But he didn't have a chance. He couldn't cut into what's inside you. That's what he couldn't bear."

"Please don't." Virginia turned her head away.

"Weep for him if you like. I know you hate me to say his name. But be glad of him too. You did what you could for him, and it wasn't your fault that it wasn't enough. But don't forget, he did something for you too. When he found he couldn't destroy you, he gave you back yourself." She swept to the door with her braids and her voluminous garments, as if she were part of a Wagner opera. From the pillow, Virginia returned her smile, before Mrs Benberg switched off the light and sailed across the passage to the room where Mr Benberg could be heard coughing and calling out feebly to know what was the matter.

17

VIRGINIA sat in the airport lounge and waited to board the plane that would take her to New York. Other people were waiting with her, but she paid scarcely any attention to these strangers with whom she would soon be imprisoned in a tiny world pursuing its orbit high over the Atlantic. She did not want to look at them, because she did not want them to look at her. Over her head she wore a soft scarf which was pulled forward on one side of her face, but it could not completely hide the dark, ugly scar that stood out in a thick welt against the pale skin of her cheek.

The loudspeaker drew a breath and spoke. "Mr Harold Martin wanted at the ticket desk. Will Mr Harold Martin, passenger for New York, please go to the ticket desk."

A tall, middle-aged man with dull grey clothes and tired eyes got up, disentangling himself from his coat and hand-baggage, and walked to the door of the lounge. Virginia saw the stoop of his shoulders and the way his jacket bulged with too many things in the pockets. When he had gone through the swing-doors, she remained sitting perfectly still with her eyes fixed on the doors to see him come back.

The passengers had been called to the plane before he returned. As she went forward with the crowd, Virginia looked back, and saw him come into the lounge. He walked just behind her into the blazing night of the airfield, and then he went ahead, his long legs striding across the tarmac, one hand up to keep the wind from taking his weather-beaten grey hat. He went into the plane before her, and when she climbed in and saw that he was sitting alone, Virginia pushed past a hesitating woman and sat quickly down on the seat beside him.

He was sitting on the right side of the plane, so that when he turned to her with a brief smile, he saw the scar at once. He did not look away awkwardly, as most people did. He remained looking at her for a moment with pity in his eyes, and then he gave her a wider smile.

When the plane began to taxi out into the night, Virginia leaned forward, pulling the scarf across her cheek. "Do you mind if I look out? It's my first flight."

"Sit by the window," he said at once. "Change places quickly. You're not supposed to stand up." He unfastened his safety-belt and helped her with hers, and then she was clutching the arms of the seat and watching the runway lights glide by, faster, faster, until suddenly they were below her and dropping away and she was part of the earth no longer.

"Like it?" he asked, as she settled back into her seat with a sigh. "One never quite gets over the thrill of being safe on the ground one moment, and safe in the air the next."

Virginia took off the scarf and shook out her hair. He could not see the right side of her face now, and so she could talk to him without being conscious of the scar and of his eyes either dwelling on it, or deliberately looking away. But, of course, he knew how to look at a woman with a blemished face. She had forgotten that.

For a while, she did not say anything. She had twelve hours in which to say the words. There was no hurry. He was looking through papers in his brief-case. Virginia opened a novel and tried to read, but her eyes kept sliding round to the long, lined face with the bony temples from which the thin hair had long ago receded. The stewardess brought coffee and sandwiches, and when the little trays were taken away, he took out a tarnished silver case and offered Virginia a cigarette. On the little finger of his right hand he wore a signet-ring with the seal carved into a red stone. Virginia did not need the evidence of the ring, but it was the memory of the red stone shining under the light above the piano that finally touched her into speech.

"Excuse me," she said in a small voice. "This is going to sound very odd, but I think you are my father."

They talked most of the night. When the lights in the plane were turned off, and the other passengers settled themselves with grunts and rustlings to uneasy slumber, Virginia and her father switched on the little reading lights and talked their way into each other's lives again while the plane beat its way across the sea with a thick roar that was no longer a noise but an unheeded part of the atmosphere.

Virginia's father told her that his wife had died two years ago, soon after her baby was born. "Something went wrong," he said. "She never really recovered from the birth. She was ill all the time, and then one morning, she just went, quite quietly. She was a very quiet woman. Peaceful to be with. I wish you had known her."

"I did." Virginia told him about her visit to the house.

"Typical of her not to tell me. She was always thinking about not upsetting me, and the irony of that was that with her I never felt like getting upset. Since you met her, perhaps you can understand how much she did for me. You never liked me very much when we lived together, did you? I don't blame you. I was a rotten father, and a rotten husband, and a pretty rotten person altogether to have about the house, I should imagine. Vivien—that was my wife's name—she didn't think so. She didn't despise me like—well, she really loved me, I think. That makes a lot of difference to a man. If a woman believes that a man is something, he can become it. Vivien thought I was worthwhile, even when I lost my job and we were on our beam ends. Your mother now," he paused and kneaded his large-knuckled hands, frowning at them, "your mother never thought I was worth anything, and so of course I wasn't, to her. But I learned a few things after I left Helen. Pity she couldn't benefit from any of them. I learned about being lonely. I learned what can happen to you if you think about nothing but yourself. I tell you, Jinny—I can tell you this now that you've grown up without my help—there were times when I thought of coming back."

"Why didn't you?"

"I didn't think Helen would have me. And then, of course, I met Vivien and everything was changed. I had a home, and Vivien showed me how to enjoy a child, a joy I never allowed myself with you."

He took out his wallet and showed Virginia the pictures of his children, a serious-faced schoolboy and a two-year-old baby, fat and pleasing. "We have a house in Richmond. Modest, but there's a garden, and Andrew does well at the school. I have a housekeeper who looks after them, and looks after me in a sketchy way when I'm at home. I do these trips quite often. I'm with another travel firm now, and we're pushing holidays in Britain on to the Americans for all we're worth. I was damn lucky to get the job, and I have to go where I'm told, but I hate being away so much. Mrs Leavis is—well, adequate. I can't stand the woman myself, but she's reliable with the children. I've talked too much, and you've been sitting there listening so quietly. You never used to be so quiet. But, of course, I only remember you as a schoolgirl. You used to drop things and fall over your feet all the time. I suppose you don't do that now. Tell me what happened to the schoolgirl. Tell me everything. At least," he glanced at her uncertainly, "as much as you want to tell. I don't even know where you're going now, or why."

"I'm going to stay with Helen. I've been ill."

"I can see that." He put his hand under her chin, and, turning her face, gently touched her cheek. "An accident?" It was the first time he had mentioned the scar.

Virginia nodded. "That's why I'm going to America. I'm going to have plastic surgery. Helen's going to pay for it," she said, and realized how odd that sounded. It was natural that a mother should pay for a daughter's operation. Natural, unless you knew what had happened between Virginia and Helen. "Did you know she had married an American?"

"I heard about it. That's nice for her."

"He's very rich. Helen is going to send me to Mount Sinai Hospital in New York. I wanted to have it done in England, but Helen is so Americanized now that she doesn't believe that any English surgeon could do it properly."

They both laughed. "You know," Harold said, with a note of surprise, "after all these years, I'm really rather fond of your mother. I don't remember the quarrels and bitterness now. I remember how bright and smart and attractive she was—always so much too poised for me. But that wasn't her fault. It was mine. A rich American." He smiled. "Much more her style."

He paused. Virginia thought about her mother, wealthy and discontented, running to fat and losing her looks from idleness; and about her father, finding out from Vivien what marriage could be, losing her, and plodding along in the wake of her guidance, with his hopes pinned on the two children who meant so much more to him than Virginia ever had.

After a while, her father said diffidently: "Do you want to tell me about the accident?"

"Not now. There's too much to tell. I don't want to start telling you now when we're only just getting to know each other again. I'll tell you another time. When I get back to England. Helen thinks I'm going to stay in America, but I'm not. When it's over, when I look human again, I shall go back to London and get a job."

"Will you really come and see me?" Her father's lined face looked younger and happier. Virginia could see what he must have looked like during the serene years with his wife.

"If I may. It will be something to look forward to."

They were silent for a while. Her father closed his eyes. Virginia switched off the pencil of light, and presently her father switched off his light too, and she thought he fell asleep.

In the darkness, his hand came over to her arm. "Jinny," he said, "I've no right to say this, no right at all. But the night is going by, and when the plane lands, you will go off with your mother, and I'm afraid of losing you. I don't want to tie you down, and I don't want to stand in the way of marriage for you——"

"I've been married," Virginia said shortly. "He died three months ago."

"My God," he said, "I'm sorry. How appalling that a man's daughter should go through that, and he not know. You're young and lovely, Jinny. There will be someone else.

Forgive me. No one wants to hear that, but there will be. And until there is—won't you please come and live with me, and be my daughter, and help me bring up my children?"

The stewardess passed quietly up the aisle like a night-nurse in a hospital, checking briefly but competently on her charges. When she had gone, Virginia said: "Yes, Father, I'd like to."

Soon after that, they fell asleep. They woke and smiled into each other's travel-weary faces. They breakfasted together, talking easily. They were father and daughter travelling together, leaning close to each other to gaze down at fabulous Manhattan, looking like a collection of grubby child's bricks perched precariously on end. Windows flashed in the morning sun. As they passed over the Hudson river, crawling with craft of all sizes, the Statue of Liberty waved at them with the hopeful, useless gesture of a stay-at-home woman watching the trains go by.

They dropped on to the runway. The plane braked, slowed, and gathered speed to run towards the buildings. As it approached, Virginia could see her mother clinging to the rail on the airport roof.

Helen wore a mustard-coloured suit. With one hand, she held on to a large blob of scarlet hat. No one but the woman Helen was nowadays would dress like that to meet a plane. "Is Helen there?" Virginia's father asked. "I'll stay in the background. I don't want to meet her, but I would very much like to see what she looks like."

"She's not there," Virginia said. "She's waiting for me at the house." It was going to be distressing enough for Helen to learn that Virginia was going to live with her father. This much at least Virginia could do for her. She could allow her to remain a bright, attractive memory, and not let her be exposed as a spoiled and selfish ageing woman who looked for contentment in money, and looked in vain.

The plane stopped. Virginia drew her scarf forward across her cheek and got up to join the people crowding to the exit, the people who had sat submissively in the plane for twelve hours, but now could not wait to get out of it.

317

Her father sat in his place, searching in his brief-case for his passport. He reached up, took Virginia's hand, and held it for a moment to his lips.

"Hurry back to England," he said.